KILLIAN

First Edition.

ISBN: 978-9-0832501-2-0

Cover Design: © The Pretty Little Design Co.

Editor & Proofread: Nice Girl, Naughty Edits

Formatting: NRA Publishing

KILLIAN

BILLIE LUSTIG

AUTHOR'S NOTE

Okay, so think Peaky Blinders.
If you just blurted out *'fuck yeah, #teamshelby!'*, you're good to go.
If you don't know what that means, I'd like to know what rock you've been living under so I can hide there when my level of tolerance for people is at zero.

But in all seriousness, the questions are: Blood? Guns? Organized crime? Brooding criminals that will make you sweaty in all the right places?
The only right answers are: yes, yes please, sign me up, and what chapter?
If your answers do not correspond with the ones mentioned above... go back to your rock and pick up a B. Lustig book instead.

Happy reading!

P.S. This one holds a mention of suicide that might be confrontational. Just a heads up.

To Katie,

You saw this boy for what he was from the get-go.
He's yours.
Even though he's mine.
You get me. Thank you for getting me.

1

PROLOGUE

KILLIAN

EIGHT YEARS AGO

"Hey, I thought you'd bring Reign with you?" I look at Sienna strutting through the door of Dunks as I stand beside the counter. Her long black hair sways around her almond face, her brown eyes lit up by the sun. She shakes her head, holding up her denim coat.

"I needed to pick up my jacket. Reign said he'd stop by Emma's and they'd come together. They'll probably be here any minute. Did you already order?" She glances at the donuts on display, but I know she'll go for some munchkins like she always does.

"Nah, I was wicked impatient waiting for the three of you." A smirk curls my cheeks and she rolls her eyes dramatically as I pull my phone from my pocket. "There was a time when you were always on time, Sienna Brennan. My little brother's bad habits are rubbing off on you."

"Well, they can't be worse than yours." The fierce look in her eyes makes me laugh.

"Touche."

I run a hand through my brown hair, ruffling my fingers through it to get rid of the itch on my head, then swipe through my phone to call my brother. It doesn't take long before I hear him pick up, but his voice stays quiet. A tight knot forms in my stomach as I wait for him to say something.

"Reign? Are you there?" The frown on my face has Sienna arching her eyebrows, her pink lips a little pinched. "Where are you at? Did you pick up Emma?"

The silence is deafening, but I can hear him breathing through the phone.

"She's dead." His voice lacks that jovial tone I'm used to from him, instead it's laced with defeat, sorrow, and grief. A tightness grips my chest as I blink into nothing, the blood rushing from my face.

"What? What are you talking about?" I want to ask if he's pulling some wicked lame joke, but I know my brother. He wouldn't joke about this. Not after the shit he went through over the last four years before he moved back home.

"She's dead," he repeats.

"Who's dead?" Sienna's eyes lock with mine, her face falling as she looks at me in fear. All I can do is blink at her, unable to break the connection while she does the same. She softly shakes her head, her hand covering her mouth.

She knows, she knows before Reign lets her name fall from his lips, because I know it too. I can feel the loss settling in my bones right before it pulls me down, but I refuse to let it get me.

"Emma. She's dead." I hear my little brother start to sob into the phone, and it threatens to tear me apart. I don't dare to repeat her name to Sienna, who's holding on to my arm with her eyes growing moist. I want to break down, shout in anger as he calls out the name of the one I fell in love with. But I can't fall down, I can never fall down.

"What? Where are you? Are you at her house?"

He lets out a groan, which I take as a confirmation, and I grab Sienna's arm, dragging her behind me.

"Stay there! We'll be right there!" I shout, hanging up the phone as I storm out of the store with Sienna on my heels.

"Kill!" she shouts, barely keeping up with me. "Killian! KILLIAN!"

I turn around at the corner of the street, locking my teary eyes with hers.

"Emma?" Her voice is small, and a tear falls down her cheek. Her shoulders are slumping and my face already gives the answer she needs, but she still waits for my answer. For my confirmation that something has happened to her best friend.

When I nod, her knees buckle, and I quickly reach out, pulling her up before she can hit the cobblestone of the Boston streets. She sobs against my chest, wetting my shirt with her tears before she brings her chin up.

"How?" she asks quietly, her voice breaking.

I hold her face in my hands, pushing my own tears back with every ounce of strength I have. "I don't know, okay? I don't know. But right now, we need to get to Reign. Do you hear me?" I blurt out the last sentence with more force, making her wince in the process. "We don't have time for this, Sienna. We need to get to *Reign*," I growl, thinking about my brother all alone right now. Anything to stop me from thinking about Emma.

Sienna nods, her eyes closed as she takes a deep breath to settle her tears.

"We. Need. To. Go."

She nods again, and I pull her with me as we jog toward Emma's house while I hold my phone pressed to my ear to call Franklin.

"What's doing, Kill?"

"Franky! Emma is dead."

"What?" The deep voice of my big brother is laced with dread. "What do you mean, she's dead?"

"I don't know, okay!? Reign just said she's dead."

"Where is he?"

"Emma's house. We're heading there now."

"Stay there!" Franklin booms. "Connor and I will be right there."

When he hangs up the phone, I tuck my phone back into my pocket, glancing over my shoulder to Sienna, who's still holding a steady pace behind me.

"Come on!" I shout, breaking out into a run when we reach the final block that leads to Emma's house. I barely register anything on the street, and when I see her white house in the distance, I pick up speed to close the final yards until I stomp up the front steps to the door. Noticing the door is already open, I push through with Sienna heaving behind me.

"Reign, where are you?" The panic is now creeping up on me, the silence in the house feeling as if the reaper will be coming for me any second now. But I've never been a coward, so I run up the stairs, two steps at a time, until I see my brother sitting on the other side of the hall. His back is pressed against the wall, his eyes closed, as he lets his head rest against the yellow painted drywall.

I fall to my knees in front of him, shaking his shoulders, needing to see his green eyes peering back at me. "Reign!"

When he finally opens his eyes to look at me, they are vacant. Gone are the vibrant specks of gold that always dance around his irises, but it still fills me with relief to see he's okay. That feeling quickly vanishes, though, when I hear Sienna gasp in shock from behind me.

I slowly turn my head to my left, my gut already telling me what is about to cross my retinas. They grow wide when I see my girl hanging in the stairwell of the attic. A thick rope sits around her neck, making her skin even more pale, her arms slung limply at her sides. Her blonde hair covers half her face, but I can still see her bloodshot eyes that will probably haunt me forever.

"What the–" My mouth gapes, my gaze filled with a horror that's quickly taking over my body.

I stand on shaky legs to get closer to her, my heart plummeting as I stare at her in shock before the reality of what I'm looking at truly sets in.

Grief, hurt, pain, despair, they all crash through me in the next second. If there is an emotion that can cause anguish, you name it, I'm feeling it. But the biggest emotion of all has me angry as a bull with a red cloth dangling in front of him.

Rejection.

She said that what we had was all she needed, that *I* was all she needed. That she was going to get better. That whatever the fuck we had was going to be enough for her to heal. To let go of the past and focus on the future. *Our future.* But the fact that she's hanging lifeless on the stairwell in front of me tells me she fucking lied. She bullshitted me, even though I gave her everything I had.

I was hesitant, because my history didn't show me any good outcome that comes from love, but she wore me down and eventually, I believed her. I believed that we could make it work, because my feelings seemed to grow for her every single day. Her bright smile. Her sparkling eyes. Her silly comments that made me laugh. I fell in love with her, because she convinced me I was enough for her.

"Kill? Killian, where are you?" Franklin's voice booms through the house.

"We're up here!" I call back, keeping my eyes trained on the girl that decided to take my heart to Heaven with her.

You're a liar, Emma Walsh.

I wasn't enough.

I will never *be enough.*

2

PRESENT DAY

KILLIAN

What the fuck is she doing?

An amused smile pulls on the corner of my mouth while my hands stay tucked in the pockets of my leather jacket. The air is brisk, showing the warmth of my breath every time I exhale, like a one-second fog. I watch the petite brunette walk back out of the building with a scowl on her face. I have a feeling she isn't a day over twenty-one.

Her ivory skin sticks out against her black jeans and black bomber jacket, her outfit making her look like the ultimate rebel. She's walked in and out of the building three times now, holding a Glock in her slender hand. I can see she's not familiar with guns by the tension in her fingers as she keeps a tight grip on the handle, but the determined look in her eyes tells me she doesn't care about that. She's more worried about the people on the street and walking in and out of the building, retreating back to the alley next to it every time someone crosses her path. She probably hopes she blends in with the night, and on a busier street I probably wouldn't have noticed her, but her nervous behavior makes it obvious she's out of place.

She presses her back against the brick of the alley, in the comfort of the darkness, and I see how her chest moves up and down with deep breaths. To calm herself down, and find some courage, I assume.

My curiosity moves my feet forward, and I cross the street with big strides until I almost reach the alley and moderate my pace to see what she's up to. As if she's going for another shot, she takes one more deep breath, then struts back around the corner and toward the entrance of the building. She checks the barrel of her gun, making me believe she's really going for it this time, and I quickly close the distance with three big strides, then pull her back by her jacket.

Her shocked gasp is loud, and in one swift move, I jerk the gun from her hand, throwing her back against the brick wall. A shriek bursts from her mouth as her eyes widen, and she brings her knee up to kick me in the groin in defense, but I'm quicker. I easily grab her neck, squeezing just enough to make it hard for her to breathe, and unable to scream, while I place the tip of her own gun on her temple. She freezes, fear lacing her eyes.

"What the *fuck* are you doing?" My tone holds more of an edge of incredulity than a growl, and her expression changes to that determined frown creasing her brow again. I let my gaze trace along her features, taking her in as I keep her in place.

Her face is fresh and free from make-up, showing freckles across her nose and cheeks. Chocolate brown hair frames her face, flowing around her shoulders. The navy blue in her eyes stands out with the fierce gaze she's giving me, showing every ounce of her bravery through the angst I'm sensing from her throbbing pulse. She's a pure beauty. And undeniably young.

Clearly, she's in a place she shouldn't be.

"Speak," I command when my eyes lock with hers again. When she stays silent, not removing her defiant gaze from mine, I tighten my grip on her neck to enhance the seriousness of my command.

"I'm going to kill him," she finally snarls with an amusing level of sass, and I raise my eyebrows in surprise.

"Cryptic and entertaining." I chuckle around my words, since she doesn't seem capable of *killing* anyone. Beat some kid up in high school, sure. But she hardly looks like a coldhearted criminal.

"Who exactly is on the top of your shitlist?"

"Sullivan." My brows arch at that answer.

"You're here to kill *Chief* Sullivan?"

She nods.

"You," I snort. "Why?" I give her a dull look because even she must realize how ridiculous that sounds. It's like asking a mouse to fight a lion. She doesn't stand a chance. Besides, no matter where in the United States you live, everyone knows a cop killer doesn't get a happy ending. Especially when he's the Chief of Police.

Her pretty eyes flash with a sadness that has me cocking my head a little and my brows knit together.

"He killed my family."

I let out a grunt at that explanation, a feeling of unexpected sympathy creeping up on me. It reminds me of my years in foster care, where I felt alone, missing my brothers. I hated the world, and I can relate to the feeling of wanting to do something about it.

"How old are you?"

"Does it matter?" she spits, her voice filled with disdain.

"How old are you?" I repeat, more demanding this time.

"Old enough to avenge my family."

My fingers move up, cupping her chin in a forceful grip that has to hurt, or at least it's meant to hurt.

"Don't make me ask you again, kid," I say in a low and menacing tone.

"I'm not a kid!" she growls, baring her teeth. "I'm eighteen."

Huh, proves my point. Definitely a kid.

"Barely out of diapers," I reply, amused.

Realizing she's no threat, I let go of her, and she squares her shoulders, then crosses her arms in front of her chest.

"I stopped being a kid the day that bastard slaughtered my entire family," she adds.

I keep a straight face, but the revelation does something to me.

Even though I don't know if it's true, it's easy to believe. Chief Sullivan is a son of a bitch, the dirtiest cop I've ever met, and I wouldn't give a damn if someone blew a bullet through his head. That is, if he wasn't on our payroll. He's a big part of why us Wolfes have the influence in this city that we have and I'm not going to let some kid with a grudge ruin that. Even if she looks good doing it.

"He'll kill you." I hold her gaze, watching how her fear seems to simmer down. As much as I appreciate the audacity of her plan, it's also filled with stupidity. She couldn't keep me off for a second just now. She doesn't stand a chance against any grown-ass man. Let alone an experienced cop.

"Then help me." She pushes out the words with a growl, but I can hear the desperation etching through it. She tries to keep a bold stance, but her age doesn't work in her favor, showing me how out of her element she is.

"Why the fuck would I do that?" I huff, followed by a laugh.

"Because you're Killian Wolfe." My brows lift, surprised by her balls to take my name into her mouth. "If anyone can help me, *you* can." She shoots me a daring look that turns me on as much as it annoys me, bringing out my desire to show her exactly who she's talking to.

Vigorously, I wrap my fingers around the front of her neck once more, this time slightly lifting her from the ground as I bring my mouth flush with her ear and breathe in the rose scent of her hair. A scent that fucks with my mind for a split second, making it harder to make the following threat.

"Since you know exactly who I am, you also know I can be your worst nightmare. Don't piss me off, or Sullivan will be the least of your problems. You don't want to mess with him, but you *definitely* don't want to mess with me." Abruptly, I let her go, taking a step back before I give her a final glance. Her hand moves to her neck, rubbing the sensitive skin.

"Go home, little girl." I hand her back her gun and hesitantly, she takes it from my hand before I push her out of the alley. She throws one last dirty look over her shoulder while I watch her take off with a smile haunting my face.

Kid or not, I appreciate her spunk.

"Don't let me see you again, or I'll feed you to him myself," I call out behind her back. When she lifts her hand, flipping me off, but never turning her head, a wide smile splits my face. I shake my head, a little stunned by her brazen attitude, then turn around to walk into the building.

3

Lexie

"Ugh. Stupid, stupid, stupid," I mutter to myself, with my hands tucked deeply into my bomber jacket. My palm is still clasped around the cold metal of the gun hidden in my pocket, acting as my beacon of confidence while I stomp down the pavement, pissed as fuck at myself. The adrenaline still rushes through me, making the pounding of my heart sound like an ominous drum with every step.

That didn't go as planned.

I had it all worked out, even had a checklist to follow to make sure no one saw me.

Wear dark colors to make sure you don't stand out. *Check.*

Wear gloves to prevent DNA from spreading. *Check.*

Double check the gun. *Check.*

Make sure no one sees you as you enter the building. *Check.*

But naïve as I was, I forgot that last one after I chickened out the first time, like the fucking *little girl* he thinks I am. If I didn't, I'm sure I would've seen Killian Wolfe as soon as he walked onto the block, simply because he's not someone you can overlook.

He's not bulky like his brother Connor, looking like the fucking hulk, but there is something about his energy that makes him appear huge. His green eyes are more compelling than any of the other brothers', acting like lasers as he scans his surroundings. He's the kind of man people part for on the street because he forces you onto a different path with a single glance. They say he's the one you should fear.

He looks dangerous, like the ultimate bad boy.

But as always, the bad boys are more alluring, and Killian Wolfe is no exception.

I've seen him around the city more than once, and every single time my eyes are drawn to him like he's pulling a cord to direct my attention, even though he has no clue I exist.

I always catch myself staring a little too long, because although he causes fear to ripple through my body, there is also something that makes it impossible to ignore his presence.

Yeah, if I just didn't hesitate the first time, all caught up in my fear, I would've definitely seen him and I would've made sure he'd *never* seen me.

My heart almost fell from my chest when he tossed me back into that alley. For a second, I thought he was there to finish what Sullivan's guys started. I figured my days were over since meeting a Wolfe in a dark alley is almost as daunting as murdering a cop.

Maybe even worse.

I tried to fight him off, but it was clear from the moment he put his hands on me I couldn't match his strength. I knew for certain that he was going to kill me right then and there and now minutes later my racing heart still has a hard time settling down. Internally, I was already giving up, yet still trying to keep a fierce stance. I was basically shitting my pants, giving everything it took to not crumble under his touch, right until he showed me an inch of sympathy after I told him what happened to my family.

It was only brief and gone before I could blink, but I saw it. Or at least I think I did. I felt my pulse calm down a little, but without my gun, I still had to surrender to his mercy.

I was already cursing myself for potentially getting killed in a dark alley, until he started to ask questions and I realized he wasn't aware of my last name. The fear of dying gradually simmered down enough to feel confident he might let me live, and when he finally sent me on my way, I even thought about turning around and shooting him.

But my common sense told me to drop the thought and keep walking. I know the entire police department will be looking for me when I kill Sullivan, and I also know it will be a tea party compared to what would happen if I shot a Wolfe.

I don't know how much they are woven into the administration of this city, having their influence everywhere, but I'm aware of the stories about them torturing people, Killian being the worst of them all. I once heard a rumor about how he likes to make his victims scream for his own pleasure before peeling their skin and burning them just for fun.

Messing with the Boston Wolfes is the stupidest thing you can do, even I know that.

Especially Killian.

I suck in the cold air of the night, keeping a firm grip on my gun. And with a steady pace, I march back to Dorchester, taking deep breaths to settle down my heightened senses, until I reach my building.

Glancing around me, I make sure I'm not being followed inside by some creep looking for drugs or a quick fuck, then make my way up the stairs with two steps at a time. I don't live in the worst part of the neighborhood, but I certainly don't live in the best part either, and since I'm on my own, I'm definitely more cautious about my surroundings. If anything, the last year taught me I can't trust anyone and I won't make that mistake ever again. By the time I reach the sixth floor, I'm slightly heaving, and I open the front door with my keys while I try to catch my breath. I move my chin over my shoulder one more time to make sure I'm alone, then get in and close the door behind me. My fingers swipe the deadbolt as I lock up, before I throw my keys on the side table next to the door and take off my jacket.

I let the piece of clothing fall to the floor, knowing no one will nag me about picking it up anyway, while I take the two steps to the couch, turn around, and let my back fall against the cushions.

Wallowing in the loneliness that has become my life for the last couple of months, I push out a deep breath in the comfort of the silence. In the first few weeks, it was overwhelming, catching me by surprise every time I walked into this empty space. But now I don't know any better.

With my hands resting on my stomach, I look up to the ceiling as my chest slowly moves up and down, my muscles relaxing.

The adrenaline of meeting Killian Wolfe is slowly wearing off, and all that is left are his moss-green eyes that keep flashing through my mind. I knew exactly who he was the moment his eyes locked with mine. It's not the first time I've seen him. Since I moved into my grandmother's one-bedroom apartment, I've seen him making appearances in the neighborhood. Doing business with the scum of this city, I'm sure. My father warned me about all of the Wolfes to really make me understand how I needed to stay far, far away from them.

So I have.

While I've been preparing my hit on Sullivan, I did my best to fly under the radar, blending in with the crowd wherever I go. But every time I saw Killian around the area, I couldn't help but stare at his fearless stance as a shiver ran down my spine. A shiver that is as terrifying as much as it's addictive. His appearance always acts like a magnet drawing me in.

But it's nothing compared with his gaze boring into mine. He was intimidating, like the Devil waiting for you at the front gates of Hell. The daunting look in his eyes had me worried he'd snap my neck within a second, and then the lethal look he gave me the moment his hand pushed me against the wall froze my muscles in fear.

I knew I was in a wicked amount of trouble. He was everything I imagined he'd be when I saw him from afar, secretly peeking at the Devil, but in reality, he was so much more.

Scary, yet alluring.

Intimidating, yet captivating.

Aggressive, yet beautiful.

God, he was so fucking beautiful.

A sharp jaw that was covered with a light stubble. His green eyes were even greener when he was only three inches away from mine, reminding me of a clear water lake in spring, where the water is so transparent you can see all the way to the bottom. His light brown hair fell a little in front of his forehead, giving him a boyish look that was mesmerizing, and for a second, I needed to remind myself who I was dealing with.

I remember in high school, we would romanticize these men ruling over the city we were born in. Thinking they would sweep us off our feet, acting like the men we read about in novels. All dreaming we'd one day be that special girl he'd change his character for. When my father shared the story he was working on, I didn't fully want to believe him, still dreaming about these men like a silly teenager.

But that all changed on a Thursday night in March.

The night, I realized not every cop is there to serve and protect the people in this city.

My happy bubble filled with silly senior year worries like what to wear to prom and graduation parties was burst overnight when I learned people can be ruthless and there is more ugliness in this city than I cared to believe. A time that feels like ages ago, when really, it's only been eight months.

Now here I am, living in my late grandmother's tiny apartment until I get my perfect shot to avenge my family.

One shot, that's all I need.

All I need to do is give Sullivan a one-way ticket to Hell like he deserves.

After that, I'll pack my bags and start over somewhere Midwest. Part of me wants to stay in Boston, but I have nothing to stay for. There is nothing left for me here but bad memories. A new city, a new name, a new life. Maybe I can get a job that will allow me to go to a community college. Maybe I can even start dancing again.

It's as far as I'm willing to go right now, because I can't get myself to think that far just yet.

I push out a deep breath, then get up and head into my small kitchen to grab a glass of water. When it's completely filled, I bring it to my mouth, chugging it down as I glance at the family picture on the refrigerator.

A smile cracks through as I think back to that last family day we spent at the Franklin Park Zoo. Sofia and I complained we were too old for that shit, but when grandmother threw out the *I am old, I decide* card, we went with smiles on our faces. It was fake for the first hour, but after a while we started to enjoy ourselves, our heads warmed by the summer sun.

The memory fuels my determination as I take in our bright smiles, silently promising my family that I'll get the revenge they deserve.

Tonight really was a bust.

As much as I hate the way Killian Wolfe treated me like some little girl, he did point out an important thing; I'm exactly that compared to a grown ass man.

Little.

Inexperienced.

And insignificant.

Killian Wolfe cornered me within a heartbeat, and the only reason I'm still alive is because he allowed it. I can come a long way with a gun and determination, I'm sure of that, but if Sullivan got a chance to fight me, I'd probably be dead within a minute.

Not to mention the fact that someone close to Sullivan now knows I'm alive, which won't work in my favor. I'm sure he knows Jameson Lee had more than one daughter, and even though he's not searching very hard for me, I know he will want me dead as soon as he knows I'm still in the city.

The last thing I need is getting on anyone's radar, especially the Boston Wolfes', but thinking back on tonight, I realize my original plan was flawed like a leaky boat in the middle of the ocean. And then, I asked him to help me... what the hell is wrong with me? As if Killian Wolfe will help a clueless girl on a vengeance mission like me.

Though... It could be the only way. It could be the thing I execute this with success and actually still be breathing at the end.

I need a better plan.

I need someone to train me, and I need someone who can get me close to Sullivan.

I need a Wolfe.

I snort at my own silliness when the stupid thought slips into my mind, but as I keep repeating it in my own head, memorizing the small hint of sympathy I found in his eyes, it becomes a better idea with every second.

If I can get Killian Wolfe to train me, and teach me everything he knows, I might stand a chance. It will be risky to ask for his help. But if he wanted me dead, I would be already.

Killian Wolfe can be my one shot at vengeance.

A deal with the Devil is just what I need.

4

KILLIAN

I glance at the screen of my phone while two of my men follow behind me, walking down the street to get to the next shop to collect our fees. My oldest brother, Franklin, does these rounds in his fancy town car, showing up like the mob boss that he is, but I like to roam the streets of our city, breathing in every smell, registering every sound and blending in with the crowd. Well, as much as you can blend in being a Wolfe in this city.

In the last decade, my brothers and I have created a presence in the city of Boston that is undeniable. We have control in every layer there is, and one thing Franklin has always been focused on is earning the respect as well. The people respect us because we also give back, contributing to the community and helping those in need. But I, unlike the rest of my brothers, also enjoy the fearful glances I get as I walk downtown. The ones that know I don't hesitate to inflict pain if you cross me.

"What's up, tool?" I pick up the phone while pushing out a breath.

"She bailed," my youngest brother Reign pushes out with frustration.

My feet stop for a moment, assuming he's talking about his ex-girlfriend, Sienna, whom he's trying to get back, and I roll my eyes when they go back in motion.

"You stupid fuck. You finally got her to go to dinner with you and you fucked it up." Sienna and Reign have a history. One where my brother screwed up royally, but I understand why. His issue is that I'm the only one who understands because I'm the only one who is aware of the demons he's battling. I've been trying to get him to open up for years now, but he only recently shared the ugly truth of his time in foster care with our two oldest brothers, and he refuses to tell anyone else. I'm sworn to secrecy, but it's tempting to share his struggles with the girl he's in love with just so I don't have to listen to their bullshit fights anymore.

"Did you at least eat?" I ask.

"No-suh. She ran out on me after her first glass of wine."

"What did you do, you idiot?"

"Called her *baby*." There is a guilty tone in his voice that has me letting out a feral grunt.

"For a fucking whizz-kid, you are wicked stupid half the time. Why would you do that? You know it ticks her off when you call her that."

"I know!" he screeches. "It just happens, okay? It just rolls off my tongue out of habit." He pauses. "She just drives me nuts, man. I've been holding back for weeks now, trying to get her to loosen up around me. But the minute she does, I take another step, and she backs up. I know she still has feelings for me. I can see it in her eyes. But she's stubborn as fuck."

"She's Italian," I reply matter-of-factly. She has always been feisty and he broke her heart. What more reason does she need to have to give him a hard time?

"What the fuck has that got to do with it?"

"They are stubborn." I shrug.

"Gee, thanks for this mind-blowing revelation. Any more useless comments, Kill?"

The annoyance in his tone has me chuckling through the phone.

"Look, she's a proud woman. You broke her heart and stomped on it the moment you decided to stay in New York for Callie."

"I didn't stay in New York for Callie," he snaps, referring to his ex-girlfriend turned best friend. "I wish everyone would stop saying that."

"I know that. But she doesn't," I concede.

"If she let me speak for two seconds, I could explain to her. Instead of her jumping to conclusions all the time."

"Oh, yeah. This sounds familiar," I reply, the judgment clear in my voice.

"What's that supposed to mean?"

"You know exactly what I mean," I blurt with a bite. He and our oldest brother, Franklin, have been fighting like cats and dogs for years because Reign refuses to put on his big boy pants and ask Franklin the truth about the past. About what happened before CPS split us up and shipped us to different foster homes. He's one to talk about people jumping to conclusions. "Look," I continue when he doesn't reply, "if she was any other girl, I'd tell you to fucking put her on the spot and tell her what the deal's gonna be. We ain't got time to pussyfoot around women. But this is Sienna. She's had a thing for you since you were twelve." I bite my tongue, refraining myself from saying anything else because I know he doesn't need more reasoning after that. He has loved the girl since he was a kid. As much as his past haunts him, so does Sienna, and he just needs to suck it up and make it work.

"I know," he finally admits.

"So, you have two options. You can either be a damn chucklehead about it and keep pushing her to forgive you. Or you can do it at her pace. I don't know, maybe try to become her friend again first. She doesn't trust your stupid ass." The sarcasm is dripping from my voice as I wait for the traffic light at the crossover to turn green.

"Since when are you the wise one?"

"Always. I just never bother to share my opinion." The light turns green, and I saunter over the pedestrian crossing toward the sports bar at the corner of the street.

"You're a real asshole, do you know that?"

"Ya-huh."

"Did you tell Franky about the roses?" Reign asks, referring to the package with roses he received this afternoon. It could be a sweet gesture from a secret lover, but the dozens of worms it was accompanied with tell us that's probably not it. My baby bro got a wicked problem with a stalker. Or an angry ex. Who the hell knows?

"I did. He told me to look into it."

"Did you find anything?" I hear a beep of what sounds like an elevator coming through the line, and I assume he's home.

"I did, but it's a dead end. I went to EPS, found out their routes to check the driver. There were no packages delivered today."

"No-suh," he huffs.

"Turns out the guy doesn't work at EPS. I need you to check if you can find more, pull the street cams, see where he comes from." Reign is the best hacker on the East Coast and if there is anything else to find, he will find it. Even when he was twelve years old, he managed to hack into the police station and get Franklin out when he was arrested for first degree murder. Tampered with some evidence and shit. It didn't matter because CPS still took away my brothers and me, but at least Franklin was no longer behind bars.

"I'll do that now. I just got home," he informs as I hear the elevator doors open up.

"Wicked. You wanna—" My thoughts trail off when my gaze catches a familiar face standing on the other side of the street. She's wearing the same black clothes, her hands tucked into her black jacket. At first, her expression turns pale, shocked at my eyes finding hers. But then a daring scowl washes over her face. Her blue eyes keep staring at me intensely, unfazed. "What the fuck."

I move to the edge of the sidewalk, the road with cars the only thing that's separating us. The vehicles rush between us, making a gust of wind fan my face every second as our eyes never untangle. She holds my gaze, challenging, and in that brief moment, I know her being here is not a coincidence. She's here for me and she doesn't even try to hide it.

The girl has got more nerve than I gave her credit for the first time we met.

"What's doing?" I hear Reign bark through the phone with worry, and I tear my eyes away from her. "Killian?! What's wrong?"

"Nothing," I snarl, then twist my body while feeling her eyes still burning on my back as I continue to set a steady pace to my destination.

"Right," he drags out skeptically. "Random, but whatever."

"I'll tell you later. You gonna watch the game?" I ask him, doing my best effort to change the subject. I'm not sure with what motive that girl is following me, but I sure as hell am going to find out before I share anything with any of my brothers. Reign's stalker is giving us worry enough, no need to bother them with some kid following me around like a lost duckling.

"Yeah, you wanna come over?"

"Might as well, since you are definitely not getting laid tonight." The taunt brings a smile to my face, appreciating my own comment. I expect my brother to throw out a snarky response, but instead, the line stays quiet.

"Ay, are you still there?" I call out to him this time.

"She was here, Kill." There is confusion in his voice.

"Who? Sienna?"

"Aubrey."

"What? Aubrey is dead. Drowned herself in the river in Providence, remember?" I huff, a little worried when the name of his foster sister falls from his tongue. I never saw the girl alive, but from what I heard, she was fucked up in more ways than one, and the last thing I want is my brother worrying over a ghost.

"Then why is there an origami swan sitting in front of my door?"

I nudge my chin in greeting to the bouncer, and he instantly opens the door for me.

"What are you talking about, Reign?"

"He's in the back," the bouncer informs me as I walk past him.

"One of those damn swans," Reign continues. "It's sitting in front of my door. Folded. Paper. You know the ones Aubrey used to make when–" He cuts off his sentence, and I breathe out through my nose, not feeling like reliving the story of his time in foster care. "I'm telling you, Kill. I have a bad feeling about this. It has to be someone from Providence."

My hand aches to rub my face, but I keep my unbothered stance as I walk toward the back of the bar to the owner. His eyes meet mine and by the satisfied gleam on his face, I'm assuming the big bag on the table contains the money he owes us.

"Maybe you're right. We'll figure it out, okay? In the meantime, I'm sending two men to guard your building."

"Yeah, okay."

"Get some sleep. We'll talk tomorrow." Without waiting for his reply, I hang up the phone, then direct my attention to the man in front of me.

"Sullivan, what's doing?" I cock my head, blinking. He's changed his uniform for a navy polo, bringing out his fake tan. His gray hair is short, showing how much baldness is creeping in on top of his head. He seems different, more of a tool than normal. I can't help wondering if it's because of the information I learned a few days ago.

A wicked grin lifts the corners of his mouth.

"Killian Wolfe." He speaks my name with respect. "Are you playing?" He holds up the deck of cards, and I glance at the other two men around the table. I've seen them before. They each have a stack of chips in front of them, giving me a side-eye that tells me they don't want me to join. Can't blame them because the last time I made them go home empty-handed. But the fact they clearly want me to leave makes it that much more fun to join.

With a smirk, I take the stool in front of me. "Deal the cards."

5

Lexie

Yeah, so I guess I need to work on my stealth mode.

After he basically caught me red-handed that first night, I became more careful. I kept my distance and put a Red Sox cap on my head to hide my face, now completely aware of the fact that I won't go as unnoticed as I would've a year ago. He now knows what I look like, and I need to make sure I never appear in his line of sight.

Luckily, he hasn't spotted me again and I managed to trail his every move.

I've been shadowing him for days now.

Trying to learn his behavior.

Become familiar with his customs and habits.

But other than him doing business at almost every corner of the street in this city, I got nothing. Most days, he drives to the Wolfe's family mansion in his black Audi, has supper, then goes back downtown to do his rounds of whatever he's doing. After that, he either goes for a drink until midnight or he heads to his penthouse around eleven and the lights go out less than thirty minutes after that.

He spends a lot of his time with his brothers, but I already knew that. There is Franklin, the oldest and leader of the pack. Connor, the one who has a permanent scowl on his face and seems to be the most feared after Killian, who is the third Wolfe. The youngest is Reign. He looks like Prince Charming, and from what I gathered, his mouth matches that comparison. Rumors are he can hack into anything, finding whatever piece of information he needs. I thought about getting Reign's attention because he looks like the one who's most approachable with his boyish grin, but if he finds out my name and does a background check, I'm pretty sure I'm fucked.

I thought they'd have an interesting life, where they go to parties every night, always have supper in restaurants, and sit in strip clubs and all that shit. Pick up a few girls. You know all the stuff you see in mob movies.

But in reality, Killian seems to have a routine that he sticks by, never doing anything out of the ordinary.

Tonight is different, though. From what I've figured out, they are reopening the Pack, the bar they own, after some renovations, and all of the Wolfes are present. I've watched them all walk in with the oldest brothers' girlfriends while Reign's girlfriend, Sienna, seems to be organizing everything.

The girls are gorgeous; all grown up and sophisticated.

Kendall Ryan, Franklin's girlfriend, has brown hair that falls over her shoulders with big waves. She's wearing a skin-tight gray dress that's covered by a black trench coat as she struts into the bar on Franklin's arm. Connor's girlfriend is wearing a little black dress, which is a big contrast with her light blonde hair, making her look like an angel that has a date with the Devil. I think her name is Lily. Whispers say they even have a kid together, but I haven't seen a glimpse of him yet. And Sienna? Sienna is breathtaking, with her black hair that runs all the way to her waist. She looks like a businesswoman that's got all her ducks in a row, and if I was still in high school, these women would act as my role models.

Right now, I just wonder why they are crazy enough to run with the Wolfes.

My breath is clear in the cold air as I keep my position in the alley across from the bar while repeating my plan in a mantra like I have for the last hour. The aim is to force him to listen to me, threaten if need be, but I have no doubt doing that on Wolfe territory will get my neck snapped within seconds.

So, instead, I'm standing here, hopping from one foot to the other to keep myself warm and hoping he will be either the first to leave or the last. Hoping I will be able to catch him alone. I'm even praying for a miracle of him being drunk, giving me a better opportunity, but in the last week I've never seen him even remotely intoxicated, so I guess that's a long shot.

Finally, after a few hours, Franklin and Connor walk out of the bar, followed by the blonde girlfriend, getting into the town car waiting on the sidewalk.

A minute later, the rest of them walk out, heading down the pavement. I spot Killian and Reign while in front of them walks Kendall, her arm linked with Sienna's. They are laughing, looking like a group of friends going out, and I follow them in the shadows until they reach one of the clubs downtown. The pink neon sign says Club 72, and the ridiculous line of people waiting on the cobblestones tells me it's a popular place to be. A red carpet is spread out in front of the door that's guarded by two bouncers looking like they could be extras in a Game of Thrones episode.

As soon as the bouncer spots the Wolfe brothers, he opens the velvet rope for them and they disappear into the club like they come here every night.

Dammit.

I suck in a lungful of the cold air, then clench my jaw as I decide on my next move.

Pulling out the ID card in the back of my jeans, I glance at the picture. I slowly push out my breath, keeping my tears in the back of my head.

I know I can easily get in with this, but the birth date has my heart aching. It feels weird, as if I'm tainting her memory, but I push away the feeling, knowing I just need to suck it up and do whatever it takes.

Not willing to let my nervous streak get the upper hand, I quickly cross the street before I can convince myself otherwise, then join the queue. I ignore the curious glances of people, probably from looking underdressed in my black jeans, until finally I'm next in line.

"ID," the bouncer grumbles. With parted lips, I stare at his height as he peers down at me with dark brown eyes. When he clears his throat, arching his brows in question, I snap out of it, giving him a tight smile. I hand over the ID and he takes it from my hand with suspicion in his gaze. His eyes move back and forth between the card and my face while my heart pounds against my ribcage and pebbles move down the skin on my arms. The seconds tick by and it feels like minutes until he opens his mouth.

"Sofia. Pretty name." He hands me back the card and I take it from his hand.

"Thank you."

His grumpy appearance softens a little as he gives me a smile, then opens the rope to grant me access, and the corners of my mouth curl thankfully in relief. Without hesitation, I put my feet in motion, a rejoicing feeling taking over when the sound of the music becomes louder with every step.

"Oh, Sofia!" My feeling of triumph falls down the drain when he calls out the name that lifts the hairs on the back of my neck. I freeze, closing my eyes for a moment as I take a deep breath, and turn around with a fake smile splitting my face in anticipation.

"Yeah?"

"Happy birthday." He throws me a wink and my fake smile turns into a real one before I rear my body back and move through the door as fast as I can. Relieved, I push it open, my cheeks being hit by the damp air of the club. My eyes need a few seconds to adjust to the strobe lights and my nose scrunches when the penetrating smell of alcohol attacks my nose.

I welcome it with a contented sigh.

Since I've been alone, I haven't touched a drop of alcohol, feeling a deep desire to keep my senses sharp. But for some reason, I feel out of my element and in desperate need of a drink. I spot a row of free stools at the bar and take a seat as I shrug off my leather jacket, followed by my zip-up hoodie to adjust to the humidity, then I order a glass of vodka. The bartender looks at me in suspicion. I wonder if I should add something cool, like, *on the rocks,* but luckily, he keeps his mouth shut, and when he places my drink in front of me, he takes my money without any remarks.

I put the glass to my lips, the burn coating my throat and warming me internally. I repeat the action three more times before I feel my senses settle, then I twist my body a little to roam around the club to find my object of interest. It's filled with people clearly older than me, dancing and having a good time.

Ever since freshman year, I would fantasize about when I was old enough for this kind of night. Having fun with my friends. Flirting with older boys. But right now, it does fuck all for me. If anything, it feels like a fake form of enjoyment, now that I know the world isn't all rainbows and unicorns.

It doesn't take me long to find the girls dancing in the middle of the dancefloor, and when I see one of them glancing at something on the other side of the club, I follow her line of sight until I notice the two Wolfe brothers.

Bingo.

6

"You really gotta stop smiling." I give my brother a teasing smirk, then take a sip of my whiskey.

"I can't." Reign looks like a love-struck fool, and I'm enjoying it just as much as he is.

"Have you kissed her yet?"

"No." He glares at me with pursed lips. "Because my tool of a brother has fucking bad timing."

"Sorry about that," I titter, not meaning shit of it.

"But I guarantee you that my lips are on hers within the hour."

The smile he's giving me is smug, as if it's already in the bag. But Reign wickedly fucked up his relationship with Sienna, and I know she ain't going to jump back into his arms that easily. The last couple of weeks have proven that.

"Don't fuck it up, Reign." He meets the knowing look I'm shooting at him with a serious one of his own.

"I won't. Not again."

I hope he's right, for his sake. But the cold shoulder she kept giving him for the last few weeks tells me he's gonna have to work a little harder than that. She's going to make him grovel for it until his knees bleed.

"There is a girl staring at you from the bar."

I take a sip of my drink, never following Reign's line of sight. "I noticed."

The truth is, I saw her from the second she walked in here.

Alexandra Lee.

Missing for the last eight months, but clearly not vanished since she's been following me around like a damn puppy for the last week. She tried to be a good little spy, doing her best to stay out of my sight except for that first time on the street, but I've seen how she's followed my every step like a shadow. Not because she stands out in a crowd, because she looks like any other teenage girl, but now that I've seen her face, I can't seem to unsee it. It made it easier to spot her since she has been tailing me for days.

Our men noticed it too, since her stealth mode needs a wicked amount of work, but I told them to let her go, simply because I'm curious how far she'll take it before she makes a move for whatever she wants. The fact that she's no longer keeping it a secret that she wants my attention, staring at me with her navy-blue eyes, tells me that's probably now.

"You gonna do anything about that?" Reign asks with raised eyebrows.

It's tempting, because as much as I want to teach the little girl a lesson to not play with the big boys until she's older,

I'm fucking curious about what's ticking her confidence to make her think she can outsmart me. I've been seeing her face every day, and I've become a bit addicted to it. I like waking up in the morning, knowing we're playing this game of hide and seek.

It's been putting a smile on my face.

A devilish one, but still.

"Yeah, why not." A wolfish grin splits my cheeks, and I knock down the rest of my glass. Then I slide off the stool, giving my little brother a mock salute, to saunter off to my latest stalker.

"Wrap it up, man," Reign bellows behind my back. "You don't want to get any cooties."

"Shut up, you tool."

When she sees me approaching her, she turns her head, sipping her drink as if she's unaware. I notice all the muscles on her back tense under her black skin-tight t-shirt, her chest slowly moving up and down, but the nervous twitch in her jaw tells me her pulse would be racing underneath my palm if I placed my hand around her neck right now.

We really need to work on her ability to blend in and act indifferent, because she looks as unaffected as a well-trained dog, wagging her tail until she's allowed out of her crate.

Taunting, I brush my chest against her back, moving past her, then sit down at the empty stool next to her. With my knees caging her in from the side, I pop my elbow onto the bar, resting my head in my palm with a cocky grin. Most women would drop to their knees if I gave them the focused attention I'm giving her, but she just twists her neck, glaring at me with fiery eyes. Uncertainty crosses her face, but she quickly tries to swallow it away.

"I need to get the bouncer fired since he clearly didn't ask you for an ID."

"He did."

My brows raise, my expression turning mocking as I breathe out a quiet laugh.

"That's right. I forgot you were this teenage ninja turtle, wicked slick and all."

She presses her lips together, keeping her glare pointed at me with her chin held up high, bringing my attention to her slender neck. Her fair skin teases me, my fingers aching to touch it as I wonder how soft it might feel. The freckles on her nose light up every time the strobe light flashes over her face, and I want to hold her cheeks in my hands so I can count them.

She lowers her eyes to her glass, ignoring my sarcastic comment.

There is something about her that keeps me intrigued, something that wants to push her buttons, while at the same time she forces a level of respect from me, even at eighteen years old. She doesn't act like a warrior princess, but she holds her own, even though I can see her heartbeat bouncing in the crook of her neck.

She tries to keep her hands busy, her chin dipped, and from behind her back, I glance at my brother acting like a chucklehead with his hand motioning like a claw. His upper lip lifts, and I don't have to hear him to know he's giving me some kind of feline stupidity. I press my tongue against my cheek, flipping him off without her awareness, and he replies with a teasing smile. I roll my eyes, then put my focus back on the teen in front of me. My eyes rake down her entire body, before I move them back to her face, peering at her as she quietly keeps sipping whatever sits in her tumbler.

Feeling brash, I pull it out of her hand, brushing my fingers against her with the intent to catch her off guard. To make her snap at me.

"Why are you following me?" I ask as I bring the drink to my lips, staring at her from over the rim of the glass. The cheap vodka attacks my tongue and I do my best to not knit my brows together at the disgusting taste. "That's wicked awful shit."

She snorts, her blue eyes finally finding mine. They look like blue diamonds, captivating and unbreakable.

"Do I look like a loaded crime lord? If you think it's shit, how about you buy me a real one?" There is sass in her voice that has me licking my lips. Part of me wants to grab her neck and forcefully remind her who she's talking to, but instead, I lift my hand to the bartender, holding up two fingers. Our gazes stay tangled until the bartender places two glasses of his best whiskey in front of me, and she boldly takes a glass before pouring it down her throat like a fucking shot.

A full laugh ripples from my chest when she slams the glass back on the bar, a smug grin written on her pretty face. "You're right. Way better."

Amused, I bring my face closer to her, getting into her personal space. My hand sits on the back of her stool, my breath fanning the skin underneath her ear. She smells fresh out of the shower, with a hint of something floral that shows the soft edges I know she's hiding so well. It's exhilarating being this close to her, bubbling up senses I thought would be numb until my last breath.

"Why are you following me, *little girl*?"

She slowly turns her head, looking into my eyes with a fearless expression.

"Help me." It's a mix between a question, a command, and a plea, and for some reason, I feel my organs shriveling. That same sympathy I felt before wants to crawl up to the surface, but I shove it back down like an unwanted guest.

"What's in it for me?" I push her brown hair to the side, brushing the tips of my fingers on her velvet skin, giving me a clear vision of the goosebumps trickling down her slender neck.

"Whatever you want."

Interesting.

"What do you have to offer?"

"Myself," she replies without hesitation, though I'm not sure she understands the true meaning of that answer. "I'll do whatever you want."

At this proximity, my lips are dying to taste her body as I breathe her in like she's my gulp of oxygen underwater. As if the air in my lungs is vanishing and she's the only thing that can save me from drowning. It completely demolishes the sweaty people and bad liquor around us, my mind now only focused on the delicious scent in front of me. Now that I'm taking my time, hovering my lips close to her artery, I recognize her scent from that first night. It's that same subtle rose, combined with the tang of bergamot.

"Whatever I want is a pretty broad statement." Teasingly, I press a kiss on the crook of her neck, and I feel how she tenses under my touch. With a smug grin, I continue to let my lips linger under her ear.

"Are we talking sex?" I ask, my voice husky, deciding to call the animal by its name.

I watch how her throat bops when she swallows, making me wonder if she's scared or turned on by my question.

I have a feeling it's both.

I *want* it to be both.

I want her to fear me like I'm a demon, and I want her to be tempted enough to forget about that fear, deciding there is no better thing than to give in to the Devil himself.

"If that's what you want." The words sound like music to my ears, her tone daring, etched with a hint of apprehension.

"You're a child," I tell her bluntly, my lips still lingering on her skin.

"I'm a woman," she snaps, a little offended. Her tone is harsh and leaves no room for argument, but the fact that she keeps her attention on her glass shows her uncertainty. She is in way over her head, and she knows it.

I could enjoy myself, taunting her a little while longer, but I realize it's not a fair match.

Pulling my head away from her, albeit reluctantly, I let out a chuckle. "Yeah, okay." I slide off my stool, ready to end this conversation, while my dick twitches in protest. She turns me on, but I don't interact with women as young as her. No matter how hot or entertaining they are. She should be in school, hanging out with kids her age, all that bullshit college kids do. Anything but trying to piss off a criminal like me.

Her hand lands on my arm, and I glance at it with irritation, then move my gaze up to hers. The warmth of her palm seems to burn through my shirt, but I ignore it, keeping a stoic stance.

"*Please*. Just help me."

"I'm curious," I mock. "What exactly do you want me to do?"

That same desperation I've seen before washes her deep blue eyes, forcing me to keep looking at her. It ignites a feeling that cascades heat all the way up to my neck, crawling under my skin in the most inconvenient way.

"Train me. Teach me how to fight." She pauses, squeezing my arm. "Help me kill him and I'll leave Boston," she mutters the last words, and I push away my concern.

"Why would I do that?"

"Because he's a bad man," she scolds.

"Ah, come on, Lexie. That's all you got? I'm way worse than some dirty cop." Her eyes widen in shock when she hears part of her name fall from my lips, and I lick them with an arrogant smirk. "What? You think I wouldn't find out who you are? I'm a *Wolfe*. You can't follow me and expect to stay unnoticed."

She lifts her chin in defiance, reclaiming her bold stance. "It's Alexandra."

"Whatever." I roll my eyes.

"You're an asshole, but you don't seem heartless," she foolishly continues. I should end this conversation, and not even tolerate how she's wasting my time, but my feet fail to move forward as I keep staring into her determined gaze.

"Then you're blind." I smile.

"Or I see right through you."

A guffaw erupts from my belly, and I throw my head back in laughter. "Oh, you're cute."

When I dip my chin back to the firecracker in front of me, I feel the tip of a knife pressed in my stomach, and my smile slides off my face as I glance down. When my sight moves back up, I am met by a devilish gleam that stirs up a big pot of emotion inside of me.

And not all good, might I add.

She looks sexy as hell with that glint in her eyes, her lips pursed in a *I don't give a fuck* look. But the undeniable desire growing in my groin is accompanied by a flaring anger that wants to strangle her, wants to knock her head on the bar for having the balls to threaten me. I don't care if you're eighty or eighteen.

No one threatens me.

"You still think I'm cute now?" she taunts, lifting her brow.

I hold still, not uttering a word, making her perish under my gaze. My jaw ticks, and I can see the fear overtaking her courage as her pupils dilate, her eyelids moving up just a tad more. It's barely noticeable. But I see it. My entire stance becomes more domineering as I square my shoulders and dip my chin, bringing my face close to hers. Her sweet scent prevents me from making any rash decisions, like yanking her out of here by her neck or snapping it all together.

She swallows roughly when my fingers move over hers, softly pulling the blade from her hand. As if she's shrinking under my energy, she doesn't move a muscle, then flinches when I slam the knife onto the bar top. I wrap my hand around her neck, pulling her close enough to put my lips flush with her ear.

"Next time I see you, you better have found a way to impress me enough to keep you alive. Because let me tell you one thing, *Lexie*. No one threatens me and lives. Unless there is a fucking good reason for me to not slit your throat while I sip on a glass of whiskey." I pause to look into her eyes, admiring the defiance that's still shining through. "Get out of here, before I tell the bouncer he let through a teenager with a big mouth. I'm too busy to babysit." I let go of her neck with a growl, and she gasps when I release her, then I saunter off with a building fury flowing through my veins.

I feel like stomping my feet, but I hold on to my anger with composed steps. Confusion crosses my face when Reign isn't standing at the table anymore and I whip my neck around to scan the dancefloor. With a scowl, I strut through the club, looking for the dark-headed girls that belong to my brothers. When I can't find them, I make my way down the hall to check the restrooms, right in time to see my brother stalking into the ladies' room with Kendall on his heels. Kendall's eyes are wide with worry, causing my feet to pick up pace before I storm through the door.

My jaw clenches so much it hurts when my eyes land on Sienna sitting on the floor. Her slender hands rub the skin on her neck as if someone has grabbed her, and instantly my lip lifts into a snarl. Alexandra Lee runs through my mind, igniting the ticking time bomb inside of me. If I find out she's behind this to get my attention, I'm going to wrap my hands around her velvety neck and watch her life slowly simmer out of her.

"Who did this?" Reign grits out as I move my gaze up and down Sienna. She seems startled, maybe even a bit uneasy, her other hand holding her head.

"Some girl," she croaks, building up tension in my jaw.

"What does she look like?" I grunt. My hands ball to fists, and with the anger that is already seeping from my pores, I feel like I'm destructive to anything that will find my path in the next few minutes.

"Where were you?" Reign scolds, snapping his head to me, but I keep my eyes on Sienna, dying for her to give me something to rage about. To give me the chance to take my anger out on someone, preferably a girl with brown hair and navy-blue eyes.

"What does she look like?" I command again.

"Long platinum blonde hair. Red dress."

A twang of disappointment slams through my chest, but I ignore it, and before she's done talking, I twist on my heels, storming out of there to look for whatever blonde I can find.

Forcefully, I push everyone in the club aside, baring my teeth like the Wolfe that I am. People give me questioning looks, with the occasional brave dirty glance, but I can't find a blonde that's wearing a red dress. The DJ arches his brows as I step into the DJ booth, giving me full access to the entire floor, before he continues his set and I let my eyes roam the area. Unintentionally, they hold still at the bar. The seat Lexie was in is now occupied by some guy. With a pinched mouth, I give up to find my brother and the girls.

Two minutes later, I walk outside, welcomed by the brisk air of the fall night that's hitting me in the face. I suck in a deep breath, shaking my shoulders to hide my aggression from Reign as I watch him put Sienna in the SUV waiting for us.

"Are you okay?" I ask Kendall as I come to stand beside her. I feel how she eyes me before fixing her attention back to Sienna.

"I'm fine," she breathes out. "But Franklin isn't going to like this."

"Don't tell him just yet. We need to know if it's related first." I grab her arm, pleading. Her blue eyes remind me of Lexie's, and that fucks with my head until I see her pink lips smirking.

"I won't. But you can't hide this for too long, Kill."

I shoot her a thankful smile. At the beginning of this year, Kendall and I started on the wrong foot, and I made her life a living hell. She has every right to hate me after the shit I pulled, but she took it all like a queen and has never brought it up once. In fact, in the last few months, we've been getting along better than I ever expected.

"I know. I'll look into it tomorrow." We share an expression of understanding as my brothers shut the car door with a loud thud and then spin to face us.

"I want you to check the feed for me," Reign grunts. "Find out who that girl was."

I nod, but it's followed by a shrug and an expression that shows my skepticism. "Could've been any girl with a history with you, though. You're not a saint."

He glares at me before rubbing his face. "I haven't slept with any girls in months, and the only blonde I slept with is Callie Reyes."

"It can't be her?"

"Don't be fucking stupid, Killian. She's my friend. Besides, she's a Carrillo now. She doesn't have a thing for me."

I know. His relationship with Callie is nothing more than friendly and, from what I hear, she isn't the petty kind.

"So any blonde one-night stands you can remember?"

"None," he replies.

I slap his shoulder in encouragement. "We'll figure it out. Go home. I'll take Kendall home."

Reign gives me a tight smile, then takes Kendall into a quick hug before getting into the car.

We watch as they drive away, and I put my attention back on Kendall.

"Let's get you home."

"I can get home myself." She holds back my arm as I take out my phone to call for another car to pick us up. "It's okay. You look like you need another drink, Killian. It's okay. I'm not helpless, you know." An encouraging expression flashes through her kind eyes, and I shake my head with a smile.

"You don't say?"

The corners of her mouth curl as she holds her lips pressed together.

"Fine, but I'm waiting for the car to get here, or Franklin will want my head on a platter."

She chuckles, holding her trench coat close with her hands. "Sure thing."

7

Lexie

Thirty minutes after my night club fiasco, I storm through the front door of my studio, pressing my back against the wood as soon as I lock up behind me. I close my eyes, resting my head against the surface as the feeling of defeat washes every inch of my body, exhausting me. Licking my lips, my chin trembles and tears slip down my cheeks.

For the first time in weeks, I let my emotions suck me into a vortex, spinning me around like I'm merely a bubble failing to reach for the surface.

A wail sounds through the room, showering my skin with pebbles as if it's not even mine, while my shaky legs collapse beneath me, and I fall to the floor. I press my face into my hands, unable to keep my feelings in check. The nervousness that's been boiling all night finally spills over, and I'm too weak to stop it. To hold it back.

As soon as I pushed the tip of that knife into his stomach, and his eyes locked with mine, I knew I wasn't going to do it. I wasn't capable. I don't have the guts to pull through, and he knew. I could see it in his deep green eyes. I swam in them, completely frozen as I feared the result of my stupid decision, and when he let me go with nothing more than a threat, I ran.

I stumbled out the door, jogging off like the big bad wolf was on my heels and I needed to hide in the safety of my house.

And now I sit here, behind my front door, like a scared little bunny, helpless as fuck.

A year ago, I was worried about what to wear to graduation, if I'd be able to get into the University of Indiana, and if I could hang out with friends after ballet practice. I'm not cut out for this shit. I'm not some fearless spy or assassin.

I'm Alexandra Lee, daughter of Jackson Lee and Anna Lee-Kulakov. Little sister of Sofia, senior at Boston High and aspiring ballerina.

Or at least that's who I was before.

Now, I have no clue who I am other than a lost orphan. The desire to quit, to pack a bag and run as far away as I can, is strong. But the tight knot in my stomach prevents me from doing that. I've been living with nagging dread since the moment I saw the life slipping out of my sister's body in front of my eyes and I know it will always stay there if I don't kill the man responsible for it.

I stare into the emptiness of the apartment, my eyes pointed at something, but I don't see anything. My mind wanders until I bring my feet under my body, rising up as I wipe my nose with the back of my hand. Without thought, my feet slowly carry me to the duffel bag in the corner of the room, and I feel the energy shift. I dig out my pointe shoes, and with my tears still sliding down one by one, I take off my boots. I place my jacket on the bed, running my hand over it as if I'm removing my armor. My breathing has slowed, the trembling of my chin now stopped. A stone still sits in the back of my throat, as big as Mount Rushmore, unable to swallow away. But I ignore it, just like my stained cheeks, as I put on my toe shoes with care, wrapping the satin around my calves.

When I'm done, I reach for the old record player on the vanity desk across the bed while my eyes stay fixed on the city lights out of the window. I used to feel at home in Boston, enjoying every corner of every street. My room, in our old house in Chelsea, looked out over the main channel, with downtown and South Boston staring back at me every night. I would stare at the city lights until my eyes grew heavy, and I'd drift off to a blissful sleep. A sleep where dreams were still outshining the occasional nightmare and wishes would always come true. Now, living on the other side of town, that feeling seems ungraspable, but I can see it dangle in front of my eyes the entire time.

They feel as familiar as a long distant cousin, family by blood, but no real connection by heart.

I place the tonearm on the vinyl, knowing my grandmother only owned one record to play on this old thing, and I push out the air in my lungs when the classical notes of Adolphe Adam reverberate against the walls. With my toes pointed, I get into first position, counting to three before I let the music drift me away. Letting my body take over, I dance the first act of Giselle like I've done hundreds of times before. My muscles act from memory, not even making me actively acknowledge what I'm doing, and within seconds I feel the fog in my mind settle, replacing the nuisance with clarity. The stretching of my muscles with every move gets my blood pumping in a way I've always loved, forcing me to push hard like I know I can.

Dancing is the one place where I've always excelled. Where I'm strong and completely in control. The last few weeks I feel like I've been losing my sanity with every passing day, but right here, right in this moment, I feel stronger than ever. As I go through the entire melody, I stand still when the music stops, my gaze still fixed on the night sky outside my window.

My tears have stopped flowing.

A small smile creeps onto my lips.

And as I breathe in through my nose, I wait until the record repeats before my limbs start to move on autopilot again, this time feeling lighter than five minutes ago. My smile grows wider as I close my eyes, sensing my strength returning with every move I make.

And by the time the record plays for the fifth time, I feel revived, tapping into my endless will to thrive.

Whatever happens, happens.

But I will not stop.

Killian Wolfe cannot intimidate me.

And Sullivan will pay for what he did to my family.

8

Killian

I wake up the next morning with a pounding headache and a warm body pressed against mine. With my eyelids barely open, I try to recall last night. I quickly remember how I drank way too much after I went back inside the club and flashes of a brunette dance in front of my face. Pleased, I glance at the girl lying beside me, softly pushing her brown hair from her face. Hopefully... I hold my breath, disturbing myself by the action as I look for freckles on her cheeks. *None.*

When I realize it's not the brunette I want it to be, I let out a grunt and nudge her awake with anything but delicacy.

"Ay, wake up," I bark, already annoyed by the fact that her body is touching mine.

She looks at me through squinting eyes, lets out a moan, then closes her eyes again.

Growling, I tap her arm. "Get out."

This time, her eyes shoot open and she gives me an incredulous look.

"Are you serious?" she huffs. I twist my head to her, contemplating if she's hot enough for a morning fuck, but frustratedly my question is answered when Lexie's face flashes through my mind again. I'm not sure what the fuck is happening, but it seems like in twenty-four hours, Alexandra Lee has ruined brunettes for me. Now the only brunette I want to feel underneath me is the one who can give me a look like she doesn't give a fuck. Like she's not intimidated by me, even though every single part of her body language tells me she is. I want to smell her fear, making her combust in my hands with a single touch.

"Dead. Now get the fuck out of my house or we're going to have some wicked issues."

She pushes out a breath, with her mouth agape, but doesn't dare to say anything else when she becomes aware of the glare sitting on my face. Without giving me another glance, she gets out of the bed, collects her clothes, and retreats to the parlor. I cock my head at her peachy ass, giving myself a pat on the back for picking up a girl that hot while being drunk as fuck.

Not bad, Kill.

"You're the biggest asshole I've ever met!" she yells as she gets dressed.

"Thanks. Close the door on your way out, will you?" An offended grunt is audible, doing jack shit for me, and I close my eyes until I hear her open the front door, followed by a loud thud as it slams shut. I throw my arm over my eyes, not ready to start the day because my mind keeps going back to the one thing I shouldn't be thinking about; Lexie.

I told her to stop following me, so I only grew angrier with myself every second after, when I noticed how my eyes kept searching for her as I got back into the club. My body wanted to feel her lips against mine, and my mind wanted to taunt her one more time. To push her buttons and see how far I could go with her. To play.

Luckily, my thoughts are interrupted by the ringing of my phone, and I groan when I see my brother's name popping up on my screen.

The fact that he's calling at eight in the morning after spending the night with Sienna is not a good sign.

"For fuck's sake, Reign. What did you do now?" I rub my hand over my face.

"I didn't fucking do anything! She just tried to sneak out on me."

"You must have done something." I get out of the bed, heading to the kitchen for some coffee.

"I gave her three orgasms in an hour. Does that count?" he jeers.

"Well, maybe that did scare her away," I joke. "Thinks it's too much work to keep up with your stamina."

"Funny, Kill."

I grab a cup from the cabinet and place it under the coffee machine, then press the button. "Come on, Reign. You must have said something?"

"I swear, I didn't do shit. We had sex. It was great. No, scratch that, it was mind-blowing, and if she tells you otherwise, she's fucking lying. We fell asleep fucking spooning and this morning she tried to sneak out, thinking I was still asleep."

"That's fucked up." I feel for him, because knowing my brother, he probably wanted to make her breakfast and all that romantic bullshit.

"Tell me about it."

"She's just scared, you know that, right?" I tell him, playing the devil's advocate. I know Sienna loves my brother, but Reign really hurt her, and I understand why she's staying hesitant. Especially since he refuses to tell her about his past.

"Yeah, but I'm really trying here, Killian."

I sigh, taking my cup from the machine, and turn around to press my back against the counter. "I know you are." The nutty aroma enters my nose, simmering down my own frustration, and I take a sip. "Where is she now?"

"Stormed out. Can you just do me a favor and check if she gets home okay?" There is worry in his voice, and I can't help the smile that's forming because of it.

"Yeah, sure."

"You picked up some pussy last night?"

"Something like that," I mutter, thinking about a way to not talk about my night. The last thing I want is to tell my brother how, for the first time in my life, I didn't enjoy whatever woman I brought home. My mind is searching for an opening to bring the subject back to something else until I hear noises coming over the line without my brother uttering a word.

"Reign? What are you doing?" Frowning, I pause, waiting for his reply, then call out when it stays quiet. "Reign? Are you still there?"

Still nothing.

"Reign?" I yell this time.

"Yeah." His reply is small, laced with what sounds like shock.

"What's going on?"

"We got a problem."

"Why?"

"I got another package," he informs.

"Fuck." I let my head hang, realizing this stalker shit my brother is dealing with is getting out of hand. As much as I want to keep brushing it all off, we need to deal with this.

"I'll call Franky."

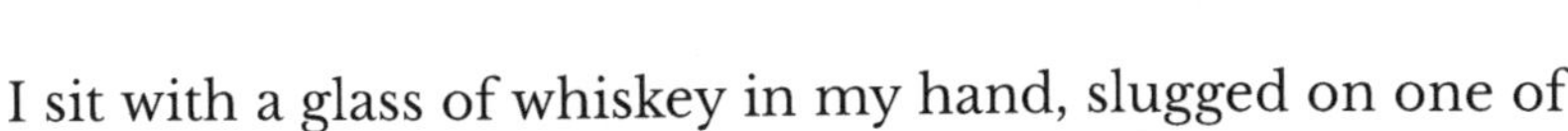

I sit with a glass of whiskey in my hand, slugged on one of the chairs in my brother's office at our family mansion.

"This is getting out of hand." Franklin scowls at Reign, repeating my thoughts. Franklin and I have the same cunning character, giving us the ability to look ahead, strategize, and always be one step ahead of our enemies. We both didn't really take these weird packages seriously, but we have to acknowledge someone is angry at Reign and this is no longer just a scorned girl.

This is now a threat.

And a threat to one Wolfe, is a threat to all.

Franklin is sitting behind his desk, looking completely calm and composed, with a *don't give a fuck* look in his eyes. But there is an urgency in his voice. Ever since our biggest enemy kidnapped Connor's baby boy Colin, we've been taking any risks even more seriously. A year ago, he'd make less of a fuss about it, but since our family expanded with Kendall, followed by Lily and Colin, he doesn't leave anything up to chance. Our family is growing and so is my oldest brother's worry.

"How can we not find anything about this–" He pauses, rubbing his five o'clock shadow. "This *girl*?" Franklin pushes out. "Is it a girl?"

"It has to be, right? Disgusting romantic gestures?" Reign shrugs. "I've been breaking my head over who it could be. I even checked Providence High, went through the yearbooks to figure out if there were any girls I might have hurt in some kind of way. But I came up blank. I can't remember making any enemies or breaking any hearts other than Sienna's. But the swan references tell me it has to be someone who knew both me and Aubrey." His face is showered with frustration.

"Unless he broke a guy's heart once." Connor chuckles, standing in front of the window with his arms crossed in front of his body. There is a smirk on his lips and Reign replies by pulling a face.

"Pretty sure there is no one with a bromance in their head."

"I wouldn't be so sure. You're not called Prince Charming for no reason," Connor counters.

"Bite me, Con."

"You got anything on the delivery guy?" I question, and he shakes his head.

"Haven't found him. All I know is I have him walking in Seaport with a little girl. I can trail them all the way to Harbor Street and then they disappear. I'm not even sure it's a guy, though. Could've been a girl in disguise. He wasn't a fat ass like Connor." He nudges his chin toward Connor, who flips him off.

"Maybe we should check underground," I say, taking a sip of my drink. "See if there are any blueprints of the area that show any cellars or tunnels."

"Good idea," Franklin agrees. "Connor, arrange that. I want those prints on my desk first thing in the morning. We need to comb out the entire area as soon as possible."

I waggle my head, giving Franklin a knowing look. "There is an event this weekend at the ICA. The cops are not going to let us roam the area without another wicked bag of money."

"We pay those *tools* more than enough."

"We could push it over the weekend?" I suggest.

"No. Reign, find some dirt on the officers on duty this weekend. I don't want to wait five more days before we can find out what's underground in the area."

A deep sigh comes from Reign's lungs. "Fine."

"Kill." Franklin rears his attention back to me. "I want you to do another round. See if you can find anyone who wants to talk. Dangle money, dangle your knife, I don't care. I want something."

I nod, downing the rest of my drink.

"In the meantime, I want more security for the girls and Colin. I want three men with them at all times. Reign, what about Sienna?" Reign looks up at Franklin with irritation.

"What about her?"

"It would be safer if she stayed at the mansion for a while. Stay under our protection until we find out who's after us."

"Pff, yeah, doubt she'll go for that," he scoffs.

"Did you screw it up again?" Franklin cocks a brow, giving him a reprimanding look, and I keep quiet.

"I didn't do shit. We had sex. She freaked. We fought. She left."

"Story of your life." Connor grins.

"Can't you go piss someone else off, Connor?"

"I can," he replies like the asshole that he is. "But I don't want to."

"Should we send her protection?" Franklin asks, ignoring my brothers' banter.

"She'll freak out if you do that," Reign tells him.

I clear my throat, looking at Reign with a serious expression.

"But we have to, Reign. Remember that girl who assaulted her? If it isn't for this stalker we're looking for, we still need to have someone keep an eye on her for the sole fact that she's being associated with us again. If the city thinks she's one of us, she'll have a target on her back."

He stays quiet, then rubs a hand over his face. "Yeah, just make sure she doesn't know."

"Alright. We'll send some men to her to make sure nothing happens to her," Franklin announces, and Connor and I get up to get back to work.

"Hold up, Kill." Connor's hand falls on my chest as we stroll into the foyer, and I turn to face my brother. His blond hair is a big contrast with my brown strands, but like all of us four, he possesses the same green eyes we inherited from our mother. His scowl stays glued to his face, but knowing him my entire life, I don't know him any other way.

"Security is telling me some girl is following you around," he says, a frown crossing his face.

"I know." A smile wants to slip through, but I hold it back.

"You know?"

"Yeah. Her name is Alexandra Lee. I met her the last time I went to Sullivan. Cornered her in the alley next to his building when I was doing the rounds. She wanted to shoot the bastard, giving him a permanent spot at the cemetery."

His brows move to the ceiling. "She wants him dead? Why?"

"Something about revenge. She says he killed her family." I believe her, but as long as I don't have proof, it doesn't mean shit to me or my brothers.

"Did he?"

"Probably." I shrug, bouncing my car keys around in my palm. "All I could find was her family being murdered by a burglar in April. Their jewelry was gone and every member of the family had a bullet to the head, except the youngest daughter who wasn't home. Alexandra Lee, a senior at Boston High. She's been officially missing since that night."

"She's in high school?" Connor exclaims. He nods his head, impressed, then fixes his gaze back to me. "Except she's not missing if she's following you around."

"Right," I muse.

"Did Reign dig up anything else?"

"I haven't asked him to."

"Why the hell not?" Connor hisses, eyeing the office door. His voice is low, making sure no one hears us. It's what I appreciate the most about my brothers. Even though we trust each other one hundred percent, we know sometimes we don't need to worry each other about every single detail going on. Connor can question why I'm letting Lexie follow me around like a stray dog, but he'll respect my decision to handle it myself before he'll pass it on to Franklin.

"Because he has more important things on his mind, doesn't he?" I counter, rolling my eyes as I dart a look toward the door. “Besides, the girl is not a threat. I’m handling it.”

“How can you be sure?” he calls out behind me.

I turn my head with a smirk flashing across my face. “She’s an eighteen-year-old girl, Con. I’ve faced hotter fires than a high school senior with a want for vengeance.”

He shakes his head, crossing his arms in front of his chest. His bulky arms almost burst out of his skin-tight t-shirt, making his shoulders even broader.

“Don’t underestimate a woman with a mission, little brother. She might be young, but sounds to me she has nothing to lose either. Those are the most dangerous.”

I stand still, staring at him as I take in his words. The annoying thing is, I don’t want his words to be true, but while he throws them in my face, I know they are. The reason she’s still trailing my every step is because she’s got nothing else to do. She’s not going to quit, simply because she doesn’t have anything else to live for.

But I also saw the innocence in her pretty blue eyes. She is no match for me.

“I can handle it.”

9

Lexie

"You better impress me."

His last words have been replaying in my head over and over again, knowing I get one final shot and one shot only. If I piss Killian Wolfe off even more, there is a big chance he will bring me to Sullivan himself, just so he can watch me squirm in fear as he ends me.

But this time, I'm prepared.

This time, I'm not leaving without getting what I want.

He wants to be impressed? Fine.

I followed him to a bar in the Seaport District, and I watched him get in before trailing after him.

I'm no longer hiding. I have a gut feeling Killian Wolfe likes to hunt, and I'm not willing to be his prey. I need something from him and I'm going to get it head on, forcing the respect I deserve by showing him I'm not some silly little girl.

When I let my feet fall over the threshold of the bar, the brisk air is a big contrast with the heat inside. The humid atmosphere hits my cheeks as I glance around the space.

Killian takes a seat next to his brother Reign, who's scowling, with a glass of liquor dangling in front of his face.

I take the stool on the other end of the bar, close to the door, and across from the two brothers so I can keep them in my line of sight as I silently wait for him to notice me.

Reign seems aggravated, talking to his brother with attitude clear on his face. Silently, I order a Coke, trying to decipher the nature of their conversation. There is frustration flashing over both of their faces and I can't say I'm not curious as fuck. But Reign's mouth stops moving when he locks his gaze with mine, a surprised expression forming as his eyebrows arch.

I can feel my heart rate picking up, but I keep my indifferent stance as he says something to his brother.

Slowly, Killian turns his head, and our eyes connect. For a split second, I can feel my heart jumping out of my chest when his mesmerizing eyes fully point at me, but it's quickly settled, vanished at the same time Killian rears his head back to his brother like I'm insignificant.

A few days ago, the move would make me feel small like a mouse, but now it's responsible for the smirk traveling my face. I lick my lips as he takes a sip from his glass, faking his indifference. But he can't hide the amusement ghosting his sharp jaw and green eyes.

I know they are talking about me. I can feel it in every fiber of my being, and knowing my name sits in his mouth excites me more than it should. I like being noticed by

Killian Wolfe. I like giving him no other option than to acknowledge me like I'm one of his business acquaintances. Or enemies.

I drop my chin to my glass, stifling a chuckle as I take a sip of my Coke. When I bring my gaze back up, my eyes quickly lock with his again, like a steel cord connects them. Holding them in place without our will. His body is slightly turned, provokingly giving me his full attention.

To unnerve me. Scare me, I'm sure. But not tonight.

Not today.

Not ever.

You see, what he doesn't realize is, I got nothing to lose.

I shoot him a defiant look, finishing my glass in three big sips before slamming it on the wood of the bar.

My eyes never dart away from his, feeling the oxygen in the air becoming scarce. He challenges me, trying to tick me off, but I'm ready for him. I slide off the stool, flipping him off as I walk backwards toward the exit. He thinks he got me.

That I'm leaving because he won.

Good. Let him think that. Killian Wolfe thinks he's got it all figured out, and that I'm cowering under his intimidation attempt, bailing before the tension gets the best of me.

But he shouldn't underestimate me.

Let's play, Wolfe.

10

It's a little past eleven when I open my front door, tossing my keys onto the side table next to it. I take off my leather jacket, throwing it over the couch before making my way to my open kitchen, then halt in the middle of the room.

A shiver runs down my spine, lifting every hair on my back as my senses come to life.

She's here.

I *know* she's here.

I can sense her. I can feel her presence fall over me like a warm blanket, but that's not what gives her away.

It's her perfume. Her scent.

I can smell a rosy whiff that is equivalent to her and I suppress a smile, biting my lip.

Good girl.

I hear her take four lightweight steps behind me, giving me enough time to turn around and improvise to disarm her, but I don't. I stand statue still with a grin on my face until I feel the cold metal of the gun pushed against the nape of my neck.

"Impressive enough?" There is a cockiness in her sweet voice that turns me on, heating the skin on my neck as I feel my insides burning up.

"How did you get in?" I growl to hide my amusement as I turn around, the barrel of her gun now aimed between my eyes. I have to give it to her; I didn't think she'd have the balls to break into my apartment. She made it clear tonight that she was challenging me, but I didn't think she was resourceful enough to resort to breaking and entering.

Connor was right. I underestimated her.

"Picked the lock." She sounds smug.

"The alarm?"

"Removed the AC power."

"How did you find it?"

"Google."

Okay, I need to get a better security system. With a slight frown about my failing alarm, I take a minute to revel in the sight before me.

She's standing there with her gun pointed at me, looking way too hot and fire blazing. Her brown hair frames the fair skin on her cheeks, her freckles undetected because of the dim light, but I know they are there. She's wearing the bomber jacket I've always seen her in, and her black boot-covered feet are slightly parted, giving her a confident stance to match the scowl in her narrowed eyes.

For the first time, I don't see an eighteen-year-old girl.

I see a damn warrior.

A fucking shield maiden in the twenty-first century.

My heart races at the realization, a thrilling feeling crashing through me, but I hold her gaze with a straight face. With a slight swagger, I swipe the bottle from the counter, grabbing a glass that sits next to it, before I take a seat on my dining room table. I relax in the chair, nudging my chin to her as I splash the liquid gold into the glass.

"Have a seat."

Reluctantly, her blue eyes narrow to slits. She keeps the gun held up, but shuffles toward the seat across from me.

When she sits down, I shove the glass in front of her.

"Drink?"

"No."

I shrug. "Suit yourself."

I take a swig of the bottle, enjoying the caramel notes and biting my tongue as I watch her. Her elbow is propped up, keeping a firm grip on the gun. Her confidence has grown, her insecurity replaced by even more determination.

It's a wicked difference compared to the first time she crossed my path.

It's sexy as fucking sin.

Her pink plump lips are slightly pursed as she waits for me to say anything.

"You got spunk," I muse, playfully pressing my tongue against my cheek.

She rolls her eyes, adding to my merry feeling.

"Will you help me?"

The answer should be no. I don't have time to take care of little girls who think they are spies of the city. I got shit to do, businesses to run, criminals to keep in line.

"What do you want from me?" Impatiently, I tap the table.

"Train me."

I hold her gaze, taking another swig from the bottle. I expect her to cower under my piercing greens, but she only tips her chin, provoking me with her alluring blues. Without words, she's making it clear she's not going anywhere. She's persistent, bold, and brave as fuck for challenging a Wolfe. *In his own home.*

I want to strangle her for it until she's begging me for mercy.

I want to smell her fear on her silky skin and see the depths of her eyes drowning with fear.

But I also respect her for it, wondering how much she's willing to push her own morals to get what she wants.

How much I can corrupt her in every way possible.

She winces when I abruptly shove my chair back to get up, leaving the bottle on the table. I saunter toward her, trailing my finger along the edge of the piece of furniture. She doesn't move, keeping her gaze fixed in front of her and her fingers clasped around the gun. I peer down at her, the tension rising to a thick cloud above us. She doesn't falter, not moving a muscle. But when I softly push away her hair from her neck, I see her pulse throbbing. She closes her eyes briefly when my fingers touch her skin and I watch how her skin pebbles.

Pleased, I breathe out, loving the effect I have on her.

It's tempting to wrap my hands around her neck and take her any way I want, hoping she'll put up a fight.

But I know she won't. I can feel it in the electric energy when we share a room.

She hates me.

But she also wants me.

She just doesn't know it yet.

"I'll pick you up tomorrow at 8. Be ready." I walk through the parlor toward my bedroom, leaving her sitting at the table.

She's confused, I'm sure. But it's only adding to my amusement. She wants to play. Let's play.

"You know where I live?" she calls out.

"Get out, Lexie." I ignore her question, dropping my body onto my bed. "You got yourself in. You can get yourself out."

I wait, staring up at the ceiling with a smile.

Until finally, I hear the door open, then close behind her with a thud as she walks out of my house.

Good girl.

She got my attention, so now all she has to do is keep it.

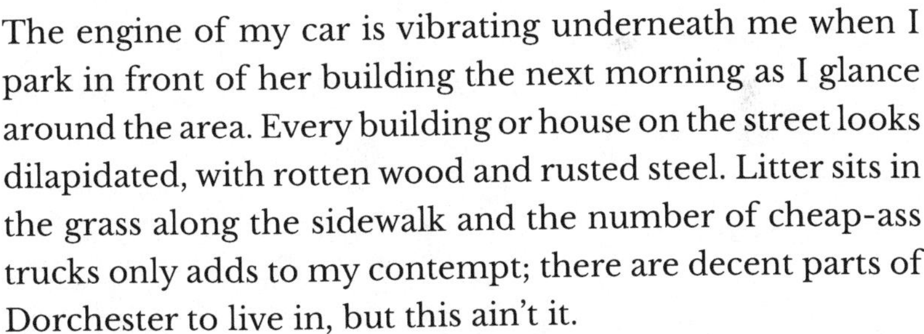

The engine of my car is vibrating underneath me when I park in front of her building the next morning as I glance around the area. Every building or house on the street looks dilapidated, with rotten wood and rusted steel. Litter sits in the grass along the sidewalk and the number of cheap-ass trucks only adds to my contempt; there are decent parts of Dorchester to live in, but this ain't it.

This is a wicked shit hole.

I push out a yawn, bringing my sunglasses up to rub the sleep out of my eyes. I couldn't sleep last night. The fact that she broke into my apartment, that she was *in* my personal space, got my entire body on high alert, making it impossible to get any rest. My mind kept wandering off, her fresh face popping into my head like a Jack-In-The-Box whenever I drifted off. She irritates me with her pushy behavior, but her fierce stance on enemy territory earned my attention. Something that will quickly vanish again if she doesn't come through that door in the next thirty seconds.

It's 8:05 and, annoyingly, I stare at the front hall, waiting for her to walk out. I'm tempted to drive off, because I lack patience for anything or anyone other than my two-year-old-nephew, but before I can act on my displeasure, she saunters out like she doesn't have a care in the world. She looks smug with another all-black outfit, topped off with her signature bomber jacket.

There is a little sway in her hips every time she takes a step forward, but her eyes show a nervous glint that gives her insecurities away.

She opens the door, lowering her gaze to face me, but not in a hurry to get in as she keeps a steady hold on the backpack resting on one shoulder.

"Where are we going?" The tone of her voice is defiant, making me flex my hands to ignore the aching feeling that runs through my fingertips.

I keep my mouth shut, cocking my head at her with an arched brow.

"I'm not getting into your car without you telling me where we're going," she presses.

"Yeah, you are," I titter, my foul mood instantly pushed to the back of my head.

She straightens her back, folding her arms in front of her chest. "No."

I lower my head, letting my sunglasses slide to the tip of my nose so I can look into her eyes without any barriers.

"You're the one breaking and entering because you want *my* help. If I wanted you dead, I wouldn't go through the trouble to get you to a secluded place and bury you. You'd be dead by now and I'd be happily calling the cops to pick you up in a body bag. Besides, who exactly is going to be looking for you when you go missing?" I taunt. The skin around her eyes twitches into a glare, her nervousness now completely gone.

"Get in the car, *Lexie*." Without waiting for her reply, I twist my head back to face the windshield.

She's a wicked fool for thinking she can blackmail me into anything, but I admire her attitude. She doesn't stand a chance against me, but she never loses the urge to push me and set her own limits. She's persistent, and even though I can't wait to demolish all the boundaries she's trying so desperately to keep, I'm also starting to respect her more for them.

She stares at me for a few more seconds before she reluctantly drops her body into the passenger seat and closes the door behind her. Placing her backpack between her legs, she quietly waits with her palms resting on her knees. I turn to her, and her brows raise in question as she meets my gaze with her piercing blue eyes.

They hit me straight in the heart, burning a hole through the soft flesh like lasers. I've never seen them in daylight and it's the first time I notice they are laced with silver specks like the damn milky way. My lips part a little in awe, the air changing to a palpable tension that has nothing to do with her fear or my irritation.

I blink, snapping myself out of it. "Put your seatbelt on."

With her lips still pressed together, the corners of her mouth lift, amusement hitting her face as she does as she's told.

"What?" I hit the throttle with enough force to toss her into her seat and she grips the handle to steady herself.

"Nothing. Just didn't think you'd be the type of guy to scowl at people for not wearing a seatbelt," she mocks.

I push down my foot to the left pedal, holding a tight grip on the wheel. The sound of the brakes holding back the tires and the smell of burning rubber reach my nose before the car comes to an abrupt stop. Her head jerks forward at the sudden motion, followed by her brown hair, before she gets slammed back into the seat, hitting the back of her head against the headrest.

With shock written all over her face, her chest moves up and down in shallow breaths.

"What the *fuck*?!" She turns her head against the seat to look at me, and I reply with a smirk, peering at her from above my sunglasses.

"Your pretty little face would be crushed if you didn't wear your seatbelt just now."

"You're an *asshole*."

"Oh, I know. But *you*"—I grab her chin, forcing her eyes to stay on me—"need to stop pretending that isn't the exact reason why you're in my car right now. Isn't that what you asked for, little Lexie?" She clenches her jaw, and I know she's inwardly squirming under my touch. When I let go, she twists her head to look out the window, her arms crossed in front of her body.

"Whatever," she pouts.

"Yeah, whatever." I chuckle, driving off again.

The rest of the drive is done in silence, although I see her shift in her seat when she reads the sign that says Lynn Woods Reservation. I expect her to pull out another snarky comment, but she keeps her mouth shut and when I park my car, I can't help poking her to get rid of her discomfort.

"Okay, you'll get a ten second headstart."

She swallows, blinking at me with her eyes widened. I can see the cogs in her head turning while I keep a straight face, knowing it's throwing her off.

"Are you serious?" I expect her voice to skip, but it comes out in a steady beat that's messing with my head when I can see a spark of excitement in her blue eyes.

I feel my cock jerk alive as she holds my gaze with less fear than I anticipated and this time it's my turn to swallow. My mind takes over, dying to chase her through the woods, like a wolf going after his prey, until I find her between my hands to claim my prize. I want to tear her flesh with my teeth as I plow deep inside of her, knowing she'll be damp from the sweat of her failed attempt to escape me.

"Are you trying to scare me?" she asks with less confidence this time.

"I'm joking," I huff, letting out an awkward chuckle, breaking my daydream.

She lets out a long sigh, and I exhale deeply, trying to calm the ache forming in my groin.

"Let's go." I exit the car to open the trunk and she does the same, coming to stand beside me. Her backpack rests over her shoulder, making her look like a dark Dora the Explorer.

It's fucking cute.

With one swift move, I pull the big duffle out of the back of my car before yanking her bag from her body and tossing it into the trunk.

"Hey! I need that!" She scowls.

I step closer to her, challenging her. "Yeah? What's in it? Your Glock 42? Maybe an extra knife, just in case it turns out you can't trust me and you need to stab me to make sure I don't dump you in the pond?"

11

Lexie

I hate it when he belittles me.

Half of the time, he intimidates the hell out of me, making me walk on eggshells to make sure I don't step on the Devil's toes, but the other half, I want to smack the grin off his face for mocking me. For treating me like an annoying little girl.

I stare back at him, pressing my teeth together with my brows in a frown that hurts my forehead. His green eyes are hypnotizing and painfully confrontational at the same time. They make my skin crawl in the most agonizing way, but I'm addicted to them, regardless. I equally love and hate the feeling he gives me when he pins me down with his gaze. It physically hurts, making it hard to breathe, but simultaneously, I've never felt more alive than staring into the vibrant eyes of Killian Wolfe.

Like he's the only one who really sees me, effortlessly digging into my soul. I feel like I can't hide anything from this man, and I have no clue how to handle that.

"Am I right?" With a smug look, his tongue darts out, licking his lower lip.

The move is slow, sensual, and creates a flutter between my thighs that I shouldn't be feeling.

"You don't have to be an asshole all the time, you know?"

He snorts with a chuckle, averting his gaze before he snaps it back, grabbing the front of my neck. I gasp at his sudden movement, my lips parting as my heart falls to the floor.

"Wrap your pretty head around it, little girl. I *am* an asshole," he snarls, though I can see the smile haunting his sharp jaw. His eyes hold a craving that is easily mistaken for a hunger to kill, but when he moves his free hand around my waist, tugging me against his body, I know killing me is not on his agenda. "But you already knew that. Because that's the whole reason you've been demanding my attention for weeks."

"I need your help because you're the only one who can train me to kill Sullivan," I counter, trying to dismiss his words.

"Nah-huh," he tuts, tightening his grip on my neck. "We both know that's some wicked bullshit, baby." He lowers his lips, the warmth of his breath burning against mine as he brushes his mouth over my skin. "I know you did your research as much as you could. You know my brothers are as equally lethal as I am. We all kill when we need to, but the difference between my brothers and me?" He pauses, his fingers pressing into my throbbing pulse. "They are more approachable. You could've gotten your eyes on Kendall or Lily, knowing your sob story would trigger their kind hearts to tell my brothers and they'd help you. You could've gone to Reign, knowing my youngest brother has a soft spot for human life in general. He would've given you all the information you needed and helped you kill Sullivan within a heartbeat. But you didn't. Instead, you went after the one Wolfe who is known for the kill and feared for the torture." I swallow under his touch, my knees feeling weak with his mouth so close to mine. My heart feels like a baseline, steady but loud as fuck as I try to contain the urge to give into the pull his body has on me.

"You went after *me*," he continues. "Want to know why?"

A hum leaves my throat, forming a smug smirk on his face.

"Because you like the thrill. The fear. The pounding of your heart. It reminds you that you're alive. You chose me, because I make you feel alive in a world that made you numb when your family died."

His words land straight in the gut, hitting the right spot of my annoyance.

He leans in, moving his mouth flush with my ear, and I close my eyes when they connect with the shell. "Stop kidding yourself, and just roll with it, *Alexandra*."

Abruptly, he lets go, and I need to steady myself at his lack of touch. He grabs the duffle, throwing it over his shoulder before he slams the trunk closed, then takes off with big strides. He leaves me standing there, stunned, and I watch him as he marches up the trail without a care in the world.

His use of my full name hasn't gone unnoticed, and I feel the smile creeping on my face, feeling like I just won the battle. My annoyance simmers down, because even though he might have gotten me all figured out, he also just showed me his cards in this game of push and pull we keep playing. I breathe in the fresh air through my nose, fueling my confidence.

"Move your ass, Lexie!" His deep voice echoes through the woods, jolting me back with a shriek before I jog behind him.

After five minutes, I follow him off the trail, deeper into the woods, until we reach a picnic table in a little clearing that isn't bigger than ten square yards. Unable to hide my leftover suspicion, I glance around the secluded area, wondering how he found this spot.

"Do you come here often?" I joke.

"Every Saturday until I was fourteen." He throws the duffle onto the table with a loud thud. "This is where my brothers and I learned to shoot."

Not the answer I was expecting, but okay.

That makes sense. I notice a few broken bottles sitting on a stomp about thirty yards away, leftover from whoever tested their skills here last.

"What made you stop?"

"Foster care."

Awkwardly, I bring my gaze to the ground, then take a seat on one of the benches as he opens the bag, pulling out two hunting rifles, an automatic gun, a pistol that looks like a Magnum and a sniper rifle. Tentatively, I watch how he places them all in front of me, feeling his eyes examining every response on my face. I've made myself familiar with guns in the last few months, knowing every part of my Glock, but watching these big guns spread out in front of me unsettles me. Like I'm living someone else's life.

"Now, I only come here to blow off some steam if I need to," he clarifies. "Which one do you wanna fire first?"

"We're going to do them all?" I nervously fidget with my fingers, annoying myself with my sudden lack of confidence.

"Yah-huh." He gives me a look that says *duh*. "What's the matter? Chickening out?"

"Never," I scoff.

"Then let's go, baby. Pick one."

A warm feeling runs through my body, moving all the way up to my cheeks.

I like it when he calls me *baby*. My sensible mind keeps telling me he probably calls all the women in his life baby, but my heart can't avoid getting all giddy over it. It leaves his tongue in a smooth, yet gruff tone, speaking to every nerve in my body.

My eyes move up and down the row of guns as I try to ignore the blush on my skin.

"That one." I point at the Magnum. The barrel is at least four fingers thick and the length takes up my entire lower arm. It looks like it's heavy, making me believe it will test my skills more than the other guns.

I bring my gaze up, catching Killian cocking a brow, and for a split second, I feel like I failed a test.

"What makes you pick that one?"

I glance at the gun again, touching the metal with my fingers. "Because it's big, thick, and intimidating compared to the others. If I can handle that one, the others will be a breeze."

When he doesn't say anything, I look up through my lashes. He keeps a straight face, but I think I can see the satisfaction in his eyes, as if he likes my answer. It makes my heart expand a little with pride, igniting another flutter in my stomach.

"Good choice," he praises, then pulls a box of bullets out of the bag. With ease, he drops out the magazine and starts loading it with bullets. "This is a Desert Eagle Magnum. It holds 0.44 bullets, big enough to blow an unrecoverable hole through anyone and anything." He holds up the bullet in the air. "It's a heavy gun. And to really wield it, you need a lot of strength in your wrists. But the most important thing"—he jams the magazine back into the gun with a fast move, then cocks it before I jerk in shock at the gunshot that follows unexpectedly—"is the kickback. Look at the barrel."

I stare at him with wide eyes. He fires another shot, making me mutter as I wince, but this time I see how much the gun snaps back after he fires a shot.

"You see how much it kicks back? You need to be prepared for that, or it will hit your head."

"Pff, it won't hit my head. I'm not *that* stupid," I puff, offended. He might be a pro, but I've been practicing enough to know I'm not an amateur either.

"Okay, hotshot. Show me your skills, then."

I boldly walk up to him, shooting him a daring look as he places the gun in my waiting palm. My hand quickly lowers at the sudden weight before I wrap my fingers around the handle. I grind my teeth, cursing my own cockiness now that I feel how fucking heavy this thing is. But determined to show him I can handle this, I bring the gun up with both hands, spreading my legs a little to steady myself.

"Elbows in. Relax your shoulders. Breathe in when you aim. Breathe out when you pull the trigger," he tells me.

"Okay."

Completely aware of his eyes fixed on me, I try to drown everything out, putting my focus solely on the rear sight. When I have the bottle centered, I don't hesitate and pull the trigger, ready to follow my bullet. But my eyes are quickly shut by a knock on my forehead, followed by a loud laugh echoing through the woods. It's deep, it's hearty, and it instantly pisses me off, but the stinging pain has me too occupied to scold him about it.

"Motherfucker!" I cry out. The cold steel hit my head with a force I wasn't expecting, and my skull feels like I walked into a door. A sharp ache makes me grip my forehead while I try to not drop the heavy gun.

"Fucking hell!" I stomp.

Killian gently pulls the gun from my hands, and I bury my face in my palms, feeling embarrassed as fuck. He keeps chuckling, placing the gun back on the table while I focus on my breathing to get rid of the pain.

Leave it up to me to make a complete fool out of myself the first chance I get.

His hands land on my hips and he tugs me against him as he plucks my hands from my face. Ashamed, I hesitantly let him, keeping my eyes fixed on his chest. I'm scared to look him in the eyes, because I know I'll have a wicked hard time holding my own when he pins me down with his stare. It's like as soon as I feel his body close to mine, I tense up, as if my body is begging him to help it relax by his touch. Add his hypnotizing eyes, and I'm done for.

"Let me see." His laughter has simmered down to amusement, and I dare to look up at him as his thumb caresses the skin on my forehead. His gentle touch is scorching, and when his green eyes fall to mine, my pussy literally stirs to life in delight, dying for him to kiss me.

I've had one boyfriend. His name was Brad. He was the team captain of the football team and looked like a dream with his shaggy blonde hair and his captivating smile. I felt on cloud nine when he first asked me out, and when he asked me to be his girlfriend at the start of senior year, I was over the moon. He was sweet, funny, and a little rough around the edges. The guy every boy looked up to and every girl wanted to date. He was my first in every single way, and even though I know I definitely had genuine feelings for him, he didn't spark my body alive like Killian Wolfe does. I try to remember how it felt when Brad would touch me, looking for something familiar, but with only a few light touches, Killian seems to have erased my high school crush from my memory.

"It's all good. Not a scratch. It might get a bit bruised, though." There is a softness in his voice that I haven't heard before, making me squirm, desperate to feel his hands everywhere. His gaze drops to my lips, and I drag my teeth over them to keep myself from closing the distance while at the same time my mouth turns dry. The craving in his eyes is primal, and I know with the wrong motivation he can be lethal. But, as much as I fear him, I also sense my body growing hungrier for him every time I'm in his proximity.

"Do it again." Breaking our connection, he takes a step back. He switches back to business mode in a heartbeat, and I can't completely hide the disappointment that comes with it. Sucking in a lungful of air, I pick up the Magnum. This time I feel more prepared, hitting the tree twenty yards in front of us without getting the barrel slammed in my face.

That's more like it.

I fire again, hitting the same spot.

Show the big bad Wolfe what you got, Alexandra.

I keep going, the hole in the tree growing bigger and bigger with every shot as I lose myself in the thrill every time I pull the trigger. I drown out Killian's burning gaze, feeling my confidence grow every time I refill the empty magazine. By the time I reload the gun for a fourth time, the tree shows a big hole from all the bullets piercing into the bark while Killian watches me, sitting on top of the picnic table.

"Yes!" I jeer. "Did you see that?"

He sits with his legs spread wide, and an amused smile creeping onto his face. There is pride laced there, and it pushes my confidence as high as the sky. Excited, I do a small dance as I reload the gun.

"Let's spice it up, baby." Killian jumps off the table, landing directly in front of me with barely a foot between us.

He moves to stand behind me, whispering in my ear, "Ignore me. Whatever happens, I want you to block everything out and focus on the target."

I narrow my eyes in suspicion, but keep my mouth shut, ready to take his challenge. I can do this. Breathing in through my nose, I focus my eyes on the target while I look through the rear sight. The closeness of his body makes it hard for me to concentrate, creating a fog in my head that's becoming thicker with every second. I take a deep breath, doing my best to remember everything he told me to do, but I get completely thrown off when I feel his hands grab my hips, digging his fingers into my sides and his chest moves even closer to my back. My head is cocked, and I lick my lips to ignore the heat of his fingers above the hem of my black jeans. He brings one hand up, pushing my brown hair away from my neck, then slowly pulls my jacket a little away from my shoulder.

"What are you doing?" I croak with parted lips. His breath is whispering along my skin, resulting in every single hair raising in a freaking wave that's followed by a shiver along my spine.

He replies by pressing his lips against the crook of my neck, and I hiss as I suck in a deep breath with clenched thighs. It's a sound of agony, tortured by the desirable burn of his mouth against my skin. My heart races as I feel my eyes roll to the back of my head when he continues to pepper my nape with kisses. Firm, affectionate, some open-mouthed, but all of them are lingering and excruciating in the best way.

This man is the Devil and I can't resist.

"Killian." The way I speak out his name is meant to be scowling, but even I can hear the craving in my voice and when he replies, I can hear the smile in his.

"What?" he asks innocently.

"What are you doing?" I'm still holding up the Magnum, completely still as I enjoy every second of his touch. His hands now snake underneath my shirt, kneading the area with a delicate yet demanding grip while his lips never disconnect from my neck.

"I'm kissing you."

"I didn't realize this was part of my training."

"I need you to be able to focus while holding a gun." His teeth scrape my skin and I let out a whimper. "To not be distracted by *anything*."

"You're seducing me," I hiss, a little incredulous.

"If you can't handle *me*, how can you handle anyone else?" he challenges.

"You don't think I can make this shot?"

His lips move to the area below my ear as he puts his tongue into the action.

"Show me."

I drag my teeth over my lip when he takes my earlobe into his mouth and the desire between my legs grows to an agonizing proportion. The son of a bitch is effortlessly distracting me, and I'm dying to just throw the gun aside and press my lips against his. But I know this can't be as easy as that. He's unpredictable and part of me is worried he will turn me down if I try to take control. It could still be a big test. To see if I'm serious about this. He can pick up any girl he wants if he drives into town right now. But he's spending his morning with me because I have something that intrigues him. Something that makes him want to sacrifice his time because I know he probably has a ton of other shit to do. I need him to keep respecting me, to make it interesting enough for him to stick around or he will find someone else to entertain him.

"What do I get?" I sass.

He quickly grabs my chin, twisting it toward his lips as he pushes out a breath with a wide grin. Our lips are only an inch apart, our breath mixing in the most intoxicating way. The green in his eyes darken, a clear hunger dancing around his irises.

"What do you want?" It comes out in a growl. Low, deep, and terrifying. A year ago, I'd be running off by now like the young girl that I am, knowing I have no business hanging around with the leaders of the dark side of Boston. But that life feels like a lifetime away and right now, all I want is for him to touch me like I'm his. To surrender to him, like he has the ability to jolt me back to life after a long, unbearable slumber.

"To finish what you started," I disclose boldly. I try to push away my insecurity, triggering him by playing his game. He's not a guy that's tempted by a hot body. He's a guy that's tempted by a challenge. If I want him to see me, really see me, I have to make sure he has no choice but to acknowledge me.

"You want me to fuck you, *little Lexie*?"

YES, my body screams.

"If I'm that little, you wouldn't be pressing your lips against my neck."

Amused, he licks his lip, the corners of his mouth curled.

"Hit the mark. Hit the beer can."

I glance at the only visible beer can sitting on the trunk, untouched. It's blue with white letters showing off the brand of Boston's most popular beer.

Bud Light.

Determined, I rear my head back, squinting one eye while the other peers through the rear sight and I give it my best effort to ignore his hands that are still trying to distract me. I take another deep breath, closing my eyes for a moment when he presses another scorching kiss on my neck. When I open them again, I have a clear vision of the bullseye and I breathe out as he told me, then pull the trigger with confidence as I'm drowning out everything else happening around me. Happening to my body. Ignoring all the nerves that are thriving under his lips. When the sharp sound of the bullet leaving the barrel has passed, the beer can flies through the air, and my eyes widen in surprise.

"I did it," I say, pleased with myself.

Killian never looks up as he continues his trail of kisses, this time pulling the gun gently from my hands.

"Did you see that?" I rejoice.

He responds by roughly spinning my body toward his, with his hands clasped in my shirt. He places the gun on the picnic table as he moves his chest closer to mine, his eyes now moving from my eyes to my lips.

"I guess you're going straight into my reward, huh?" I nervously place my hands on his arms, and a smirk washes his face as he pulls me flush with his body.

"Didn't realize it was *your* reward."

"It's yours?"

"To be honest? I don't care." As soon as the last word leaves his lips, they're on mine, and instantly I'm addicted. His tongue is rough and gentle at the same time, his taste a toxic mix of alcohol and something sweet that makes me crave more with every stroke. I moan into his mouth, and he replies by fisting my hair so hard it burns my scalp.

It's painful, dominating, and it does exactly what I want him to do; *make me feel alive.*

12

I let out a grunt when her soft tongue connects with mine. My hunger has been watching the game unfold like a benched player, but when the warmth of her mouth overtakes me, it's not willing to sit on the sidelines any longer. I pull her head back so I can deepen the kiss, wanting every inch of her fucking body pressed into mine while my hands are off to explore the skin hidden underneath her shirt.

I was just planning on teasing her, whispering shit in her ear as she made the shot, but when my eyes glanced at the velvety skin on her slender neck, I couldn't resist. Compelled, I had to touch her, even though I knew it was a wicked stupid choice to make. I also knew it was inevitable. Now that I've felt her throbbing pulse against my lips, I'm desperate for more. Ignoring all the reasons in my head why I shouldn't do this.

You don't know her. *I know enough.*

She wants Sullivan dead. *He's a bastard anyway.*

He's on your payroll. *I'll find someone else.*

She's too young. *She's legal, all I need to know.*

Franky won't agree. *Franky can go fuck himself.*

You can't trust her. *She can't trust me.*

I push her back against the table, a small gasp leaving her lips at the sudden movement as I stare at her with a feral look.

"You get one shot to back out of this."

She swallows, but her fierce blue eyes never show any insecurity as she gives me her answer by saying nothing at all.

I grab her neck, pressing my chest against her. "One shot to tell me you don't want this, and I'll let you go."

Her chin rises. "I didn't think the infamous Killian Wolfe had an ounce of chivalry inside of him."

My eyes move back and forth over every inch of her face, searching for any distress. But as I suspected, I can't find any. Alexandra Lee might be young, but she isn't afraid to dance with the Devil, showing me more guts than I've ever seen in a woman.

"I don't." I smirk, then crash my mouth against hers in a bruising kiss. She eagerly takes off her jacket while I put her on the edge of the table so I can stand between her legs. Her fingers reach out, snaking underneath my shirt before she digs her nails into my back, scratching my skin as she slowly drags them down again.

I wince, throwing my head back from desire.

"Fuck!" My call reverberates through the woods. I spread my hand along her cheek, holding her in place while I bite her lip. My hands lift her up to put her back on the ground and I pull her jeans and panties down in one swift move before I place her bare ass back on the cold wood of the table. The chill in the air around us reminds me we're outside, but the heat of our bodies keeps us both warm and comfortable. She holds on to my shoulders, watching me as I lick my lips, then I run a finger through her folds. Her eyes snap shut, letting her head fall against my chest with parted lips.

She's soaking wet and my fingers are quickly coated with her cream.

I rub two fingers over her clit, before I start to tease her entrance in slow and gentle circles. Never really entering, just gracing the wet skin while I feel how she drips on my hand.

"God, I can't wait to taste you." I bring my hand up, sucking every drop of her off my fingers as her eyes grow wide. Shock is written on her face, combined with an excitement I can't place. "Next time, I'm spreading you wide with my tongue down your pussy."

She blinks at my bluntness, and I cock my head in suspicion.

"Are you a virgin?"

"No," she huffs, suddenly hurrying to unbutton my jeans. Relieved, I let out a chuckle at her eagerness, pleased to see the same desperation that I feel.

"Good, because this is going to be rough, *little girl*."

I can still see that bit of innocence in her gorgeous blue eyes, and like the asshole that I am, I want to destroy it. I want to corrupt her, pushing out the warrior swimming to the surface.

Before she shoves my pants and boxers down, I pull out a condom, then tear the wrapper with my teeth. Rolling the rubber around my hard shaft, she grabs my shirt to yank me closer and I look up at her, brushing my nose against hers.

"Will you hurt me?" Her voice is low and cautious.

"Probably."

"Will it be a *good* hurt?" Her question surprises me, and I look at her in awe. I expect her to tell me to be careful with her, but instead she's giving into the pain I might inflict on her. She's welcoming it, even though I can still see the worry lacing her expression. A weird feeling hits my chest, and I answer her question by giving her a bruising kiss, then I press my forehead against hers while I place my tip at her entrance.

"It will be the best feeling you'll ever experience." I push inside of her in one deep thrust, giving her no time to adjust until I reach her wall. I grunt when my cock is surrounded by her heat, making me bite my lip in blissful agony. She winces and I hold still, giving her a second to get used to my thick lid inside of her, but when I watch her eyes roll to the back of her head with a whimper coming from her lips, I take that as my cue to hit home.

I pull back, then start to thrust inside of her with firm moves, fueled by the longing moan that erupts every time I'm fully seated inside of her.

My hand wraps around her t-shirt covered breast, and while I feel her walls touch every nerve on my shaft, I regret not taking her to my bed, making sure I could lick, stroke, brush, and taste every inch of her body. This started in my mind as a quick fuck, but now that I feel her body linked with mine, all I want is to cherish her and eat her out until my entire face is covered in her wetness. Having a quicky in the woods doesn't feel sufficient now that I've had a taste of her.

She hisses when I bring my thumb to her clit, drawing slow circles around the sensitive nub. Her shriek reverberates through every bone of my body, bringing out that bone-deep need to make her shatter in my hands as I keep plowing inside of her. We both grunt with every move, sweat forming on my skin as I huff against her skin. I keep slamming against her, keeping a close watch on every muscle in her face.

"Does it hurt?" I rumble.

"Yes!" she admits. Her answer makes me smash inside of her even harder and a screech sounds loud in my ear.

"Do you like it?" I demand, pulling her hair so she can lock her eyes with mine. Her eyes are teary, her pink lips sitting in a snarl as I keep going like she's my personal toy.

"Yes!" she sneers back at me, a primal hunger in her gaze.

"Do you want more?"

"Yes!"

"Good girl." I smirk. "Touch yourself."

Like the obedient girl that she can be, she does as she's told, and it doesn't take long before she throws her head back at her own touch. I feel her relax more with every moan that flies out of her mouth, and I keep a steady pace as I chase us both down the path of ecstasy.

"Oh, shit," she mutters, crying.

I know she's close, because I can feel her quads starting to tense underneath my palms, noticing how the movement of her fingers grows more frantic.

"I'm coming," she says, her voice filled with desperation. "I'm coming! Please! Keep going! Don't stop!"

I pick up the pace, feeling my own orgasm building with every plea she makes, loving how she has no choice other than to let go.

"Oh, God. Oh, FUCK!" Her normally sassy and steady voice is now high-pitched, like a screaming siren, falling from the sky without a parachute. Her walls tense, milking my shaft, and I keep going while her hips start to shake with a long wail coming from her little body. She holds onto my shoulders, her eyes pressed shut, and it doesn't take long before I feel my mind check out, completely focusing on the incredible feeling surging through my groin. I roar out in pleasure when I feel my cum spurting out at the same time Lexie's legs start to relax. I hold tight to her hips, riding out my own wave of release until I feel my orgasm simmering, and I press my forehead against hers. We're both heaving, and her breath fans my thumb when I brush it up and down her plump lips.

Her eyes look a little glossy, and I can see the uncertainty slowly creeping back inside of them. I give her a peck on the lips, slipping out of her, and she immediately jumps up to pull her jeans back on. The sexual tension is rapidly replaced by an awkwardness that pisses me off, and I sigh as I tug off the condom before throwing it on the ground.

"Are you okay?" I zip my pants, arching my brows at her.

"Yeah, I'm fine." She offers me a tight smile, but I press my lips together at the discomfort that's dripping from her face.

Clearly, she's not fine.

An hour later, I drive back onto her street with a knot in my stomach. She hasn't said a word the entire time, and I feel like a tool for making her uncomfortable like that.

I never planned to fuck her in the woods, but at the time it felt completely right, and I don't regret it for one second. I've been wanting her ever since she pressed the tip of her knife into my stomach. But there are small moments that remind me of her age. Of the fact that she's an eighteen-year-old orphan who keeps her walls up because she's got nothing else left. Not enough innocence to still be a normal teenage girl, but barely a woman either.

I know she enjoyed that just as much as I did. I can feel it in every bone in my body. She was desperate for someone to make her feel like she wasn't built from porcelain, and I gave it to her in spades. I didn't expect her to change her behavior toward me, suddenly act like she actually likes me, but I didn't anticipate her to close off either.

With a big sigh, I park the car, pushing my annoyance away, then turn my head to face her.

Reluctantly, she meets my gaze, and I offer her a coy smile.

"Look, that was fucking *great*," I tell her honestly, resulting in her eyebrows lifting in surprise, "but *this*"—I move my finger back and forth between us—"is unnecessary. You don't have to be awkward around me. You can still be the little brat that you have been since that night in the alley. It was sex, Lexie. *Just sex*."

"Right," she says. "I knew that. I'm fine, really."

"Are you?"

"Are you still going to train me?"

"Sure." I shrug.

"Then, yeah. I'm fine." The corners of her mouth curl and she opens the door to exit the car and I watch her get out with a short wave. Rubbing my hand over my face, I let it fall to my lap as I stare at the decaying entrance of the building. She walks in with her petite frame, her backpack hanging around her shoulder, and I make a snap decision.

I hit the stop button, exiting the car.

"What are you doing?" She turns around with a frown.

"I'm walking you up."

"Why?" she asks as I stride over to her.

I shoot her a bored look, then point my hand at the door. "Lead the way, little Lexie."

Warily, she narrows her eyes to slits, but when I don't budge, she just sighs before making her way into the building. The inside is even worse, with paint chips on every inch of the walls, the wood on the stairs looking like it will fall apart just from looking at it, and a mouse runs through the garbage back in a corner of the hall as we walk by. It smells moldy, combined with the smell of beer, and I glance up at her when she takes the first step of the stairs.

"Is this thing safe?"

She turns around, her lips pursed in defiance. "Probably not."

Right.

"What floor?"

"Sixth." She keeps ascending, unfazed.

"No elevator?" I follow behind her with a scrunched-up nose as I try to ignore the disgusting mix of smells attacking my nose.

"Broken."

"Of course," I mutter, running a hand through my hair.

When we finally reach the sixth floor, my lungs are heaving a little, and my legs feel heavy from the amount of steps I needed to take to get here. She stops in front of a door that once was red, but now looks more brown.

I eye her as she fumbles with the keys, then opens the door. She takes the lead before turning around to face me, spreading her arms in an inviting way.

"This is your place?" My eyes scan the area, and I'm immediately shocked by the size of it. It's a small studio, with barely any room for a living. The space around her king-size is the biggest, holding at least two yards between her vanity desk and the bed. There is a couch that can't fit more than two people and the kitchen looks clean but outdated, like the rest of the furniture. A door separates the living from the bed, and I assume it's where we can find the bathroom. I look for any personal belongings; pictures, odds and ends, anything that tells me a little bit more about sassy little Lexie, but there is nothing.

She stands beside me, a sad look washing her face.

"It was my grandmother's. My father inherited it. I moved in here after my family died. Didn't have anywhere else to go."

"Your father never rented it out?"

"No," she replies firmly. "It has been sitting empty since my grandmother died last year. He wasn't ready to go through her stuff just yet. I came here after..." she trails off. "I just don't want to risk anyone finding out I'm alive before I..."

"You won't be able to pull it off if you can't even speak it out loud."

She pushes out the air in her lungs, swallowing the agony that I can see in her eyes.

"Kill Sullivan," she says.

"Good girl."

She walks to the kitchen, grabbing a bottle of water.

"Don't really have anything to offer. I'm on a tight budget, so tap water is the way to go." There is sarcasm in her voice, and I wonder if she's trying to hide her embarrassment. Our eyes align, and I feel something gripping my heart.

"Pack your bags."

"What?" she shrieks. "Why? Where are we going?"

"You're staying with me." I fumble with the keys in my hand as I impatiently wait for her to get moving. She's not staying here another night. This place might hold some memories for her, and one day I'll help her sort through her grandmother's shit, but I don't feel comfortable leaving her here. The neighborhood is filled with scum, mostly druggies, and I have a feeling I'd only feed my worry if I found out how many sex offenders are living in the next five blocks alone. Now that I've seen where she lives, I don't think I can sleep without worrying if there is anyone bothering her.

"What? No."

"Pack your bags, Lexie," I order, boredom in my tone. She should know by now that I don't take no for an answer. I like her sass, but it's not something I will let change my mind.

Ever.

"It's Alexandra." She folds her arms in front of her chest.

"Pretty," I mock. "It's also too long. Now pack your bags or I will send a few of my men over in an hour to do it for you."

"Why?"

"You're an eighteen-year-old girl living by herself in a studio in a very bad part of Dorchester. What do you live off anyway?" The reprimanding tone in my voice is undeniable, only adding to her defiance.

"None of your business."

I saunter toward her until I'm completely in her personal space.

"I'm making it my business."

"My parents' savings." I close my eyes at her answer. I still remember vividly what it's like to be alone in the world, trying to get by. I always had Franklin making sure I had everything I needed while Reign and I were stuck in foster care, but it still made me feel alone as fuck. Something ticks me off, knowing that this young girl is all alone, with no one looking out for her. No one to make sure she's fed, taken care of, and safe.

For some fucked up reason, I feel this big responsibility to keep her safe.

"Let's go."

"Killian," she huffs, incredulously.

"You got ten minutes," I tell her as I make my way to the door. "I'll wait in the car. If you're not down by then, I'll come get you."

"You're an asshole, you know that?"

"I'm aware, baby," I say with a smirk, before I slam the door behind me.

13

Lexie

"*It was just sex,*" he said.

But that's the thing, it wasn't. It was short. It was rough. It was fast. It was fucking *primal,* and it was nothing like the sex I ever had with Brad. Sex with Brad was sweet and affectionate. I enjoyed sex with Brad, but he never made me come, and the handful of times I did have an orgasm, he wasn't even in the room.

And then Killian Wolfe happened.

The big bad Wolfe takes me out to the woods and makes me see stars in broad daylight. It was out of this world and nothing like I could ever imagine. He's scary as fuck, but also sexy as hell, and our encounters over the last few weeks have made it no secret to me that I'm attracted to him like crazy. Every time he came close, I wanted him closer, and every time his lips ghosted my skin, I wanted him to press them against my body.

But the memory of my family kept my focus on the endgame, knowing I'd not only fail my family if I let Killian blur my vision, but I also can't afford to get distracted by his sharp jaw and compelling eyes. I vowed to myself I wouldn't go there. Getting into bed with one of the biggest criminals in this city is a bad idea. One that possibly will get me killed quicker than I can say *revenge*. But when his hands landed on my hips, traveling under my shirt with his mouth exploring my neck, I couldn't stay in control anymore.

I wanted more.

I wanted *him*.

I got carried away, completely turning into mush under his touch, not even giving a shit that he'd probably toss me aside when he was done, like I'm one of his many conquests. He surprised me when he agreed to keep training me, but he surprised me even more when he demanded I stay with him, like he was concerned about my safety. I've been so lonely for the last couple of months, I can't even remember what it feels like to have someone care about my wellbeing, and as much as I don't want to make a big deal out of it, my heart seems to be pleased by the fact that I'm now sitting in his car as he drives back to his apartment in Southie. I know I should keep my distance, but I can't help squirming in my seat when I think back to the woods, dying for him to touch me again.

I want him to keep kissing me until my lips are numb.

I want to feel the thrill of his hands exploring every patch of my skin.

I want to leap myself into his lap, straddling him as I get totally lost in him.

But instead, I'm looking out of the window, sitting on my hands to prevent them from reaching out to touch his leg. I sense his gaze falling on me every now and then, making it hard to not turn my head, but I keep staring ahead to avoid any kind of interaction.

After a few minutes, he drives his car into the garage under his building, the rumbling sound of the engine echoing against the concrete walls.

We both exit, and before I can grab my big weekender, he pulls it out of the trunk, throwing it closed with a loud thud. His feet take him to the elevator and my eyes stay fixed on his breathtaking appearance. His back is covered with his leather jacket, but you can see how fit he is through his broad shoulders, his ass hugged by his black jeans. Even walking away from me, he looks like a force to be reckoned with.

He intimidates the hell out of me, but at the same time, I feel this magnetizing pull toward him that I can't deny.

"You coming, little girl?" He glances over his shoulder with a lopsided grin that almost makes me do a double take. With bulging cheeks, I blow out a breath, wondering if this is such a good idea.

How the hell am I going to keep my distance if I'm living with Hades, God of the Underworld?

When I enter the elevator, he finds my eyes as he rests his back against the wall.

"You okay?"

"Great," I mutter, putting on a brave face.

I can sense his amusement coming at me in waves, pissing me off a little, but I keep my jaw tight. When we get off, I wait so he can open the door, then trail behind him as he gets in.

I hold still, a shiver running down my spine. It looks different in daylight.

The parlor is lit by the big windows, highlighting his gray furniture under the rays of sunshine shining through. There is a cream rug in his sitting area that I didn't even register the last time I was here, and his wooden dining room table looks lighter than I remember. There aren't any personal belongings around the room other than one picture of his brothers and him, but I have a feeling this is just who Killian is.

Simple and straightforward.

"What's wrong?" He places my bag on the couch, turning around to face me.

"Nothing." I shrug. "Kinda weird being in your house. *Invited*."

"You want me to throw you out so you can break in?" For most people, this is the part where you laugh, thinking it's a joke. But Killian Wolfe rarely jokes and his straight expression tells me he's dead serious.

"No, I'm good."

He jerks his shoulder a little, then turns around to grab a drink from the fridge.

"Where did you learn to pick a lock anyway?"

He pulls out two bottles of water, throwing one at me before I catch it against my chest.

"YouTube."

His snort is followed with a chortle as he takes a sip from the bottle.

"What?"

"You Gen Z kids."

I roll my eyes, twisting the cap from the bottle. "Don't pretend you didn't grow up with technology."

"I grew up in the time when we thought Facebook was a real source, Blackberry would survive as a brand, and YouTube was mostly filled with funny cat videos," he mocks.

"Right."

He saunters toward me with a big smirk splitting his face. He's holding the bottle in his hands, pulling his car keys out of his pocket, then halts right in front of me. I peer up at him, feeling his warmth radiate against mine. My hands want to be pressed against his chest, and my lips part when his gaze darts to my mouth.

"I need to head out," he says with a gruff voice that vibrates through my muscles. "I'll bring back dinner. What do you want?"

Inwardly, I feel my suspicion growing, filled with a jealousy that pops up a lot of questions in my head; *where are you going? Are you leaving me alone? When will you be back? Are you going to see a woman?* But I keep it together, swallowing my insecurities away like an inconvenience.

"Pizza is fine." I reach into my pocket, holding up a twenty-dollar bill, as his eyes never leave mine. Hunger crosses his face, and I'm pretty sure it's not for food. My neck is flushed with heat as he keeps staring me down, then he grabs the twenty-dollar bill from my hand. When his hand touches mine, I swallow hard, doing my best to ignore the pounding of my heart against my ribcage as if it wants to jump out. He takes another step closer, leaning in to press his forehead against mine, and I close my eyes in anticipation. It feels like forever, but finally, his searing lips connect with mine in an affectionate kiss while at the same time, he pushes the bill back into my pocket. It's shorter than I want it to be and when I pull back, brushing his body to move past me, it takes everything inside of me to not yank him back, but I hold still as he pushes his mouth against the shell of my ear.

"See you later, little Lexie," he whispers before he walks out, leaving me completely frozen in the middle of the room until I hear the loud thud of the door closing behind me.

I bring my fingers to my mouth, thinking about his lips against mine as I stare at the door he disappeared through.

I'm in some wicked shit.

***

It was two PM, after he left me alone in his apartment, and I've learned two things about Killian Wolfe. One, he has more whiskey in his house than actual food, and two, he only has one bedroom.

The only thing that was sufficient enough for lunch was a box of Dunks in the fridge, and I strolled off to explore as I sunk my teeth into a strawberry frosted donut. With my mouth full, I froze in his bedroom, realizing there wasn't another room in the house. My heart was jumping in excitement while my mind was scowling at the situation before I turned on my heels and decided to postpone the problem until later today. I plopped myself onto his couch, settling in to watch some TV before I drifted off.

I wake up from my dreamless sleep when my phone rings in my pocket, and I pull it out with a big frown. I haven't been called in months, simply because I've been living in solitude for so long and no one even knows I still exist. I glance at the unknown number, contemplating if I should answer or not. Sucking in a deep breath, I make the decision to give in to my curiosity.

"Hello?"

"What do you want on your pizza?" Killian's voice booms into my ear, gluing my brows together.

"How did you get my number?"

"Lexie," he growls.

"Right. Stupid question." *He's Killian Wolfe, for crying out loud, Alexandra.*

"Margherita."

"You want a pizza with just cheese?" I can hear the taunt in his voice and I purse my lips, a little offended.

"What's wrong with that?"

I hear him chuckle through the phone. "Nothing. I'll be up in a minute."

He hangs up, and I put on one of my favorite movies, waiting for him to walk through the door. When he finally does, the smell of fresh pizza proceeds him, and my stomach roars awake. Like the cool person that he is, he nudges his chin to me in greeting, setting two boxes on the coffee table. He takes off his jacket, throwing it on the armchair next to the TV, then hands me a box.

"Thank you." Eagerly, I open the box, my mouth watering at the smell of melted cheese combined with tomato sauce. I grab a slice, glancing at his pizza when he opens the box, then take a bite. He notices how my eyebrows move to the ceiling when I notice the chunks of pineapple and ham on his pizza and the muscles in his face form a big scowl.

"Don't even dare to scold me that pineapple doesn't belong on a pizza."

"Never," I mutter, suppressing a smile. "I just expected you to be a meat lover or something."

"Well, I never really cared what anyone expected of me." He chews his bite, licking the sauce off his lips. I'm sure he doesn't try to be sensual about it, but unintentionally my vagina wakes up on high alert and I take another bite to distract myself.

"What are you watching?"

"The Longest Ride."

"What's that?"

"A Nicholas Sparks movie." He holds still, giving me an incredulous look. "What's wrong with that?"

"Everything," he says with his mouth full.

"You are such a guy."

"You're such a girl."

He daringly holds my gaze, pinning me to submission as he tears off a piece of his pizza with his teeth, but I can't resist rolling my eyes at him first before I turn my head to the TV and continue eating.

When we're both finished, he props up his feet on the coffee table, spreading his arms over the back of the couch.

"I didn't expect you to watch a chick flick," he tells me.

"Why not? I'm an eighteen-year-old girl. Not that weird, right?"

"Well, maybe because the first time we met you were on your way to blow someone's brains out, and the second time you threatened me with a knife." He cocks his head at me, then shrugs as he continues. "Thought you'd like the bloody shit. Slasher movies and all that nasty crap."

"I've never seen a slasher movie," I confess.

"No-suh."

"Ya-huh. Never really been a fan of horror shit. Makes me feel sick."

"We're watching one." He sets his feet back to the floor, grabbing the clicker from the table.

"What? When? Now?" I rear my head back.

"Right now." He turns off my movie, flicking through Netflix.

"No! I just ate."

"So?" He shoots me a dull look.

"So, I want to keep it in my stomach." I might look like a tough girl, acting like nothing scares the shit out of me, but the truth is somewhere in the middle. I feel fearless thinking about the revenge I want for my family, but I've never been a fan of scary movies. They tighten a knot in my belly and make it impossible for me to sleep at night. The unsettling feeling creeping up on me tells me that hasn't changed just because my family died.

Like a viper, he grabs my ankle, yanking me flush with the entire couch, and I let out a startled shriek. He places his palms beside my head, hovering above me like he's about to swallow me whole and I hold still, waiting.

"Do you want to kill Sullivan?"

"Yes," I huff with a firm tone.

His face lowers to mine, his lips only an inch away from my face. "You think you'll just get a clean shot and it's done? You think he won't put up a fight? You need to prepare for the mess, baby. If it turns out cleaner than expected, that's just an added benefit. If you can't handle the blood"—he brushes his lips against my cheek, his words leaving in a whisper—"the hunt, the kill"—he softly bites my skin, and I close my eyes for a millisecond—"you'll never be able to take your revenge."

My skin feels like it's burning, wanting to be cooled down by his touch.

"Fine." My voice cracks a little, and I clear my throat.

"Good girl." He moves back into his corner of the couch, and I hurdle myself back up into mine while he puts on The

Texas Chainsaw Massacre. Out of protection, I grab one of the pillows, holding it tightly against my chest as the movie starts.

I make it all the way through the second kill without hiding behind my hands, but when the killer appears to be dead and then isn't, I yelp out in agony. My nerves are killing me, and my heart feels like it will jump out of my chest any minute now.

Killian's full laugh makes me glare at him, even though I also enjoy the relaxed stance he has. It makes him even more attractive, approachable, and when he lifts his arms, I can't hide the smile that sneaks onto my face.

"Come here." I crawl against his chest, settling into the crook of his arm. A sigh leaves my lips, enjoying the comfort he gives me when he wraps his arm around me like we've been doing this forever.

"Pay attention. First rule. Never assume they are dead just because they are down. They are never dead. Remember that." He emphasizes the last lines and I nod my head in understanding before we both put our focus back on the screen. With my body pressed against his for the rest of the movie, I don't feel as scared as before. My hand rests on his stomach, while his thumb brushes against my upper arm in an affectionate way that makes my mind run wild.

Before I lost my family, I had a secure life. I had a roof over my head, loving parents, and a sweet boyfriend. I felt safe, like nothing could destroy my world like it did. After that night, I thought I would never feel like that again. But lying with my head against a man I'm supposed to fear, I have never felt more invincible than I do right now. He's daunting, making me uncomfortable at least half of the time, but there is something about him that builds my confidence. That pushes me to be brave and fight my demons, no matter how insignificant.

I listen to his heartbeat pounding against my ear, soothing me like a beating drum until the credits are shown. My mind wanders off, recalling the movie and wondering if my intuition is playing a joke on me. Killian Wolfe is the most feared man in this city. The most cunning of his brothers, and merciless when you piss him off. How can someone as bad as him make me feel more safe, more alive than I've ever felt? How can I so desperately want to trust someone who is known to be untrustworthy? And how can I trust myself for wanting to believe he's not all evil? How can I dance with the Devil without becoming a part of his world?

He brushes my hair from my neck, stroking his fingers over my veins.

"What's on your mind, little Lexie?"

"Nothing," I bluff.

"Don't lie, baby." I feel my heart jolt when he calls me *baby*, instantly pushing away my apprehension toward him.

"Is it true that you like to torture people?" I know the question might make him angry, feeling like I'm sticking my nose into something that isn't my business. But one thing I'm starting to understand about Killian is that he appreciates honesty more than anything. He doesn't like to beat around the bush. He faces his problems head on and he respects the people who do the same. Even if that means they don't agree with him.

"Sometimes."

"Why?"

He sighs, slow and loud, but I can't decipher if that's because he doesn't want to answer or because he doesn't like the answer he's giving. "Because they deserve it."

I like that answer. I know it's not completely fair, because he'll be the judge and jury in every situation he finds suitable, but it still gives me hope that he has some morals. That he doesn't kill people just for sport.

That I'm not putting my trust in a psychopath.

I sense him lowering his head, a soft touch of his lips in my brown hair as he taps my thigh.

"Time for bed, baby."

Right, bed. *Shit.*

He must feel the tension in my muscles, because he answers my question before I can even ask him.

"I'll take the couch. You can take the bed." He gets up, walking toward his bedroom, and I follow in his steps. I eye him as he grabs a blanket from the closet, then shoots me a wink that creates a flutter in my stomach.

"Are you sure?" Am I? There is a desire deep in my bones that wants to drag him to bed, hoping he will hold me until dawn. But even though he makes me feel brave, he doesn't make me brave enough to voice what I really want from him.

"Goodnight, Lexie." He smirks as he walks out of the room, then closes the door behind him.

Goodnight, Killian.

14

KILLIAN

The next morning, I got off the couch, regretting that I gave her my bed. My back is sore, and my eyes are heavy from waking up every fucking hour. I don't even know why I decided to be the gentlemen, because I could've easily let her sleep on my couch, or next to me, even better. But she felt so vulnerable in my arms last night, I didn't want to give her the feeling I was taking advantage of her.

And trust me, it has been a challenge.

I thought our adventure in the woods would be enough to get my hunger for her out of my system. At least enough for me to train her how to defend herself before I send her on her way again. Now I feel wicked stupid for taking her home, because I can't keep my hands off of her. I like to taunt her, to scare her, just enough so she'll come crawling against my body for comfort. She likes the thrill, the excitement of not knowing what I'll do next, and I love the lazy look that sinks into her blue eyes every time she surrenders to me.

I grunt, pushing myself up to stroll to the kitchen, grabbing myself a cup of coffee. Enjoying the nutty liquid, I let the caffeine wake me up a little before I tiptoe to my bedroom.

With my chin high, I try to get a glimpse of her pretty face while her body is wrapped in my sheets. She looks as comfortable as a cloud, and I swallow the urge to settle my body next to hers, tugging her against my chest with my nose buried in her brown hair.

Instead, I shuffle through the room, softly closing the bathroom door behind me before turning on the shower. The fact that she's sleeping in my bed fucks with my head, testing my willpower to defy the temptation, because I'm dying to wake her up with my tongue on her pussy and tear her apart. To taste all of her.

I settle for a quick, cold shower to rein in my twitching cock, then brush my teeth before I saunter back out with a towel wrapped around my hips.

When I open the door, I'm met by her striking blue gaze, turning my frown upside down in a heartbeat. She looks innocent, almost angelic, as she peers at me with sleepy eyes.

"Morning, sunshine. Sleep well?"

"I did." She stretches her arms with a yawn, giving me a peek of her stomach. But it's the recognition that she's wearing one of my shirts that makes me want to jump her.

"Good." I turn my attention to my closet, rapidly pulling out boxers and jeans to hide the wood growing between my legs again. "There's some leftover Dunks in the fridge."

"No, there is not," she replies. There is a familiarity in her tone that I like, as if she's slept over many times before last night.

"What do you mean?" I rear my head back. Her relaxed look is still in place and I quickly decide this is my favorite look of hers. Her messy hair, her cheeks blushing as she slowly wakes up, her blue eyes fresh and open, like she isn't fully awake to be aware of the ugliness the world has to give.

"I ate them yesterday because you left me without any food."

"There were five donuts in there."

"So?" She cocks her eyebrow.

"You ate them all?"

She shrugs, unfazed. "I was hungry."

"Where do you put that crap?" I continue to get dressed, and by the time I get my shoes on, she gets out of the bed with a reluctant look washing her face. My t-shirt almost comes to her knees, and I lick my lips at her long legs moving toward me. My hands are aching to pull her to my chest and explore what kind of panties she's wearing underneath, but I tuck them into my pockets as I resist the urge to rake my gaze up and down her body.

"Are you leaving?" she asks.

"Yes."

"Where are you going?" She folds her arms in front of her body, looking at me with an expression that seems insecure.

I keep my straight face, ignoring her question.

"What about our training?" she adds.

"One of my men will pick you up at eight. He will bring you to Louisa's Shots. She will give you a whole arsenal of weapons for you to practice with until noon and after that, someone will drive you to the gym my brother owns. One of the trainers is going to work out with you and work on your self-defense, then someone will drive you back here."

"Louisa's Shots?"

"It's our shooting range," I explain. "It's run by a woman named Louisa."

She frowns, a little confused.

"Why did you bring me to the woods if you own a shooting range?"

"Because I wanted you for myself." My honest answer clearly throws her off, but I have no reason to lie to her. I wanted to see what kind of wood she's carved out, wanted to see if she can really handle a gun or if she's all talk. I also wanted to see how far I could push her. Taking her to our shooting range gives us an audience I didn't care for.

"So, you won't be training me?" She's unhappy. I can see it in every muscle in her pretty face, even though she's trying to appear indifferent.

"I got shit to do. They will help you with whatever you need to learn to protect yourself. See you later today, baby." I walk out of the bedroom, dismissing the conversation.

"Wait!" I hear her footsteps stomping behind me. "When are we going to kill Sullivan?"

I spin on my heels, giving her an amused eyebrow lift. "We? Who said anything about *we*?"

"What do you mean? You said you'd help me."

I take another step closer, my eyes narrowed.

"I said I'd *train* you. I never said I was going to help you kill him."

"What the? Are you serious?" she yelps. Her gaze is on fire. Gone is the relaxed look as she shoots daggers at me.

I smile cynically. "Why would I help some girl to kill my business partner?"

"Well, I don't know?! Maybe because you have a heart?" She sounds desperate, looking like the frustrated teenager that she is. The air leaves my lungs, and I cup her cheek, brushing the skin with my thumb.

She's so filled with contradictions. I can see the strength in her eyes, her ability to be fatal like a lion, but she's also still so innocent and flawless like her skin.

It's soft, pure, delicate, and nothing like me.

My selfishness wants to destroy her, corrupt and claim her as my own, until I'm done with her.

But something holds me back.

"I don't have a heart, baby."

"Then why agree to train me?" The disappointment in her voice is killing me, and I let go of her, darting to the door to get out of here.

"There is no fault in helping a young woman to learn how to defend herself."

"Please help me," she pleads softly when I open the front door. When I turn to face her, her eyes are laced with pain, her tears showing in the corners of her eyes.

"If you want me to take a life for you, you have to prove yourself. Prove yourself to be of value to me. Nothing is for free, baby."

"How?"

"You'll figure it out. See you later, little Lexie," I tell her, then walk out, slamming the door behind me.

"How is she doing, Louisa?" I have my phone pressed against my ear as I walk into my building for my daily checkup. She's been going to the shooting range every morning for the last four days, followed by some excessive self-defense training from one of my best men.

"Growing angrier every day." Louisa's thick southern accent seeps into my ear like a comforting melody, giving me a familiarity of a grandmother I never had.

I know she's right. I've been eating at the apartment with her instead of having dinner at the mansion with my brother, but she's been getting more and more snappy by the day. I could pry, force her to tell me what's up her ass, but it's made me able to keep a certain distance from her and fight the urge to wipe the scowl off her face with my tongue down her throat.

"Not what I meant." Strutting forward, I get into the elevator, then push the button up while I keep a steady hold on the Chinese takeout I brought home tonight.

"Good. She's been practicing with the sniper rifle the entire morning."

"Is she getting any better?"

"She took a bet with Sniper Jack today."

"No-suh!" I blurt, surprised. Sniper Jack is Louisa's unofficial lover. A guy from bumfuck Alabama who followed her after a one-night stand. The man is a redneck to the core, and he shoots like a damn professional.

"Damn right, she did."

"And?"

"She won."

"Nah, you're playing me."

"Don't insult me, boy. I'm telling you, your girl can shoot like she's getting paid for it."

A feeling like pride fills me, and one cheek lifts in a lopsided grin.

"You think she's ready for some real action?"

"Only one way to find out, sweetheart."

"Thanks, Louisa." I hang up the phone, stepping into the hallway before I walk through the front door of my apartment. Like magnets, my eyes instantly move to Lexie shuffling from the kitchen to the couch as if she's in pain.

"What's doing, baby?"

She averts her gaze, another clear scowl set as the features of her face tense up.

I press my tongue against my cheek, my annoyance instantly reaching a peak before throwing the takeout on the coffee table. There is this innate need to reprimand her and tell her not to fuck with me. I can feel it rattling the gate, dying to get out.

Ignoring me, she drops her ass on the couch, then grabs the clicker to turn on the TV.

She flares my anger like a drop of water in hot oil, and I viciously slam the thing out of her hand, towering in front of her.

"Hey!"

"Get your ass up, Lexie."

"It's Alexandra." She keeps her gaze in front of her, unable to look at me, but holding her defiance in place.

"I don't fucking care." She could be named Queen Elizabeth the fucking third. I call her whatever the fuck I want, which will be *little bitch* if she doesn't drop her childish act real soon. "Look at me, little girl." My growl is deep, coming from behind my teeth.

She doesn't move.

"Look at me, Lexie, or you'll fucking regret it."

Her entire body stays frozen, except for the ticking of her jaw, as if she's unimpressed.

With one swift move, I grab her by the back of her neck, pulling her to her feet as I press my fingers deeply into her skin.

"Get off of me! You're hurting me!" She tries to push me off, but I switch my grip to the front of her neck, squeezing a little to make her more compliant.

"Don't, little girl," I warn. "I don't have time for this wicked bullshit. You either tell me what the fuck is messing with your mind, or I throw you in my bedroom so I don't have to look at your damn frown the entire night."

"You'd like that, wouldn't you? Keep me cooped up here like your damn prisoner." Her blue eyes are fire blazing, making my dick twitch as I let out a sarcastic, huffing laugh.

"You are the one who wanted *my* help, baby. I'm not keeping you here. Go if you're desperate to leave." I let go of her, taking a step back with spread arms.

I don't give a damn if she stays or goes. She can walk out right now, and I'll remember her as a good fuck in the woods.

"I did, yeah! I wanted *your* help!" she shouts, furious as fuck. Her brown hair falls in front of her cheeks as she pricks a finger in my chest. "But you just ship me off to the soldiers in your army!"

"And that's an issue, why?"

"You think I couldn't go to the shooting range myself? You think I couldn't find myself a trainer? Take some self-defense classes? I wanted *your* help! Not your hired minions!"

Well, I didn't see that one coming.

I don't even know why I agreed to train her, but there was something in her entire appearance that felt like she deserved the help. Reminding me of how helpless my brothers and I once were after my mother died, I wanted to give her the tools to survive in this world. To make something out of herself and never fear anyone ever again. My mind is dying to do it myself, to make her the little warrior I know she can be. But I also know it will be wicked hard to not throw her in my bed if I spend my days with her. Letting her get trained by my men was the safest option.

For both of us.

I have a feeling she doesn't agree with that, though. With my tongue pressed against the back of my teeth, I look at her intense expression. There is a hurt in her eyes that slices through my gut, and I want to take it away. I pull her shirt, yanking her flush to me as her hands fall over my chest.

"You're here spitting fire at me because you want more of my time?"

Her eyes narrow, scolding. "You make it sound like I want sex."

"Do you?" I huff against her face as my own darkens at her eyes flaring with excitement. "Because I do. *Desperately.* Now that I've had a small taste of you, I want more every fucking minute like you're my shot of heroine. I want to tear you apart and taint you with my cum, but I'll ruin you."

She swallows hard, glancing up at me through her thick lashes. Her rage vanishes in front of my eyes as the air electrifies around us as if lightning could strike us at any second now. I expect her to show fear, but I know I'm in trouble when all I find is a craving that matches my own.

"What if I'm already ruined?"

I cup her cheek, my face softening as I trace her jaw with my thumb. The freckles on her skin blend in a little more with her flushed cheeks and there's a glint of sadness in her eyes, showing the innocence she tries so hard to hide.

"You're not ruined, baby. You're far from ruined. But you will be if we blur the line too much."

"I don't trust them," she confesses with a pinched mouth, her gaze dropping to my chest.

"Who?"

"Anyone. I don't trust them."

Realizing she's talking about the people training her, I push two fingers under her chin to force her to look me in the eye. "And you trust *me*?"

"Most of the time."

A ghost of a smile slides onto my face at her answer.

"You shouldn't." There is amusement in my voice, but I mean it. She shouldn't trust me, because in the end, she doesn't mean anything to me. She's fun. She's entertaining. But she's nothing more than that.

"I can't help it."

"Why do you trust me?"

She averts her gaze, thinking about my question. Her eyes snap shut for a moment before they look up at me with a sincerity that hits me in the heart.

"Because you don't hide who you are. I fear you sometimes. But at least with you, I know exactly what I'm fearing. I'd rather know I'm dancing with the Devil than get stabbed in the back by an angel."

Her answer catches me by surprise again, making me think I misjudged her. In my head, I keep seeing her as this eighteen-year-old girl, thinking she needs someone to protect her from the demons in her world. To protect her from *me*, but still give her what she needs.

Maybe I was wrong.

"Okay," I concede. "I'll train you from now on."

"Really?"

"Yeah. But I'm warning you, I'm worse than any of my men."

She nods. "I'm ready."

"Good. Come on. Let's eat."

It's the middle of the night when a screeching sound stirs me awake. A voice murmurs in the background and I arch my back to stretch the sore muscles around my spine, wondering what I'm registering before I hear Lexie wail from the bedroom.

"What in the–" I mutter as I rub my eyes. The scream sounds even louder, and I quirk my body up, grabbing my gun from the table. For a brief moment, I'm wondering if I'm hearing shit that isn't there, but then another shriek reaches my ears. It's piercing, going straight through every bone in my body, and I stumble over my feet as I storm into my bedroom with my gun drawn. On high alert, I scan the room for anything out of the ordinary, expecting to find a burglar with wicked bad timing or something. But the room is empty, and I swing my eyes to the girl in my bed. She's tossing and turning, distress etched on her face.

"No! No!" Her cry is filled with despair and every hair on my back rises before I jump on the bed. I quickly put the gun on the nightstand, then try to jolt her awake by shaking her shoulders.

"Wake up, Lexie. Wake up, baby!"

Her muscles tense by my touch and she lashes out with her hands, her eyes still completely shut.

"Fucking hell!" I bark, ignoring the sting on my cheek when her hands connect with my face. I lock her arms by wrapping my own around her upper body, holding her tightly against my chest.

"No! Let me go! Let me go!" Tears are streaming down her face, the sight alone gutting me.

"Wake up! Wake up, Lexie!"

She keeps going, her cries growing more frantic by the second.

"Alexandra!" Her eyes fly open when I shout her full name in her face, her lashes fluttering because of my breath. She's staring at me in terror, her muscles completely rigid under my touch. It's knocking the air out of my lungs, physically hurting me as she looks at me like I'm the Devil himself.

"Sssssh, it's me. You're safe. I got you. Nobody is going to hurt you." I hold her cheek in my hand, peppering her tear-stained cheeks with kisses, trying to calm her down. Finally, I feel her relax in my arms, before she presses her forehead against my chest and I start to rock her like a baby. I keep her head tightly against my heart, sucking in a breath as I glance around the room, a little worried about the extent of her nightmare.

"They are coming for me. They are coming for me. They are coming for me," she sobs, not completely back in the real world.

Her words make me clench my jaw in agony, needing to protect her from whoever she's talking about.

"You're safe, baby. I will keep you safe."

Her breathing changes, and she pushes me a little away, bringing her gaze up. Her blue eyes are bloodshot and laced with embarrassment.

"I'm so sorry. I-I had a night–"

"A nightmare. I know." I hold her face in my hands, unable to let her go just yet.

"I'm sorry. Di-did I wake you?"

"It's okay, baby."

"Yeah. I'm sorry. You should go back to sleep. I'm alright. I'll be alright." She offers me a tight smile as she tries to put up a strong front, but I see the lies written all over her tired face. She fears being alone right now, probably knowing her nightmare will continue as soon as her head hits the pillow again. I twist half her body, pressing my chest against her back before I lie down, taking her with me.

"What are you doing?"

"Going to bed." I tug her closer against me, spooning her from behind while I bury my nose into her neck with my hand resting on her stomach.

"I thought you didn't want to blur the lines."

"I changed my mind. Goodnight, Lexie."

She loosens up, pressing her ass a little more against my groin, and I feel a growl coming from my throat.

"Why?" There is victory in her sleepy voice that I should demolish right away, but I can't. I can't crush her after the state I found her in mere minutes ago.

"Goodnight, baby," I say, dismissing her question.

15

Lexie

"You weren't kidding when you said you were even worse." I pull out an ice pack from the freezer, then place it on my shoulder. He wore me out today, but I knew the second he took me to a backroom at the shooting range that this day was going to be different than the ones before.

"Where are we going?" I asked.

"Time to level up." He smirked.

"To what?"

"Moving targets." There was a devilish gleam in his eyes that had me worried for a second, thinking he was expecting me to kill innocent animals or something. Or worse; humans. But I sighed in relief when a simulator was waiting for us as we walked through the door. He explained to me that it was a hypersensitive machine, acting just as

accurately as real life. I pushed back the question on my lips when he told me it was used by the military, making me wonder how the hell he got his hands on it. But I learned that it's a waste of energy to ask certain questions, simply because he won't answer them anyway.

We practiced the entire morning, and by noon, my shoulders were sore from holding up the gun for an hour straight. But that was just a warmup, because when we arrived at the gym, he had no mercy. He threw me on my back more times than I can count, showing me I wasn't ready to fight him over and over again while he kept screaming at me to do better. Within the hour, my legs felt like Jell-O and my lungs were heaving to catch some breath. There was a vicious glare on his face most of the time that had the ability to cripple me. But I refused to give him the satisfaction, only using it as fuel to keep going until he decided to call it a day.

I'm completely exhausted, but I also feel stronger. More capable.

He's leaning with his back against the counter with his arms crossed in front of his chest, his eyes raking up and down my body with a blank expression.

"I warned you."

"I know." I feel my body tense under his gaze, wishing he'd touch me to relax my muscles. How I want him to stroke every piece of my skin with his rough palms while his lips are connected to my neck. I hold his gaze, dragging my lip between my teeth.

He keeps a straight face.

He's a star at keeping a straight face, acting like he isn't affected by anything. But I've been spending a lot of time with him. I can see the small changes in his eyes. The small movements in his face. They are tiny as hell; barely noticeable if you don't know him.

But I see them.

The slight flare of his nostrils.

The subtle tick in his jaw.

The heat flashing in his deep green eyes.

I know he was right when he told me we shouldn't blur the lines. Killian makes things in my body ignite that are dangerous. The kind of things that can easily turn into feelings and that's a trainwreck waiting to happen. But I can't resist the pull I have toward him. I can't control my thoughts when I think about all the things I want him to do to me. I tried my best, but now that I woke up with his arms wrapped around my stomach, the little spoon to his big spoon, I can't do it anymore.

I want more, even though I know I shouldn't.

"You can't look at me like that, little Lexie."

"I'm not that little, you know," I counter.

"Oh, I know." He drops his gaze to the floor with a sigh.

"Then why do you keep calling me *little Lexie*?"

"Because it's my only reminder that I shouldn't touch you." His mouth is pinched, a look of pain clear in his eyes. He's having a hard time just as much as I am. He wants me. I can see it in the way he looks at me every time I walk by or the small smiles he shoots at me every now and then. Boldly, I close the distance between us, until our bodies are only an inch apart. With my hip leaned against the counter, he twists his torso to mirror my stance as his tongue darts out the lick his lip.

"You already did," I remind him.

"And we can't go there again."

"Why not?"

"I'll hurt you." He rubs a hand over his face, followed by a grunt, before it lands on the side of my neck. His thumb brushes the skin on my jaw and when his eyes drop to my mouth, he bites his lips as if he's preventing himself from kissing me.

"I'm not made out of sugar."

"No, you're made out of something even sweeter than that."

He dips his chin, his mouth now close enough for his breath to fan my face.

I want him to kiss me so desperately. I want our breath to mix, sucking in the air in his lungs like life support. I want to feel his hands on my body like he will be able to find places that are only reachable by his touch. I want him to ruin me, like he promised me he would if he crossed that line. I close my eyes, waiting for him to press his lips against mine, but the moment is ruined when his phone starts to vibrate in the pocket of his jeans. His forehead connects with mine, pushing out the air in his lungs as he exhales with annoyance before he pulls it out.

"What's doing?" he answers with a growl.

"Kill, it's me." I can hear the woman's voice coming over the line, instantly flaring my ugly green monster. I try to take a step back, but Killian holds my elbow in a firm grip, not willing to let me create the distance between us that I need as he keeps his gaze locked with mine. The muscles around his eyes are tensed up in agitation, and I glare at him with the same intensity.

"What's wrong?" Killian asks with worry in his voice, and I listen to the female answer.

"I fucked up," I hear her say.

"What do you mean, you fucked up?"

She stays quiet and I make another attempt to escape from his grasp, but he only presses his finger tighter on my skin, hurting me in the process.

"He knows," she says.

"Shit," he mutters, finally letting go of me as he stalks off to the parlor. "Where are you? I'll pick you up in five minutes."

"Where are you going?" I throw the icepack on the counter, glaring at him as he puts on his leather jacket.

"I have to go."

"When will you be back?"

"Goodbye, Lexie." He barely gives me a second glance before he darts out the front door, slamming it behind him, leaving me stunned in the middle of the room.

"Asshole!" I shout through the door, hoping he heard me.

16

"Anything?" Sienna gives me a worried look as she gets in the car.

"He's not answering. I'm pretty sure he's going to the mansion to find Franklin."

I hit the throttle, and we're launched forward through the sound of the roaring engine while I maneuver my car through the city as fast as possible.

"He was really upset, Killian," Sienna says cautiously.

"It was long overdue, and we all know it. He will be fine." It was about time that Reign found out the real reason why Franklin killed Declan Murphy when he was eighteen. There was a very good reason we got sent away to foster homes because the Boston government considered my brother a criminal, unsuitable to take care of his four younger brothers.

"Another generation of Wolfe men without morals, who will be a risk to this city," one of the cops on his case said to us.

He was right about me. About Connor. But Franklin and Reign have more morals in their pinky than Connor and I combined. He didn't kill Declan for sport. He did it to protect our friend. *My friend.*

"He will hate us for not telling him about Emma." Her name echoing through the car makes my chest constrict. An image of her bright smile flashes before my eyes, knitting a knot in my stomach.

Emma didn't tell me Declan raped her until a few months before she died. I was relieved he was already dead, because otherwise I would've buried him six under myself. I was so angry, but she begged me not to tell anyone. Said she just wanted to look forward and focus on us. That our love was enough. I stupidly believed her.

"I know."

"Does he know about you two?" I glance at Sienna, giving me a tentative expression.

"No." No one knew about Emma and me. It was puppy love. It sneaked up on me, until I realized she was responsible for the smile on my face and I grew serious about her. But she was also Reign's oldest friend. He was having a hard time adjusting to life after foster care, and I didn't want to fuck things up for him again. He had been through enough change for a lifetime. So, Emma and I kept it quiet. Sienna was the only one who knew, and there is no need to taint Reign's memory about Emma after all these years. My relationship with Emma was fun, brief, and nothing more than a first love and last love.

A few minutes later, I drive my car onto the gravel before parking it in front of the big stairs that lead up to the entrance. Without waiting for Sienna, I dart out, bursting through the front door.

"Reign? Are you here?"

It stays quiet before I hear Connor's booming voice coming from the office while Sienna's footsteps trail behind me.

"He's in here!

We both jog to the office, halting in the doorpost when my eyes land on Reign.

"Reign? Oh my God, are you okay?" Sienna questions with worry.

He looks like he just saw a ghost, the blood having completely disappeared from his normally cheerful face. He swings his gaze to mine with a pained expression that makes him look more fragile than I can handle.

"I'm fine. Or I will be."

"Reign. Sit down, man," I tell him.

"What's going on?" Connor moves his gaze back and forth between us before Reign pulls out his phone.

"He *knows*." I hold Connor's gaze, explaining the situation to him with two words and a knowing look. Connor's eyes widen a little as lips part, forming a silent 'O'. When he rears his neck back to Reign, he pulls out his phone from his hand with a frown creasing his forehead. Reign's face falls, the shock undeniable.

"Who's that?" Connor asks. "What the fuck?!"

He holds up the phone in front of me and Sienna gasps beside me.

A photo of Franklin and Kendall is on the screen. They are both tied up with blindfolds covering their eyes.

"Dammit," I mutter, then snatch the phone out of Connor's grip to look at the messages that come with it.

UNKNOWN NUMBER: Roses are red, lovers are dead. Thank you for giving me your brother to play, you can collect his body by the end of the day.

"I want everyone on our team here within ten minutes!" I growl. "We are ending this bullshit tonight. Is it true Carrillo is in town?"

Connor nods.

"Call him. I want him guarding Lily and Colin. Everyone else goes with us."

A feral growl echoes through the room and Reign pushes everything off the desk, fueled by a rage I've never seen from him before. Like a madman, he throws every book off the shelves that he can find, trashing the place while he screams as if he's losing his mind. His cheeks are flushed, his eyes crazed while every muscle in his body is tensed like steel.

"What the fuck, Reign! STOP!" I demand. But Reign keeps going and we all stand there, completely thrown off by his lack of control. His anger makes him bare his teeth as he keeps going, letting go of his anger for the first time in his life until finally, he falls to the floor, tears streaming down his cheeks, his hands on the back of his neck.

"It's my fault. It's all my fault. It's my fault. I ruined us."

Connor drops to his knees in front of him, wrapping his arms around him.

"It's okay, Reign. I got you," Connor says.

"I was wrong, Con," he wails. "I was so wrong. I'm so sorry."

"I know. It's okay. It's okay. I got you."

"What are we going to do?" Reign sniffs.

"We are going to get him back and you two can work your shit out, okay?"

He nods, taking a short breath. "How?"

Connor twists his head to me as I watch them with grinding teeth. "Any ideas?"

"Yeah, I got a few ideas."

17

Lexie

I hate him.

I've been sitting on the couch watching some kind of telenovela with the TV on mute because I'm too busy sulking to register anything happening on the screen.

I'm getting so sick of the hot and cold treatment he's giving me. I know whatever the fuck he does is not my business, but he doesn't have to be an asshole about it, does he? Every time I start to relax around him, he finds a way to piss me off until I want to bite his head off.

By ignoring me.

By talking to me like I'm a child.

By treating me like I'm a bug on his shoe that he can't wait to get rid off, and I freaking hate him. Maybe I should just take my chances, kill Sullivan on my own, and get the fuck out of here. I'm sure I can get a rifle somewhere. I could shoot Sullivan from a distance, aiming for his leg or something before I blow a bullet through his head while looking him in the eye.

He's the only reason why I'm still in Boston because, other than that, I have nothing to stay for. But every time the thought enters my mind, Killian's face flashes before me, combined with a strong feeling of not wanting to leave him.

I let out a frustrated breath when my phone buzzes and I glance at the screen to check the messages coming through. Killian is sending me a location, but before I have the chance to check where it is, he's calling me.

"What?" I bark, still pissed about him walking out on me without an explanation.

"I need you to go somewhere," he replies, completely unaffected by my annoyance. "I've sent you the location."

"I saw."

"Do you see the jewelry box on the liquor cabinet?" I snap my head to the right, my eyes finding the box next to his favorite bottle of Bourbon.

"That's a jewelry box?" I always assumed it was solely there for decoration or something.

"Yes, Lexie," he groans, annoyed. "There is a Range Rover in the garage. The keys are in the box. The double bottom of the trunk holds a sniper rifle. I need you to be my sniper tonight."

"*What?* Are you serious?"

"Do I ever joke about anything?" I guess not.

"What if I screw up?" Suddenly, my throat constricts, fear shivering down my arms.

"You won't, baby," he says with ease, like it's the most normal thing in the world. "Leave now. Park the car a block away. Someone from my team will meet you there."

He hangs up the phone, and I stare into the night, blinking.

I swallow hard at his request, not sure if I'm ready, but realizing I don't have any other option. If I want him to help me kill Sullivan, I have to prove myself to him.

I have to show him I'm capable of the kill.

I have to be his sniper.

This is my chance.

18

It only takes me a few minutes before I have everyone instructed and ready to head out while Connor tries to calm Reign down with a few shots of Bourbon.

"Just stay put, okay?" I move my attention between Lily and Sienna, reloading my gun on the kitchen counter. "Kane Carrillo will stay here with a few of his men. If anything happens, he will take the three of you to a safe house." My head swings to my little nephew playing on the kitchen floor with his firetruck.

"I wanna come!" Sienna sputters.

"No." I glare, and she purses her lips in disagreement. But she knows better than to argue with me when I'm on edge like this, so luckily, she doesn't utter another word.

Lily gives me a coy smile in agreement, overruling Sienna's defiance, while she puts her light blonde hair up in a ponytail. "We're not going anywhere."

"Good." I slam the magazine into my Glock while Connor and Reign walk through the swing door. "Let's go." Moving past them, I exit the kitchen, the sounds of their footsteps comfortably echoing behind me. I don't mind working alone, getting shit done. But when it comes to the big shit, the important shit, I like having my brothers around. We are a team, acting like a pack. If all four of us are together, there is a level of loyalty that's irreplaceable. I can conquer the world by myself. I can take over Hell with my brothers.

"What are they doing here?" Reign asks when he notices Kane and Callie Carrillo stepping out of the SUV parked in front of the house.

"Keeping an eye on Colin and the girls," I reply.

We all give them a nod in recognition as we descend the steps, then make our way to the SUV waiting for us. Connor gets behind the wheel and I take the passenger seat while Reign slides into the back, his gaze still vacant and filled with worry.

I don't have time to be worried. It's a wasted emotion that's unnecessary because it doesn't gain you anything.

I need to act.

I put my phone to my ear, instructing my final asset to put the plan in motion.

"Yeah?" There is still annoyance in her voice, but to my pleasure, it has simmered down a little.

"Yeah. Be there in ten." I pause. "Oh, and hey! Don't screw this up. This is your shot to prove yourself."

I hang up, then put my arm out of the window to signal the cars in front of us to go.

"Who was that?" Reign asks.

"My secret weapon." I grin. Maybe it's stupid to put my faith in an eighteen-year-old girl, but she's a fucking good shot and I've seen the determination in her eyes. She's capable of killing if it's for a good reason. I know getting my approval to kill Sullivan will be a good enough reason for her to do whatever I ask her to do.

Right before we drive out the gate, the door on the driver's side flies open and I snap my head over my shoulder, watching Sienna hop into the car like it's nobody's business.

"What the hell? Get out, Sienna!" Reign orders.

"No!"

"What the fuck, Sienna?" I growl.

We can't have another stressor right now, and Sienna going with us is exactly that. We have no clue what we're up against, and I'd rather not have another body to protect. Especially when that body is my brother's girlfriend.

"Baby, this is not a game. Con, stop the car!"

"No! Reign Wolfe, I just got you back. I'm not losing you again." Sienna's eyes well up, giving him a pleading look.

"For fuck's sake, baby." Reign grabs her hand. "You're not going to lose me. I'll be back before you know it. Connor, stop the car."

"No, Reign. I'm coming with you!"

"Stop the car, Connor!" Reign barks. My aggravation reaches a peek, rolling my eyes at their squabbling like they are already married. This is serious and we don't have time to make a list of pros and cons.

"Reign!" I jerk my body to face both of them. "We don't have time for this shit." I point my finger at my soon-to-be-future-sister-in-law, or whatever the fuck kind of label they want to put on it when they are done with this wicked nonsense. "Not cool, Sienna! You're one of us, and I love you like a sister, but right now you're not helping! You're only making this harder. You can come, but you're staying in the car or so help me God, I will put you in the trunk until we get my brother back." I pause. "Got it?"

She shifts in her seat, nodding with a guilty look washing her face, and I fix my gaze back in front of me.

"You think he's serious?" she whispers to Reign.

"Dead. And so am I. You're staying in the car, or we'll tie you up, gag you and blindfold you before we throw you in the trunk," Reign tells her.

"What?" she shrieks. "You wouldn't."

"I would if it meant keeping you safe for the next few hours."

"And I sure as fuck will," I blurt without hesitation. Reign might carry the girl in his hands, but I'll happily be the bad guy in this story if it means she'll be alive and making my brother happy after this. Free will is overrated when it comes to this kind of shit. Sometimes you need a dictator to make the hard decisions, and I happen to be the fucking best there is.

Fifteen minutes later, I exit the car with Connor as we wait for Reign to do the same.

When he does, he comes to stand beside us, and I give him a questioning look.

"Are you ready for this?"

"I guess." He moves forward, but I hold him back with my hand on his chest.

"Look. There is a big chance a part of your past is in that warehouse. *Are you ready for this*?" I keep my gaze fixed on Reign. My gut is telling me this has everything to do with his fucked up time in foster care and after the night of revelations he's had, I can't have him breaking down again. It could be the difference between a minor setback to a full-blown disaster. I need my brother to have a straight head so we can make sure we walk out of there alive.

All of us.

"I'm ready." He squares his shoulders with determination, and I hope he'll be able to keep this level of confidence.

"Good. Let's go." I twist on the spot, instructing the rest of our men to surround the entrance while three of them are ordered to guard. Sienna stays in the car because, well, we don't have time to worry about her as well.

"Is she in place?" I whisper to our head of security.

"Yes, sir. She's all set."

I nod, then take the lead entering the warehouse while my brothers fall into step beside me. My hand stays close to the gun tucked in my jeans as the union of our steps echoes through the empty space.

There is no light, and we slow down to let our eyes adjust to the stuffy darkness until we're in the middle of the warehouse.

Suddenly, a single light turns on, the bulb swinging from the ceiling by the sudden movement of the cord.

I breathe out through my nose, grinding my teeth when I look at the sight in front of me, bringing my vicious side out in its full glory. Connor snorts with the same rage, probably wanting to kill someone. Franklin and Kendall are both tied up to a chair with Kendall's mouth covered with duct tape.

"Evening, boys." Franklin grins.

He looks completely relaxed, not even bothered, but I know having his girl tied up to a chair kills him inside. My eyes travel to the blonde standing right under the light bulb. She's shooting us a smile that doesn't reach her eyes and I recognize her as the girl that kidnapped my nephew, Colin, a few months ago.

"You," Connor growls in recognition.

"Bella," I huff, balling my hands into fists.

"Aubrey," Reign stammers. "You're dead."

19

Lexie

"Aubrey?!" Connor and Killian yelp with incredulous looks.

Both men seem to be growing by the second, rolling their shoulders in anger with clenched jaws. Their green eyes are looking even more feral than normal, making me realize I haven't seen Killian truly scary just yet.

But I'm about to.

When I arrived at the warehouse, some of their men helped me on top of the building, giving me access to the entire floor plan through an open window in the roof. Now I'm resting here, on one of the beams, feeling completely out of my comfort zone. Heat is flushing my neck, and I keep wiping the sweat off my forehead. I feel like I'm pretending to be a spy, though the seriousness of the situation is nagging at me.

One single lightbulb lights a small part of the empty hall with Franklin and Kendall sitting tied up to a chair. A crate with a little girl locked up sits in the dark near the wall, making my heart squeeze ever since I came up here. Even though my eyes keep drifting to take everything in, my rifle stays aimed at the girl named Aubrey, who's wearing white jeans and a red leather jacket, standing in the middle of the light with a smile splitting her cheeks.

"Really? Because I feel pretty alive." She's clearly enjoying being the center of attention, but there is an ominous look in her eyes that makes me want to wipe the grin off her face.

"Your hair," Reign says in shock.

She plucks a strand of her blonde hair. "You like?"

"I don't understand."

"It's not that hard." Aubrey rolls her eyes, sauntering a little closer, with her slender fingers wrapped around a handgun. "I faked my own death. Aubrey's life wasn't much fun anyway. Bella, on the other hand, she is fun."

"Bella," Reign repeats. "You kidnapped Colin."

"Yeah, sorry about that."

His shock is replaced with an anger that matches his brothers', standing beside him like wild animals waiting to be unleashed.

"You drugged him."

"Don't be so dramatic. It was innocent. Just something to keep him unconscious."

"And the gifts?"

"Just wanted to let you know I was thinking about you." Her lashes flutter.

She reminds me of Harley Quinn, looking pretty but completely fucked in the head.

"Why are you doing this?" Reign grunts, frustrated.

I feel for the guy. I've only seen him happy with a constant smile on his face and right now he looks like his world is crumbling underneath his feet because the twisted mind from his past seems to have come back to haunt him.

My gaze swings to Killian, who quickly acknowledges my presence by locking his eyes with mine. The rigid muscles in his angry face make him even more breathtaking than normal and I blow out a breath to settle the adrenaline surging through my veins with my sweaty palm tightly around the rifle.

Aubrey cocks her head with a psychotic look.

"Why are you looking at me like that? Aren't you happy?"

"Happy?" Reign parrots, his expression indignant.

"Your brother ruined your life. I'm here to save you from him. We can finally start our life together."

Killian's snort could wake the dead, mocking her with a single sound.

"Together? Aubrey–"

"Aubrey is dead!" She cuts Reign off with a vile look. "It's Bella!"

"*Bella*, I don't understand." Reign emphasizes her name, trying to placate her.

She clears her throat, the impatience clear on her face. "You said we would leave, build our own family. Look, I already started." She points her gun to the crate with the little girl and all three men follow her gaze with horror in their eyes.

The girl clearly is delusional, making me even more curious about what her history is with Reign. Either way, it's definitely not a good one.

"That's fucked up," Killian says, and Connor growls with a deep scowl.

"Is she yours?" Reign questions.

"Isn't she cute?"

"She is." He smiles, but it's reluctant.

"We can make more, honey. You, me, her. Let's go like we were supposed to with Nova."

Who's Nova?

Reign shakes his head. "That was never the plan. I was going to help you. I was going to save you. But I never intended to start a new family. I already have a family."

"But you came back for me." She shakes her head, her gaze dropping to the floor. "I saw you. You killed my dad for me. *I* was your family."

"I am." He slowly moves closer to her. "You can be. But if you want to be part of my family, you can't hurt the people I love. You're hurting my brother. My *friend*."

He points at Kendall, staring at him with her blue eyes wide and filled with fear.

"No! Your brother deserves it! He took you away from me!" Aubrey shouts. She quickly lifts her arm, pointing the gun at Franklin, and I straighten my shoulders, keeping the scope aimed at her head.

"Franklin tried to get you out!"

"Lies," she sputters.

"He tried to get you out, but you were too old. He tried to get you out until you turned eighteen. And then you *died*."

She lets out a feral wail that showers goosebumps on my arms, then points her gun to the ceiling and shoots twice.

Dust falls down, a trapped pigeon flying through the hall in distress. The sudden sound tightens my chest, and I blow out a breath to calm myself down again.

Aubrey lowers the gun back to Franklin with a vicious glare.

"Shut up, Reign! You've always had him on a pedestal. Too stupid to see he's the root of all problems."

Reign takes a big step forward, and my breath catches in my chest, my finger set on the trigger.

"Aubrey, if you hurt my brother, I *will* kill you," he grates out.

"Oh, I see how it is now." He takes another step closer. "Don't move!"

Reign lifts his hands in surrender. "Calm down. Just let them go."

"Reign?! Are you okay?" I glance over my shoulder, my eye catching Reign's girlfriend jogging into the room with panic in her eyes. My lips part in shock, annoyed with her timing while fixing my gaze back at Aubrey, knowing she's the loose projectile in this situation. Killian didn't tell me to kill her, but I'm confident he wants me to blow a bullet through her brain if she's hurting anyone in his family.

"Stay back, Sienna," Connor grunts. He looks scarier by the minute, the frown on his forehead getting deeper and deeper.

"I heard gunshots. Oh my God, Kenny?" Sienna gasps, throwing her hand in front of her mouth.

"Stay back," Reign barks.

"Well, well," Aubrey titters, "look what the cat dragged in. Sienna Brennan, how are you?"

"You," Sienna pushes out, surprised. "*You* attacked me."

At this point, I really wish Killian told me everything that was going on. Aubrey attacked Sienna? Do they know each other?

"Geez, you people sure like to overreact. It was a little bump on the head." Aubrey rolls her eyes.

"You hurt her?" Reign slowly breathes through his nose, his eyes hardening.

"Honestly, Reign, if she can't even handle that, she ain't woman enough for you." Aubrey rolls her eyes.

"She's more woman than you'll ever be," he sneers.

"Is that so? You think she has the balls to do this?"

She quickly brings herself to Kendall, putting the gun on her forehead and I glance at Killian to give me some kind of confirmation to pull the trigger, but when his eyes find mine, he still gives me the tiniest shake of his head.

"No!" Reign shouts at the same time Sienna yells, "Stop!"

"You are dead, girl." Killian chuckles like the Devil himself. If he's worried, he hides it like a damn pro, standing there like he's watching a street performer do his trick. It's breathtakingly scary, but it's also turning me on. He has a level of confidence that is inexplicable, showing me how big of a threat he can really be. It's never the angry ones that you should fear, it's the ones that don't seem to feel anything at all.

"She's innocent. Sienna, get in the car." He points his finger behind him and she shuffles backwards to do as he says.

"No, actually, Sienna. *Stay*." Aubrey smiles.

"Leave," Killian presses with a grunt, the Wolfe inside of him baring his teeth.

Aubrey shakes her head, her glare now aimed at Killian. "Tut, tut. I said I wanted her to stay." She pauses. "How about a trade? Your brunette for my brunette?" She nudges her chin to Kendall.

"No," all the brothers blurt out in unison, to my surprise.

"I'll do it."

I glance at Sienna, who's putting up a brave face as she's offering herself up.

"Don't you dare," Reign roars, never letting his eyes avert from Aubrey.

"Sienna." Killian tries to grab her arm, but she swings it in the air to escape from his grasp.

"Oh, such a noble little wifey," Aubrey taunts as Sienna moves past Killian.

"Sienna, don't you dare," Reign calls out behind her back, glancing at Killian in despair. He brings his gaze up and I hold still as both men look up at me before I give them a small nod in understanding.

"Maybe I was wrong, maybe she is woman enough for you." Aubrey's eyes are fixated on Sienna, and Reign lowers his gaze before yanking her behind him.

"Sienna, stop!" he orders.

Aubrey's arms tenses, pointing the gun at Reign.

"You really don't want to do that, Reign."

Reign shoves Sienna toward Killian and he drags her behind him with one quick move. Reign's stance grows more vicious, now matching the big energy of his brothers. His features are stern and there is a relaxed grin on his face that reminds me of Killian, ready to lash out in the blink of an eye.

"I'm sorry, Aubrey," Reign says. There is no sincerity in his voice and I feel the tension rise in the room. I keep my aim sharp, ready to pull the trigger at any time. "I really, really am. I wish I could've helped you more. Helped you better. Helped Nova better. I failed you and for that, I'm truly sorry. But you failed to have seen one thing from the start."

"Now you sound all cryptic like your brother. Your *alpha*," Aubrey mocks. "It's pathetic how all you grown ass men let your life be dictated by one man. As soon as he leaves the building, you're nothing but a few stray dogs looking for your leader."

A devilish snicker falls from his lips. "But that's where you are wrong. We are a pack. The *Wolfe* pack. You know what the characteristics of a pack are?"

"Please, do tell." She swishes her gun in the air with a bored look.

"Family." He pauses with every answer, thickening the tension in the air. "A team. Careful planning. Strategy and unlimited patience."

I can see the truth in his words, just by watching their places and stance in the room. It's amazing how these four men are all completely intertwined, able to think the same in the heat of the moment. They truly are a pack in every single way.

Aubrey lets out an evil laugh that brings me chills while I keep my aim pointed at her.

"Not sure what that's going to do for you now?"

"You might think we are an unstructured group of dogs without Franklin, but we continue to function as a pack. With or *without* him."

I watch Killian give me a jerk of his chin from the corner of my eye, and I let the red dot fall to Aubrey's chest. The adrenaline pumps harder through my blood, the sound of my heartbeat pounding in my ear. My mouth turns dry as I keep my focus on Aubrey, who now fearfully starts searching the room around her, and I pray for her not to look up.

Reign smiles, this time as malicious as Killian. "You didn't really think you could beat us, right? It's over, Aubrey. Drop the gun."

She holds still, as if she's going over her options.

"Drop the gun," Killian commands.

Despair crosses Aubrey's face and she shakes her head.

"You were mine, Reign. *Mine*. When you came to Providence, I knew you were going to be my savior and you just bailed." She pushes the last words out with a growl, then stomps off to Franklin. "How are you going to pay for that? With his life, or hers?"

She pushes the barrel against Franklin's temple and my heart speeds up when I see the look on her face. She's serious this time. My fingers are aching, as I keep my finger on the trigger, aiming for her neck. I slowly feel the fear creep in, knowing I need to make a decision within the next second, and my eyes fix onto the potential movement of her finger.

"No!" Reign shouts.

"Say goodbye to your brother, Prince Charming." The jerk of Aubrey's finger is minimal, but I don't hesitate, pulling the trigger, and the gunshot reverberates through the entire hall.

Aubrey falls to the floor with a loud thud, her eyes wide as she gasps for air.

I'd expect to feel something. Guilt. Regret. Anything. But instead, I just stare at the girl from above, seeing her life slipping through her fingers as everyone stands frozen around her. I hold the rifle up, ready to fire another shot just in case, the fast beating of my heart never slowing down.

"Are you okay?" Reign swings his body to Sienna, the stress still dripping from his face.

"Yeah," she huffs.

Satisfied with that answer, Reign looks up to me, then looks at Killian.

"Is that—?" He looks at Killian. "The girl from the bar?"

Killian swings his gaze up at me, giving me a beaming smile that almost knocks me down before they fall back to his brother.

"Told you I had a secret weapon." He smirks with a wink, then cuts Franklin and Kendall loose while Reign squats down next to Aubrey, cocking his head in a taunting way, showing the dark side of Prince Charming.

"At some point in our lives, we have to stop blaming everyone else for our misery. I wish there was something better for you. But I knew that very first day how much your dad's evil had already rubbed off on you, Aubrey. I desperately wanted to save you. But I never truly could." The tone in his voice is cold. Venomous. And now I realize it's not just Killian. Or Connor. Nor Franklin. All four of them are capable of things the Devil would fear. All four of them don't hesitate to kill if you threaten them.

"Help me," Aubrey gurgles, her eyes widened in terror.

I know it's useless. Even if Reign doesn't end her himself, the vicious grin cutting Killian's face in half tells me she's not going to live much longer than this.

"You tried to hurt my pack. *No one* walks away from that alive."

"Reign, no," she whispers, her words barely audible.

"Goodbye, Aubrey." He moves to get up, but with her last strength, she grabs his arm and he rears his head back to her.

"Take care of my girl, please." My gaze drops to the girl still sitting in the crate with a blank expression. She scares the shit out of me, her eyes peering from the darkness like headlights.

Reign gives her a short nod, then gets up with a glare, his piercing eyes finding Killian.

"Kill her."

Killian licks his lower lip, gloating over the opportunity his brother just gave him while Reign glances at Franklin holding Kendall in a tight grip. Killian saunters toward her with a mischievous grin as he pulls a knife from his back pocket. It's not big. But it's shiny and looks sharp as hell, even from up here.

He crouches down, chuckling before he shoves the blade into her slender neck, and the blood gushes out. I want to look away, the excessive amount of blood making my skin scrawl. But I suck in a deep breath, swallowing away my nausea as I remember what Killian told me: *"You need to prepare for the mess."*

So, I watch.

I refuse to let my gaze falter as he pushed the blade in one more time, tearing her flesh like he's prepping her for dinner and when he gets back up, his eyes immediately find mine. I show him my straight face, until the corner of his mouth lifts, giving me a look of approval.

"Good girl," he mouths.

My heart swells and I can't help returning his smile with one of my own. His approval does something to me. It builds my confidence in a way only he can, and even though I know I shouldn't let my heart feel whatever it wants to feel, it makes me wonder what I'm doing. I demanded his help because my goal was to be able to kill the man that slaughtered my family. But in the last few days, I seem to be living for the looks of approval Killian Wolfe gives me. Always hungry and in need of the next one.

20

It's a little past midnight when I arrive at the apartment, finding Lexie watching TV on the couch. She drove my Range Rover back as soon as we cleared the area, while I drove back to the mansion with my brothers to pick up my Audi.

Her gaze lifts to mine, a tentative look coming my way as I keep my eyes locked with hers. She still looks exactly the same, pure, beautiful, *young*. But her eyes show a level of maturity that wasn't there earlier, making her even more desirable than before. A lustful smile wants to creep through, but I keep a straight face as I lock the door behind me and take off my leather jacket, throwing it through the room casually.

She arches a brow in question before they grow wide with every step I make toward her.

I didn't forget how jealousy flared across her face when I left her earlier tonight, and it's been on my mind ever since. I like how she's growing possessive of me, even though I shouldn't encourage it. It makes me want to leave my mark on her even more than I already did, making her untouchable for anyone else.

When I'm standing in front of her, I hold out my hand. Her eyes narrow in suspicion, a little defiance still etched in her gorgeous blue eyes, and I roll mine at her lack of movement. Accepting a little curl of my lip, I pull her up by her waist while a shriek comes from her throat. With one swift move, I spin us, then take her with me as I let my body sink into the cushions. I grab her hips, adjusting her thighs so she straddles me. Her warm hands land on my chest, feeling like a hot iron burning into my skin while she drags her teeth over her lips. Her gaze is hesitant, a little uncomfortable, as if she's not sure if she wants my hands on her body. But the electrifying energy when our bodies connect confirms that she's dying to feel my hands on her. Our little get together in the woods was quick, and primal, giving her a taste of how good I can make her feel, and she's been craving more ever since.

"You were jealous." I run a hand through her soft hair, and a whiff of her rose scented shampoo welcomes me. Inwardly, I feel a flutter biting its way through my organs, wanting to breathe her in, but I hold still, catching the change in her expression.

The frown that forms is wicked cute.

"I wasn't."

"You're a shit liar." I pull her neck, forcing her face only a few inches from mine, but she quickly pushes back.

"Get over yourself." Her glare is steady, almost believable.

Almost.

"Don't even try, little Lexie. Admit it." She can't hide her feelings from me, no matter how hard she tries. Maybe it's her inexperience, maybe it's her age. Either way, I see right through her, staring into the deep pools of our matching yearning.

"What do you wanna hear?" she asks, the defiance clear in her tone and expression.

"I want to hear what you felt, hearing another woman's voice coming through my phone. I wanna hear what it did to your body." I fist her hair, tilting her head a little as she holds my gaze with grinding teeth. "Did it make you squirm in frustration? Did it make your blood boil? Did it make you want to kill her? Kill *me*?"

Her mouth is pinched, her eyes shooting daggers at me as if she actually stands a chance against me. She knows better.

"Yes." It's a growl. Sharp. Satisfying me more than it should, even though it's filled with venom.

"Yes, what?" I want to hear her spit out the words. I want her to dive into that dark emotion and own it.

"I hated it," she snarls. "I hated her. I hated *you*."

My tongue darts out, taking in her heated stance. My unpredictability keeps her on edge, her eyes never feeling comfortable enough to avert their gaze. I like that about her. The fact that she's uncomfortable, but never allows herself to show it. She'd rather die with her chin up in the air than curled up in a corner. Her species is rare. One of a kind, even. She didn't get that because her family died. No, it's something that's embedded in your soul, reaching the surface when life forces you to let it out.

"You're so gorgeous all worked up." My groin grows tightly against my jeans. "Dripping with jealousy. Makes me want to shut you up with my tongue in your pussy. Are you wet for me, little Lexie?" The tip of her fingers tense on my chest.

"I hate you."

"I know you are," I continue, a smirk slowly taking over my face.

"You're an asshole."

"Humor me," I titter. "Why?"

Her posture changes a little as her shoulders slump and the sharp edges of her eyes soften just a little. Enough to show a spark of vulnerability.

"I don't even get a *thank you, Alexandra*? A *you did good*?"

Her disappointment shatters through me like broken glass, reminding me of her age. She shrinks a few inches underneath my gaze, the lost orphan coming through even though she's trying her hardest to not let it show.

I'm not the one to give sympathy to those who lost, or to anyone in general. If you want someone to listen and give you a hug to make it all better, you go to Reign. Maybe even Franklin. I don't have time to tell you it will all get better when the world is too ugly to ever really get better. But right now, I'm having a really hard time ignoring the fact that the upset expression she's shooting at me is affecting me.

"You want a pat on the back for shooting someone."

"I killed her. Thought you'd be proud."

"You shot her," I clarify in a mocking tone. "I killed her."

"You really are an asshole." She tries to get off my lap, but I hold her tight against me.

"What do you wanna hear, baby? That you're a badass?"

She shrugs. "Something like that."

"I won't. But I'll reward you." I guide her lips to mine, nibbling her lower lip as I softly pull it between my teeth. My hands connect with her warm skin, pushing her shirt to the side, and she shifts on my lap. "You looked wicked sexy with that killer gaze in your baby blues."

"Killian." It's supposed to sound like a reprimand, I'm sure. But it only sounds like music to my ears, demolishing every ounce of restraint I have left.

"I love it when you say my name like a plea."

Eagerly, I grab the hem of the soft fabric, pulling it over her head before throwing it somewhere behind me. I lean back, staring at her chest as I drag my teeth over my lip. I haven't forgotten how good she felt while her warmth hugged my hard shaft. But I haven't had the pleasure of feeling her bare breasts underneath my palms. To suck her nipples and notice them tense under my tongue. I could've easily thrown in a sneak peek whenever she hit the shower. I could've claimed them as my own while she was tucked against my body in the middle of the night. But I'm glad I didn't, because now it's like I have a present I haven't completely unwrapped just yet. Like I was postponing the evitable for my own heightened pleasure as soon as I tore all the layers off. But really, I knew I wouldn't be able to resist as soon as I had her body completely surrendered in my hands.

I move my hands around her waist, locking my lips with hers. Her hesitation completely vanishes, and her hands drop to my neck with an urgency that makes me moan against her tongue. I reach up, unclasping her bra, then push her back to look at the sight of her. They are perky, covered by flawless, creamy skin. Her nipples harden under my gaze as I brush my thumb underneath the swell of her breast. I gently keep stroking her, and her lips part as she waits for my next move.

I'm completely transfixed by the gorgeous sight in front of me. The longing in her eyes. The vulnerability of her bare chest. It brings all my senses alive to watch her opening up to me in anticipation of me guiding her.

I gasp when she slowly grinds her hips, rubbing her center over the bulge in my jeans. When I bring my gaze up, there is a dare in her eyes that rips a laugh from my mouth.

"Growing impatient, little Lexie?"

She dips her chin, her mouth flush with my ear. "I want you."

Her breath brushing over my skin grows my cock until it's painful, eager for the same attention. Shutting my eyes in a fleeting moment of weakness, I relish in the feel of her plump lips against the sensitive spot behind my ear. She trails seductive, open-mouthed kisses down all the way to the crook of my neck, her hot breath whispering with every swirl of her tongue across my skin.

"I want you to make me feel alive." Kiss. "I want you to hurt me." Kiss. "To torture me." Kiss. "To make me beg for more while you make me crumble in your hands."

"Fucking hell," I mutter.

Unable to hold back, I throw her beside me on the couch, then crowd her body as I crawl on top of her. She's giving me a smug smile, pulling my shirt over my head. When her eyes land on my bare chest, she presses her lips together, taking all of me in with a single gaze.

"You wanna feel alive, baby?"

She nods.

I get up, pulling her legs in the air so I can yank her jeans off her hips until she's sitting on my couch with nothing more than a thong covering her core. When I'm done, she goes for my jeans like a hungry little lioness. She unbuttons them quickly, then slides them down with my boxers until they're pooled around my feet. I step out, then pull her back into the pillows before she can reach for my throbbing dick.

"You want me to set every inch of your body on fire?" I place my knees beside her hips, directly lining my cock in front of her face. "Lick my balls."

She gasps at my brazen order, but she doesn't fight me. She licks her lips, then looks up at me through her fluttering lashes as she takes my balls into her mouth. A hand wraps around my cock, and she starts to slowly move it up and down my shaft while she swirls my balls around her mouth, one by one, like they're a damn jawbreakers.

She moans as she looks up at me, the sound vibrating against my skin, and I let my head fall back as I thread my fingers through her hair. Her tongue moves to slide up and down my shaft, making every single nerve tingle like they're about to sing me a Christmas song, and my knees slightly buckle when she takes my tip into her mouth. Her small hands play with my balls, slowly massaging them with a finesse that I've never felt before. She sucks my cock like it's her favorite thing to do and when I swing my gaze to her beautiful face again, her blue eyes link with mine. My cock reappears and disappears into her mouth as she sets the pace and I just hold still, enjoying every single second of the sight in front of me.

"Fuck, you're so gorgeous."

A smirk twists my lips, admiring the fragile position she's in. She's at my mercy, pleasuring me with a drive that liquifies my organs. It shows the level of trust she's giving me, making my heart purr. She's had a defiant stance every minute of every single day, but here she is, showing me she's willing to give me her insecurities. To drop her walls just for me.

Her hands move up my legs before she presses her nails into my ass, pushing my hips so she can take me deeper into her mouth.

"Fuck." Her moves grow more demanding, sucking my shaft like she's thirsty for every drop of my cum. A groan echoes through the room, fisting her hair as I set the pace, fucking her mouth with my eyes fixed on the ceiling. Small whimpers resonate against my tip every time I hit the back of her throat, and it's so tempting to shoot my load into her mouth. But I want to be deep inside of her when I fill her up.

I pull her back by her hair, my cock plopping from her swollen lips, and she blinks at me with a pout. My thumb wipes the saliva from the corner of her mouth, smearing it all over her glistening lips.

"I want to taste you," I tell her.

Her eyes flicker with excitement as she swallows, before her lips part as she takes small breaths.

"You'd like that, wouldn't you, baby?" I peer down at her, my hand never leaving her cheek. She's sitting in front of me, looking so innocent, except for the crazed look in her eyes. Her tongue darts out, and she swipes it along my thumb, igniting a flutter in my core when a thought crosses my mind.

"Has someone ever licked you, little Lexie?"

The shake of her head is tiny, but clear.

I'm not surprised. She is fierce like a warrior, but she's still as inexperienced as a schoolgirl. I've been certain from the start that someone took her V-card a while ago, but I have a feeling there hasn't been a teenage boy that completely accommodated her needs. That put her skin on fire and made her mind explode with a single touch, a single stroke, or a longing kiss.

I drop to my knees, settling between her thighs as I place a kiss on the inside of her leg. She never averts her gaze from mine, watching every move with a palpable tension.

"Has someone ever sucked your clit until you couldn't breathe anymore?"

Another shake of her head.

"Do you want me to?" I drag my tongue along the crook of her thigh, slowly pushing underneath the fabric of her thong.

She stays still, her mouth agape, a desperate look written on her face.

I take her thong off, then place her legs over my shoulders. A shriek comes from her lips when I pull her center closer to my mouth, her ass now up in the air in the palms of my hands.

"Do you want me to?" I repeat, my growl fanning her folds.

Her wetness is taunting me like frosting on a cake, begging me to lick it off and devour the taste. I push the tip of my thumb inside, then swirl her wetness around her center.

"Oh, damn," she cries at my soft touch.

"Do you want me to?" I hover above her center, my mouth only an inch away. I can smell her, her growing arousal tempting my nose to dive in.

"Yes!" she finally yelps. "Yes! I want you to."

The urgency is clear in her voice, creating a wolfish grin on my face.

"Good girl."

I collide my lips with her center, sucking up the juices that are already dripping from her core. It's salty, sweet, and even more intoxicating than I expected. It's a perfect balance, an accurate representation of the girl whose body it's dripping from.

"Holy shit!" she shouts. Her fingers dive into my hair, fisting it like she needs something to hold on to. Her pull burns on my scalp, adding to my desire as I devour her pussy like a delicacy. I kiss, lick, stroke, brush, and suck every inch of her pussy, never getting close to her clit so I can build her up to the point I want her to be. She squirms above my palms, but I hold her close to my mouth, never giving her any room to escape my grasp.

"This is the best pussy I've ever tasted," I murmur against her folds. "It's addictive. You're addictive." I slide my tongue up, flicking her clit, and she jerks in my hands.

She sucks in a deep breath, her shocked eyes finding mine.

"Do that again," she orders.

"What? This?" I can feel the amusement on my cheeks as I take her clit into my mouth. I gently suck it, knowing exactly how much pressure her sensitive nub needs.

"Oh, my God!" she cries out, her head dropping back to the pillows. Her eyes roll to the back of her head as I keep kissing her center. The tension in her muscles is alternated by complete relaxation, and I know I can make her come within five seconds. But the view is too gorgeous to cut things short. I want to frame the vision of her like this, forever staring into her eyes while my mouth locks onto her pussy. Her mouth is tense, the skin around her eyes knitted together as I drag out her orgasm.

"Please, Killian," she cries.

I ignore her, having too much fun looking at the sight of her completely surrendered to me. It's the sexiest thing I've ever seen, exceeding all my expectations of having her spread out naked in front of me.

"Please!"

The tip of my tongue draws small circles around her bud, while my lips fall around it with every few swirls and sucks.

"Hmm, I can do this all night," I hum, never missing a beat.

"Please, Killian. It's too much." She tightens her grip on my hair, keeping my head in place as she starts to ride my face. "I'm close. I'm *so* close."

I bring my head up, denying her my tongue while our gazes align. Hers filled with sexual pleas, mine showing how much I'm enjoying holding the power.

"Don't stop," she whispers.

"How badly do you want it, little Lexie?" Teasing, I run my tongue down her folds, and it's followed by another moan from her throat.

"Badly," she huffs.

"But how badly?" I like poking her. I like ticking her off, simply because I love seeing her all worked up and spitting fire at me. She's beautiful when she's giving me her pure and innocent side, tempting me like an angel, but she's breathtakingly gorgeous when she's showing me that she's not afraid to taunt the Devil.

The corner of her mouth lifts into a snarl, her eyes darkening like I want them too.

"Make me come, asshole, or so help me God, I will do it myself."

I launch for her neck, wrapping my fingers around it with a vicious glare, loving this push and pull between us. She fears me, but she never lets it get in the way of reaching her goal.

"I'm the one who's going to make you come, little Lexie. Me and no one else."

I hold her glare, squeezing her neck a little tighter.

"Then. Make. Me. Come," she grits out the words, baring her teeth, and I can't hold back the evil grin that falls through. I hold my hand wrapped around her neck, then cover her clit with my mouth. I let her ass drop to the cushions, pushing a finger inside of her tight walls while my tongue keeps twirling around her clit.

"Oh, fuck!" she cries.

My eyes roll to the back of my head, the sensation of her warm juices over my fingers creating a fog in my mind. Her thighs fall over my shoulders so she can press her core closer to my mouth and within seconds, she tenses underneath me. My grip around her slender neck tightens more, giving her barely enough space to breathe while I flick her clit a few more times until her legs are shaking on my shoulders.

"Killian!" The scream of my name brings a shiver to run down my spine as her orgasm ripples through her. A pained moan follows and soon I taste a wave of her saltiness coat my tongue as I suck it up like it's my life elixir. When she relaxes, I look up from between her legs, lazily licking her clean until her eyes open and lock with mine.

"That was–" She searches for words.

"Delicious." I press a final open-mouthed kiss on her center with a smirk lurking in the corner of my mouth. "Taste it."

I climb over her my body until my lips find hers, and I press my tongue inside her mouth. She moans deeply, her fingernails digging into the skin around my spine. My cock jerks, ready for more action, and I lower my hips so I can align myself with her center.

"Are you on the pill?" I hum between kisses.

"Yes."

"Good." I shove my shaft inside of her and her eyes spring open at my sudden movement. I give her no time to adjust, slamming my cock against her wall before I hold still.

"This is–" I'm lost for words. Feeling her warm flesh hug mine with no restraints feels better than I ever imagined, like letting your body fall in a hot bath after a long day of labor. Every nerve on my shaft is heightened, wanting to stay inside her tight pussy forever.

"This is wicked divine," I huff, pressing my lips against hers.

She meets my eyes with a lazy look, completely spent. If I ever wondered if she was capable of submitting to me, the picture in front of me is the answer.

"I'm yours. I'm yours, Killian Wolfe. Take me however you want."

"You're damn right you are." I move my hips forward, vigorously pumping inside of her. She worked me up so perfectly that my cock is already chasing my release like a dog in a fox hunt, desperate for the kill after an excruciating tease. She holds on to my shoulders as I grip her hips, angling her body as I please to get the most friction with every thrust. I groan when she arches her back, silently begging me to take her deeper.

"Fuck me, Killian. Fuck me like you mean it." My fingers dig into her soft flesh, keeping her tightly in place. It only takes a few more thrusts, feeling her walls milk my cock, and I let out a groan as the muscles in my back tense. My chest falls forward, my forehead pressed against her neck, and when she cries out in pleasure with her hands fisting my hair like I'm hers, I'm exploding. The sensation ripples through my entire core, bringing me a release I've never experienced in my life. My eyes are shut, and for a few seconds, I feel like I've reached a high no drugs can ever replicate.

I'm drunk.

Drunk on little Lexie Lee and it's the most blissful feeling I've ever felt.

My hips jerk a few more times until I let my weight fall completely on top of her, her chest heaving underneath mine. I breathe her in, her rose scent now laced with sweat, creating an intoxicating blend. She hugs my torso, resting her cheek against mine, and the sigh that leaves her lips makes my heart twitch. It's filled with contentment. Satisfaction. And I allow the thought that maybe there is even a little peace in it.

When my lungs are no longer heaving, she releases a moan.

"You okay, baby?" I murmur against her damp skin.

"You're suffocating me."

I laugh, then pull her into my arms so I can switch our positions as I rest my back on the gray fabric of the couch. I tuck her on top of me, our naked bodies merged as one. Her ear is pressed against my heart, and I can feel the lopsided grin that tenses the muscles in my cheeks, unable to pinpoint what triggered it, but letting it sit there nonetheless.

"You did good, baby. I'm proud of you."

"What?" She tilts her head, resting her chin on my chest to look up at me, but I keep my eyes closed. My hand strokes her spine, loving the feel of her soft skin underneath my fingertips. My mind still seems to be drifting in purgatory, dancing in front of the gates of Heaven. That's how it feels. A little taste of Heaven, clearly visible, but always a little out of reach. But at this moment, I'll take anything I can get.

"I feel like I should record this." I hear the smirk in her voice. I don't even know why I said it. I'm not the kind of guy that gives out compliments, but the words left my mind faster than I could process.

I bring my head up a little, softly biting her lip in a reprimand.

"Shut up."

"Who was she to you?"

A frown creeps onto my forehead, getting pulled out of my afterglow by her question.

"Who?"

"Aubrey." I hate that name, and I always hated the girl that it belonged to. I heard the stories from Reign. He spoke about her with pity and despair, wanting to save her, but I always knew she was a rotten apple. He has the ability to see the good in people, making him a better person than me. I choose to see the ugly; that way you can never be disappointed.

Aubrey was definitely ugly. Rotten to the core.

"To me, nothing." I shrug. "To Reign? The ghost of his past."

Her cheek connects with my body again as she melts into my arms. She feels small in my arms, but at the same time stronger than I feel. Like she should be saving me, instead of the other way around. But either way, it feels like she belongs right here. Right now. It should frighten me, but weirdly enough, it doesn't.

"What is your story?" she asks.

"I don't have a story"

"Everyone has a story."

"I'm a Wolfe. That's my story." The Wolfe name has been famous and infamous in the city of Boston long before my brothers and I turned it into the successful name it is now. But it has always been powerful. My grandfather was the biggest arms dealer in the state, bringing not only wealth with the name, but also fear.

Franklin runs the city, trying to be just and fair whenever he can, but the generation before us was anything but that. We've always been criminals, just some better than the others since my old man was nothing but a petty thief. Franklin took his position before he was sixteen, and when my grandfather passed away, it was a given Franklin would take over. Not only did he take over, but he flourished the business, having the brain to see the bigger picture. He created a legacy for us that will allow us to one day live from our legal businesses, existing in the light instead of hiding in the dark. I don't know if I'm cut out for the light, but I'm proud of my brother for creating the option.

"Is it true you've been in foster care?"

"You've been busy." I arch a brow. "Two years. Upstate New York."

"Was it awful?"

"It wasn't great. But compared to my brother, it was a fucking walk in the park." My stomach can cope with anything, and I'm rarely grossed out by any dirty shit. Connor pulls someone's toenails out next to me, and I'll happily keep eating my fresh donut from Dunks. But thinking about all the horrors Reign had to witness in his four years in foster care, that makes my stomach somersault in agony, before it flares into an untamable rage.

"Why?"

"Not my story to tell, baby."

"Is he okay?" Her sweet voice sounds caring, and I push away the painful history of my baby brother's teenage years.

"He will be." I keep brushing her skin, enjoying her weight on top of mine. "Why do you care?"

She stays quiet, as if she needs to think about the answer. The room fills with silence, soothing us both as our chests keep breathing evenly together.

"I don't know." Her shoulders move up toward my chin. "I guess because I know what it feels like to be alone."

I close my eyes at that answer, hating the feeling it brings me. She has built her walls so high; I sometimes forget how fragile she still is. She's strong ninety-nine percent of the time, but the remaining one percent is so easily forgotten when you get a fearless know-it-all for the most part. I don't want her to be alone. I know what it feels like to be alone, but at least for me, I know my brothers are there in the end. I still have family, even if I'm not the family man like my brothers are.

She doesn't have anyone. Her entire family was murdered like an inconvenience.

My nose brushes against her hair before I press a kiss on top of her head.

"You're not alone, baby."

21

Lexie

"*Hit me in the face and you get to pick what we do tonight,*" he said.

I like a challenge just as much as the next anger-filled teenager, but most of all, I want to punch the taunting smirk off his face. He's been pushing me all afternoon, scraping every ounce of energy from me by yelling in my face. Telling me I'm little. I'm young. I'm naïve. Anything to piss me off even more while I try to get that clear shot to his nose.

Sweat is dripping from my forehead, my wrapped hands in front of my face as I bounce back and forth across the mat to find the right time to charge. I swallow to get rid of the dryness in my mouth, trying to control the heaving of my lungs while my eyes stay locked with his, darting around him. I'm getting sick of the stuffy air in the gym, but my ego won't let me stop when I look at Killian's smug face. I've been dancing on my toes for at least an hour, and every single muscle in my body feels sore and completely worn out, but I *need* to win this.

Suddenly, he stops, the sharp look in his dark green eyes softening, and I lower my hands with a frown.

"You're tired, aren't you? Maybe we should call it a day?" He takes small steps forward, his gaze never leaving mine. Suspicion fills me, but I take the time to catch my breath, my chest moving up and down to get as much air in my lungs as possible.

"Really?"

A lopsided grin builds on his cheeks before a devilish glint flashes in his eyes. I gasp, seeing his demeanor change right in time to catch the swing he's aiming at me. Dropping my chest, I dodge his punch before getting up to slam my fist into his stomach and dart out of the way.

"Asshole!" I glare, putting my hands back up to hold my defense.

He hunches forward only slightly, then straightens his back as he starts to take a few more ominous steps toward me.

"Come on, little Lexie. You can do better than that," Killian mocks, a mischievous grin splitting his face that shows how much he's enjoying this. He circles around me like an animal surrounding its prey, wearing nothing more than his gym shorts that aren't even slightly damp.

"You don't play fair!" I shout, growing even more frustrated than I already am.

He quickly lowers his body, trying to kick my feet out from under me, but I jump up to avoid my body from crashing to the floor.

"You think your enemy will play fair?" He snickers, then gets up, aiming his fist at my nose. I dive, slapping it away with my lower arm before I create some distance between us. "You think they will wait for you to gather your breath?"

The fatigue is taking its toll, and I do my best to keep my head on straight.

"Think harder, Lexie! This is your life!" he shouts, showing his teeth.

I lash out, but he blocks my fist with ease, and I grind my teeth as I keep going.

"Harder!"

My feet never stand still, not wanting to give him an easy shot, ready to dodge his attacks, but I'm starting to realize this isn't going in my favor. If I want to win, I need to play his game. I charge him, trying to hit his face as much as I can, and he quickly overtakes me, spinning me in his arms. I fall against his hard chest before he kicks my feet underneath my body and I fall to the ground. I try to roll away, getting on my hands and knees to get up, but I'm not quick enough, and he covers my body entirely as I feel his chest against my back.

"Where are you going, little Lexie?" he growls with amusement in my ear. His hand reaches to the front of my neck, forcing me to submit, and I feel a smile creeping onto my lips. I suck in a breath to gather the strength I need, then arch my back as much as I can to push him off and onto the floor. When his weight falls over my body, I roll us both over, forcing myself on top of him. I catch him by surprise when he's situated beneath me, my back on top of his chest, with my gaze aimed at the ceiling.

"What the–" he mutters, right before I slam my elbow in his ribs, followed by my feet connecting with his groin. He cries out, squirming, and I rapidly throw my legs in the air so I can spin and twist myself around to face him. I straddle him, my thighs gripping tightly around him, locking his hands under my hips as he's gripping his groin in agony, then connect my fist with his cheek without mercy. It's harsh, it's painful, and it almost makes his eyes pop out of his head before they shut with a clenched jaw. Like a Jack-In-The-Box, they spring open again, knocking the air out of my lungs. His hands are pulled from underneath me and he swiftly grips my hips, rolling us over so he has the upper hand again. The glare in his eyes is straight from Hell, as he grabs my neck, closing around my windpipe.

"You think you're smart, little Lexie?" he seethes in panic from the lack of air. His full weight sits on my hips, making it impossible to buck him off as my legs writhe underneath him while I try to pry his hands off my neck. "How are you going to get out of this one?"

A fog forms in my brain, triggered by the alarm that rushes through my body at his firm grip. The adrenaline pumps in my ears, making it that much harder to stay calm and look for a solution. I fold my arms over his, then press them against my chest, hoping to break his hold. I feel his grip loosen, unable to keep the pressure on my throat. He lowers his head, trying to put my strength into his constraint, and when he's close enough, I slam my palm against his nose with all the power I still have.

A loud grunt echoes through the gym when his eyes shut and he falls from my body.

"Jesus Christ!" he cries out.

I scramble away from him, panting, as I get on my feet with a vicious glare.

"What the fuck was that?" I yell.

He wipes his nose with his palm, then glances at the blood smeared over his skin.

I hold my stance, fearless, but I can't deny the unease that creeps in, not knowing how he will respond. The ticking of the clock on the wall sounds loud and ominous as I wait, catching my breath while my gaze stays fixed on the man sitting on the floor in front of me.

Finally, he twists his head, glaring, but I see the ghost of a smile that is fighting to get out. It's lurking, and it takes mere seconds before he shows me a full grin.

"I told you, you could do better than that."

The tension leaves my shoulders, and I let my head hang, shaking my head with a smile before I swing it back to him.

"For a minute there, I thought you were going to kill me."

"I was." He chuckles, then gets up with a serious look coming my way. My cheerful mood falls as quickly as it rises as he approaches me with that intimidated energy I've become familiar with. I search his eyes, looking for a hint that tells me I need to keep my distance, but when I can't find any, I let him pull me against his chest, a hand falling onto my sweaty neck.

"But you weren't really going to fight if I didn't."

"So, it was a test?"

"It wasn't a test. It was showing you how badly you want to live. Take that. Use that. You'll need it for the rest of your life." I feel my heart expand, bringing a boldness to the table that is seemingly fueled by the leftover adrenaline.

"I won." I smirk, my palms pressed against his bare chest.

The laugh that makes my lashes flutter conjures a wide smile on my face.

"You're right. You did win." He drags his thumb over my lips. "What do you wanna do?"

With my lips pressed together, I smile, his thumb resting in the corner of my mouth. Our lips meet, slowly parting in an affectionate kiss that makes my toes curl.

"What is it, baby? Because I already know what I want to do."

"You didn't win," I huff against his lips.

"Oh, baby," he taunts, pressing a kiss to my lips with every word. "Don't you know I always win?"

"You do if all you ever want is sex," I titter.

"Not sex. Sex with *you*."

"If you play your cards right, you'll get that too. But I want my reward first."

"Your reward?" His grin grows wider.

I nod. "I get to pick what we're doing tonight."

He brings his gaze to the ceiling, then releases the air from his lungs.

"Wicked," he says, sarcastically. "What do you want?"

"Three things." I raise three fingers in the air. "Popcorn, candy, and the movie of my choice."

An eyebrow arches up. "You want to watch a movie when we could have sex?"

"Yes."

"No."

"Yes."

"No."

"Why not?" I screech.

"Because movies are a waste of time."

I roll my eyes at his childish comment, countering it by raising my chin, unwilling to give in. "I don't care. I won. We're doing what I want. I want a movie."

His hands stroke the bare skin of my back, his fingers reaching underneath the hem of my sports bra while he moves past my ear to trail kisses down my neck.

"I want *you*."

"You can have me." I feel him sigh in satisfaction. "*After* the movie."

I push him off, shooting him a wink as I saunter away from him. He holds my gaze, pressing his tongue into his cheek with playful eyes.

"Or I can just take you right here," he dares.

I cock my head at him. "You're not a man of your word?"

"Rarely."

Lust crosses his face as he comes closer, and I lift my hand.

"Movie *first*."

He continues his steps, yanking me to his chest by the fabric of my bra.

"You're being annoying."

"I won. Don't be a sore loser." That seems to tick him off because he lifts his hands, taking a step back.

"Fine. But I'm having you as soon as the first line of the credits hits the screen."

"Okay."

"And no fucking chick flick."

"Pinky swear, baby." I chuckle, then make my way to the dressing room to clean up, but he pulls me back by my ponytail, my back connecting with his chest. His mouth sits flush with my ear and his arms snake around my stomach.

"Ouch!"

"You called me baby." The contentment is audible in his voice, and I swallow to settle the butterflies flying through my belly.

"I did."

"Keep doing it. I like it." A kiss lands in the crook of my neck before he pushes me forward, slapping my ass in the process. I can't resist a pleased glance over my shoulder, my blues connecting with his greens for just a quick moment. I feel a shiver wash over my entire body, his words making me glow like a damn lantern. A sensation that I've been feeling more often lately. Part of me tells me to be cautious, to not let it settle in my bones, but my heart tells me I don't stand a chance.

It's already too late.

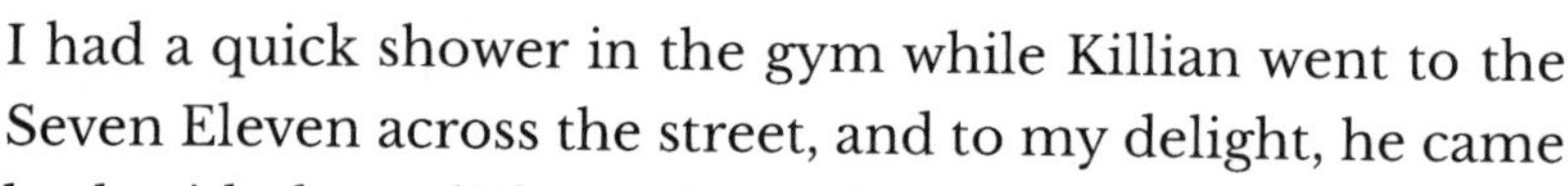

I had a quick shower in the gym while Killian went to the Seven Eleven across the street, and to my delight, he came back with three different bags of popcorn.

"I bought them all, because I didn't know what you liked," he muttered, barely audible to me. I thanked him with a bruising kiss, which frustrated him even more when I refused to let him drag me into an alley. Something I only did because I don't want to give in, not because I didn't want him to fuck me against the cold bricks hidden in a corner as people still walk down the street. The thought alone makes my skin crawl in delight, burning up my already aching core whenever he's close.

We walked home, with him telling me in ten different ways how I was a tease and me scolding him for it like we've known each other for years. It's a big contrast to the first time we met and the fear that came with it.

Today in the gym I had a moment of weakness, letting my fear slither in as I felt the oxygen decreasing by the second, but deep down I knew he wasn't going to hurt me. Deep down, I know he cares. Even if he hides it behind his stoic gaze and indifferent attitude. I know Killian Wolfe cares about me, because I can feel it every time he touches me.

When we get home, Killian disappears into the bathroom to grab a shower and I settle on the couch to find a movie while I order some pizza with my phone.

Five minutes later, I'm scrolling through all the Marvel movies when the front door swings open without any warning. My eyes grow wide, a little shocked when his youngest brother strolls in like he owns the place. He halts when he sees me, cocking his head with a boyish grin slipping onto his face.

"You did something different with your hair, Kill?" He smirks. "It needs some adjustments from my side, but I do like it."

I know he's the Wolfe you should fear the least, but still my heart jumps up at the sudden Wolfe standing two yards away from me without knowing his intentions. My mind flickers up and down with panic when it rapidly goes over his possible intentions.

What if he found out who I am?

What if he's here to take me to Sullivan?

I jump up, grabbing my gun from the coffee table before pointing it at his head.

"What are you doing here?"

"Whoa, take it easy, darling." His expression stays the same, clearly unimpressed about the gun pointed in his direction, but he brings his hands up in surrender.

This is the first time I've seen him up close, and he looks even more handsome than he does from afar. His honey brown hair is messy, almost matching his lammy coat that brings out his signature green eyes, but the smile on his sharp jaw really does make him look like fucking Prince Charming.

"I would appreciate it if you don't shoot my brother," Killian says with a straight face as he saunters into the room with navy sweatpants hugging his hips. His chest is still damp from his shower and I swallow my desire away as he walks up beside me. "I know he looks like a douchebag, but I still like him. *Sometimes.*"

A devilish grin haunts his lips as he softly pulls the gun from my hand, placing it back on the table, then gives me a reassuring smile with his hands on my hips.

"I don't look like a douchebag," Reign scoffs, then tilts his head to Killian. "Aah, you love me?"

"I said *like*. Not love." He glances over his shoulder before his green eyes roll to the back of his head, then nudges his head to me. "Reign, this is Lexie."

"Alexandra." I scowl as he lets go of me, brushing his body against mine when he makes his way to the kitchen. I fold my arms in front of my chest, a glare still aiming at his youngest brother.

"Nice to meet you, Lexie."

"Alexandra," I repeat with a growl.

"I like Lexie more." Reign shrugs as if that's the end of it, then flops his body onto the nearest corner of the couch.

"Yeah, me too," Killian chimes in from the kitchen.

Hesitantly, I flick my gaze between the two brothers, both looking unfazed by my defiant posture, and neither of them giving me a second glance. A grunt rolls over my tongue before I decide Reign is not a threat, and I let my body sink into the cushions.

"Thanks, by the way." Reign turns his head, his face dripping with kindness, making it really hard to keep my scowl aimed at him.

"What for?"

"Shooting my foster sister."

"Oh, right." A little jolt of appreciation enters my chest, and I feel the corner of my mouth lift with pride. "You're welcome. Is your girlfriend okay?"

"A little startled. She'll be fine."

Killian strolls back and plants himself between the two of us, holding up three open bottles of beer.

"Beer?"

"Ya-huh!" Reign eagerly takes the bottle of Budweiser from Killian's hands while I eye it with suspicion.

"You don't want one?" Killian frowns.

"You never give me beer."

"I'm giving you beer now," he deadpans.

Reluctantly, I pull the bottle from his grasp, then take a sip. The malty taste falls on my tongue and I try to keep a straight face as it runs down my throat while Killian keeps staring at my face.

"You never had a beer?"

"I've had beer," I scoff.

Killian chuckles, taking a drink of his own. "Just luke warm keg beer?"

"Yeah, basically," I confess, suppressing a laugh at his perceptive behavior. I can't hide anything from this man, no matter how unreadable I try to remain. Something that pisses me off something fierce, since he has the poker face of a statue.

He wraps his arm around my shoulder, tucking me against his body, and I welcome the warmth of him, settling into the crook of his arm. I like these moments. They are always alternating with his cold behavior, but every time I get relaxed Killian, I feel my worries diminish, even if it's just for a few minutes.

"So, what's the deal with you two?" Reign asks, zapping through the menu on the TV to pick a movie. He asks it casually, making me wonder how much he knows.

My eyes stay fixed on the TV at the direct question, wondering what Killian will respond with. What is the deal with us? We share a bed. We sleep together. We spend most of our days together. Share our meals together. If our relationship wasn't unconventional as fuck, I'd say we're dating. But I know Killian Wolfe doesn't date. He doesn't even have to voice it, I just know.

I hear Killian slowly breathe out, and I glance up, just in time to watch his jaw tick.

"Why are you here, Reign?" He cocks his head to his brother, silently telling him he's overstepping, but Reign just peers back at him with a grin splitting his face.

"Because Sienna is with her mom and I'm bored."

"How is that my problem?"

"It's not."

"It sure as fuck feels like it."

"Oh, please. You like me, remember?"

"I really don't."

Reign shrugs. "I'm sure Lexie likes my company. Don't you, Lexie?" He leans his head forward to look at me for support, but I take a swig of my beer, averting my gaze.

"I'm going to kick your ass," Killian growls.

"Fine, can we just watch the movie first?"

A snort escapes my mouth, chuckling at their brotherly banter. It's a nice change to see someone go against Killian without an ounce of fear, showing me he's actually human.

"You think that's funny?" Killian dips his chin close to my face and I give him a smile, guilt written in my eyes.

"It's a little funny."

"Why?" he questions, bemused.

"He's not scared of you."

"Are you?"

I think about his question, cocking my head as I look at him. His jaw is sharp, covered with a stubble that I love feeling against my skin. His brown hair is still damp, sitting messily on his head. He gives me somewhat of a glare, probably wanting me to say yes, just because it seems to turn him on, but I'm not scared of him. Not anymore, anyway.

"You can be scary," I explain, keeping my smile in place. "But I'm not scared of you."

Unexpectedly, approval travels through his gaze. "Good."

"You don't have to be scared of him, Lexie. He can growl like a wolf, he can bite like a wolf, but he's loyal like a love-struck puppy. You won't get rid of him even if you tried."

The bluntness of his words has me muffling laughter while Killian gives his brother a death glare.

"Get the fuck out."

"What?" Reign screeches. "No."

"Get. Out."

"Ssssh, the movie is starting." Reign waves his brother to silence and I cover my hand with my mouth to not burst out into laughter. It's hilarious to see how Reign mocks him, completely unfazed by the scowl sitting on his face that comes straight from Hell. It's the same scowl he wore like a permanent mask in the warehouse, and I remember how it gave me chills just looking at him, but Reign is not even slightly impressed.

Killian snaps his head to me and I blink, pressing my palm harder against my mouth.

"I'm sorry," I murmur from behind my hand.

I expect him to sneer something at me, but instead he presses his shoulder into my stomach, picking me up with one swift move as he gets to his feet.

"What are you doing?" I shriek when he carries me away from the couch as I hang over his shoulder, locking my wide eyes with Reign's amused ones.

"Bringing you to bed where I can punish you." Killian slaps my ass and I yelp, jerking my body up.

"Killian! I won!" I slam my fist into his rock-hard back as he saunters toward the bedroom. "You promised me a movie! I want to watch a movie!"

"Me too!" Reign bellows.

"I changed my mind, and I didn't invite you." He spins his body, glaring at his brother, I'm sure.

"You never invite me," Reign counters.

"Yet you still sit here all the time."

"I don't see your point."

"Bye, Reign," Killian rumbles before his body rears back to continue his steps and I'm facing Reign again.

"Bye, Lexie." Reign gives me a short wave with a smirk and I bring up my hand to do the same.

"Bye, Reign."

22

A little sleep drunk, I walk back into the parlor, my stomach roaring with hunger.

"You're still here?" Rubbing my hand over my face, I look at the sleepy face of my brother, lit up by the light of the TV.

"The movie just ended."

I glance at the clock hanging on the kitchen wall.

"It's two a.m."

"I know. Didn't say it was the first one."

I continue my strides to the refrigerator, and I hear Reign getting up from the couch to trail behind me. "Why aren't you at home with Sienna?"

He shrugs, running a hand through his honey brown hair. "Her cousin, Isabella, is staying over at her mom's house.

They were having a girls' night." There is fatigue in his eyes, but when I search for the pain that I've gotten so familiar with, I can't find any.

It's a relief, giving me a bit of hope that maybe he found some closure now that his past is no longer dominating his future.

"And you weren't invited?" I mock.

"Trust me, I was offended too." He cocks his head with his brows raised, then swings his eyes to mine. I wait in anticipation, giving him a dull look.

"What?"

He sighs deeply, and I do the same when I realize where this is going.

"Why didn't you tell me about Emma?"

I run my hand over my face, letting out a grunt, then shake my head.

"Fuck, Reign. I don't know."

"Did Franklin tell you?"

"No, she told me." No one understood how close Emma and I really were. When I moved back to Boston at sixteen, Emma was the first one who gave me that familiar feeling that I'd been missing in my time in foster care. She was the friend that never changed, the one that would still give me her friendly gaze with the same indigo blue yes. She matured in every single way, but her eyes were still there. Still capable of giving me a warm and fuzzy feeling inside. Everyone thought she was Reign's best friend, but she quickly became mine when Reign was still living in Providence.

"How long had you known?"

"Not long before she died. She swore me to secrecy." I swallow, still getting chills when I recall that conversation.

At the time, our friendship had evolved and even though we never told anyone, I'd seen her as mine to protect and to hold. Learning how she was raped at age twelve ignited a ball of rage that made me want to kill someone.

"Why?" The look in Reign's eyes is a little confused, but I'm glad it lacks the torment he's been showing for years.

"Because she cared about you. We all saw the way those years in Providence changed you. The trouble in your eyes. She didn't want you to worry about her."

"You should've told me."

"It wasn't my secret to tell." I pause, holding his gaze. "You know that."

He presses his lips together. I know he doesn't like this answer, but I also know he respects it. Reign and I share almost everything, but we'd never share a secret that's not ours. We might be ruthless and lack empathy at times, but we wouldn't betray someone's trust like that. Emma was no exception. She didn't want anyone to know. I honored her wish.

"You told me you slept with Emma once," he says with a tentative look.

"I lied."

He nods. "I figured. Tell me."

"There isn't much to tell, Reign." I wag my head, raking my hand through my hair.

Reign tuts with a little aggravation. "Don't, Kill. I know you. Better than anyone. I'm not mad at you, just sad she didn't tell me. It could've saved everyone a lot of heartache, but I get it. I hate it, but I also get it. But she was still my best friend. Tell me the truth."

I want to throw a snarky comment at him and be done with it, but I know he's right.

"I don't even know what happened. Or how it happened. It started right before Franklin pulled you out of that hellhole. We were spending a lot of time with her and all of a sudden, I found myself kissing her. One thing led to another. You know how it goes."

"She told you about the rape?"

I sigh, then nod. "A few months before she killed herself. I tried to help her. To be there for her. I even went to therapy with her to support her. Anything to show her she wasn't alone. But it didn't matter."

"Did you love her?" Though his question shoots an arrow through my heart, my reply is firm and honest.

"No." I shake my head, lying at first out of habit before I blurt out the truth. "Yeah, I guess I did."

I tried to hold it off, but at some point, I couldn't deny the weird feeling in my stomach when she'd end up in my line of sight or how I always wanted to kiss her. She wasn't just a meaningless fuck. She was the one I wanted near me all the time, and the one I wanted to protect like she was one of us. And I would've if she didn't end her life when she did.

I shoot my brother an apologetic look right before he counters it with one of his own.

"I'm sorry," I tell him.

"I know. It's okay. Just no more, okay? No more secrets between you and me." Our green eyes stay locked and without needing any more than that, the understanding quickly comes full circle.

"Cool," I concede.

"You're still an asshole."

Chuckling at his response, I dive into the fridge to grab the box of Dunks before putting it on the kitchen island. I pull one out with chocolate frosting, then shove the box to Reign, sitting down on the breakfast bar. The chocolate wakes me up from my half slumber state I was still in, my roaring stomach settling down a little bit.

He takes one out, sinking his teeth into the dough while his eyes stay fixed on me. With a stoic look, I shoot my annoyance at him because I know what's about to come next.

My little brother is really good at knowing when to talk and when to shut up, but when it comes to the two of us, we just blurt out whatever the fuck we want. His question earlier tonight was just the tip of the veil, and he will keep nagging me if I refuse to tell him what the deal is.

"What?" I finally blurt, rolling my eyes, then take another bite of my donut.

"I like her."

I sigh, knowing he's talking about Lexie. My brother is a sucker for pretty orphaned girls, so I'm not surprised she has no trouble getting on his good side without even trying.

"I like her too," I confess.

I like how she goes head-to-head with me every chance she gets, even though I can see the insecurity still dripping from her eyes. I intimidate her, but she refuses to show me, and I've become addicted to her snarky replies and sweet smile. She wormed herself into my life, and I don't even remember what it was like when she wasn't around.

"What's her story?"

"I told you, she wants vengeance," I tell him with my mouth full.

"Did you find out why?"

"Only what's stated in the police report." For most people, that would be true, but if you are born and raised in the dark side of the city like we are, you take a police report as serious as kindergarten when you're four. It might look serious, but it's really not that big of a deal.

He tilts his head, swallowing the bite in his mouth. "Want me to do some digging?"

"Please." The only reason I haven't asked him to hack into whatever system he can get access to until now is because I knew his head was clouded with Sienna and that stalker bullshit. Now that it's all over, I need him to turn over every rock so he can tell me exactly why the Lee family needed to die.

"Might be dirty." He raises his eyebrows with a knowing look.

I know he's right. You don't murder an entire family for not paying a parking ticket. If the Chief of Police wants you dead, there is a lot more going on than you'll be able to find in the public records. He will have had a good reason to bury Lexie's family, and I'm sure it's wicked ugly.

"I expect it to be." I plop the last piece of my donut into my mouth, then brush my hands together to get rid of the excess dough.

"Go home," I tell him while putting the box back in the fridge.

"Fine." The sound of his stool shifting on the floor sounds loudly through the room, before he grabs his lammy coat from the couch, putting it on as I walk past him toward the bedroom.

"Goodnight, tool."

"Night, asshole," he replies, walking out of the door.

When the front door closes with a loud thud, I shut the bedroom behind me, crawling back into my bed to wrap the little brunette in my arms like I've been doing it for years.

I sniff her hair, sucking up her rose scent while she lets out a sleepy moan.

She looks angelic, her pure soul shining bright, when she's unable to keep her walls up while sound asleep. I wish I knew her before she changed, wondering how much more captivating she must have been when she was still innocent and sparkling. I still see the girl she used to be before someone ripped her life away from her soft hands. It's small, but it's still there, and I press a kiss to her neck, knowing I will do anything to protect that tiny spark with my life.

"Kill! Is that you?" I hear Reign call out from the office as I close the door of the mansion behind me, looking up to see Sienna is decorating the door on top of a ladder.

"Hey, Kill," she sings, then fixes her gaze back at the door.

"Hey, Sienna."

"He's in the office."

Already expecting that answer, I make my way through the foyer to find my brother.

"What's doing, tool?"

He's sitting behind Franklin's desk, frantically tapping on his laptop. His green eyes swing to mine when I walk through the door before they drop back to the screen.

"I found some stuff."

I cock my head at him.

"You look like you've sneaked into the principal's office to change your grade." When Franklin sits in here, he's suited up most of the time, looking like he belongs behind the big wooden desk, surrounded by the thousands of books that cover the walls. Watching Reign in here with his Winter Soldier t-shirt, lammy coat, and messy hair makes him look completely out of place. Add his everlasting boyish grin and he looks like the college boy from Hell, ready to kick the party alive.

"What do you mean?" He drops his gaze to his chest, plucking his coat. "Are you mocking my lammy?"

"No, I'm mocking everything. You look like a hooligan. Is Sienna letting you wear that to Thanksgiving?"

"Sienna doesn't get to tell me what to wear." He fixes his eyes on me before they fall back to the screen. "And no."

I chuckle. "You are so whipped."

"Whatever. Do you want to hear what I found or not?"

"Sure. How bad is it?"

"It's bad. I just don't know how bad just yet."

My stomach turns, not liking that answer one bit, and I lean forward, resting my elbows on my knees as I crack my knuckles.

"Apparently, her father, Jameson Lee, was a journalist at the Boston Daily News. He lived in Boston his entire life and graduated from Northeastern, where he met his wife, Anna. They had two daughters, Sofia and Alexandra."

"Yeah, I know all this shit, Reign," I huff, annoyed. "Stick to the important shit. Why did Sullivan want them dead?"

"Okay, *grumpy*." He pulls a face, and I pull one of my own when he stays quiet.

"Well?"

He rubs a hand over his face, filling his lungs with air.

"I don't know."

"What do you mean, you don't know?" Reign always knows. It's what he's good at. He finds the answer we can't find by hacking into shit. I don't like him telling me *I don't know*.

"I mean, there is nothing out of the ordinary. Dad was a journalist. Mom was a dance teacher. They bought a four-bedroom apartment after they got married. They paid their bills on time. Their kids did well in school."

"There must be something."

"Yeah, I agree," Reign says with a pained expression. "And there always is, but I clearly need to dig deeper than going through the obvious channels. Did Lexie mention anything about her sister?"

"What do you mean?"

"I don't know," he growls. "Maybe she got in trouble at Northeastern? Maybe she was dating Sullivan's son and pissed him off. I don't know, Killian. Just anything."

"You think Sullivan would order a family to be murdered because his son's heart was broken?" I deadpan, mocking his ridiculous assumption.

He tsks. "Wars have started for less."

I roll my eyes, not even going to entertain his bullshit, as I get up to pour myself a glass of whiskey in the corner of the room.

"Fine, look into it," I tell him, splashing the gold liquid into two glasses, then offer Reign one while planting my ass on the corner of the desk.

"What about the mother?"

His brows lift in response, twisting the chair to face me. "What about her?"

"What did her mother do again?"

"She was a talented ballerina before becoming a ballet teacher."

"A ballerina?" I scrunch up my nose, not expecting that answer.

"Yeah, you know. Petite girls. Pink tutu. Walking on their toes the entire time."

"I know what a ballerina is, you tool," I snap.

A laugh rumbles from the base of his chest, enjoying my response a little too much.

"Unless her mother was having an affair with Sullivan, I doubt a prima ballerina managed to piss off the Chief of Police."

"I wouldn't rule it out. Aren't most murders crimes of passion?"

"Yeah, but that would mean Sullivan would've done the killing. In this case, he sent out a team to clean up the mess. Did you ask Lexie about it?"

He has a point. If Sullivan was ready to strangle his secret lover because his affection wasn't returned in a way he wanted, he probably would've been the one pulling the trigger. Witnesses state that multiple men entered the building at the time of the crime, which suggests an execution instead of a crime of passion.

"Not yet." I've been holding it off, because I don't want her to have to relive that night again, but in order for us to turn every rock and prepare myself for whatever I'm getting myself into, I don't see any other option.

"You need to ask her. She might be able to tell some more. How did she escape anyway?"

I shake my head. "I don't know."

Reign's brows arch up, shooting me an incredulous look. "No-suh."

"What? I haven't asked."

"Why the fuck not?"

I take a sip of my drink, not wanting to answer that because it shows my cards, and I don't like to show anyone anything. But I don't have to because my brother knows me well enough to make his own conclusion.

"Because you've been too busy fucking her?"

"For fuck's sake, Reign."

"What? It's true, right?"

I run a hand through my hair, not sure what to tell him simply because he's right. Lexie can be a fucking pain, but I like having her around. I'm never one to divert from the hard questions, but for some reason, I've been too occupied by finding ways to get on her nerves than getting the answers I need.

"Shut the fuck up."

"Fine," he concedes. "My bet is on the dad. I'm trying to find out what he was working on, but so far all I found was that he was a sports journalist."

"That doesn't sound exciting."

"No, but he took criminal justice classes next to his major at college. Maybe he really wanted to be a true crime journalist or something." He takes a sip of his drink. "But whatever it is, it's buried deep."

"Alright, keep digging," I say before I pour the contents of my glass down my throat, then slap him on the back as I get up. "You think Lily's got some cookies in the kitchen?"

He snorts. "It's Thanksgiving. She's got it all, brother."

"Right." I chuckle, then find my way to the kitchen.

When I open the swinging door, Franklin and Connor are sitting on the breakfast bar while Lily and Kendall are preparing dinner on the other side of the kitchen island. My little nephew flies against my legs and I look down to rub his fluffy blonde hair before pulling him up into my arms.

"Uncle Killian!"

"Hey, little man." He gives me a tight hug, and I enjoy his tiny body in my arms while I wave at the girls, who're both shooting me wide grins.

"We decided you're doing the dishes." Connor raises his chin with a grin, then takes a swig of his beer while Franklin chuckles beside him.

"I'm sorry, what?" I bring my hand to my ear, looking at Colin's rosy cheeks. "Do you hear that, Colin?"

"What?" He giggles.

"It's your father. He's talking *shit*."

Colin cries out in laughter when he hears the word shit, folding his small hands over my lips and Connor's grin falls to the floor.

"Killian!" Lily's reprimanding eyes find mine, and I offer her a sweet smile to get back in her good graces. Luckily, she lets me off the hook and continues to stir the pot in front of her.

"Don't cuss in front of him, Killian." The scowl on Connor's face is hilarious, since I know he's only putting up an act for Lily right now.

"Yeah, whatever."

I flip him off behind Colin's back, pursing my lips in a look that tells him to watch himself before I throw him in front of the bus by selling him out to his girlfriend. When I see the glint of amusement flaring from his eyes, I can't hold back the smile.

"Tell me, Colin. Did your mom make any cookies?"

The boy replies by frantically nodding his head, then he points his finger to a plate on the kitchen counter. My eyes widen, my mouth agape as I stroll us both in that direction.

I take two cookies shaped like pumpkins, the orange frosting making them look even more appealing, then bring my hand up to put one in Colin's mouth.

"No, Killian!" I freeze at Lily's voice. "He's already had two! It's dinnertime."

I pull a face to Colin, shrugging my shoulders. "Sorry, buddy."

Putting a cookie in my mouth, I hold the other between my fingers while Colin curls his lip in a pout. Chewing, I glance at Lily, who's turned her attention away from us.

"Open up," I whisper.

Like any kid would, he does as he's told, and I shove the cookie in his mouth right before Lily's glare makes me wince.

"Killian," she growls.

"Come on, Lil. It's Thanksgiving." I grin.

"All you Wolfes are corrupting my child." Giving up, she shrugs while shaking her head. "Colin, can you please go get Uncle Reign and Aunty Sienna? Dinner is ready."

He beams in agreement, and I put him down before he darts out of the kitchen.

"You okay, Kill?" Franklin's green eyes bore into mine and I step closer, resting my elbows on the counter, my gaze fixed on my brother.

"Yeah, I'm good."

"Reign told me he's digging into your girl's background."

I ignore the mention of *my* girl. "Yeah. So far, no luck. But I'm sure he'll find something." I pause. "You cool with this, though?"

"I am." Knowing my brother, I know there is a but lingering on his tongue, so I cock my head, waiting for him to continue. "But I want the full reason before you can give her what she wants."

"I understand." As much as I want to help Lexie, we can't go around killing cops, then clean up the mess if we don't have a damn good reason for it. Nothing in this world is for free and when the Chief of Police drops dead, a lot of people will be coming to collect something to keep their mouth shut.

"How is she doing in the gym?"

My grin splits my cheeks at his question, thinking back on our training sessions. She's getting better and better every day, making me work hard for my win, when the first few weeks were a breeze. She's been paying attention and her strength has been growing with every session, something that eases my mind when I need to leave her for work. I still don't like leaving her out of my sight, but at least now I know she can somewhat handle herself.

"Really, really good. She is becoming a real asset."

Connor nods his head in approval. "Maybe she wants to join the team when you give her what she came for?"

The thought of her staying flushes my neck, a feeling of glee running through my stomach. I haven't thought about what she would do when this is over, but I'm definitely not against her joining our team. I still remember how she told me she plans to leave the city, but deep down I can't deny I hope she won't. The city won't feel the same without her in it.

"Yeah, maybe."

Our conversation is interrupted when Sienna runs into the kitchen with Colin on her arm, squealing in excitement.

"Help! Help!" Sienna shrieks, almost drowned out by Colin's infectious laugh as she hides behind Franklin. "Pirate! Pirate!"

I glance over my shoulder when Reign comes through the door with big strides and a fake scowl on his face. The look screams mischief, making me chuckle at the sight of it.

"Help us, Uncle Frank! Help us!" Sienna whispers loudly from behind Franklin.

With a playful smile that matches Reign's, Franklin turns around, taking Colin out of her arms. "Come here, I'll help you. Come, little Wolfe."

A smug grin forms on Sienna's face before Franklin hands over Colin to Connor and it changes to confusion instead. Her eyes snap back and forth between Reign and Franklin, and when she realizes Franklin is not on her team, it's too late because Franklin pushes her straight into Reign's chest.

"Run, Aunty Sienna! Run!" Colin shouts when Reign dives into her neck, wrapping his arms around her, and the laughter of the rest of us bounces around the kitchen.

"Too late for that, buddy." Reign grins.

"Traitor." Sienna sticks out her tongue to Franklin, and he just laughs while I give my attention to Lily putting a plate of meatballs close enough for me to reach one.

"Wow, Lily! This is amazing!" Sienna bellows behind me while I grab a meatball and sneakily toss it into my mouth. I let out a quiet moan when I chew and the juices coat my tongue in a flavorful explosion, making me reach out for another one.

This time Lily catches me like the real mom that she is.

"Take your paws off, *Wolfe*." She slaps my hand, and I retract it out of the way, scorned, though a smile haunts my lips at the same time the doorbell rings.

"Who's that?" Sienna asks.

"For me."

I straighten my body with a blank expression, ignoring their curious looks.

23

Lexie

Ringing the doorbell, I nervously toss my brown hair over my shoulder, taking a deep breath to gather my confidence.

"Come to the mansion around five," he said, then threw the keys of his Range Rover at me before he walked out with a wink.

I haven't failed to forget what day it is today, although I wished I had, but I assumed I'd be spending it alone on his couch while he was off with his family. So when he left me standing there, blinking at the door, I had a major freakout about a ton of shit. What should I wear? Not that I have anything to wear other than my jeans. What if it's not dinner? What if he just needs me to do another job for him? What if it *is* dinner? What does that mean? Thirty minutes later and a dry throat from all the heaving I was doing, I decided to just wing it. Which means I'm now standing in front of this huge house, wearing my usual black jeans and black bomber, wondering if I'm underdressed.

Of course, you're underdressed, Alexandra.

When the door swings open, my heart jumps in excitement when I look into Killian's devilish smirk before my cheeks lower.

"I didn't know what to wear," I blurt, scowling. "You didn't tell me what we were going to do?"

He pulls me over the threshold and into his chest. "It's Thanksgiving. What do you think we're going to do?"

"I don't know. That was hardly an invitation, Killian."

"I told you to come by the mansion at five."

"Exactly! You didn't give me any heads-up!"

His hand falls on my neck, the heat of his palm burning my scowl away. It's been happening more every day, his touch pushing my dark thoughts or foul mood to the back of my head. His touch magically seems to make my day better, and it scares the shit out of me as much as I live for it.

"Do you want to spend Thanksgiving with my family? Or do you want to spend it on my couch? Alone." There is a taunting tone in his voice and he cocks his head a little while his palms land on the small of my back.

"No." Spending today alone sounds as daunting as spending it with his family, but at least they can be a distraction.

"No, what?"

"Stop being a dick, please." I fix my blues on his greens, narrowing my eyes before dropping them to my chest. "Is this okay?" I ask, glancing at my outfit.

My mother would've had a fit if she was still alive, wanting us to dress up for every holiday there is, but I failed to pack any dresses when I left, and to be honest, I don't feel comfortable in them anymore. That girly girl left the moment my family took their last breaths.

"You look great, baby." His lips touch mine briefly, then he grabs my hand, tugging me behind him. Reluctantly, I let him lead me away on the white marble floor while I take in the grand foyer of the house. On the left is a big staircase with a gold railing, and when I look up to the balcony, I notice the huge chandelier hanging on the ceiling.

I'm still gaping when he walks us both into the kitchen and six heads turn my way, making me push out an awkward smile.

"Everyone, this is Lexie."

My smile makes room for a glare pointed at Killian.

"It's Alexandra." My words don't get any more reply than a shrug and I just give up, glancing around the room.

"Hello." The pregnant pause that follows feeds my discomfort, and I fold my arm around my body, holding on to the other while I wait in anticipation.

Finally, Reign's girlfriend brings her body a little closer to mine, reaching out her hand.

"Hi, I'm Sienna." Her black hair falls over her shoulders, and now that I see her up close, I notice how soft it looks. She gives me a friendly smile while I take her hand. "You're the girl that saved us. Thank you."

I shoot her a coy smile, not sure how to reply until the rest of them move closer to introduce themselves. They all offer me kind smiles, and by the time I meet Colin, Connor and Lily's son, I feel a bit more at ease. Still, I'm grateful when

Killian slugs his arm around my neck, tucking me into this side.

"Now that everyone is here, I have a few things to say," Franklin addresses the room, raising his whiskey glass. "This year has been a lot. But in the end, we grew our pack, and I couldn't think of a better way. You *all* have my unconditional loyalty, because from now on, you are family." I don't miss how his eyes briefly link with mine, a warm feeling expanding my chest like a hot-air balloon before I push it away. "But there is one person who deserves most of what I have to give."

"Ah, man!" Reign whines, a grin splitting his cheeks. "You didn't have to put me in the spotlight like that!"

Franklin rolls his eyes, the rest of us falling in laughter. "Shut up, *tool*."

He puts his glass down, then goes down on one knee while he grabs Kendall's hand, who's still sitting on one of the stools. My limbs feel heavy at the sight of her entire body freezing, a gasp escaping her lips, before throwing her other hand in front of her mouth while Franklin pulls out a small jewelry box. My sister and I used to daydream about our weddings, waiting for that longing proposal like most girls do. A touch of a smile traces my mouth while at the same time a dreadful feeling fills me at the thought of my sister never getting her happy ending.

Or me.

Getting married and living a happy and blissful life seems out of reach now that life as I know it has been completely destroyed. There is a part of me that still wishes for it, but it's fully buried under the darkness that surrounds my heart.

"Kenny, I spent at least an hour today finding the words to tell you how much I love you, but I finally threw them all in the trash, realizing I'm not Reign."

The room fills with chuckles.

"I don't have many words. All I know is that I love you, I refuse to spend a day without you, and I want to wake up next to you for the rest of my life." He pauses. "Will you marry me? Become a *Wolfe*?" The little girl inside of me is squealing in delight for her while we all wait for her to say something. Her pretty blue eyes well up, and, unable to utter another word, she folds her hands in front of her mouth.

"See, man. This is what you get when you propose in the fucking kitchen! Who does that?" Reign jokes.

Franklin snaps his head to Reign. "As soon as I got this ring on her finger, you better fucking run."

"I don't know, man," Killian pitches in beside me. "He kinda has a point." A taunting smirk sits on his sharp jaw when I look up, a flutter rushing through me when he quickly locks his eyes with mine.

Franklin points his finger back and forth between his youngest brothers with a glare. "Dead. Both of you." When he puts his focus back on Kendall, he tugs her hand.

"I kinda need you to say yes, pretty girl," he tells her with an encouraging smile.

She nods, followed by a yes, and we all start clapping in relief. My chest lifts before I push out a deep breath, keeping my gaze fixed on Kendall as Franklin slides the ring over her finger. He then presses an affectionate kiss on her lips before he whispers something in her hair with a mischievous smile pulling at the corners of his lips.

When they break loose, the smile moves from his face, a blank expression back in place that would scare those who don't know him. He locks eyes with Reign before doing the same with Killian.

"Oh, shit," Reign and Killian blurt at the same time. Before I know what's happening, he disappears from my side as he bolts out of the kitchen with Reign on his heels and Franklin chasing behind them. Laughter makes my shoulders shake as I watch Colin running after them.

"I help, Uncle Franky!" he yells with his cuteness before he disappears through the swinging door. When I rear my head back, Connor is rolling his eyes, sauntering behind his son. Lily and Sienna both let out a squeal, then dart to Kendall to look at the ring and I suddenly feel totally out of my comfort zone. I keep my gaze on them, awkwardly, not sure what to do but also not wanting to interrupt their moment.

For what feels like forever, I just stand there, my eyes scanning the kitchen with unease.

"Oh, my God! I'm so sorry! Come! Come!" Lily waves her hand, asking me to approach, and I do so with hesitation. "We're so rude. I'm sorry, Alexandra. Do you want something to drink?" Lily walks past me to the fridge while Sienna takes the stool next to Kendall, then gestures for me to take the one beside her.

"Sorry, Lexie." Sienna gasps, bringing her hand to her mouth with wide eyes. "I'm sorry. *Alexandra*."

"It's okay. I'm not sure why I'm still trying," I say with a smile while sliding next to her.

"Do you want wine? A beer? Coke?" I bring my attention to Lily's blonde hair, her nose in the fridge.

"I'm not twenty-one yet."

"Pff, we won't tell if you won't tell."

"Beer, please." She spins around, holding up a beer, sliding it my way before she leans her elbows on the countertop, facing the three of us.

"Congratulations." I twist my head to Kendall.

"Thank you! I did not see this coming! Did you know?" With suspicion, she flicks her gaze between Sienna and Lily.

"No!" they both shriek.

Kendall gives them both a look that isn't sure about their denial before she focuses on me. "So, can we call you Lexie?"

"Sure." I smile.

"Well, Lexie, are you from Boston?"

"Born and raised."

"Do you still live with your parents?" Kendall's question sounds genuinely interested, but instantly a lump forms in the back of my throat, too big to swallow away.

My gaze drops to the counter. "I'm alone. My parents died a few months ago."

"Parents?" Sienna parrots. "Both of them?"

I nod. "And my sister."

"Oh, my God." Sienna's eyes look like they are about to pop out of her head as horror crosses her face. "I'm so sorry. What happened?"

I bite my lip, not sure how to answer that. I know they must be used to something since they are members of the Wolfe family, but I have no clue how much Killian wants to share with them, considering he seems to be a pretty private person.

Sienna replies to my lack of words by placing her hand on my arm, giving me a reassuring gaze. "I'm guessing you're not allowed to share?"

"I don't know," I reply honestly.

"It's okay. Either way, you earned Killian's loyalty if he brought you to a job that's as important as getting his brother and sister-in-law out of the hands of a psychopath."

I snort, cocking my head. "I'm not sure if I earned his loyalty." I earned a movie night that I never got because he was too occupied working me into a fucking frenzy. I get his attention, his affection even if he's in a good mood, but I'm confident Killian's loyalty is solely reserved for his brothers. Whatever arrangement we have, I'm sure it will be over as soon as Sullivan gets a one-way ticket to Hell.

"So, hold up." Lily grabs my attention. "You're the one who shot psycho Aubrey?"

Her angelic face is written with awe, and I can't help sitting a little straighter.

"Yeah."

"No-suh! Where did you learn to shoot like that?"

I grab my beer, realizing it still has the cap on, so instead, I let the cold glass cool down my warm hands. "Killian taught me."

"Killian taught you how to shoot?" Sienna asks, a brow arched.

"Yeah."

All three of them exchange a look that's filled with surprise.

"Why is that so weird?" I ask, sheepishly.

"Killian isn't usually the one who takes interest in anything unless it revolves around the family and the family business," Sienna explains with a glint in her eyes that looks like triumph. "The fact that he has in you means you're something special."

"I'm hardly something special."

She nudges her shoulder against mine. "I have known Killian since I was twelve. The only time he took an interest in anything else was when he was–"

"You three! Stop talking about me."

Sienna is interrupted when Killian walks through the door, followed by Connor.

"We weren't talking about you!" Sienna cries out, a guilty look on her face.

He glares, amused, at the three of them before he comes to stand behind me, covering my ears with his hands.

"You're a shit liar, Sienna. Always have been. Don't feed her lies."

"We're not feeding her lies."

He moves his mouth flush with my ear. "Were they telling you how secretly I'm a good guy?"

"Something like that." I chuckle with a smile while the girls gasp around me.

"Did you believe them?"

I spin on my stool to face him. "Not a word."

His tongue darts out, licking his lips as he dips his chin to hold my gaze. "Good girl."

Pulling the bottle of beer out of my hand, he presses a kiss on my lips. It's deep, pressing, and even though there is nothing sexual about it, it packs a punch more than any other kiss he's given me. The fact that he's showing me this level of affection in front of his family has me questioning what the hell is going on between us. I'm doing my best to keep my desire and my heart separated, knowing one day whatever we have will be over. But when he does small things like this, it makes me doubt everything.

When he breaks loose, I quickly glance at Sienna, who's giving me a shocked look, then try to hide my own confusion by swinging my eyes to Connor as Killian hands him my beer.

Connor takes the bottle, bringing the cap to his teeth, before it comes loose and he spits it through the kitchen.

"Connor!" Lily scolds. "Pick that up!"

I laugh at the barbaric action while Connor rolls his eyes. He looks like the hulk, with his bulky arms and strong physique, sure giving you the vibe you shouldn't mess with him, but he still does what she says while we all watch him in amusement.

"You are so whipped, brother," Killian taunts.

Connor snaps his head to his brother, licking his lips with a daring spark flashing in his green eyes. "Don't even start, Kill."

Killian tenses beside me and I glance up at him. His lips are pursed, his jaw ticking, his nostrils slightly flaring as he holds his brother's gaze. The air in the room thickens to something awkward, and I'm wondering what I'm missing.

I let my hands graze over the soft skin underneath Killian's t-shirt, snapping him out of his stare off, and his features soften when he fixes his attention back on me.

"Where are the boys?" Lily asks.

"Out in the yard," Killian replies, never taking his eyes off me. My eyes catch gold specks dancing around his irises, alongside something that reminds me of the way my father looked at my mother, but I'm too chicken to name it. Even in my head.

"Connor, can you get them? It's time for dinner."

I'm slouched down into my chair, my eyes roaming around the table while I rest my hands on my stuffed stomach. Dinner was amazing. There was cornbread, sweet potatoes, mashed potatoes, cranberry sauce, and the turkey? Oh, my God. It was to die for. My mother made a good turkey for Thanksgiving, but Lily? Her cooking is something else. It took me about three bites to realize I hadn't had a freshly cooked meal in months, before I indulged like I was starving. Now my stomach is stuffed and my heart is full from spending the entire night with Killian's family. I've learned to fear these men, have been told they are the worst of the worst when it comes to the people in Boston. But so far, Franklin's shown me a level of intelligence and fairness that reminds me of my father, Reign shows love like my sister did, and Connor seems to be the big brother I never had. Funny enough, the one that scares me the most is Killian. In more ways than one.

"Remember that time Connor had to pick you up from the theater, because you two got caught in the janitor's closet?" Franklin says when Reign tries to argue that he's the sweetest of the four of them. Gasps are erupting from the girls' mouths and I feel my jaw drop.

"Franklin, really?" Reign scolds his brother.

Killian and Connor burst out in laughter.

Franklin lifts his drink to his mouth. "It's true, though! In fact, I think Connor and I got you out of more than one sticky situation."

"Bullshit!"

"Oh, yeah, what about that time you hacked into the security systems of the high school so you could have a sleepover at the gym? Buying off all those cops cost me some serious money!"

"Oh, please," Reign puffs, "it's nothing compared to the shit he pulled!"

"What?" Killian barks next to me, indignant. "No-suh!"

"Dude, you challenged the head of the Italian mob into a poker game!"

"So?"

"So? You were seventeen and you stripped him for thirty grand! He was ready to rip your head off. Whatever I did was child's play compared to you."

"Fuck, that was a mess to get out of." Franklin shakes his head.

"I'd won the game!" Killian argues.

"Yeah, but forty-year-old men don't like to lose to seventeen-year-olds. You were lucky I found you when I did, or your ass would be hanging out at the cemetery right now." Franklin holds his glass up in the air, his finger pointed at Killian with a tilted head.

A low chuckle sounds from Killian's chest. "Well, he shouldn't have taken that bet. I'd been going to underground poker games with Emma for months. When his right hand mocked me, I told him to play instead of talk."

"You went to those games with Emma?" Sienna arches a brow, fixing her gaze on Killian, who nods in confirmation.

"She was really good at poker. She had a poker face that couldn't be stopped by the Devil. We both knew who he was. We just knew we could beat him."

"How Bonnie and Clyde of you," Reign adds.

"The fucker underestimated me, and I showed them."

"You showed him you were a seventeen-year-old with a big brother in his league," Reign mocks. "I bet you did it to impress Emma, didn't you? Throw a little money in the air, acting like the big guy." Reign's taunts make laughter reverberate through the entire dining room and I feel how my cheeks lift with it.

"Who's Emma?"

They all fall silent, tight glances going back and forth, suddenly erasing the comfort with an awkwardness that makes me curious as hell. I turn my head to Killian.

His green eyes are fixed on Reign across the table, and when he feels my gaze pointed at him, he clears his throat before he meets my eyes.

"A friend. She died." With that, he brushes away any more room for more questions by bringing his glass to his lips.

"What about you, Lexie?" Reign questions in a clear attempt to change the subject. "What do you do for fun?"

I let a deep sigh escape my lungs, trying to get rid of the heaviness of the question now that I don't do anything *fun*. It was all I ever lived for when I was still in high school. Parties. Pep rallies. Going out with friends. *Ballet*. It all revolved around having fun. When you're a teenager, if you weren't in school, you do things for fun.

"I used to dance."

Eyebrows are raised around the table.

"You did?" Killian's hand moves to the back of my neck, giving me an encouraging squeeze.

"Hmm," I muse, nodding. "My mother was a ballet teacher." Reign locks eyes with Killian as if they are having a silent conversation and I tear my head to Kill.

"Ballet, huh?" Killian shoots me a small smile and I resist the urge to frown at him.

"Yeah. The first time I saw her dance, like *really* saw her dance, I was four." I swing my attention back to the table when I feel the corners of my eyes watering. "She got lost in the music, dancing through the room, and I remember how I wanted to be her. I've been dancing ever since. My dream was to go to the University of Indiana. They have one of the best ballet programs." I swallow my tears away, refusing to break down with a full table.

"Do you still dance?" Sienna asks.

"Sometimes. When my head is too cluttered."

They all give me sympathetic glances, clearly taking pity on me, and I break the tension by getting to my feet. "Can I help clean up?"

"No, no! Sit down. We'll do it!" Lily quickly mimics my move, starting to pile the empty plates while Kendall and Sienna do the same, followed by Connor.

I want to protest, but when I feel Killian tugging on my hand, I turn.

"Come on, let's go outside."

Giving everyone a small smile in apology, Killian leads me outside while I follow in silence. It's dark out. I tilt my head to look at the stars, enjoying the noises of the leftover crickets that sound through the silence of the night. He brings me to a corner of the yard, and when my eyes are adjusted to the night, I notice a firepit in the middle with benches around it.

"I bet you had a lot of fun nights with friends here?" I ask while he takes a seat before pulling me onto his lap. His arms lock around me, and I enjoy the feeling of his body close to mine as I let my eyes travel to the firepit that's yet to be lit.

"You don't even know. But mostly, this is where Reign and I hung out before we had places in the city. We used to sit here for hours, just enjoying the peace."

I rear my head back, feeling the need to see the features on his face. He changes when he talks about Reign. He loves all his brothers equally. But Reign is more than his brother. They are best friends and it's clear when you see how they interact. Killian is stiff, unapproachable, intimidating. But when he's with Reign, he loosens up, like he knows Reign will always have his back and he doesn't have to be on edge the entire time.

"He really is your best friend, isn't he?"

"He is," he confirms.

"That's nice. I used to be like that with my sister. We fought. But at the end of the day, she was my best friend." The emotions of the night suddenly come rushing in now that it's just the two of us and I'm no longer capable of holding them in. When I shut my eyes, tears stain my cheeks, and I'm not capable of covering my frown.

"Sssh, baby. Don't cry." He starts to wipe them off with his thumb as they fall.

"You're lucky, Kill," I tell him, my voice breaking with every syllable. "At least you still have your family." He pulls me to his chest, his hand holding me tightly against him at the back of my head. I let my emotions take over, wallowing in his touch like he's my lifeline. "At least you're not alone." For months I've been comforting myself, letting myself break before I pull myself together, but right now, I just want to break against him. Hoping that he will hold me long enough for me to not feel alone for a few minutes, desperate to remember what that feels like.

"Ah, baby." His voice sounds pained. "You're not alone. I promise you that."

I appreciate his words, feeling my heart beat faster. I should just let them comfort me, knowing and preparing myself for the realization that he can't make me that promise. That he will never keep it. But my heart seems to fly away on a cloud that's driven by the faith that maybe, just maybe, he actually means every word.

24

KILLIAN

Lexie is tucked under my arm, her eyes fixed on the TV. Her body is curled up next to mine, my cheek resting on her head.

I don't know what I was expecting yesterday, but I didn't expect it to feel as familiar as it did. I knew I couldn't keep her in the apartment for Thanksgiving and I also couldn't tell my brothers I wasn't joining them for dinner. Not to mention Lily would probably serve my head if I didn't show. So, when I told Lexie to take my Range Rover and come to the mansion, I expected a whole lot of awkwardness between us all. But it was a wicked surprise when the awkwardness never came. She fitted in with my family like a missing piece, and I couldn't hide my contentment every time I glanced at her.

I thought it would be hard for her, considering it was her first Thanksgiving since her family died, but the vacant look in her eyes shows me she's having a harder time missing her family today. She didn't tell me what today was, so I decided to let it pass, assuming she didn't want to be reminded of it. All of this morning, I've been desperate for the smile that was plastered on her face last night.

Grabbing the clicker from the armrest, I turn off the TV.

"Come on. Let's go." I press a kiss to her hair, then get up from the couch.

"Where are we going?" Her eyebrows furrow, her lips pursed in suspicion.

I put my leather jacket on before throwing hers in her lap, keeping my mouth shut. I can see the defiance in her eyes, the urge to demand me to tell her where we're going. But we've been spending a lot of time together, so she knows it's futile.

With a sigh and a slight glare, she lifts her body and puts on her jacket. I open the door, letting her stomp beside me while she rolls her eyes, and her reaction raises the corner of my mouth.

She follows me into the elevator and onto the street without saying a word, our feet moving simultaneously as we strut over the gray cobblestones.

I glance at her, a smile forming quickly.

Her hands are tucked into her black bomber, her brown hair hanging over her shoulders. There is a slight scowl on her pretty face that she's keeping in place for the lack of information I'm giving her, but I can see she's lighter than when we first met. There isn't a constant cloud hanging over her head, and I like seeing her this way.

After ten minutes, we arrive at the Pack and I push the door open until I feel her halt behind me.

"What are we doing here?" Her eyes lift with uncertainty to the sign above the entrance.

"Grabbing a drink."

"I'm not allowed in."

I roll my eyes at her, then take a big step so I can pull her elbow to direct her in front of me. "Don't pretend you don't know it's my bar," I murmur in her ear. "Get your ass in there, little Lexie." I slap her ass, and she lets out a shriek that amuses me.

I nudge my chin up to greet the bartender before I round the bar to grab a bottle of Royal Blue whiskey. Lexie takes the barstool at the head of the bar, her blue eyes looking at me in anticipation. With a ghost of a smile, I pour us both a glass, before taking the stool next to her.

I hold up the glass in front of her. "Happy birthday, *Alexandra*."

Her lashes fly high, her mouth parting in surprise.

"How do you know it's my birthday?"

"I know everything." I smirk.

A ghost of a smile is washing her pink lips as she takes the glass from my hands. We raise our glasses, clinking them together with our eyes locked. The appreciation is clear in her eyes, and I'd be lying if I said it didn't do anything to me. There is something about the looks she's giving me when she's relaxed and a little less worried. They are as mesmerizing as her smiles, and every day I'm looking forward to the first one she'll show me.

"When is your birthday?" She takes a sip of her drink and I do the same.

"Na-ah. I'm not telling you." I shake my head.

"Why not?"

"I don't give a damn about my birthday." Reign always makes our birthdays a big deal, but I'd be having a great day with just a bottle of liquor and some good food. My birthday is just another day.

"But you give a damn about mine?"

"I figured it would be a hard day for you." She's been keeping up her walls, never wanting to show her weaknesses, but I can read her better than she thinks. Two years in foster care taught me that. My foster parents used my foster brother and I as pickpockets and with it I learned the craft of body language. You can tell me as many lies as you want, but your body will speak the truth.

"It's not," she argues.

"Don't lie."

"I'm not lying."

My hand drops to her knee, squeezing it to grab her attention.

"Look, baby. You're a tough cookie. Tougher than I expected you to be when I found you in that alley. But I've been with you the entire day. I've seen the hurt in your eyes every time you've looked away from me." I lift my hand to cup her cheek, my eyes peering into her with an urgency I hope she sees, because I want her to hear me. "I see you."

She blinks and I watch her eyes grow moist, her chin quivering a little.

"Don't cry, little warrior."

She blows out a deep breath.

"Thank you." The gratefulness on her face goes straight to my heart, making my stomach somersault like a gymnast. "I just miss them." She tears her gaze away from me, fixing it on her glass. "I just miss them."

"What happened?"

"Don't you know?" She glances at me with a frown and I shrug.

"I know what it says in the police report."

"I'm sure that's wicked bullshit," she sputters, her fiery stance returning in his full glory.

"Tell me what happened." My voice is soft and encouraging, because I want her to open up to me. I want to know what she's dealing with every single day, and I want to know what is haunting her when she falls asleep.

25

Lexie

His luminous green eyes never deviate from mine, and I do my best to search for a reason to not tell him. I'm starting to trust him, and it feels so fucking good. It makes me feel less alone, like I have a partner in crime, literally. But I also know this is still Killian Wolfe I'm dealing with. We might not be enemies anymore, but I'm not sure he's my ally either. He keeps me on my toes, even when I feel confident enough to relax in his arms, because I never know when he'll snap at me and keep me at arm's length. But as he keeps staring at me, I can't find anything but understanding, compassion, and maybe even a little affection.

I take another sip of my drink, letting the soft notes of the whiskey fall on my tongue as I hope it will wash away the lump in my throat.

"We were having dinner," I start, doing my best to keep my tears at bay. "My dad saw them coming. He heard the screeching of tires and he got up from the table. I'll never forget his face." It's forever engraved in my mind, and I hate it. I hate that the fear in his eyes is the last thing I remember of my father. "He had honey brown eyes, but they dilated until they almost looked black. His skin paled to an off white, at least three shades lighter than his skin tone. But it was the fear in his normally confident voice that still makes my skin tingle when I think of it." The tiny hairs on my arms shoot to attention, pebbling my skin. My breath hitches, and I swallow hard before sucking in a lungful of air. Then, I take another drink to gain some liquid courage before I continue, while Killian never drops his attention.

"There was an air vent in his office. My sister and I used to hide there as kids. It wasn't big enough for the both of us, so with me being the smallest, he shoved me in there before he closed it again, telling me to be quiet. My sister hid under the desk, right in front of me, and I kept looking at her. She was a wildcat. Wicked popular at Northeastern because of her big mouth. I looked up to her. She was fearless." I shake my head, a deep frown cramping my face when I think of her vibrant face. "But, her blue eyes were showing me nothing more than panic." I stop, closing my eyes for a moment to hold back the tears that are pooling up, ready to fall. "All of a sudden, they were there. My father had a gun. I had no clue he even owned one. But before he could fire a shot, he dropped to the floor. The screaming from my mother was excruciating, and I wanted to get out there.

Fight." I scoff at my own stupid response, knowing I didn't stand a chance anyway. The last few weeks have shown me how naïve I was before I met Killian. "Pff, as if I could've done anything."

I roll my eyes, my lips pressed together in disdain. After my family died, there was so much rage within me. There still is, but now I see how I never even stood a chance against the men who killed them. My attitude might have gotten me close to Sullivan, and I probably would be able to shoot him through the head, but I wouldn't live long enough to enjoy it. I was nothing compared to the men that surrounded him. They would end me before I even attempted to walk out the door.

Killian's hand snakes into my hair, his warm hand burning on my neck, and I tear my troubled gaze to him.

"Sofia couldn't see me," I tell him, then sway my eyes back to my glass. "But I could see her and it's like she knew. She kept shaking her head." My voice breaks a little as tears start to run down to my chin. "Silently telling me to stay put. So I did. I covered my mouth to muffle my sobs, keeping as quiet as possible. I knew they were going to die. I just knew it. My mother was next. I closed my eyes." I close them now, putting myself back into that air vent. I still remember every sound, every smell, and every feeling. It was torture. And even though the bar is crowded enough to drown out the noise in my head, it won't. I'm still able to relive it all when I close my eyes, terror and sadness gripping my heart, and I snap them open again. "I couldn't look at her, but the loud thud on the floor told me enough. God, I felt so small." I huff, wiping my tears away with the back of my hand. "So wickedly stupid."

I sniff, then swallow to get rid of the big lump in the back of my throat before I raise my chin to force myself to not wallow in my misery.

"You're not stupid." His voice is soft, speaking to the butterflies inside me as he brushes his thumb over the crook of my neck. "You have nightmares about this?"

I shake my head. "No. It's Sofia. She was last. But she didn't get a bullet to the head. Someone rounded the desk." A snarl forms on my lips when I think about the man who killed my sister. "I still remember his big boots pounding on the hardwood floor. He chuckled like he won the jackpot and I just prayed that it would be painless and clean. But he reached out with a hunting knife, chuckling. He gutted her, enjoying the horror in her eyes, then he sliced her neck like she was roadkill. I'll never forget that chuckle. It still haunts me at night. Only those times, he's coming for me instead of my sister."

I hate my nightmares and I hate that they make me feel like I'm never completely rested. But it's those same nightmares that fuel me when Killian is telling me to give more during a boxing session. They drive me to the edge, because I know no one will come to save me. I'm on my own and I need to be able to rely on myself, no matter how big or bad my opponent might be.

"No one is coming for you." He grabs my chin, offering me a coy smile. It's in these moments that I let my thoughts wander, wishing Killian would be there in my future. The moments that he's kind and soft. When he's brushing my skin with his fingertips or when he presses a kiss to my hair. I don't need him to save me, but there is a little voice that hopes he's part of my future nonetheless.

"You don't know that. They thought I wasn't there. They could still want me dead." There is a big chance they will kill me when they find out I'm alive. If it was just my father who needed to go, they would've shot him on the street. But they didn't. They came to our house and murdered everyone they could find. They weren't just there for Jameson Lee. No, they were there for the entire Lee family.

"How did you escape?" Killian takes another sip of his drink, his hand falling from my face.

"When they left, I waited more than an hour, staring at Sofia's dead body. At some point, my mind took over and I got out, packed a bag, and fled to my grandmother's house in Dorchester. The only thing I took from my family is their jewelry and a few pictures."

"What happened to the house?"

"I never had the balls to go back there." I wanted to, but I was scared that it might be staked out, that they thought I would come back one day and they'd be waiting. Part of me wishes I could go back there, even if it's just for a day to take all the personal stuff like photo albums and my sister's favorite books. But I've come to terms with the fact that it will probably never happen.

"Is your family buried?"

"I don't know. I laid low as much as I could."

"What makes you think it was Sullivan?" I snap my head to Killian, drilling my gaze into his until I see his genuine expression.

"The guy. The one who slaughtered my sister. He was mentioning to the other guy how he was going to keep her for himself. Have some fun with her. Someone told him that wasn't what Sullivan ordered to do. He replied that he didn't care, but he gave in when the other one told him he didn't want to go against the Chief of Police."

Killian shakes his head, his jaw twitching as he brings his glass to his lips.

"Asshole," he mutters, with fire dancing in his eyes. Seeing his anger simmers down my own rage, as if I have someone to share it with.

"I want him dead, Killian." The tone in my voice is firm, determined, and leaves no room for negotiating.

"I know," he breathes, followed by a chortle.

"Will you help me?"

"Yes," he answers without hesitation, never skipping a beat.

"You work with him."

"I work with a lot of people."

"What about your brothers?"

"Don't worry about my brothers," he says with ease, like there is nothing to it. But I know my place. I'm not Killian's girlfriend. I'm not part of their family and I'm not even in their inner circle. If I tell them my story, they might all understand my desire for revenge, but they won't help me if it jeopardizes their own position.

Killian takes my glass out of my hands to put it on the bar, then pulls my stool closer to his, turning my body with his hands on my hips so that I have to face him, before he cups my cheek. His intimidating eyes search mine.

"You don't trust me." It's not a question. It's also not true. Not completely. I trust him. I just don't know if I trust him enough.

"Why are you helping me?"

He holds back a smile. "Because you begged me?"

"You could have easily killed me a hundred times. Shoved me into the canal and no one would find me. No one would be looking for me anyway. Why help me?" He thinks he's got me all figured out, but I know a few things about Killian Wolfe too. He never does anything without a good reason and there is no goodwill in his vocabulary. He's not the do-gooder like Reign. He has his eyes on the prize, always. But right now, I don't know what it is.

I can see the cogs in his head turning, as if he's contemplating how much he wants to tell me while I wait in anticipation.

"When my brothers and I got split up into foster care, we were all alone. I was all alone. I've been living my entire life surrounded by my brothers and all of a sudden, it was just me. I know what it feels to be alone in the world."

I blink as I watch Killian Wolfe change in front of my eyes. I did not expect that answer, and I'm trying to detect the bullshit, but I can't find any as he keeps our gazes tangled with a softness in his eyes that I haven't seen before. Not completely. I've seen it lurk under the surface, but I never thought it would actually come out for anyone other than his brothers.

Certainly not for me.

I try to push back the grin that wants to split my face, but I fail miserably.

"You have a heart." My gaze drops to his lips, dying to feel them pressed against mine.

"I really don't, baby," he says quietly.

"You do, Killian Wolfe." I close the distance, entwining my lips with his as I wrap my arms around his neck, and he replies by tugging me closer. My tongue darts out, demanding him to open up for me before I lap it around his with teasing strokes.

"You know I can easily fix this for you and kill him right now?" He brushes his nose against mine, keeping our lips only an inch apart as he whispers the words.

"You'd do that for me?" I pull back, looking into his straight face. His eyebrows make the tiniest movement, giving me a bored look that silently calls me out on the question. As if the answer should be clear to me, and maybe it is. "It needs to be me."

It's tempting to let him fix my shit so I can be on my way, but I can't let anyone else clean up my mess. I might be young, but I stopped being a child when my family got slaughtered and I can no longer rely on anyone but me.

"Look, I will help you," he says in a serious tone. "He will suffer for what he did. But let me warn you, baby, it's not going to make you feel better. It's not going to heal your broken heart." His thumb trails along my jaw with gentle strokes. His words constrict my throat, not even wanting to think about that. I'm not looking for redemption or something to take away my pain. *I am looking for revenge.*

"Maybe I don't have a heart. Like you."

The sigh that comes from his throat is loaded, his brows furrowed with trouble.

"You have a heart. It's just covered in blood." He pauses, meeting my lips. Our breath mixes as I take in his words. "Don't expect closure, little Lexie. You won't find it killing Sullivan."

I hear him. And I know he's right, but I have to do this.

My shoulder twitches. "Maybe. But I can't live in a world with him living his life like he's the hero of Boston."

Satisfied with that answer, he holds a tight grip on my hips as I see his worry being replaced by a mischievous grin.

"So, what is your plan?"

My gaze slumps to his chest, trying to avoid looking at him, because I know I already told him what my plan in. It hasn't changed.

"Kill him. Then move somewhere Midwest. Start over."

"Leave Boston?" His surprise makes my eyes trail up to his again, quick enough to spot the glint of disappointment before it's gone.

"I have nothing to stay for." It falls from my lips followed with unshed tears that I push to the back, because I realize for me everything has changed. I know exactly what could make me stay. I just don't have the guts to speak those thoughts out loud.

26

KILLIAN

From the corner of my eye, I catch her glancing at me. I don't have to see how her eyes are scrunched up in suspicion, her lips slightly pursed, because I can feel her energy coming at me in waves ever since I drove a different way home. In the last few weeks, I imprinted the facial expressions that sum up Lexie Lee, every single one of them cute as hell.

There is her scowl, when her eyes are all fire blazing and her jaw ticks with sharpness.

There is the suspicious one, like she's giving me now, when she narrows her blue eyes to slits with a slight pinch of her mouth, which is beyond entertaining.

But my favorite, by far, is her happy one. It's the one where the deep blue in her eyes pops, and she gets a natural blush on her cheeks that highlights her freckles. It's the one she gives me when she laughs, tickling the senses in my stomach alive like the start of an engine. Her laughter feeds my energy during the day and I can't seem to get enough.

"What?" I finally chuckle, feeling her gaze boring into my cheek.

"Where are we going?"

"You'll see."

"Killian." Her reprimand is filled with doubt, and I notice how she fumbles with the ring on her finger. Without thought, I grab it, linking it with mine.

"Don't worry."

She stays fixed on me and I meet her eyes briefly, then turn my attention back to the wheel. I expect her to argue with me, or at least nag me to tell her where we're going, but she lets her gaze fall to our hands before placing them on top of her lap. She gives mine a small squeeze before she relaxes beside me.

Content, I continue the drive, loving how she's literally putting her trust in my hands.

It builds a weird feeling in my chest, like my heart will explode any second now. It's a feeling that's been popping up more and more every day and even though I know I should deal with it, I can't get myself to push it away.

"Killian." The fear in her voice is gripping my heart, and she quickly lets go of my hand. The loss of our touch annoys me and I grab the back of her neck as I keep my other hand steady on the wheel.

"Relax."

"This is *my* street."

"I'm aware."

"That's–that's my house." She has difficulty pushing the words off her tongue like the realization is flaring up the fear she felt when she was last there.

"I know, baby. Don't freak."

"Don't freak!?" She slaps my hand away. "What if someone sees me?! They think I'm missing! Or dead!"

I park the car in front of her house with a growl, then twist my torso to face her as I put my hand back on her neck. Her eyes are darker now, like the depths of the ocean, laced with a sliver of fear.

"Drive, Killian! Before someone sees me!"

"Hey! I'm with you, right?"

She nods, but it's reluctant.

"No one is going to hurt you."

"You don't know that," she hisses.

"Yes, I do," I bellow with force, trying to snap her out of it. My eyes grow wider as I hold her terrified gaze, my fingers digging into her skin. "I don't give a damn who's coming for you. I rule this city! My brother runs this city. If I tell you you're safe, you're safe!" Her lashes flutter with every word that leaves my lips, making me feel bad for yelling at her. But seeing her fearful builds my frustration and I just need it to leave. I want her smile back.

I sigh, lowering my eyes for a second. Her chest moves up and down with harsh breaths from under her black jacket and when our gazes tangle again, she's just blinking at me.

"When I'm with you," I tell her, my tone now soft, "you never have to worry about your safety, okay?" I pull her face close to mine, regretting the way I handled this.

When she's being a badass, kicking my ass in the gym, I forget she's still young, still traumatized. It makes me forget that she's not as brave as she tries to be.

"Do you trust me?" I whisper against her lips.

She swallows, then nods her head.

"Good." I briefly connect my mouth with hers, trying to reassure her with a kiss. "Come on, get out."

Letting go of her, I exit, then round the car right in time to pull her out when she opens the door. With an ominous look, her eyes trail up and down the bricks of the building as I push her back against the car. I cage her in, pushing my leg between hers, demanding her to put her focus on me when I lift my hand to cup her cheek.

"It's okay. *You're* okay. Do you hear me?"

Her chest rises as she takes a deep breath. "Yeah."

"We're just going in. And you can grab whatever you want to grab, okay? My men are here, covering three of the surrounding blocks." She glances at one of my men, exiting the SUV on the corner of the street. "No one will take you from me."

Her eye twitches with a hint of a smile, and she grabs my shirt, yanking me against her lips. Her kiss is pressing, bruising, like it's giving her the courage she needs.

"Promise?"

"I promise, baby." I grab her hand, and before she can protest, I tug her behind me up the stairs of the building. She cautiously follows me, accompanied by a few of my men who are instructed to keep the building secure. Silently, we ascend, step by step, until we reach her floor. Her hand falls from mine and I turn around.

"Are you okay?"

She stares at her front door with a vacant expression crossing her face.

I hate this. I hate seeing her crippled with fear, and the resentment toward Sullivan makes my teeth grind. I still don't know why Sullivan killed her family, but I sure as fuck know she didn't deserve to live with the damage it has done.

"I got you, baby." I hold out my hand and, to my relief, she grabs it before I slowly direct her to the front door. It's cracked, because I told my men to make sure it was empty and safe, not wanting any surprises, and I push it open.

With a creak, it flies open and hits the wall, showing the hallway of Lexie's childhood home, and I rear my head back to her. As if she's flipped a switch, her fear is gone, and she steps past me to enter. The relief in her eyes is accompanied by a sadness that overwhelms me, and all I want to do is wrap her tightly in my arms. I pull her back, doing exactly that, giving her a hug with my nose buried in her hair.

"Take your time," I hum.

"Are there–is there," she croaks out. "Will there still be–"

"Blood?" I finish her sentence. "They cleaned the most and obvious when they took out the bodies and the investigation was done. But it's not all gone, it's up to the owners to get it completely cleaned and livable again. Because your family owns the place, they are looking for someone to claim the inheritance. Since they can't find you. It's just sitting here."

Satisfied with that answer, she breaks loose, disappearing into the house.

27

Lexie

It's weird.

It feels the same. It looks the same. And for the most part, it also smells the same, except for the excessive scent of bleach hanging in the air.

But it's the silence that echoes like the elephant in the room. I walk into the parlor, glancing around the room with a vacant stare. A coffee cup with a stain of my mother's lipstick still sits on the coffee table, my sister's English book still open in front of it. The sight of her studying in front of the TV on the floor flashes through my mind and inspires the tears blurring my vision. I blow out a breath, continuing my way to my father's office. My feet feel heavier with every step, my heart beating faster by the second.

I know I shouldn't go back and relive the moment that changed my life, but I can't help it. It's like a trainwreck waiting to happen, a moth drawn to the light. I have to see it.

I have to relive it, even if it will kill me all over again.

I stop when I reach the open door, glancing at the floor. The blood spatter still stains the rug my mother shipped from Russia, and I feel a rock drop in my stomach. It tears through me, my knees collapsing under the weight of it. When I go down, I'm welcoming the pain of the hardwood floor, hoping I'll land hard, but a pair of hands catch me as I feel Killian's body pressed against mine.

"Whoa! I got you, little Lexie." Tears roll down my cheeks while I hang limply in his arms, too paralyzed to use my muscles while I keep my gaze fixed on the desk that haunts my memories. I want to push back my tears, but the quivering of my chin makes it impossible, so I just let it go with Killian holding on to me, keeping my body from falling to the floor. I haven't cried this hard since that day, and as much as it hurts, physically causing my chest to ache and constrict, it also feels like consolation to let it all out. My sobs are loud, hysterical even, but for the first time in months, I don't care. I let the grief flow out of me, like breaking a dam.

"Shhh, it's okay. It's okay." Killian's soft breath graces the skin on my ear.

He holds me like that, with my gaze fixed on the desk in the room, until I find the strength to spin in his arms so I can bury my face into his chest. He lets me, keeping his arms tightly around my back, giving me the safety that I need to let go while I keep a strong hold on his leather jacket. For just a little while, he's allowing me to be

Alexandra Lee, an eighteen-year-old senior at Boston High, allowed to be sad about the things that happened to her. He's giving me the option to lower my walls even if it's not permanent.

The weight of his hand runs through my hair, cupping the back of my head, and I breathe him in. The freshness of his fabric softener enters my nose, and I feel how slowly my senses calm down. I press my ear against his heart, letting the steady beating act like a guide for my own. When my breathing becomes more even, I lift my chin.

His normally sharp eyes are filled with sympathy, joined by a soft smile that chips away some of the grief I'm still surrendering to. He takes my face into his hands, then gently brushes away my tears.

"It hurts," I confess, swallowing the sob that still wants to break through.

"I know."

"What if it never stops?"

He presses his forehead against mine, never letting go of my face. "It will never stop, baby. It will hurt for the rest of your life. But you will grow stronger, and one day it won't weigh you down anymore, because you're strong enough to carry it."

His words are blunt, but still, I welcome them like a cozy blanket on a cold winter night. They are pure, honest, and not what I want to hear, but it's what I've come to love about him. He never hides the truth. He never protects me from reality. He lets me deal with it, expecting me to be able to handle it. It gives me the confidence that I can survive whatever comes my way.

"I want him dead, Killian." My sadness is being pushed to the back as my impatience to kill the man responsible for it grows, and I find myself grinding my teeth before I realize.

"And he will be. I promise." A soft kiss lands on my lips, as if he's trying to calm me down with it and I let him. "Go. Grab some of the stuff you want to take with you."

He turns us both, before spinning me in his arms, then gives me a nudge into the parlor and I do as he says. I glide past the dining room table, my fingers trailing the slick wood as I continue my way to my bedroom.

When the different shades of blue on the walls align with my sight, I feel a smile curl my lips. I grab my blue bunny sitting on my perfectly made bed, then let my weight fall into the mattress.

"Ah, Bluey," I muse, pressing him against my chest as I breathe it in. I got it from my mother, who got it from hers when she was younger. She called it *Siniy*, which means blue in Russian, but I just stuck to Bluey my entire life. I took him everywhere with me until I was eight and even after that, my mother was never allowed to wash it. I hold it against my nose, still smelling the rosemary potpourri that reminded my mother of home. I never got to meet my Russian family, but now it feels even more needed, considering I don't have anyone left in Boston.

I get back up, grabbing a bag from my closet before I start going through my room to look for the personal stuff I want to take, but when I glance around, it seems useless. Everything around me feels like a lifetime away, part of a life I no longer have. So, instead, I head into the master bedroom, taking some things from my parents, before I do the same with Sofia's room. When I'm done, I go back to my own, tucking Bluey into the bag.

"You got everything?"

I rear my head, our gazes colliding comfortably as I offer him a smile. He's leaning into the doorpost, his usual smirk restored to a coy one, with his arms crossed in front of his chest. A strand of his brown hair falls in front of his face when he rests his head against the wood, and I swallow at the sight of it.

It's not fair how he steals my breath away whenever he gets the chance.

The sexual tension has always been there, and when we first had sex, I knew it wasn't going to be the last time. Our pull is too strong. But lately, something's changed.

He's been showing me a different side, one that's caring, affectionate. The version of him that makes me wonder if there is more going on than a simple agreement. The version that sparks my hope that maybe, just maybe, he feels as much as I do when I look at him. Maybe he needs me as much as I need him.

I hum in agreement, placing the bag over my shoulder before I slog over until I'm right in front of him. Instantly, his hands reach out, placing them on the small of my back to tug me closer.

"Why did you bring me here?" I cock my head, not wanting to miss any change in his features, but he keeps his face straight like always. The silence is thick until it's interrupted by the sigh coming from his lips.

"I don't know. So you could grab the things that are important to you." His tone suggests it doesn't mean anything, but really, it means everything. I move my hand up, rubbing it over his stubble, and he lowers his lashes with a lazy look that makes my heart flutter out of my chest and into his hands. I'm scared to ask him what he feels for me, but this looks says more than words will ever say, and for now, it's enough.

I bring his lips to mine, pushing a loving kiss on his, hoping he can sense the emotion it comes with. The sensible side of me tells me to snatch my heart out of his hands and run, but he made it impossible to take another step.

"Thank you," I breathe against his lips.

28

When I strut into Reign's apartment, he's sitting behind his desk in front of the window. His back is against the door because he likes to see the view whenever he's working, but I never understood how he was able to work with peace of mind if someone could literally stab him in the back.

"What's up, tool?" I let my feet carry me to the fridge, getting nothing more than a hum from my brother, who still has his gaze fixed on his screen.

"Seriously, Reign. Someone could've burst through that door and shot you in the back. You know that, right?" I pull out a bottle of water.

"I know you're not the brightest brother, but you do know I can see every corner of this building when I'm sitting here?"

"What do you mean?" Opening the bottle, I put it to my lips, then plop onto the couch behind him.

"There are cameras at every possible entrance. I get alerts whenever they detect movement. If someone wants to shoot me, they'll be at least two minutes too late."

"Sometimes I forget what a nerd you are."

"At least I'm a hot one."

"The judge is still out on that."

"Sienna will agree with me."

"She's biased. She doesn't count."

"Whatever." The clicking of his keyboard is the only audible sound in the room while I wait for him to tell me why he summoned me. I give him another minute before my impatience gets the best of me and I let out an annoyed grunt.

"Ay! You gonna tell me what I'm doing here or what? What couldn't you tell over the phone?"

He ignores me, the sound of his keyboard now replaced by the humming of the printer, and I roll my eyes. Finally, he spins his desk chair to face me, and I greet him with a glare.

"This." He hands me a piece of paper with a troubled frown, and I yank it out of his hands.

"What the hell is this?" My eyes start reading the document as rapidly as I can. My lips slowly part with every word, shock washing over me. This could destroy us. It's detailed. It's relentless. It's the truth, and in our best interest, to keep this shit buried as deep as possible. I grind my teeth, my body already wanting to kill someone. But it isn't until I let them travel back to the top, to read the name of the writer, that my heart freezes right on the spot. It stops beating while my ears are ringing as I feel the rage dripping in.

"Motherfucker," I spit.

"Yeah." My brother's eyes are watching me carefully, as if he's expecting me to snap.

There is a big chance.

"He was going to take us out?"

"Yeah, that's why Sullivan wanted them dead," Reign explains. The dots are being connected in my head and my anger now crashes into me like I'm hitting my car against a tree. The hit is there in all its glory, hurting me more than I would've expected, but undeniable. I'm not a fair man like Franklin. I'm not as empathetic as Reign. I'm not as caring as Connor can be if he sees you as family. I'm the cunning one. The merciless one. These moments are the reason why. *Betrayal.*

I don't handle it well and I'll never accept it. I don't give out second chances. Betray me and I'll bury you.

"We don't know if she knows," Reign offers tentatively. I can see the trouble in his green eyes, trying to calm me down with just a look, but it's not going to fly. It felt right at the time, but now I realize I made a mistake. A big one. A stupid one. One I promised myself I'd never make again.

"Oh, she knows."

"How do you know?"

"Because she's smarter than that," I say with gritted teeth.

"But there is more."

"What?" I bark, not sure if I can take it anymore.

"Her mother? She's Russian. Moved here when she was eighteen, married Jameson Lee after graduating Northeastern."

"And?" I already know all of this.

"Her last name is Kulakov." My brows knit together when the name falls from his tongue. Where did I hear that name before? I dig deep, trying to find the link I'm failing to see until finally a light bulb flicks on in my head. My eyes widen, my jaw dropping in shock.

"Kulakov? Isn't that?" I don't finish my sentence because I already know the answer. If it wasn't, Reign wouldn't even bring it up.

"Yeah, it is."

"Motherfucker. You think the Russian mob is connected?"

He shakes his head, then runs a hand through his honey brown hair. "I don't know, but we need to find out."

I let out a grunt, rubbing my hand through my stubble, as I stare at the ground. When I first took her home, she seemed like a lost little girl and I don't know why, but I wanted to save her. Now I'm wondering if I invited a demon into my home.

"Did you tell Callie?"

"That she probably has a cousin?" He gives me an incredulous look. "Of course not. Let's figure out if she's a friend or foe first."

"Oh, I'll find out." Determined, I get to my feet, stomping toward the door.

"You can't kill her, Killian," Reign bellows behind my back.

"Watch me."

29

Lexie

The classical music echoes through the entire parlor while I bring my arms up, lifting myself onto my toes as I start dancing. I feel my muscles stretching with every movement in the most satisfying way. All my steps make me feel like I'm floating, my memory taking over like always. But it's the first time since before I became an orphan that I'm doing it with a smile. I twirl and fly through the room with every step, and the more the music progresses, the deeper my smile becomes engraved in my cheeks. The last few days, I've been feeling lighter, my heart slowly crawling back from the darkness, and I know it's because of Killian. His dark soul lightens mine in the most wicked way, and I'm starting to believe the feeling is mutual. I can sense it when he touches me, when he steals a kiss whenever he walks by, and how his words to me are not as harsh anymore as they were in the beginning. He makes me believe I can fly. That anything is possible. It's an emotion I only experienced when I still had my family, but even then, it wasn't as intense as what I'm feeling now. It's consuming me, swallowing me whole, and I welcome it.

I spin on the spot, then freeze when Killian is standing in the parlor.

"Hey!" I smile.

He's staring at me with a vacant stare, but there's a craze in his eyes that's pebbling my skin. His energy is intimidating, like that first time we met, but he seems completely in a trance. My smile drops to the floor, my eyebrows raising with worry.

"Kill? What's wrong?" Reluctantly, I take one step forward.

He blinks, then there is a slight shake of his head as if he's snapping himself out of it. His absent look is rapidly changed by an evil glare, and I gasp for air.

He pulls out the gun from his waist, pointing it at my head, his eyes spitting daggers at me. "You're a lying little bitch, *Alexandra*."

With big strides, he tries to close the distance, and I stumble back as nerves rush through my body. The look on his sharp features makes him appear possessed, and my unease increases by the second.

"W-What are you talking about?" I stammer when I hit the wall. Before I can dart away, he grabs my neck with force, pressing me into the wall while the cold metal of his gun touches my temple. The hurt of his fingers makes it hard for me to breathe and my entire self-defense mechanism blacks out. The pounding of my heart sounds in my ears, realizing this might be it. This might be the moment Killian Wolfe switches on me and he'll end my life without a second thought. I thought I was safe with him, but now I realize I never was. He will kill me if he decides I'm not worth his time.

"Is your mother tied to the Russian mob?"

Russian mob?

"What? No!"

"Don't lie!" His roar makes my lashes flutter as I do my best to hold back the tears that want to escape. The tone in his voice is menacing, triggering the loneliness I've become so familiar with. For a short time, I thought I wasn't alone. I believed him. But now I know I will never be anything else. It's me, myself, and I. No one is coming to save me. If I want to live, I need to do it on my own.

"I don't know what you are talking about," I shout back at him.

"When were you going to tell me your father wanted to bring us Wolfes down. That he was writing an article about us that would get us locked up for life?!"

"I-I didn't." It's only a partial lie, but now it's my biggest regret. I've always known why my father was on Sullivan's bad side. I've always known my father wanted to fight against the criminals in the city, the Wolfes being the biggest priority. But when they died, I didn't care.

I still don't. I just want my revenge.

"You do realize I'm a Wolfe, right?" His lips brush against my cheeks as I pray he won't literally eat me alive, when I feel him scrape his teeth against my skin.

"Killian, I-I..." I try to look him in the eye, but he's completely focused on my neck, creating a barrier that makes it impossible to plead with him.

"You what?!" He tightens his hold and I gasp for air. "Didn't think I'd find out?" His voice lowers, the sweetness in his tone making him sound like a true psychopath.

"Oh, naïve little Lexie. You didn't think I was going to ruin the deal with the law enforcement of Boston without turning every single stone, did you?" I hold still, his eyes now locking with mine. "What? You thought you were special because I put my dick inside of you whenever you wanted?"

His words slice right through my heart, like a knife through butter, and all I can feel is defeat. All I can feel is how he's shoving me aside like a stray dog, realizing I'm useless. I can't hold back the tears, but I keep my chin up, holding his gaze.

"I'm sorry."

"You're not, baby," he snarls. "You're nothing but a cheap fuck."

"You don't mean that." I don't know why I said it, but I do mean it. He's hurting me. He's lashing out, but I can't have imagined the last few weeks. I didn't imagine the way he looks at me with affection and devotion or how he keeps me close to his body in the middle of the night.

"You don't know what I mean!"

His grip on my neck releases just the slightest bit, enough to give me a little more breathing space.

"I'm sorry." I shake my head. "I didn't think it was important."

"Bullshit!" He pushes my head to the side with the barrel of the gun.

"It was my father's story. It had nothing to do with me!"

"It had everything to do with you!"

"I was never going to use it against you. I swear." I twist my head enough so I can find his eyes again. They are blazing, the gold specks completely pushed away by his dilated pupils. "I just want him to pay. I don't care what you do for a living. I just want him dead."

"Yeah, you got a sweet tongue, baby." His fixation loses concentration for a split second and I take the moment to connect my elbow with his side. He grunts, gripping his flank as I dart away from him. Quickly, I jump over the couch, reaching for my gun on the coffee table. When my palm wraps around the handle, Killian storms toward me, his gun pointed at me, but when I mirror his stance, bringing my gun up until it's aimed at his head, he stills. We stare at each other, the sadness in my eyes matching his, and I feel my heart crumbling to my feet.

"I'm not bullshitting you, Killian!" I cry, waving one hand over my body. "Look at me! Look at my life! I'm nobody! I don't exist! No one would listen to me anyway! I got nothing left. I don't give a rat's ass how you make your money. Who you kill to get what you want. All I've got is my revenge. I'm not after anything else." Melancholy begins to take over, and I decide I don't want to fight anymore. I'm sick of fighting. Most of the time, I don't even know what I'm still fighting for. I have nothing left anyway. "And if you want to take that away from me as well, go for it." Holding my chin up, I put the safety on the gun, then lower myself to place it back on the glass table. His eyes narrow, his jaw ticking, and I can see the doubt bringing back the green in his eyes. He doesn't know what to do with me and I see it as a win. If he was convinced I needed to die, I'd already be lying on the floor with a bullet in my heart.

I suck in a breath when he saunters toward me, his gun still hanging in his hand. His free palm wraps around my chin, peering down at me like he needs to make sure he has the upper hand, but I know it's not a done deal.

"Give me one reason why I should keep you alive."

"Because you know I didn't start this!" I glare, finding my courage back bit by bit. "I'm just doomed to finish it."

"Not good enough." He roughly pushes me back, then places the barrel between my eyes. I swallow, my heart slamming against my ribcage as if it's about to jump out, and right when I think to myself, *this is it*, I catch my will to live. I might not have anything left in this world, but it doesn't mean I can't build something of my own. Create the life my parents wanted me to have. Heaving, I quickly let my eyes wander to find anything I can fight him with, when they land on the deck of cards in the fruit bowl on the dining room table.

"Play for it," I blurt desperately. "If I win. You let me live. If you win? You can do whatever you want." It's a stupid suggestion because I know he's good at poker. Reign told me once how they let Killian play for certain deals, knowing he'll always win.

An evil smirk forms, amusement creeping into his eyes. "I always win."

"Not this time," I counter, slowly pushing the gun out of my face. "One game. One winner. Any prize you want."

"You don't know what you're getting into, little Lexie." He turns his back to me, making his way to the table. He places the gun on the surface, easy for him to reach, before he takes a seat, then he nudges his chin to the chair across from him.

With heavy feet, I slog his way with squared shoulders, swallowing roughly to settle my nerves. I've only played poker a few times on the default game on my phone, knowing the basics. Surely not enough to be betting my life on it, but I don't have a choice. I could grab my gun and run out the door, but he's Killian Wolfe. He'll either find me within five minutes or he'll make sure I'm looking over my shoulder for the rest of my life. My heart stutters, as I'm realizing this is really it. I've hit the ultimate low. I can't sink any lower than this without actually ending up buried underground. My life now is at the mercy of someone else, mentally stripped from my freedom, whether I run or play.

I might as well be dead.

I take the seat and when his devilish eyes run over my body, a shiver slides down my spine. He shoves the deck hard, and they stop right in front of me.

"Deal the cards."

30

KILLIAN

She looks fucking hot in her tight leggings that hug every curve on her body in the best way. A crop top shows the velvet skin of her belly and even her pointe shoes turn me on with those silk ribbons wrapped around her ankles. She looked breathtaking when I burst through the door and I needed a moment to snap myself out of it, hypnotized by the carefree energy she radiates when she dances.

I can see the doubt in her blue eyes when she takes a seat, mixed with a primal sense of will to survive that I've seen since the first time I cornered her in that alley. It's as mesmerizing as staring into the moon, building a sense of awe at its ungraspable beauty. I can see her pulse throbbing from across the table, and I lick my lips, wanting to cover it with my mouth.

The adrenaline surges through my veins over and over again, like a race car going sixty-one laps over a race track. It feels never ending, keeping every sense of my body on edge. But I can't deny the tiny voice in the back of my head that's making it incredibly difficult to keep concentrating on my rage. I feel stupid as fuck, letting her crawl under my skin, but the rage, the tightness in my chest, I'm the only one to blame and I know it. It's telling me I'm responsible for this, giving her no reason to trust me. I didn't want to give her that kind of power over me, but somewhere along the way, I assumed we were building some kind of common ground. We operated as one, and I started to appreciate it. I didn't even see how much until she betrayed me by keeping secrets from me.

Important secrets.

This isn't me finding out she dropped out of high school or has a drug issue. This is vital information for my brothers and me, and she should have told me. But I can hear a question lingering in the back of my head: *would you have told her if the roles were reversed?*

The answer is short and simple: no. Not a chance in hell. Information is valuable, especially if it's about those who are close to you. I'm livid because of the choice she's made, but I do understand, which is only pissing me off more. She's thinking like me, playing my game like she invented it, and it's frustrating the hell out of me.

She swallows, taking the cards out and shuffling them before her eyes lift back to mine. "We're not using chips?

I press my tongue against my teeth, unable to hide the amusement at her effort to pretend she still knows what the hell she's talking about. I can see the unease dripping from every inch of her body. My guess is she's never really played other than some simple digital games. She probably knows the basics, nothing more than that. Yet she continues to keep her chin raised and her eyes shooting daggers at me every chance she gets. It confuses the hell out of me, both fueling my desire and my need to snap her neck at the same time.

"We're betting for your life, no need to use chips, *little Lexie*," I snarl impatiently. "One hand. One flop. Just deal."

A ghost of a smile crosses her flawless face as I fist my hands to trigger my muscles to focus anywhere else but my twitching dick.

"I know what you're doing." The tone in her voice is more confident than I expected to hear tonight, the features on her face holding an audacity that makes me want to bend her over this table and shut her up with my dick slamming inside of her. When did she grow up and get the upper hand over *me*? Killian Wolfe?

"Is that so?"

She drags her teeth over her lip until it springs free into a smirk. "You're trying to intimidate me." *Good girl.* "Trying to overrule me with your piercing eyes and fearless stance." *Smart girl.* The temperament she's displaying revs my heart to life. I appreciate her choice of words, reveling in the admiration in them. But she's not going to get off that easily. I want her to squirm underneath my gaze, to fear me, making her wonder if I'm capable of killing her or not. Even if it's just for punishment, I want her to doubt my intentions as much as possible.

"The only thing I'm trying to figure out is if I'll be dragging your dead body across my floor." Her grin stays in place, and it quickly grows into a chuckle. It sounds a little diabolical, adding to my desire. She's acting like the female version of myself and right now it's hard to believe she's just a nineteen-year-old girl. She looks like a woman in control, one who doesn't hesitate to kill if she has the right motivation.

She looks like a full grown woman, ready to take on the world and slay whoever gets in her way. *She looks motherfucking perfect.* And I hate it.

"What's so funny, little Lexie?"

"You're bluffing," she taunts, tilting her head a little.

"Are you sure about that?" A tingling feeling showers every piece of skin covering my bones, working all the way down until it reaches my toes. I want to kiss the sass off her face so badly while I squeeze her neck so I'm all she can breathe in. The need to hurt her is equivalently torturous to the need to feel her skin against mine.

"I've got to know you a little better in the last few weeks. You're mad at me." I'm furious. And fucking irked because of her level of defiance that's doing way too much to me. "But you don't want me dead. I can see it in your eyes." I feel my throat tighten, my mouth turning dry. She makes my heart beat at an exhilarating pace. It's addictive even. It creates an urgency for her that I can't afford but also makes me believe I can't live without it either. At some point over the past weeks, she's wrapped me around her little finger and I was too fucking blind to notice.

"Deal, *Alexandra*."

She lifts a finger, her attitude never faltering. "One hand. One flop. Highest combo on the table wins. I win, I live. You win, you can do whatever you want with me."

"I'm planning on it."

She shuffles the cards one last time, our eyes at no time diverting from the other's. Like they are linked by an invisible cord with a permanent tension. She shoves a card my way before placing one in front of herself, then repeats the move. Never moving a muscle in my face, I lift both cards to take knowledge of them, then place them back on the table as I watch her do the same. The thick air in the room blurs my vision, the tension shielding us off from the world around us as I hear a siren in the distance. My heartbeat pounds in my ears, nervous as hell at the outcome of this game. This one single game that can make or break either one of us, because I know I'll have to pull through on my threat. It excites me as much as it scares the shit out of me. Never has a woman stirred so many emotions within me. I didn't even know I was capable of half the things I'm feeling right now.

In any other given situation, I'd do it without hesitation, but staring back at her bright face, blue eyes, and silky brown hair, I already feel a lump the size of a tennis ball sitting in the back of my throat just thinking about her beautiful eyes without that spark in them.

She places the five cards in the middle of the table and my eyes never drop from her face as I see her looking them over. A flash of victory crosses her face. It's brief, only visible for a millisecond, but I saw it. It gives me the motivation to keep my scowl in place, not giving her an inch of my relief in return.

"You first." She nudges her chin at my cards and with a swift move, I turn them over for her to see. A smile slowly graces her lips in its full glory, making it hard for her to keep her indifferent attitude. She flips her own cards over, but I don't even spare them a glance. Instead, I keep my gaze focused on hers as relaxation slowly creeps in.

"I win, I live." The triumph rolls off her tongue, making my heart soar.

Abruptly, I get up, rounding the table until I'm crowding her space. With Bambi-like eyes, she stares back at me, her fear crawling back to the surface.

"W-What are you doing?" She swallows, her hands twitching. She's doing her best to keep her chin up and her eyes fierce, probably to silently convince herself I won't hurt her.

I grab her brown silky hair with force, fisting it with a tight grip that I know must burn her scalp when a whimper falls from her lips. Dipping my chin, I hover my lips above hers.

"I thought you got to know me better? You got me all figured out?" Her shallow breath warms my lips. "Are you scared of me, little Lexie?" I whisper.

"No."

"Liar."

"Are you going to kill me?" There is a tremor in her voice that she's desperately trying to hide, but I know her better than she thinks. The blood is slowly draining from her face, and my cock swells as I stare into her skittish gaze.

"You should know by now, baby. Win or lose, I always get what I want," I rumble against her skin.

She keeps our eyes locked, though blinking rapidly like she's about to take off.

"What do you want?" she asks, her voice gruff as she croaks the words.

I smirk, tilting her head a little with my fist, then whisper, "To tear you apart."

My mouth finds hers, but this time it feels different. Electrifying. Like we've been apart for weeks, desperate to feel each other's touch, when really it was only mere hours. It's bruising, it hurts, and it's packed with an emotion I can't afford but can't stop either. At first, she's shocked, not sure how to handle this reaction, but when I lift her from her chair, pulling her long hair to bring her closer like it's my reins, she finally gives in. Our tongues sweep together at a demanding pace as I lift her butt onto the table, pulling out my knife from the back of my jeans. My free hand moves all over her body, pushing away every piece of fabric I can find to make sure I feel her soft skin under my palm. When I break our kiss, still holding on to her hair, I press my knife against her throat, and her blue eyes find mine while I untie the silk ribbons around her lowers legs so she can push them off her feet.

They are dilated with a clear desire, laced by that level of defiance she's been giving me since the day we met. Her dismay has vanished into thin air. Not just tonight, but when I think of it, this is the girl I've seen for weeks. The girl that manages to keep my attention longer than any female ever has, making it impossible for me to keep my distance.

The sharp knife presses into her silky skin, creating a thin red line.

"What are you doing?" This time there is no defiance in her tone and inwardly I applaud her.

"Don't you dare hide anything from me *ever* again."

The hardness in her gaze softens with a sincerity that makes my heart stutter. "I'm sorry."

"You will be. Say it," I demand with a grumble.

"I'll never hide anything from you."

"Not even yourself."

“Not even myself.” I bring the knife down, slicing her shirt open with one swift move, exposing her lace black bra and heaving chest before I do the same with her leggings. Her eyes swing back up, now completely submerging into lust. I slam the knife against the table, wanting to startle her, but she doesn’t even flinch. Her response is nothing more than a look dripping with craving. *She is so goddamn sexy.*

“I’m yours.” It’s not the first time she’s said this, but tonight, the statement almost makes me shoot my load from my already painful dick. With a groan, I spring her breast free, latching my mouth over her nipple. It hardens underneath my tongue as she reaches the hem of my shirt to pull it over my head. When she stares at my bare chest, I unbuckle her bra, then take one of her tits in my hand. It’s the perfect fit for my palm, firm and rolling in my hand like it was made for me. I drive her torso back against the table, her legs still falling from the edge as I take off her black leggings, then I pull her back up. The burning heat of our skin colliding causes a grunt to escape my mouth. She moans when I roll her nipple between my thumb and index finger, my mouth moving to her neck with a scorching trail of kisses.

“You are mine, Lexie,” I huff against her damp skin.

“I’m yours.” I don’t even know why I feel the need to claim her, why I’m desperate to hear her repeat those two words over and over again. I just know they have never made me feel as high as I feel now, riding a wave of ecstasy without even being an inch inside of her.

Desperate to taste her, I unbutton my jeans, then shove them over my hips with my boxers before they pool on the floor. She’s sitting on the table, wearing nothing but her little thong and a horny grin haunting her face. I lick my lips at the sight of her waiting for me in anticipation.

"You want this, baby?" I grab my cock, and she replies with a nod as her lips part. Her arms stretch, wanting to pull my hips closer to her core, but I quickly grab the knife from beside her. She freezes at my move, holding still with her legs spread.

"Don't move," I order.

Tauntingly, I run the tip of the blade over her collarbone and her eyes close, her head falling back as if she's trying to remember how the cold steel feels on her skin. With a searing, slow pace, I drag it down the swell of each of her breasts, igniting a deep moan from her throat, then draw a circle over her belly button. She's relaxed, until I notice her hold in a breath when I reach her freshly shaven bikini line. I tear the fabric up with a single slice, and her eyes shoot open with question, but she keeps her mouth shut, showing me she trusts me. It makes my painfully hard cock twitch, silently telling me no one else will ever be enough for him. It has to be little Lexie Lee from this moment forward.

I lower the tip of the blade, until I reach her clit. Her lips part, her breathing growing shallow as she watches me. Lifting the blade, I press the tip into the wood of the table right in front of the opening of her wet pussy.

"Do you trust me, baby?"

She doesn't hesitate to nod and I smile, coy and pleased, when really I want to thunder like a caveman.

With the flat side of the blade, I slowly move through her folds, and she winces, but it's followed by a moan that makes her toes curl. When I'm all the way up to her clit, I lift it, admiring her wetness shining on it like butter.

Bringing the blade to my lips, I lick it off, a diabolical smile forming when her saltiness falls on my tongue.

"Fuck, you taste so good, baby."

"Share," she orders, and I feel a brow lift. I hold the blade in front of her, but she shakes her head, slamming it out of my hands before she yanks my face against hers. She groans when our tongues meet in hunger, never skipping a beat.

"Greedy little girl, aren't you?"

She hums in agreement, holding on to my cheeks to keep my head at the angle she desires.

"I am," she huffs between kisses. "And I'm yours, so you better fuck me like you mean it."

"You want this?" I rub the tip of my cock through her wetness, and immediately her forehead falls against my shoulder.

"You want me to stretch you wide?"

"Yes!"

I tease her entrance, never going inside but applying slight pressure to her opening with every move.

"How badly?"

She whines, "Desperately!"

31

Lexie

I hold on to his neck, my forehead pressed against his shoulder. His warmth envelops me like a blanket on a cold night, and I know at this moment that no one else will be able to keep me warm ever again. Not like he can.

The last ounce of my sanity had been hanging on by a thread for days and I've been trying to keep my grasp on it. But right here, right now, I'm falling. I am falling hard and deep and I just know I will never completely recover from it.

I'm in love with Killian Wolfe.

The words flash through my mind at the same time he pushes his fat cock inside of me, extending me with a force that makes my head spin. A feral moan echoes through the room, and my skin shivers when I realize it's from me.

"I got you, baby." For the first time, his voice completely calms me. His hand slips into my hair, giving it a tight pull before it falls to my neck. With the palm of his other hand latching onto my hip, he begins to thrust.

"Fuck, you're so wet. But I want you even wetter." His mouth lavishes the sensitive skin of my neck, and I whimper in his hands, wondering if soon I'll pass out from all the nerves that are forming an indescribable high. Every inch of my body feels like it's on fire, the only cure and instigator being the man who's completely merged with my body.

"Kill," I beg, though I don't even know what I'm begging for. My eyes well up, when every time he slams inside of me, a suppressed emotion resurfaces.

Pain.

Fear.

Hope.

Grief.

Joy.

They all run through me in a destructive combination, like a damn hurricane, not giving a damn what's in its path. He was right all along. He's the only one who's been able to make me feel when I've been numb for so long. His eyes make me feel alive, his touch makes me realize I still have a pulse, and my heart decided to beat for him without my consent.

"Kill," I whisper again.

"Sssh, I got you, baby." His soft lips grace the shell of my ear, nibbling and sucking and making me shiver. "You're mine now. *I got you.*" As he breathes his words into me, their meaning hits me right in the heart, as if Cupid had a clear shot, and the waterworks that I've been holding back until now crash and release. He pushes me into a blissful oblivion, deeper and deeper, tears now rolling freely down my cheeks. This man is cracking me open, body, mind, and soul, and it's as painful as it is beautiful.

"Don't let me go, *please*." My lips find his, longing to feel him as close as possible. Our chests collide when I wrap my arm around his neck, like he's my lifeline in the darkness of my turmoil. He doesn't realize I mean don't *ever* let me go, but right now I settle for this moment.

"I won't, baby." He pushes my back against the cold table, holding my neck so he can keep up the strength with every powerful thrust. My eyes roll to the back of my head, unable to keep up with the fire forming in my core. When his thumb circles my clit, I arch my back, crying out from pleasure. Killian Wolfe is the one people fear and I always understood why. There is a permanent glare on his face, snarl on his lips, and devilish look in his eyes, but it's insignificant compared to the way he touches me. There is a level of confidence in every single stroke of his hand, combined with a gentleness that is indescribable. This man is ruining me with everything he's got, and I'd be begging him to if he wasn't.

"Fuck, Alexandra. What do you do to me?"

"It's Lexie," I huff, snapping my eyes open to him. "It's *Lexie*."

Alexandra is the girl of the past now, the one that no longer exists.

I'm Lexie now.

A smirk slides into place as his eyes lock with mine. "Come for me, *Lexie*. Let go, baby."

I focus my attention back to the sensations building between my legs, my pants growing more shallow by the second as he moves his thumb over my bundle of nerves. First slowly, with a slight pressure, but when my moans become uncontrollable, he gives me what I need.

"Fuck!" I scream. His cock fills me up like it's made for me and when a tidal wave of rapture slams through me, I black out for a split second. In that blink of an eye, it's as if my soul leaves my body, floating in purgatory.

"Oh, damn," Killian grunts, grabbing my hips as he picks up the pace of his thrusts. My muscles feel heavy, and I bite my lip, wanting to experience every time he slides in and out of my walls as he hunts his own peak. When I come back to my senses just a little, my eyes catch the features in his handsome face tense, his jaw twitching before he throws his head back. A feral grunt erupts from his lungs when he releases his cum inside of me and my lips curl with pride. He pumps a few more times, then holds still, panting.

My hand lands on his happy trail, feeling the urge to touch him, and when our eyes lock, a smirk tugs on his cheeks. With his cock still fully seated inside of me, he leans over, his thumb brushing my jaw as he brings his lips closer to mine.

"You destroy me, little Lexie."

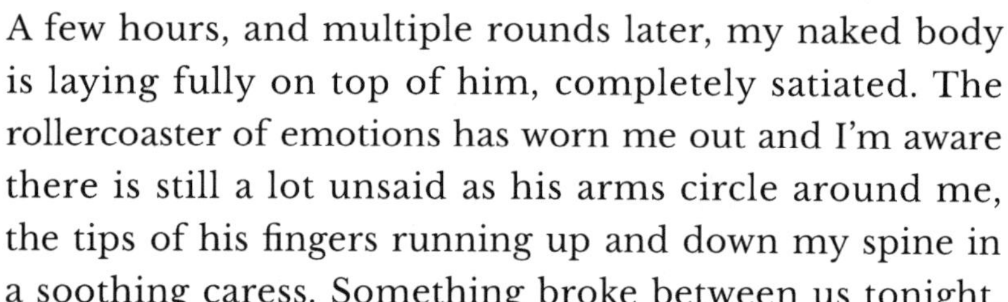

A few hours, and multiple rounds later, my naked body is laying fully on top of him, completely satiated. The rollercoaster of emotions has worn me out and I'm aware there is still a lot unsaid as his arms circle around me, the tips of his fingers running up and down my spine in a soothing caress. Something broke between us tonight.

Like we'd built a block tower together, then someone ran through it without a care in the world. In the same hour, we managed to make a new start, but we still fear someone will destroy whatever it is we're building. I can feel it lingering in the air like a fog. I want to get rid of it, but the thing is, he's the only one who can fix it. He's the only one I can build that tower of trust with, and I know it.

"Does your mother have ties to the Russian mob?" His lips brush against my hair.

"Why are you asking?" I keep my ear pressed against his heart. I like hearing his heartbeat. It shows his humanity, the one he's trying to hide.

"Her last name is Kulakov."

"I know." Of course, I know. My mother talked about her Russian name with pride. A life that has always felt like miles away because we only heard about it in stories. "What has that got to do with the Russian mob?"

"Your mother was the heir to the biggest oil company in Europe. The one that's known to be close to the Russian mob."

I jerk my head up, resting my chin on his chest. Unlike a few hours ago, his eyes are now calm and free from suspicion, and I feel my chest constrict with relief.

"She rarely talked about her childhood. All I know is that her brother was murdered, and my grandmother disappeared around the same time. She never saw her again. It's why she stayed in Boston. She didn't have anything to get back to." When I recall the story, I realize my mother and I are pretty alike. She had to leave everything behind, starting a new life because there was nothing left for her in Russia. I know she had a hard time with it, missing her family and not knowing where her mother was. But if she was able to start over, so can I, right?

"You think that has something to do with their deaths?" I can hardly believe my mother had connections to the Russian mob, because I never noticed anything out of the ordinary. After twenty years in the states, my mother was more American than Russian.

"No," Killian discloses. "But if you are of interest to the Russian underworld, I want to know." A lingering kiss lands on my forehead, building a flutter in my stomach.

"I don't know. *I swear.*"

He smiles at my firm tone, brushing his thumb over my cheek. "I believe you."

Another rush of relief settles me, knowing tonight could've gone completely differently. I know what I feel for him, and deep down I know he feels it too, but if anything, it has become clear in the last few weeks how the only thing that matters to him is his family. I'm not his family. The thought hurts, but I get it. I just want him to be able to trust me. I wouldn't betray him. Not when he's the only thing keeping me sane and alive right now.

"Kill?"

"Yeah?" He rolls us so that my back is pressed against the table, and he leans over me to look into my eyes. My emotions flare up again when he looks at me with affection, a gaze I thought I wasn't ever going to see anymore when he burst through the door earlier. It was eerie, and it made me realize I've never truly seen his anger before tonight. I feel sorry for the ones who have ever been up against him and thought they stood a chance. We might not have a future, but I want to make sure I'll never be on the receiving end of that again.

"I didn't tell you, because to me, it really doesn't matter. Maybe a year ago I would've thought differently, but I don't give a damn now after everything that happened."

He dips his chin, bringing his lips to mine. His kiss is warm, comforting, and sweet enough to curl my toes.

"I believe you, *Alexandra*." I smile at the use of my full name, knowing he does it to please me.

"My mother always called me Alexandra. She spoke it with not an ounce of an accent, making it easy to forget she was Russian. But she couldn't hide her Russian tongue when she was mad at me. It always made me chuckle."

"She didn't speak Russian to you?"

"No. Strictly English. If she didn't make Pelmeni every month, have vodka in the fridge year-round, and have matryoshkas sitting in the window, I wouldn't even know I was half Russian."

"What's Pelmeni?"

I moan, thinking about the last time I had Pelmeni, my mouth watering. "Pastry dumplings, filled with minced meat. It's nothing special, but my mother always used fresh thyme and garlic and they were so good."

Now I wish I paid more attention to my mother's cooking, not knowing the least of how to cook the Russian dishes she used to make for us.

"You know I had my first taste of vodka when I was twelve," I add with a grin that reaches my ears.

"No-suh."

"Ya-huh. It was my birthday, and Sofia and I were sneaking around. I knew she had a taste of alcohol before and, like anything she did, I wanted to be like her. She dared me to take a sip."

"And then what?"

"Before I could put the bottle to my lips, my mom walked in. At first we just stood there, scared for whatever was coming, but she just blinked. Then she pulled the bottle from my hands, placed it on the counter and pulled two shot glasses from the cabinet. Sofia and I looked at each other, having no clue what was going to happen. Finally, my mother filled both glasses with one finger, then stepped away with a straight face, nudging her chin at the two shots. We didn't dare to say anything until she said, *"Well? Go on."* Sofia broke our silence, asking if she was serious. You know what she replied?"

He hums in question, amusement audible.

"You're half Russian. Might as well treat you as such."

His chuckle warms me, acting infectious as I join him. "Your mom sounds like a badass."

"She was."

"Did you and your sister like it?"

"The vodka? God, no, it was disgusting. I didn't touch it until I was fifteen after that."

A laugh booms from his chest, vibrating against my ear. I like hearing him laugh. It comforts me, and after the words he spoke, I hope I'll be hearing it forever.

32

Her punch hits my jaw unexpectedly, and my chin rears to the side. It's filled with a power I didn't even know the little thing possessed and instantly, my face starts to throb.

"Motherfucker! That's a first," I hiss, spitting on the floor to check for blood in my mouth. It comes out clean, and I swing my head back to Lexie, who's now staring at me with wide eyes, her hands covering her mouth.

"I'm sorry."

The guilty look on her sweaty face is cute as hell, and pride quickly replaces my foul mood.

"Don't. It's a good sign. You're getting better."

She closes the distance, placing her hands on the small of my back. "I'm so sorry, baby. Do you need me to kiss it better?"

"My jaw? No. But I'm pretty sure you hit me in the groin earlier today."

"Nice try."

"Oh, I'm having your lips wrapped around my cock later tonight, baby."

She arches her brow. "What makes you think that?"

I can't resist her pouty lips and I lock them with mine. "Because we both know you're deep down a dirty little girl, loving it when I make you choke on my cock."

I spin her in my arms, then shove her forward before smacking her ass. "Hit the showers, baby."

She doesn't deny my accusation, just mutters an *asshole*, making me snort with a grin.

"We'll get to that another time, Lexie." She replies by flipping me off, gluing my smirk to my face as I start to put away the gear we used, then hit the showers myself.

Any other day, I'd be joining her for a quicky before we grab some food on the way home, but it's Friday, and Franklin is expecting us for dinner at the mansion. My brother is punctual and though I don't mind pissing him off, I know Lexie does, so I'm putting my desire to press her against the bathroom wall on hold for a few more hours, and fifteen minutes later, we walk onto the street to make our way home. We stroll in silence, getting closer with every step, until finally, I throw my arm over her shoulder, tucking her into my side.

It's a bold move, showing the world exactly who she belongs to, but after our little power-play, all bets are off. I don't give a damn who sees me. I know I should think this through, think about the possible threats it can cause, but I've been a shithead. Every time I hear a voice in my head that's telling me I'm putting her at risk by showing she's one of us in public, but I'm a selfish motherfucker. I know our time is limited and I want to live whatever I have left with her without worry.

"You want to get changed before we leave?"

She snorts, her sparkling blue eyes looking up at me for a brief moment as we keep strolling down the street. "Into what? Another pair of black jeans and shirt?"

"You seriously don't own anything else?"

Her shoulder shrugs under my arm. "When I left, I packed the necessary things. One day, when this is over, I'll get a job, find myself a place to live, and buy myself some new clothes."

I ignore her *'when this is over'*, not even tempted to know what that means, though it has me swallowing uncomfortably.

"Why didn't you bring more?"

"It's not important. They are just clothes. Plus, they don't feel like mine anymore. I'm not the same girl anymore."

"You know I can buy you whatever you want, right?"

"And act like my sugar daddy? No way. It's bad enough that you're ten years older than I am."

"What's wrong with that?" I huff, suddenly feeling old as fuck.

"I didn't say–"

"Alex? Is that you?" A blond boy interrupts as he walks past us. My lips immediately purse in annoyance as we both halt, twisting our bodies to face him. I clench my teeth together, eyeing him up and down. He's wearing washed out jeans, with sparkling white sneakers, and a thick puffy coat covering the rest of his body. His shaggy blond hair makes him look like a tool, but the confident gaze in his gray eyes tells me he's probably the prom king of his year. I instantly decide I don't like him.

"Brad?" I feel her tense under my touch, and she glances up at me with worry in her eyes that pisses me off.

"No-suh!" He takes a step closer, his arms open to take her into his embrace, and I pull her back only an inch, but enough to make him startle a little. His brown eyes meet my greens, and I can see the flash of recognition in his when they slightly widen. I expect him to back off, finding the quickest way to continue on to wherever the fuck he was heading toward, but the boy has more balls than I give him credit for and his gaze falls back on Lexie.

"How are you? Where have you been? Everyone is looking for you!" His concern seems genuine, but it only fuels my need to bare my teeth and tell him to take a fucking hike.

"Errr..." she drags out, clearly uncomfortable.

"We thought you were dead! I'm so sorry for what happened to your family." He rests his hand on her arm with a smile, his expression dripping with sympathy.

"Thank you."

There is a longing in his eyes that snaps my mouth open with a bark. "Who the hell are you?"

Lexie's palm falls on my stomach as she quickly glances up. I can feel her reassuring smile peering through my cheek, but I refuse to look away from the sorry ass teenager standing in front of me. "Kill, this is Brad."

"I don't give a damn who he is."

"We went to school together," she tries again, but I'm fixated on the tool standing in front of me like he knows her. Like he matters to her. I want to throw the stone that's forming in my stomach against his head. Multiple times. Until he's resting on the sidewalk.

"Touch her again and I will break your arm."

"You traded me for him?" He smirks, daring me with a single look.

"Don't, Brad. Just go," Lexie moans, attempting to place her back against my chest, holding me back. I shove her to the side, then grab *Brad's* neck, walking him backwards until he's glued against the brick building to our side.

"You think you're brave, boy?" I lift him by his throat and his cheeks turn red as he struggles to breathe. "You're not. You're stupid. I know you know who I am." I pause when Lexie comes to stand beside me, her hand pushed underneath my shirt to brush over my stomach.

"Kill, please."

"You do, don't you?" I continue, staring into Brad's panicked gaze.

He nods frantically.

"Who?" I demand.

"Wolfe!" It leaves his mouth in a croak, unable to form any more words than that.

"That's right! You know what us Wolfe do to sheep like you? We tear them apart. You're marked now, little shit. You better make sure I never see your face ever again, or you'll be ripped apart." I abruptly let him go and he hunches forward, grabbing his throat. Not wasting any time, he scrambles on his feet, giving Lexie a glare as he peers past me.

"Nice boyfriend you got, Alex!" he shouts, furious.

"I'm not her boyfriend, fuckface!" Grinding my teeth, I stomp toward him, Lexie pulling on my arm. Brad finally grows a brain, running as fast as he can, but I keep going.

"Killian! Please!"

When he disappears around the corner, I come to a halt, taking shallow breaths through my nose like a raging bull, while Lexie keeps a firm grip on my arm. I stand there, contemplating whether to let him walk or not until her touch disappears. Confused, I spin on my heels, then watch her carry her feet away from me at a fast stomping pace.

"Lexie? Baby, where are you going?"

"Home!" she calls out, not even looking back. A little puzzled, I follow her trail, rolling my eyes at the obvious anger that's evident in her entire stance. My own temper settles a little, not understanding where her sudden outburst is coming from.

"You wanna tell me what's wrong, baby?" I ask when we walk into the foyer of my building, and she stops in front of the elevator.

"Nothing."

"Okay, I'm not going to play that stupid game. You tell me what the fuck is going on or you don't. Whatever works for you."

The elevator doors open, and we ascend, her silence answering to comment.

"You're acting like a brat," I tell her when she opens the door to the apartment with her key.

"Well, then it's a good thing I'm not your girlfriend." It comes out in a mutter while she throws her keys on the side table, slogging toward the kitchen.

I'm frozen on the other side of the threshold with a scowl on my face, the door still open wide. The tone in her voice is undeniable, begging me to read between the lines. But it's her stance that still has me working my jaw. The tension lacks, like she's too tired to put up with a fight.

I step through the door, slamming it shut as loud as I can, expecting her to flinch. *Nothing.* Unbothered, she takes a bottle of water from the fridge, bringing it to her lips.

"That's what this is about?" I glare, making my way to the countertop of the island. My palms press against the cold surface, purposely keeping my distance. "Me telling that *tool* I wasn't your boyfriend?"

"That *tool* used to be my friend!" She swings to face me.

"I don't care!"

"Of course, you don't." She has the audacity to roll her eyes at me. I'm waiting for the unease to settle in that always goes hand in hand with her defiance, but it doesn't come.

"What the fuck are you talking about, *little Lexie*?"

"Nothing, Kill." She takes another sip.

"Clearly it's not *nothing* or you wouldn't be here sulking."

"I'm not sulking."

I cock my head at her.

"I'm not!" she shrieks, her eyes this time traveling toward mine with a disappointment that guts me. "This is my life now. *You* are my life now. But I did have a life before that and you don't have to be an asshole to anyone we might run into."

"You said it yourself, you can't be seen."

She gives me a bored look. "And you said it would be fine if we walked home from the gym every day. You knew there was a chance we'd run into someone."

I did say that. Mostly out of selfishness. I don't want her to hide who she is. I want her to walk beside me with that same attitude she gives me every day. I checked if Sullivan was looking for her, but after I learned he thought she fled, I'd become cocky for my own benefit.

"I know what I said. Doesn't mean I want you talking to your ex."

"Who says he's my ex?" she dares.

"The longing look in his eyes and the busted one in yours." Her plump lips are slightly pursed and puts the bottle of water on the counter, then crosses her arms.

"Tell me I'm wrong."

"The new guy asking about the old, not awkward at all." Mocking almost drips from her chin, a ghost of a smile haunting her features and fueling me to school her.

"I'm not your boyfriend, Lexie."

"Trust me, I'm painfully aware of that." She pushes off to stroll past me, but I hold her back with my fingers on her stomach.

"Painfully? You want me to be your boyfriend?"

Her chest lifts as she sucks in a lungful of air, then she swings her glare to me.

"What I want is for you to stop acting like a dick!"

"I'm a dick?" I snap, yanking her against my chest by the front of her neck. "After all the shit I've done for you, I'm a dick?"

"No, but you sure as fuck act like one most of the time." That same disappointment is now ten times more intense, doing all sorts of shit to me as she continues. "Just be a bit nicer, Killian. Would that hurt? I know I'm a silly little girl and up until nine months ago, I didn't know how fucked up the world is. Now I do. And I know you're not one of the good guys. But do you have to treat me like shit the entire fucking time?"

It's like she slams a knife through my heart, but the real kicker? I can't blame her. I keep her on her toes, more than necessary, and she never backs down. She sticks around no matter how much I try to push her away, and I've grown to like it more than I should. I can't tell her that, though.

I move my hand up, pushing a strand of her hair behind her ear. "I don't think you're silly. Just *little*," I tease.

"Funny."

"I can be. Sometimes." I offer her a grin, but she just returns it with a skeptical look. There is a tiredness in her expression that knots my organs together. Her gorgeous blue eyes give me a look of hope. Like she's begging me to tell her it will all get better one day.

"I'm just tired, Kill. I just want to feel safe for ten minutes of the day. To not keep my guard up every damn second."

Fuck, I'm such an asshole. Instinctively, I pull her against my chest, cupping the back of her head. I feel like I've failed her, and I shake my head, trying to snap out of it, but it's useless. I should tell her that this is life. This is what life has to offer; you can take an old estate, redecorate the place, and put up some nice furniture, but it's still falling apart. I can try to prepare her as much as I can, but it won't change a thing. I should tell her that she's on her own, that no one is coming to save her. But before I can do what's the smartest thing to do, I tell her, "You're safe with me, baby."

33

I press a kiss to her temple when we enter the mansion, then slap her ass.

"I'm heading into the office real quick. Go find the girls in the kitchen."

She gives me a coy smile, her level of exhaustion not sitting as clear on her face as before, but it's definitely still there. I follow her as she does as I say, her hips tempting me in a way that heats my body, and when I let my feet carry me toward Franklin's home office, I release the air from my lungs.

I'm objective in most situations, being able to see the best strategy and possible outcome in almost all circumstances. I don't let my feelings get in the way of anything and I'm not the guy you go to if you want something done out of sentiment. I'm not a fixer because I care. But I want to fix it all for her. I want to be responsible for her bright smile and the spark in her eyes. I want them to wake me up every morning like her happiness is reserved for me. And fuck me, up until Brad strolled down the street, I realized I made myself believe it *was* all for me. Now I realize, it's not. She might be smiling for me, but to be fucking fair, there isn't much else for her to smile about.

"What's doing, Kill?" When I set foot over the threshold, Franklin nudges his chin at me, followed by Reign and Connor, both seated in the two chairs in front of the desk. I acknowledge them the same way, then bring myself to the left corner of the office to pour myself a drink.

"Sullivan has to go," I tell them ten seconds later when I spin on my heel with a tumbler in my grip.

"Fine," Franklin says with ease. "But I want that story demolished." The judgmental look he's giving me has me glaring at my youngest brother.

"You told him already?" I ask Reign with accusation in my tone.

"Of course, I did."

Shaking my head, I rear it back to Franklin. "You know I was going to tell you."

"Don't worry about it. I asked Reign if he had any updates, and he told me. I didn't think you were keeping it from me." His pause is long enough for me to furrow my brows together. "Just that you were too occupied to pick up your phone." A smirk forms on his lips and I press my tongue into my cheek.

"What are you saying, *Franky*?"

"I'm saying," he drawls, "that I know what you're busy with and I get it. We've all been there. Hell, Reign is still there."

"Ugh, now you make me sound like a pussy." Reign scrunches up his nose.

"You are." Connor chuckles.

"No-suh!"

"One"—I lift my finger in the air, fixing my attention on Reign before swinging it to Franklin—"ya-huh. And two, I'm not *anywhere* you think I might be."

Franklin tilts his head with a bored look. "You're not spending every free minute you have with a certain perky brunette?"

"No," I huff, offended, before hating my lie. "Yes. For fuck's sake, you know what I mean."

"I do know what you mean, and you know I'm right."

"So what if I spend a lot of time with her? She's living with me." I bring my glass to my lips, my lashes low as I stare into the brown liquid.

"He's in denial." Connor doesn't even try to suppress his laugh. He flat out makes fun of me, his chest shaking more and more as he meets my glare. My other two brothers can't hold back their devious grins, but at least they still have the decency to make an effort to hold their amusement back.

"Look, I don't know what's going on in that thick head of yours"—I point my finger at Connor when he finally settles down a bit—"but I'm not whipped like the three of you. I care about Lexie, yes, I do. But that's it. Ain't no questions being popped, or titles being given out."

"Bullshit," Reign couches, his fist in front of his mouth.

"How long do you think it will take for him to realize?" Connor chimes in.

"Realize what?!"

"At least a few more weeks. He's a stubborn ass. She probably has to almost die or something." Reign snickers.

“I’m going to murder both of you.” I lift my gaze to the ceiling, then let it travel to Frank to ignore the two chuckleheads grinning at me. “*Anyway*, I need Sullivan dead. Soon.”

“You got my approval, but be careful, Kill. This is the Chief of Police we’re talking about. You need to make sure nothing trails back to us. I want to be able to stand at his funeral with a straight face,” Franklin warns.

“On it.” I slam the rest of my drink down my throat to place it back on the liquor tray, then pull out a document from my inside pocket while the liquid burns all the way to my stomach.

“Something else,” I tell Franklin, setting the document in front of him.

“What’s that?”

“I want this in her name.”

He picks up the piece of paper, his eyes tracing the words, line for line.

“Is this her parental home?”

“Ya-huh.”

“But isn’t she the rightful heir, then, anyway?”

“She is,” I explain, “but because technically she’s missing and presumed deceased by the local law enforcement, it will take a few weeks before they’ll clear the property and have everything cleaned after she turns up. I want her to be able to get home as soon as this is done.”

“Denial.” Reign coughs again and I meet his smirk with a look that comes straight from the Devil. Connor’s chortling beside him doesn’t help either, and I’m about to throw something at both their heads.

Ignoring them, I lock eyes with Franklin, whose ghost of a smile is inevitable when he glances at the two tools from the corner of his eye.

"She's been through a lot. I just want her to have a home to get back to when this is over. A safe one." She might not want to stay in Boston, but I want her to have a place she can call home, no matter where she is.

Franklin holds my gaze, both of us trying not to acknowledge how Connor and Reign are pissing me off. He then picks up the piece of paper, holding it in the air.

"I'll have this ready and cleaned up within a week. That's cool with you?"

"Ya-huh, sounds good." It sounds fucking annoying, to be honest. Up until this point, I didn't know how long Lexie would stay with me. Yeah, I know she'll move out eventually, but now that Franklin has hung a timeframe on it, I fucking hate it.

"You sure? You look like someone drank the last of your Royal Blue." Franklin cocks a brow.

"No, I'm good." I'm not even a fucking little good, but the last thing I need is to give my brother more ammo to fuck with my head. Besides, she can't fucking stay with me forever.

Right?

34

Lexie

I stroll out of the bathroom, wearing a towel around my naked body and my hair wrapped in another one, at the same time Killian saunters into the room. When our eyes lock, he stops, his hands tucked into the pockets of his sweatpants, before his eyes rake over me.

"Fucking hell."

"What?" I drop to the bed.

"You look fucking hot. If we didn't have somewhere to be, I'd fuck you senseless right now."

I lick my lips at the thought, then frown when his words sink in. "*We?* We have somewhere to be right now?"

He comes to the bed, covering my mouth with his, then moves his hand between my legs. I moan against his tongue when a finger slips through my wet folds.

"How are you always wet for me, baby?"

He smooths it up and down, a grunt vibrating through his chest when he dips his finger inside of me.

"So. Fucking. Wet." He leans in, his mouth trailing small kisses below my ear. "I skipped supper today. When we get back, I'm going to spread you wide on the kitchen counter and you can be the supper I never had." Another longing kiss falls on my lips before he pushes off of me, turning back around.

I lay on the bed, legs spread, towel half covering my body and a blush on my cheek. I bring myself onto my elbows, lips parted, stunned.

"What the fuck? Are you seriously leaving me hanging like that?"

He glances over his shoulder with a horny grin, pulling his shirt over his head before putting on a new one.

"You want me to take a picture first? It's a fucking sexy one."

"No! What I want is for you to finish what you started."

"Oh, I'll finish it, baby. In a few hours."

I get up, purposely throwing the towel to the floor as I come to his side to grab my clothes from the shelf he freed for me. He quickly dips his chin at my naked body, then continues getting dressed with an amused grin.

"You're an asshole," I mutter, putting on some black lace panties, then moving onto my black jeans. "Getting me all worked up before we head out."

"It's for a good cause."

"There is no good cause to get a girl all hot and horny and then to leave her hanging. It's just a dick move."

He throws me against the frame of the closet, his fingers enclosed around the front of my neck. The warmth of his breath coasting over my ear has my eyes closing immediately, soaking up the energy of his body pressed into mine.

"You know me well enough to know I never, *ever,* leave you hanging. When we get home..." *Home*, I love how he puts *we* and *home* into one sentence. It makes my pussy clench even more. "I will make you beg for more with my tongue rimming your asshole, but right now? Right now, I need you worked up as hell." He takes my earlobe between his lips, softly sucking it before pressing a kiss against the silky skin on my neck. "Now get dressed. We're going on a mission," he commands, then walks out of the bedroom.

Asshole.

He's the biggest mind-fuck there is. To me, in the last few weeks, he's been looking like a superhero more and more every day, but when he opens his mouth, he turns into this villain that has got me completely hooked.

I grew up thinking I'd one day meet my superhero, but it's becoming painfully clear that I've lost my heart to the villain.

***

Twenty minutes later, we're both dressed in all black, sitting in his black Range Rover as he drives through the streets of Boston. I noticed at least two SUVs following behind us in the side-view mirror, and I wonder what is going on, but I haven't asked. No point, since Killian doesn't share if he doesn't want to anyway. So instead, I just sit here, letting the city pass me by.

Once upon a time, I loved this city. I was always proud of being a Boston girl, loved hearing the slang around me walking on the sidewalk and Bruins jerseys when hockey season started. Then my family died, and I hated it. Suddenly, my bright, fun city was now dark, gleaming, and felt like it was suffocating me. But ever since I met Killian, my love for it has been growing back a little day by day. Now, I feel excited to walk the streets again without feeling the need to look over my shoulder. To suck in the atmosphere on a game night. To buy a cream pie at the nearest bakery.

I haven't forgotten his harsh words, acting like a constant reminder that we are not together. He's not mine and I'm not his. But Killian Wolfe has changed me so much over the last couple of weeks, I don't think that will ever be completely true. Part of me will always be his, simply because he saved me in more ways than one.

My eyes narrow in suspicion when we drive onto a street that looks familiar. I sit up, stretching my neck as I take in the houses along the road. I've walked them more than once.

"We're going to Sullivan's? Sullivan is the mission?" I snap my gaze to his. He briefly meets my eyes with a tentative look.

"Are you ready?"

His words ignite a cold shower of nerves raining down on me, producing a rapid heart rate that pumps the blood into my ears like a beating drum.

Am I ready?

Fuck, who even knows. Probably not, but I've been waiting for this day for months. I'm not going to waste another shot to kill the son of a bitch if Killian is giving it to me on a silver platter.

"Fuck yeah, I'm ready!"

He drives into the street before the entrance of the building, then maneuvers the vehicle into an alley on the left before putting the car in park. I cock my head, registering the other two cars doing the same, then swing my head back to him.

The engine turns off and I twist my body to face him. He throws his torso to the back, his fresh citrusy scent entering my nose in the most intoxicating way. Instantly, I feel my heartbeat slow down a little, having him close. I rub my sweaty palms against my jeans, taking controlled breaths to calm my nerves.

"Put this in." He holds up an earpiece that is nothing more than an earplug. "We'll be able to communicate. The rest of the team can only communicate with me, but I'll make sure you're never alone." I take it, putting it in my ear shell, then lift my eyes to the gun he's giving me. It's a little bigger than the gun I've been practicing with, but definitely a better size than the Magnum he gave me in the beginning. I check the magazine, then rest it in my palm to remember the weight of the firearm while it's fully loaded.

"So, what's the plan?" I ask.

"We're going in through the back. Two men will be guarding the front entrance to make sure we don't have any unnecessary witnesses while we make our way up the staircase. When we reach his floor, we'll secure the entire hall before we get in. Then you do this whatever way you want, okay?"

I nod. His green eyes are looking illuminous in the dark of the night. Weeks ago, they would scare me, staring at me like I'm his prey, ready to be torn apart. But they don't frighten me anymore. Now they bring me comfort, showing me that fierceness I need to gain energy from. He doesn't treat me like a prima ballerina. He treats me like the warrior that I need to be to complete what I started.

"He's home alone, but he's expecting his mistress in thirty minutes. It means we need to be gone before then."

Unexpectedly, he grabs the back of my neck, yanking me to his lips. I can taste the last of his whiskey on his tongue that he swipes through my mouth with an urgency that has my stomach dipping. When he breaks loose, his forehead presses to mine, our noses brushing together.

"You got this, baby." Not another question if I'm ready or if I'm sure. No, only three words that give me the push I need. Three words that tell me he thinks I'm capable of doing this.

I smile. "I got this."

"Let's go."

We both exit the car, and the men in the SUVs behind us follow when we creep toward the back entrance. Every sense in my body is on high alert, but funny enough, there is a tranquility in my muscles that I didn't expect. Like my mind goes into full hunter mode, fueled by the adrenaline that's rushes through my veins.

With light feet and a quick pace, we make our way up the stairs, guns drawn as we keep close to the wall, avoiding the stairwell as much as we can. With every new floor, my heart beats faster until I see the number five on the door of the next level, knowing this is Sullivan's floor. Grinding my teeth, I feel anxious to burst through his door. Whatever fear I still had tucked away is now replaced by a rage that flares up the closer we get.

With his back against the wall, Killian opens the door, glancing into the hall before he signals we can go. The floor is made out of brown marble, showing the luxury of the building, and it only increases my anger. This bastard is living his life in comfort, not even batting an eye that he's a fucking murderer.

When we reach the front door of apartment 402, I'm completely pumped.

"You're up, baby." Men shuffle past me, to create an armed wall on both sides of the hallway, and I tear my gaze up to Killian, waiting for him to make the next move. But he holds still, giving me a look filled with anticipation. The corners of my mouth drop when it hits me.

"You're not coming with me?"

His lips stay pressed together, though they form a small smile.

"This is your revenge, baby. You don't need me."

Suddenly, panic tightens my chest, and I frantically shake my head.

"I do! I need you! I can't go in by myself," I whisper-shout, shooting him an incredulous expression.

"Yeah, you can." He takes my face in his hands. "Remember that first night? You were ready to go in and blow a bullet through that bastard's head."

"I was stupid!" I interrupt.

"Yeah, you were. But you had the confidence to do it anyway. This time, you're prepared. You trained for this. *You got this.*"

"Kill..."

"Ssh, *you got this,* little Lexie. I'll be right here. I can hear everything you say, and if things go south, I'll be right behind you."

I keep wagging my chin.

"I'm right here, baby. You're not alone. But you need to do this without me. *For them.*"

A tear runs to my cheek when my sister pops into my mind. The memory of her bright smile almost blinds me, and I close my eyes with a deep breath. Then I use the grief to fill me with the motivation I need before I open my eyes again. There is pride in his green gaze as he looks down at me, and finally, I nod my head.

"You got this," he repeats, pushing a loose strand of hair behind my ear.

"I got this."

"Good girl," he says, holding up a bobby pin. "Go show that motherfucking pig he shouldn't have messed with Lexie Lee." Our lips lock one final time and at the same time I pull the pin from his rough fingers. His confidence in me heightens my own and, deciding there is no better time than now, I move my body past him. On autopilot, I take the final steps until I'm in front of the door, then squat down to level my eyes with the lock. Like YouTube taught me, I work the lock, but my shaking hands have me dropping the pin. Twisting my head toward him, I blindly pick it up.

"*You. Got. This,*" he mouths once more.

I purposely blow out a breath, putting in my best effort to concentrate and fully focus on the task ahead. It takes me only five more seconds before the door springs open and my vengeful attitude returns in its full glory.

Bringing my gun up, I fully swing it open, glancing into the empty parlor. My mind runs on overtime, contemplating the next move, and boldly, I slam the door shut. The loud thud makes me wince for a split second, but when I hear movement coming from one of the bedrooms, I smile at the wanted effect.

"You're early, kitten." His gruff voice grows in volume with every word, telling me he's coming closer, and I keep my gun up high. "What the—? Who the fuck are you?"

He halts, taking me in from head to toe. I've only ever seen him in pictures, but he looks even more like a douchebag in real life. His beer belly is pressed disgustingly against his dress shirt, a trimmed greasy beard covering his jaw. It's weird to me that the Chief of Police looks like he's unable to run after crooks and criminals, but then again, he clearly doesn't face the hardships anymore when you look at the smug grin on his face.

"Please tell me you don't call your mistress *kitten*," I mock. My fear vanishes into thin air, knowing with every fiber of my being that I'm better than the piece of shit in front of me.

"Don't make me ask you again, little girl." He tries to sound unimpressed, but I can detect the uncertainty in his tone.

"Or what?"

"Do you know who I am?" He takes a step forward and I tilt my gun a little, aiming at his head, just enough to make him freeze again. "I'm the Chief of Police. You don't want to shoot me. If you do that, you either spend the rest of your life in jail or the Boston Wolfes will hunt you down."

I snicker. "The Wolfes, huh?"

He hums.

"I'm not afraid of the Wolfes."

"Then you're prettier than you are smart."

"Maybe." I shrug. "But I'm also determined to get my revenge. To let your life flash in front of your eyes before I end you like you've done to my family."

His dark eyes suddenly spark in recognition, then he lifts the corner of his mouth into a lopsided grin.

"Those eyes. You really are a stupid little girl. I thought you would be well on your way to Florida or something, Alexandra Lee."

"I really wish everyone would stop calling me little, because I doubt you'll be calling me little when I blow your brains out of your skull."

"You and what army?" His waiting attitude is gone in the blink of an eye and my gun fires as he leaps for me. I don't have a chance to fight back as I'm knocked on my ass by his bulky frame, watching my gun sliding over his tile floor from the corner of my eye.

"Shit! Lex, are you okay?" Killian's panicked voice huffs in my ear while Sullivan punches me in the face. My skull bounces off the floor from the force of his hit, causing a splitting pain through my head. My world goes spinning, and the fear creeps back into my bones when he lifts me onto my feet by my jacket. Like a ragdoll, he throws me through the room, slamming me against the wall.

"You little bitch! What exactly did you think you were going to do, huh? Kill me?" His chuckle is diabolical and for some reason, I know it's a chuckle my father once heard.

"Baby, talk to me," Killian says.

Sullivan wraps his hands around my neck, hoisting me from the floor, my legs dangling below me as I struggle in his grip. The smell of cigars, combined with a spicy cologne attacks my nose, while I try to pry his fingers from my throat. I will forever have this scent engraved on my brain and all I can think of is how I don't want this to be the last thing my nose will register as I gasp for air.

"You were just as stupid as your mother." My eyes widen at the mention of her. "Oh, you didn't know?" He snickers. "She came to me, demanding I leave your father alone. But he was talking like a damn chatterbox. He just wouldn't shut up."

I try to buck my hips in an attempt to jam my knee into his rib, but he doesn't even budge.

"When I think of it, your family is pretty stupid. Or should I say *was*?" he taunts with an evil smirk.

The air starts to evaporate from my lungs, and even though I'm freaking out internally, I'm losing energy to help myself.

"Lexie! Goddammit!" I hear Killian in my earpiece, but it's all drowning out because of the lack of oxygen. I'm not able to remember even a little of what Killian has taught me in this moment, and I slowly feel my consciousness slipping away. My parents' faces flash in front of my eyes, followed by my sister, and I'm ready to give up. Despair settles in my chest, but I welcome it. I can't fight anymore. I'm tired. I feel so goddamn tired.

But like lightning in a clear sky, my eye catches Killian bursting through the door. My eyes spring open, realizing I love that face, love that man, too much to say goodbye.

I do my best to focus on him, watching his mouth move.

At first, I can't hear or see what he's saying, but as if I'm breaking through the ice, I suddenly register the way his lips move.

"You got this." There is a fierceness in his eyes that shows his own fear, combined with the desperate urge to help me with his gun pointed at the back of Sullivan's head who barely takes notice of the others joining the party. Killian's men follow his trail, with guns drawn, silently spreading out through the room, but Killian holds up his hand to let them refrain from firing.

"I'm right behind you," he had said.

He wants me to do this by myself.

When our eyes meet again, he's nodding his head, encouraging me, pleading with me, and it's like the sky bursts open. Like he's the sunshine I need to function. To grow. To flourish. *To win.*

Suddenly, my black out ends, and I slam my elbow into the side of Sullivan's neck. He winces, then quickly reestablishes his firm grip on me. I repeat the move, then at the same time, I do it with my other elbow and he hunches over with a deep groan.

"You bitch!"

I waste no time kicking him in the groin. It's powerful, putting every ounce of strength in it that I have left, and he grabs his balls in wailing agony. I push him back as hard as I can, then slide over the floor to reach my gun, scrambling back on my feet, and when he straightens his back, I'm standing in front of him again.

This time, it's different.

This time, I know Killian is right behind me.

35

KILLIAN

The pebbles on the grip of my gun are painfully pressed against my palm. It took every ounce of willpower I have to not blow a bullet through Sullivan's head when he had his greasy paws wrapped around her slender neck. My heart is slamming against my chest so hard it aches, my palms sweaty with fear, and my stomach feels like cement. I almost had a heart attack seeing her this vulnerable in another man's hands and I silently vowed to myself that I will never *ever* see it again. I'm giving her this moment, because I know she needs it and, most importantly, she deserves it. But from this moment forward, every single motherfucker who wants to come near her that doesn't wear the last name Wolfe is a fucking dead man. I will gut them and enjoy every second. I will torture them and laugh at their pain. I will let the entire city know Alexandra Lee is not to be touched or you will face the consequences.

Sullivan fixes his posture, his bushy eyebrows lifting when he sees me and my men, then it's followed by a smug grin.

"Oh, you're in trouble now, *little bitch*."

Lexie glances over her shoulders, locking our eyes for a brief moment.

"I'm not scared of a Wolfe."

"You should be," Sullivan tells her, crossing his arms, and I saunter to her back, pushing my gun against her spine. To comfort her, I run my thumb over the back of her neck, a gesture Sullivan is unable to detect.

"Killian." Sullivan nudges his chin at me in greeting.

"Chief."

"Meet Alexandra Lee."

"Oh, we've met."

"When?" His eyebrows knit together.

The smell of her rose shampoo makes me smile and I twirl a strand of her hair around my index finger, then bring it to my nose to suck it in.

"She was standing behind your apartment a few weeks ago. Was determined to kill you."

Sullivan chuckles. "She's a feisty little thing, isn't she? She's young, but I think we can still have a lot of fun with her. I bet she's still tight in all the right places."

I bring my hand over her shoulder, pressing her back against my chest as I place my palm over the front of her neck, resisting the urge to bare my teeth. Bringing my lips flush with her ear, I press a kiss to her shell, then slowly start to leave a trail of open-mouthed kisses down her neck.

"Oh, she's a lot of fun. Tastes good too." Lexie relaxes under my touch, but never lowers her gun.

In the meantime, Sullivan's grin grows wider by the minute, clearly unaware she isn't afraid.

"Lower the gun, girl. It's over."

"You're right, Sullivan. It's over," I mock, then shift my body a little to point my gun at him. It takes a minute before it clicks in his head, and I watch his face fall in horror.

"What the hell is going on? You're working with her?" His jaw drops in a stunned pause. "We made so much money together! You betrayed me for her."

"What can I say? She's still tight in all the right places." I shrug, throwing his words back at him.

He stays still, the cogs turning in his head as he tries to decipher the situation.

"You stupid motherfucker. What is she offering you? What does she hold against you?"

"What makes you think I'm holding anything against him?" Lexie questions with renewed spirit in her tone.

"Because the Killian Wolfe I know would never fuck with business!" Sullivan snarls.

"Maybe you don't know the real Killian," she adds.

"And you do?" He huffs, then shakes his head with a chortle.

"Shut the fuck up, Sullivan. Don't make this harder than it is. I know your fuck buddy is on her way over here, so please make sure I don't have to kill her because you wanted to chat for another minute. Get your fat ass on the couch." I jerk my head toward the piece of furniture. Reluctantly, he takes some sideway steps, still scowling at our guns before lowering his body onto the black leather couch.

"How do you wanna do this, baby?" I pull her flush with my chest, my nose nuzzling her neck. She leans into me, my eye catching a mischievous grin slipping onto her freckled cheeks.

"Part of me wants to torture him, make him suffer." She breaks our connection, stepping toward the couch until she stands directly in front of him and with a single signal, I let all my men point their guns on Sullivan's thick head.

"But there is also a bigger piece that just wants to blow a bullet through his thick skull. Make the world a better place with a single shot and with as minimal energy as possible."

Her posture is fierce, her brown ponytail showing off the slenderness of her neck. Though she's still dressed like the eighteen-year-old I met that first night, she's changed so much. She might be young, petite and unassuming, but she's a warrior, showing more courage than I've seen carried by most men.

But people always underestimate how quickly the world can flip on its side, changing every single thing that happened a second before. I'm not any different, and right when I think this is a done deal, and that my girl will settle her score and tomorrow the city of Boston will need a new Chief of Police... in the blink of an eye, he kicks her feet from underneath her, catching her on top of him.

"No!" My roar booms through the room, the tension making my muscles go rigid. Now I understand when people say their heart stops, because I can literally feel how it stops beating. It's like someone throws a bucket of ice on top of it, the organ being too shocked to keep pulsing.

Sullivan pressing a small caliber against Lexie's temple, and I feel like a fucking dumbass.

Fuck, I should've checked him first.

"Drop the gun, sweetie," Sullivan shouts against her ears.

"No!" She grinds her teeth, refusing to let go of the gun in her palm.

He pushes his gun harshly against her head, making it jerk at the motion. Her navy-blue eyes don't hold an ounce of fear, but when they lock with mine, I'm sure she can see mine shining through. My life has never been a walk in the park or a white picket fence with Sunday night dinners, but unlike my brothers, nothing has ever truly created an angst I couldn't overcome. But this time, knowing that asshole has her life on a thread, I fully sense the fragility of life and it's terrifying the shit out of me.

"Drop the gun, you stupid bitch!"

"No!"

Lexie squirms on his lap, showing a small stroke of her stomach, while Sullivan's eyes grow more enraged by the second.

"Better make her cooperate, Wolfe! Or I'll blow a bullet through her head right now!"

"Lexie! Stop!" The thought alone shifts me into survival mode. "Baby, stop!"

She stills at the sound of my voice, her glare softening when our eyes tangle again. I watch her chest move up and down softly, her entire body still draped over her biggest enemy. She's completely surrendered to his will, and my mind works quickly to find the solution to get her out of there. It takes me a few moments to push my fear away, knowing it will only cripple me, and I use it as fuel to control my rage. *He will not win.* The Wolfes have never failed to defeat an enemy. I'm sure as fuck am not going to stop now.

"Trade me, Sullivan."

He arches a brow, a lopsided grin forming.

"No way. Killian Wolfe fell in love with this perky little thing. Is she really that tight?" His hand snakes underneath her shirt, widening Lexie's eyes as he lowers his fingers into her jeans. "She does feel soft, but does she feel soft everywhere?"

"Touch her and I swear, Sullivan, I'll make you suffer until dawn. I don't care how quickly she wants you dead, but you touch what's mine and I will make you wish death comes sooner than it will arrive." My voice is calm and composed, but really it's taking everything in me to not pull that trigger and blow his brains out.

With a smirk, he dips it even lower, and she bucks her hips. "Na-ah, honey." He knocks the gun against her head, and she cries out, her body going limp for a moment. Her jeans move up when his hand covers her core, and my stomach feels like it's harvesting a stone.

When he pulls out, he brings it to his nose, and I clench my jaw.

"Hmm, smells good."

"Trade me." I take a step forward, desperate to find some kind of upper hand. The evil grin that splits his face marks my mistake. I showed him my cards.

"Well, I'll be damned. You really are in love with her, aren't you?"

"Trade me, Sullivan. A dead Wolfe will give you even more respect than you have now."

He chuckles while shock creeps into Lexie's gaze. "Killian Wolfe has finally turned soft."

"There is nothing soft about Killian," Lexie sasses.

"Oh, you like taking his cock, sweetheart? You do, don't you? I bet you're a dirty little slut."

"Trade me," I growl.

"I wasn't born yesterday, Killian. Your brother will kill me before I can even find a ride out of Boston." He lifts both of them off the couch, his arm firmly around Lexie's waist, the barrel never leaving her temple.

"But you can be my leverage out of here. I'll trade you. You can have the little bitch. I want you so you can tell your big brother he'll see you again when I'm safely in Mexico."

"Fine. Just let her go."

"Put your gun on the floor."

I do as he says, squatting down, then get back on my feet with my hands up in the air.

"Killian, no," Lexie pleads.

"Turn around," Sullivan barks.

Obeying, I turn my back to him. I hear him shuffle closer, my men all giving me looks in anticipation with clenched jaws. They are ready to turn him into a sieve, but I can't risk Lexie's life. I feel they are close, and I hold back the temptation to glance over my shoulder. Lexie is shoved against the floor with a shriek at the same time Sullivan wraps his arm around my neck, followed by the cold steel of his gun against my cheek.

"No!" Lexie reaches for her gun, then gets up in one swift move that has me breathing out in relief at her spirit. "Killian, what are you doing?" It's like we switched places, her blue eyes now laced with pure angst. She keeps her gun high, ready to shoot, but the insecurity that drips from her face tells me she doesn't dare to pull the trigger now that Sullivan is using me as a human shield.

"It's okay, baby."

"He will kill you!"

"I'll be fine."

"Where is your car?" Sullivan barks in my ear.

"Out the back." My words are drowned out by the shot that ricochets through the room, chased by dry wall dust falling on top of our heads.

"Don't you dare move, Sullivan!" Lexie's gaze is murderous, filling my heart with pride when I register how he tenses behind me.

"What are you gonna do? Shoot me? You can't do that without hitting your boyfriend."

She finds my eyes, a determined look in hers. "I can make it," she says with confidence.

I feel myself smiling, knowing she can. It's a big risk, but I taught her everything I know and I have no doubt in her skills.

Sullivan moves us another step to the side.

"Don't *fucking* move, asshole!"

He halts.

"You destroyed my life!"

"If your father published that piece, it wouldn't be just my head that was going to roll. The Wolfes would've been locked up like animals! You know he's just as much the enemy as I am!" Sullivan snarls back.

"Maybe, but you made this decision. You get to live with the consequences." A diabolical grin washes over her face right before she locks her gaze with me again.

"I can make it," she repeats.

She's so beautiful. She stole my heart from right under my nose, long before I realized I have one. I thought it slipped out of my hands when my first love decided I wasn't enough for her to stay in this world, but turns out it was never lost. It was just numb. Playing dead until the right person decided to poke it alive.

"I'll make you a deal, Sullivan," Lexie continues, keeping her blues tangled with my greens. "Let go of him now, and I'll make sure the Wolfes give you a headstart of an hour. Enough time to pack a bag and get the first Greyhound out of here. Maybe you'll even have luck on your side and you'll actually get to start over before Killian and I find you." Her smirk is lopsided, and though my situation is far from comfortable, considering I have a gun against my temple, I can't help dragging my teeth over my lip with desire for her. The fear I felt when she was in my position is completely demolished, knowing she's right.

She can make it.

"Not a chance in Hell," I bark before Sullivan can reply. "This was her revenge, *Chief*. It was never about me and frankly, I don't care if you live or die. But you made one vital mistake."

"What's that?" His voice is gruff and insecure.

"You touched my girl. *Nobody* touches my girl. She clearly is a better person than I am for wanting to give you a headstart. But *you* signed your death certificate the moment you touched what is *mine*. Now I just want you bleeding on the floor." I smile, exchanging a look with Lexie that says it all.

"What are you talking about?" Sullivan sounds panicked. "You're still the one with a gun against your head."

"I know. But she's a better shot."

"Goodbye," Lexie adds.

I barely see her finger move before the ringing of the gun sounds in my ear. It makes me wince only an inch, right before Sullivan's grip on me loosens and I feel blood spatter land on my skin. My entire team takes a step forward, their guns aimed and cocked as I hear him fall to the floor with a loud thud, but I don't even bother to look over my shoulder.

"I told you I could make it." Her blue eyes are beaming at me through the blood spatters that landed on her face, my heart beating in my ear like a joyful drumroll at the sight of it.

"I never doubted you for a second."

"I killed him." I expect her to hit a state of shock any second now, but she just sounds upbeat and exited, as if it hasn't land yet.

"I know." I give her a tentative gaze. "How do you feel?"

She licks her lip, jerking my cock awake. "Like I want to kiss you."

"Not sure what you're still waiting for."

Her feet move forward at a fast pace before she leaps through the air, wrapping her legs around my waist. I catch her with ease, one hand holding her hip while the other snakes into her soft brown hair.

"I want you to take me home and make me beg for more," she says, right before her plump lips crash against mine.

36

Lexie

I thought seeing the life slip out of a human being would do something to me. That it would ignite a sense of guilt and dread that would forever haunt me, even though I never doubted my actions for one second.

But it never did.

I didn't feel anything when I blew that trigger through his head. No guilt. No dread. And no satisfaction either.

It didn't give me the closure I needed, but as soon as my gaze landed on Killian's blood-spattered face, I knew I didn't need closure anymore.

I just need him.

The relief that crept into my bones was for him instead of my family. My heart pounded against my ribcage in excitement, pride and joy at seeing his arrogant grin lifting his cheeks. It was immediately followed by a craving that has been building to agonizing proportions since we got back into the car. He grabbed a wet towel from the kitchen and washed my cheeks with so much affection it almost made me burn out of my skin. Every move was thoughtful as he kept our eyes locked and I felt my desire for him building bigger and bigger with every minute that passed. When he was done, he washed his face with a bottle of water before he drove us back home, the tension growing thicker with every yard that passed. It had me uncomfortably shifting in my seat, making it hard as hell to not touch him by keeping my hands on my lap. We keep riding the silence as we descend up to his floor, but before he can open the front door, I can't take it any longer.

I launch myself at him, locking my mouth with his in a bruising kiss while wrapping my legs around his waist. Eagerly, he tucks me closer to his chest, pushing his tongue against mine with firm strokes. He moans against my throat, and the sound makes my pussy clench. We fall through the door with an urgency that has us ripping off each other's clothes while our lips never disconnect, and by the time he places my ass on the dining room table, I'm only wearing my black jeans and boots. I lick my lips, staring at his bare chest, and he presses his lips together as he takes me in. His eyes slowly roam over every inch of my body, as if he wants to remember every swell and birthmark, while I wait in anticipation. His chest is bare, looking like it needs to be touched, and I reach out to yank him to me.

"Fuck, Lexie." He places his mouth over my nipple, massaging my breast in his palm as he keeps me still by my hip.

"Take everything off," he commands while leading by example. I wait with parted lips, watching how he peels every last piece of clothing off his body until he's completely naked in front of me. I want to say like an Adonis, but Killian is so much more than that. He's more like Aries, God of War. A rebel cunning enough to bring cities to their knees.

"I'm waiting," he tuts with a slight glare that turns me on even more.

I slide off the table, then slowly unbutton my boots before kicking them through the room. My eyes never leave his, and I can see the appreciation crawl into them as I unbutton my jeans. With tentative moves, I push the fabric over my hips, until it pools around my ankles and I step out of it.

"Where do you want me?" My eyes are hooded, accompanied by a seductive smile.

"On the table. Hands and knees."

I feel my eyebrows move to my hairline, and I blink in surprise, but when he keeps his straight face, I know he's serious. Wanting him anyway I can, I do as I'm told, turning my back so I can climb onto the table. My knees and palms barely touch the cold wood before I feel two wet fingers move up and down my dripping pussy. I'm always ready for this man, but tonight, it's on a whole different level. It's like I want him to own me, to tear me apart and take care of me after. My hips jerk at the slippery feeling of his fingers through my inner lips, and I let out a cry of pleasure.

"You've been waiting for me to fuck you since we left, haven't you?"

"Yes," I admit. His touch never slows, already building my frenzy with his warm breath close to my core.

My back arches, bringing my ass up in the air, as I lean forward on my elbows with a loud moan.

"Hmm," he muses, "you smell like dinner." He latches onto my pussy, playing with my entrance before I feel him trail up. A whimper falls from my lips when his tongue swirls around my asshole in slow and thoughtful strokes. The sensation is completely new and overwhelming, and all I can think of is how I want more. How I want him to fill me everywhere, taking anything he will give me.

"Such a sexy little hole. Still tight and fresh for me to break in. Have you ever been fucked in the ass before, Lexie?" His tongue dives in, and I raise my chin at the ceiling.

"No!" I moan, my body jerking at the sensation.

"Do you want me to?"

"Yes!"

"Oh, I will, but we'll ease you into that. Right now, I just want to play with every hole you have."

"Please, Killian. Keep going," I moan. "Don't stop. Don't *ever* stop." His touch feels too good, and I slowly slip into a state of euphoria that makes it hard for me to keep up. His thumb is rubbing my soaking wet pussy, while two fingers slide into my core as he keeps working my asshole with his tongue. My body feels like it's about to pass out and I don't know what to do with this mind-blowing experience as I squirm on top of the table.

"Keep yourself up, baby. I haven't had my fill of you yet."

"Please," I beg, dying for him to drop me over the edge, but he keeps going like I'm the elixir of life. "Please, make me come, baby. Make me come, Killian."

His grunts vibrate against my wet flesh when he lowers his mouth, his nose nuzzling my perineum. “No, I’m not done yet.”

The softness of his tongue keeps licking my folds, each flick of the muscle more torturous than the other. He keeps going with an eagerness that has me believing he’s enjoying this more than I am, groans and moans humming against my core.

“You taste so damn good, baby.” He takes my clit between his lips, gently sucking the sensitive nub at a steady pace. “You feel that, baby? I want your honey in my mouth.”

My forehead falls against the cold tabletop when I feel how slowly, but resolutely, he pushes me into a rapture that has me crying through the house like an agonized demon. The rush that rips through me is intense and harsh, but at the same time, divine and out of this world. Even if there was any doubt left if Killian Wolfe ruined me for another man, this is the final shove I needed. He speaks to my body like it’s an extinct language and he’s the last human alive to be able to translate. He makes my body hum in a vibration that’s undetectable for anyone else, and I don’t think I’ll ever be able to live without it ever again.

His mouth covers my entrance, and I revel in the feeling of him sucking up my juices, the popping of his lips making me feel like the most desirable creature on earth while I ride out my orgasm until my knees buckle underneath me. With my ass hanging on the edge of the table, his chest falls over my back while he rubs his hand over my drenched pussy. My cheek is pressed against the surface, completely spent as I enjoy the lasting sensation of his hands on my body.

"You know you look even sexier completely worn out by me?" he whispers in my ear. "You make me crazy, baby. I've been wanting to bury myself inside of you since the moment you blew a bullet through that bastard's head. I need you, Lexie. I need you hard."

"Then take me."

"I own you." He growls his claim, and my heart purrs in response as he aligns his hard cock with my entrance.

"You own me." I don't even have to think about it. The words leave my lips like I don't even have a choice. Killian Wolfe owns my body, mind, and soul. His dark soul scared me at first, but I know now it matches mine. He's my match made in Hell, simply because Heaven is no place for us.

He shoves his shaft deep inside of me, a shriek erupting from my throat when he hits my wall. With his hand on my back, he holds me still, the other one fisting my hair as he pulls my head to face the ceiling. My scalp burns from his grip, but it's a pain I welcome, only heightening the sensations as he starts to pump harder and deeper.

"Good girl," he huffs, inwardly making me smile. "You're such a good girl. *My* girl."

He keeps going with force, the table shifting with every thrust, his moans making me bite my lip. I love hearing how I make him come undone. How I'm responsible for the few times Killian Wolfe loses control.

I blissfully lay there on the table like a ragdoll, his cock slamming into me with more velocity with every tension of his muscles. I let him use me like I'm only in this world for his desire and nothing else, because right now, that's all I want to be. I don't want to be Lexie, I don't want to be Alexandra, I just want to be Killian's reason to come undone.

"Fuck!" he roars, and with a rapid amount of pumps, he unloads inside of me. His fingers dig into the skin of my back as he keeps me as still as possible, and I whine at the sharpness of all my nerves underneath.

When his touch relaxes, I hear him pant behind me, a content smile lifting my cheeks. His damp body falls on mine, his weight crushing me a little, but I don't even care.

My mouth opens with a yawn, the fatigue seeping into my veins.

Lips find the crook of my neck, before he moves closer to my ear.

"You're one hot little warrior," he says, flooding my body with another rush of pride, right before he slides out of me, scooping me from the table and into his arms. With his gaze peering with everlasting lust, I hold on to his neck as he walks us toward the bedroom.

"We're going to bed?"

"My warrior needs sleep." He lowers me onto the bed, holding my face in his hands as he drops a lingering kiss on my forehead. Then, he tucks me into the crook of his body, settling his face in my hair. "Sleep, baby. Your nightmare is over."

And with that realization hitting me, I slip into the deepest slumber I can remember.

***

When I wake up the next morning, the bed is empty. But when I reach out, I can still feel his warmth lingering underneath the sheets. With a peaceful feeling, I let the night pass through my mind.

The jerking of the bullet crashing through Sullivan's head flashes in front of my eyes, but it's quickly replaced by the proud look Killian gave me as soon as he landed on the floor.

I didn't even care that he was finally gone, that my family was avenged. All I was focused on was the man standing in front of me. He guided me through my past and now all I want him to be is my future. Anything before doesn't matter. I know I'd been set on leaving town ever since it became me, myself, and I against the world, but leaving Killian doesn't feel right. I don't think I'll ever be safe in this city, though. I expect Sullivan's men to want to retaliate and it's for the best to back my bags and start a new life. I don't want to stay in Boston and look over my shoulder the entire time. It's a thought that's killing my gleeful mood, and I decide to push it to the back of my mind, ready to start a new day. With a smile curling the corner of my mouth, I get out of bed wearing nothing more than panties and a T-shirt from Killian before I stroll into the parlor barefoot.

Killian's back is pressed against the counter, a cup of coffee in his hands as he scrolls through his phone.

"Morning, baby." His eyes catch mine, and I close the distance to stand between his legs with my hands around his waist.

"Morning."

"Do you want breakfast?" He dips his chin, locking his lips with mine.

"Are you breakfast?" I ask, peering up at him through my lashes in a way that conjures a sexy grin from his cheeks.

"Insatiable, are you?"

"You corrupted me." He destroyed me in the best possible way, making me crave for more of his touch every time we're together. A path of kisses caresses my neck, and I move my head to the side to give him more access.

"Hmm, not regretting a thing," he says, tugging me closer to his chest.

"What's this?" My gaze falls on the newspaper sitting on the counter. It's still folded, but I can easily recognize my face on the front page, and I pick it up as he follows my line of sight.

"Your face."

"I see that." I swing my head back to his deep green eyes. "What's it doing in the paper?"

My eyes flick over the words as I read the article that comes with it.

Missing Alexandra found. Yesterday, the Boston PD announced that Alexandra Lee, missing since April this year has been found in healthy conditions. The teenager was believed to be staying at her grandmother's house in Dorchester.

I shake my head. "How?"

"As soon as we left Sullivan, I had someone write an article about your whereabouts." He lifts his palm to cup my cheek, his gaze boring into mine with an affectionate look. "You're no longer missing, baby. You're free to go wherever you want."

My lips part in shock, and I just blink, trying to process what he's saying. Of course I wished it was a possibility, but considering I shot the Chief of Police, I always assumed that I had to run. That I had to take a new identity and start over somewhere fresh. But this changes everything and though it's hard to comprehend, there is a slight jolt of happiness at the idea of staying Alexandra Lee. To not have to bury the legacy of my family completely by also giving up my name.

"I'm free," I croak. "Thank you."

"I got you something else." He takes two steps to the fridge, pulling a piece of paper from underneath the magnet, then hands it to me.

My eyebrows knit together, keeping my eyes tangled with his as I unfold it. Roaming the words, I notice the address, then gasp in shock when I realize what this is.

"The deed to my house? It's in my name."

He shrugs as if it's not a big deal. "I didn't want you to wait weeks before they processed everything. The house is yours. No one will ever be able to take it from you."

"You did this for me?" Tears are pricking my eyes, formed by happiness as I look at the man in front of me in awe. He's one of the biggest criminals in the city, feared by many, avoided by most. But here he is, bending over backwards to help me get back on my feet.

"You can live there for as long as you want," he adds. "Your parents had a small mortgage on it, so I paid it off. You'll never have to worry about a roof over your head ever again. You'll always have somewhere to call home. To come back to if you want."

"What? You didn't."

"It's no big deal."

I should fight him on it, but right now I'm just happy that I can go home whenever I want. I can decide what I want to do with it. I can honor my family and their things. I can find closure when I'm ready, and it's the most meaningful gift he could ever have given me.

"I'll pay you back," I offer.

"No, you won't. Consider it your belated birthday gift."

"Killian." I tilt my head, offering him a grateful smile. "Thank you."

"You're welcome, baby." He turns around, making another coffee while my eyes go over the deed one more time. A heavy weight is lifted off my shoulders and the smile it's causing almost hurts my cheeks.

"So now what?" I ask, glancing at his back.

"What do you mean?"

"What will we do? What will we do now?"

He turns around, holding his coffee in front of his chest as he continues to rest his back against the counter. He's looking like a dream with his light brown hair sitting messily on his head, his five o'clock shadow begging me to rub my fingers through it.

"I guess you go back to your life, and I'll go back to mine. You had your revenge. You have your house. Go. Be a teenager." My smile falls as the words leave him with such a casual tone that it feels like a rain cloud is hovering above me. A frown creases my forehead, at the same time a sharp feeling shocks my heart, and I cock my head.

"I'm hardly a teenager."

"You know what I mean." The realization of the direction of this conversation hits me flat in the face, my cheerful mood completely demolished by the thunder that fills the room.

"And you know what I mean!" I snarl, shaking my head. "Are you breaking up with me?"

His tongue presses against his cheek before he snaps it shut with a sharp jaw. There is an anger flaring in his luminous eyes, but they are laced with conflict. I close my eyes, preparing myself for the words that will reach my ears next, because I already know what he's about to say. I already know he's about to ruin everything we have. I already know he's about to break my heart.

"I'm not your boyfriend, Lexie."

37

Her lashes fall, her pink lips forming together in a small stripe, and I push the air from my lungs. A tight feeling constricts my stomach as I try to hold my indifferent stance. Her eyes fly open, this time drenched with hurt and pain. Pain I'm causing her. I stare into her teary eyes, and it's breaking everything in me, but I keep my face blank.

"Please, don't do this," she begs, her voice breaking with each syllable.

"Don't, Alexandra." I turn my gaze to the floor. It kept me up all night, holding her in my arms with my nose buried in her hair. I knew by the time dawn would set in, I'd have to let her go. I'm feeling way too much for her and she's already making me cross boundaries that are dangerous in my world. I've known all this time this, *us*, was just a temporary thing, that even though it kills me, I have to let her live the blissful, carefree life that she wants. To find someone who will take care of her, who will see her for the beautiful creature that she is, someone who will keep her out of harm's way at all costs.

In an ideal world, I'd make her mine and keep her close forever. But It's not. This is no fucking fairy tale and there are sure as fuck are no happy endings. Love isn't a forever thing and I'm not a forever man. But she deserves to try and find that. If anyone deserves her happily ever after, it's her.

"It's Alexandra now?" Her tone is poisonous. "Just like that? You're just gonna shove me aside like I'm *nothing*?" My instant reaction is to tell her she's not *nothing*.

She's everything.

But I know telling her that will only make her want to stay even more, so instead I rip off the band-aid quickly and without too many words.

"We both knew what this was." I've never had issues being an asshole. My brothers let me say the things no one wants to hear in every business meeting because I'm the only one that's relentless when shit needs to be done. But this time it's fucking me up. Making me wish someone else could take over and tell her what needs to be said.

From the corner of my eye, I see her head shaking in confusion.

"We're not the same. Not anymore."

"I'm still the same guy!" I shout, flicking my gaze back to hers. Her navy-blue eyes are laced with sadness but filled with anger. The sight of her breaking down in front of me is killing me, and I do my best to push it aside in rage, knowing I don't have any other option.

"Liar!" she fearlessly yells back, narrowing her eyes. "The man that threatened my life in that alley would've never given up his life for anyone else other than his brothers!"

My heart stops and I feel like time freezes, her words hitting me straight in the gut.

"You did that, Kill! You traded your life for mine! You can't deny that you have feelings for me! Whatever it is, I know you feel it too!"

I swallow, unsure what to say. She's not wrong. But I know it doesn't mean shit. I'm not the kind of man you marry and have kids with. I care about her, and I want her to be happy, but I know she'll never be happy with me. I'll never be able to truly give her what she wants. What she deserves.

"It doesn't matter."

"Why not!" She charges me, shoving my chest. With force, I grab her wrists, locking our angry gazes together.

"Because it's not me, Lexie! What do you want from me? A picket white fence? A few babies? Or do you want me to go to parties with you as you live out your teenage years because I'm neither of the two, baby."

"I stopped being a teenager before I met you," she sneers.

I push her a step back, creating some distance between us. "But you don't have to be! Go! Live your life! Finish school! Go to college! Find yourself a boy like Brad!"

"I don't want a boy like Brad! I want *you*!" Tears are rolling over her freckled cheeks, and it's taking everything inside of me to not wipe them away with her thoughts.

"I'm not an option!" I growl.

"Why not!?"

I launch forward, grabbing her neck before pulling her flush with me.

"Because I'm Killian *fucking* Wolfe!" I rumble against her lips, desperate to connect them with mine. I want to say fuck it, and give in to my selfishness. To keep her locked up in my house for my desire only and let her become my warrior princess until we've hit our expiration date. But this girl, she's survived so much. I can't do that to her. I can't let her believe we'll be together forever, that we can build a life and have a family of our own. And I know it's what she wants. It's what every teenage girl wants, isn't it? Eventually, they all want their Prince Charming and a few babies. I'll never be that guy.

I'm the villain.

"You deserve more than the criminal I am!"

She shoots me an incredulous look, like I'm insane. "I don't want more, you asshole! I want *you*! I want to stay with *you*!"

"You'll never be safe with me."

"I'm not asking you to keep me safe." The frustration is etched in her features as she replies with her palms landing on my arms. Her touch burns through my skin and I hold in my breath when I can see the bravery enter her gaze. "I love you, Kill. I'm *in* love with you."

My heart falls to my feet, growing to a proportion I can no longer carry before I slice it into pieces in my mind. I press my teeth together, closing my eyes as I breathe in through my nose. Grabbing her upper arms, I lift my gaze, and I'm met by her hopeful eyes.

I want to feed the hope and tell her we'll be alright. To be weak and give in to my impulse, but instead, I snarl, "And you'll get over me."

I push her off, leaving her standing in the kitchen as I saunter away from her. The walls seem to close in on me, the air too thick for me to breathe.

"You're not even gonna admit it?" she calls out, right before I grab my keys to get the hell out of this place.

"Admit what?" I spin on my heels, howling. "That I want you? That I want to keep fucking you every day for the foreseeable future?"

She snorts, a mix of calm and disappointment settling on her face. Nothing about her attitude would give away her age, because right now she looks taller than I am.

"No, that you love me, *asshole*." There is no malice in her tone, just surrender.

I swallow as I watch her transform right in front of my eyes. Her defiance disappears, along with her rage, and all that's left is defeat. A sight that will haunt me forever, but I know will be the best for her.

"I don't, Lexie," I tell her before I walk out of the door.

38

Lexie

I still remember the day my family died like it was yesterday. When I close my eyes, I can feel the pain that settled into every muscle in my body as I walked out of the door in shock, carrying nothing more than a backpack with some clothes. It was excruciating, almost unbearable, until the numbness settled in and I just started living on autopilot. My need for revenge made me feel anything other than grief, and I vowed to myself that after Sullivan died, I'd make sure no one could ever make me feel like this ever again.

But in came Killian Wolfe. He made me feel alive when I thought I was nothing more than an empty vessel with one last mission in this world. He brought my heart back to life, making me feel all these sensations I never thought I'd experience again. And then he ripped my heart out, leaving me with that same emptiness that I haven't felt in months. He lifted me up to the ultimate high, only to bring me back to the lowest point of all. The point where I feel nothing more than a lost soul. No life. No purpose. No family. *And no heart.*

I knew he was going to destroy me. Ruin me.

But I never knew how literally it was going to be.

For the last few days, I've been staring at the TV, not even turning it on as tears would only stop pouring from my eyes for five minutes at a time, tops. The sadness is overwhelming, and most of the day I just want to sleep, because at least that way I don't have to live with the pain. The house is filled with utter silence other than my sobs and I hate how my childhood home is now tainted with more bad memories. Growing up here, I was a normal teenager, frustrated about silly things, but happy overall. This house represents home and security, or at least it used to. Now the walls look glum, and when I look around me, it feels like the color is sucked out of everything. Like an empty shell, just like me.

With my eyes closed, I try to catch some more sleep, drowning out my thoughts, when the doorbell rings. I slowly open my eyes, the fatigue feeling too much for me to get up as I decide to let it go. It feels like I'm tied down with bricks hanging on to every limb and I'm too tired to fight it, but the ringing of my doorbell is relentless.

I let the air get sucked into my lungs, then get up as I exhale loudly. With a foggy mind, I shuffle to the front door, snatching my gun from the side table in the hallway out of habit.

I don't bother to look through the peephole, just cock my gun, then open the door as I hold it hanging beside my body.

A shiver runs up my spine when I look into a set of gray eyes that used to make my heart race with excitement. But now it just beats with discomfort as I look at Brad's smile sliding into place when his gaze falls on me.

"Brad."

"So it's true? You're back." He awkwardly runs a hand through his ragged blond hair.

"Something like that," I mutter, turning away to make my way to the kitchen. As expected, his footsteps follow behind me after I hear him close the front door.

"What happened, Alex?" He observes me with worry when I turn around to face him as I place the gun on the counter.

Alex.

I feel like she no longer exists. I've been Lexie for weeks and I don't even know if she's still there. I'm an orphan with no name.

"A burglar killed my family. I escaped. Stayed at my grandmother's condo for a while." It's a sum up from what the paper says, and I'm pretty sure he read it like everyone else in this half of Boston.

He crosses his arms in front of his chest, and I mimic his stance before I let my hip rest on the counter.

"Is that why you carry a gun?"

"I need to protect myself."

"And Killian Wolfe?" There is a judgment in his voice that I couldn't care less about, but it's his scowl that ticks me off. The contempt, as if I'm some naïve little girl. I probably was at some point, but not anymore. I've seen more ugly in this world than most people will ever experience in their life.

"What about him?"

"You dated him?" His eyes flash with jealousy. A year ago, it would've excited me, loving how Brad was possessive over me. But now it just feels like a nuisance. A ridiculous display of alpha behavior, because he can never compare to the man I've foolishly let into my life.

"No." I roll my eyes. "He taught me how to fight."

"How did you two meet?" he asks with a little more tact this time.

"Are you here to cross-examine me about Wolfe?" The last thing I want is to explain my relationship with Killian to my ex-boyfriend. Especially since I don't even know how to put it into words myself.

His stance changes, hands up in the air as he moves a few steps closer.

"No, no. I'm sorry. I just wanted to see you. See how you are doing." He takes the final steps to fill the space in front of me, his hands rubbing my arms.

"I'm fine." I turn my head away to avoid his gaze.

"You going to keep living here?"

"I don't know. I don't know what to do now."

"You can go to college." I can hear the hope in his tone. "With *me*."

I lift my eyes to his. "You're going to Northeastern?"

"It's wicked." He smiles, enthusiastic. "But I missed you."

"I missed you too." It's an automatic reply, but it isn't a complete lie. Yes, I missed him. But only because he's a part of my old life. He's part of the past that I still miss every day and a big part of me wishes that I could get that back, even if just for a minute.

"I can come stay with you," he continues with a lightheartedness that I wish I possessed as well. "Like we always planned after college. Now that you're not going to Indiana, we can live here."

Indiana, the dream I had in another lifetime and the reason we broke up before graduation. *'I don't do long-distance,'* Brad told me, *'it's for the best.'*

"Right."

"I'll take care of you." He dips his chin, lifting mine with the tips of his fingers. "Like before. Let me take care of you." The warmth of his breath heats my lips as he comes closer and desperate to feel anything other than pain, I close my eyes. When our mouths connect, I feel nothing at first, just holding on to the affection that I've been missing for the last few days, and for a brief moment, I wonder if maybe Brad can be enough. If I can start over with him. But when his lips part, and his tongue gently meets mine, that feeling is overshadowed with a Titanic-sized amount of guilt that washes over me.

"I can't do this," I huff against his touch, but he gives me nothing more than a moan while his hands fall to the small of my back.

"Stop, Brad," I plead with a little more force this time. "Stop!"

He jerks his head back with wide eyes. "What's wrong?"

"I can't do this."

"Do what? Kiss me?"

I shake my head. "I'm not the same girl."

"It's okay. We'll figure it out together." He tries to continue by lowering his lips again, but I twist my head away.

"You need to leave," I say adamantly as I try to keep my tears at bay.

"No-suh, you're kicking me out?" He takes a step back, offended, and I keep my gaze to the floor to avoid the hurt that is audible in his voice.

"I'm sorry. I need some time alone."

"Alex."

"Please, Brad. Just go."

"Baby, you're not alone."

"Just go, Brad!" I shout, pointing my finger at the door.

Shocked, he blinks at me for a long time before he finally shakes his head.

"Alex, please." He folds his hands together, begging for me to listen, but I can't. I'm sitting here in purgatory, unable to go back to the past and pick up where I left off, and having no clue when and where my future will start. I once was crazy about this boy, but now he's nothing more than a hurtful memory I can't keep.

"Go!"

"Fine," he says with a snarl. "I just wanted to help, Alex." With one last glare, he tears his gaze away from mine before he stomps away with big steps. Every step sounds less audible than the other, as he moves farther away, and I let my tears roll down my cheeks.

When the door closes behind him with a loud thud, I fall to my knees as sobs escape my throat, his words replaying in my head.

"I just wanted to help, Alex."

I know. But that's the gutting part; no one can help me. Simply because no one can give me back my family, my life, or my heart.

39

Killian

I close my eyes with pressed lips when I hear the key in the lock and within five seconds, my youngest brother jumps over the back of my couch, flopping himself onto the cushions next to me.

"Hey, fuckface," Reign cheers. His mood is chipper as fuck, only adding to my annoyance. I've been avoiding everyone for the last week, telling them I'm busy. But really I've been doing whatever I've had to do to keep the businesses running, before I get home to drink myself to sleep. It's that or shooting random people on the street. I figured Franklin wouldn't appreciate me starting a war with the city of Boston.

"What do you want?" I take a swig of the bottle of Royal Blue whiskey, keeping my eyes fixed on the TV.

"Why are you so grumpy?" he asks, bemused.

"I'm always grumpy."

"No, that's Connor."

"Whatever."

"Anyway, I want to discuss Franklin's bachelor party with you."

"What about it?" I grunt as I roll my eyes. The last thing I want to do is discuss anything regarding my brother's wedding. I'm not in the mood for a party, let alone one that forces me to stare at my brother looking all lovey dovey with his girl for the entire day.

"Well, what are we going to do? I have a feeling Kendall doesn't want some stripper all over her man the entire night."

Actually, that sounds like a fucking great idea. Seems like the perfect opportunity to bury myself in some fresh pussy to get over the one that's responsible for my sour mood.

"It's a bachelor party. I say stripper for him and a couple of whores for me," I tell him, then bring the bottle back to my lips. The content burns my throat as I feel it surge down with two big gulps.

"Oh, yeah, Lexie will love that," Reign counters with sarcasm. "Speaking of, you're bringing her for Christmas, right?"

"No." The question makes me pour even more liquor down my throat. I didn't even realize Christmas was right around the corner and now the thought of her being alone will haunt me even more.

"Oh God, trouble in paradise?"

"No."

"Fucking hell, did you two break up?" Reign huffs.

"We were never together." It's funny how the truth can feel like a complete lie. If we were never together, then why does it feel like I broke up with her?

"Seriously, Kill, please tell me you didn't dump the girl before Christmas."

"Can't dump her if we were never together. It's not rocket science, Reign," I mock, taking another gulp.

"Right, you're drinking Royal Blue like it's whatever, which might I add"—he pulls the bottle from my hands, before slamming it on the table—"it's not, so don't waste this shit on your little rampage to get over whatever is going on between you and Lexie." He twists his body, facing me with a troubled frown.

"There is nothing going on!"

The scowl on his face makes me roll my eyes. "You're drinking as much as I was when I found out Sienna was on a date with Lucas. Stop bullshitting me. What's going on?"

"Nothing," I grunt. "She left."

"Why?"

"She had her revenge, so she left. Went back to her teenage life." I can barely get the words off my lips, because I hate thinking about her like some silly teenager. She's not. She might be young, but she's more woman than most girls will ever be.

Reign narrows his eyes at me, suspicion written all over his features. "Did she leave? Or did you throw her out?"

"Tomayto, tomahto."

"Fucking hell, Kill." He incredulously throws his hands in the air before he lets them fall to his legs with a thud. "Why?"

"What do you mean, *why*?" I glare. "We killed Sullivan. What more was there to do?"

"You like the girl." He states it with ease, as if that's an argument.

"I do. Doesn't mean I'm going to get all sappy like the lot of you and start dating her."

"Why not?"

"Because." Because I'm not going to put myself through the bullshit of letting my world revolve around someone else. Not again.

Reign snorts. "You sound wicked mature right now."

I fix my attention back on the TV. "She left. Life goes on. Fucking drop it." I snatch the bottle from the table again, taking a big swig. "I don't care if you stay or go, but if you're staying, can you shut the fuck up now? I'm trying to watch a movie."

He eyes me with suspicion, annoyed with me, until he reluctantly lets his back fall against the couch, his head pointed at the TV.

"You get tonight," he discloses, "but tomorrow, you better start talking."

"Shut up, tool," I counter, putting the bottle to my lips to continue my mission to pass out before midnight.

40

Lexie

You know how people always say the holidays hurt more when you're alone? It didn't. In fact, it passed by me with chronic pain just like every other day since I've been back in my own house. But the next day I woke up, deciding I wasn't going to give up. I survived while my family didn't, and I'm not going to let the pain kill me. I'd honored boxing day and started packing while I called a realtor to list the house. Though it was where I grew up, it's also time to let it go. It'll never feel the same again without my family to fill it up, and I could use the money to start over. For the last three days I've been going through every single room of the house, separating things into categories of what to keep, what to put into storage, and what to sell, and now I'm glancing around the empty parlor.

It feels weird, seeing these walls without decoration and the spacious room without its furniture. But it also feels liberating, like I'm creating space in my head with every room I finish.

The doorbell rings and I let my head hang with a sigh. I knew Brad would come back eventually. He's a good guy and I know he'll have a hard time letting me go. When we dated, he was the one in control, the one who took care of me. It made me feel loved and secure, but I don't need that anymore.

Trying to fight the annoyance in my mind, I open the door, ready to tell Brad that I appreciate his concern, but that I'll be fine. My gaze is met by two piercing green eyes and a boyish grin that definitely doesn't belong to Brad.

"Reign," I huff, pushing out a breath.

"Hey, Lexie." He walks past me like he owns the place, his feet trailing toward the parlor. I should kick his ass for his boldness, but it's hard to be mad at Reign, so instead, I roll my eyes, slamming the door shut with a thud, before I follow his steps.

"What are you doing here?"

"Nice place." He scans the empty room, a little amused.

"Thanks."

"I think you need a bit more furniture, though. It's a bit... deserted?" He cocks his head with a lopsided grin pulling up a cheek.

"I sold it all."

"Yeah, I figured." He steps toward the window, staring out for a moment before he turns around and lets his back fall against the surface, his arms folded in front of his chest. "Including the house?"

"Yes."

He nods with pursed lips. “You’re leaving Boston?”

“New year, new life.”

“Isn’t that a bit drastic?”

I lift my chin to hold his gaze. His green eyes are so similar to Killian’s it’s eerie, gutting me from the inside, but Reign’s are laced with a sympathy Kill’s always lacked.

“I got nothing to stay for.”

“Nothing?” He arches a brow, calling me out.

I shake my head, running a hand through my hair. “I have no family left. This city is nothing more than one big memory.” I lift my hand when he opens his mouth to interrupt. “*Don’t* even try to mention your brother.”

His mouth snaps shut, and we keep staring at each other until I blink and tear my gaze away, my eyes falling to the floor as I try not to cry. I know Reign is the one Wolfe you can confide in, the *friendliest* of the whole pack, but I refuse to cry in front of a Wolfe again.

“I’m sorry you had to spend Christmas alone.”

I shrug, his words barely reaching me. “I’m used to being alone by now.”

“He misses you.” He gives me a tentative look, and I reply with a vicious glare.

“Did he tell you that?” I snarl.

“I know my brother.”

“He doesn’t want me.”

“He told you that?” Reign’s eyes widen and, reluctantly, I give him a short nod.

“Fucking idiot,” he mumbles, then swings his gaze back to me. “What happened?”

“He didn’t tell you?”

“The bastard has been avoiding every conversation we try to have with him.”

The explanation surprises me, but I keep my expression straight.

"We killed Sullivan. He kicked me out the next day, saying we were over." Tears are pricking in my eyes, thinking back to the moment I walked out of his apartment. It felt like I entered with a heart, though black and cold as ice, but I left without one.

Reign pushes off the window, taking his feet a little closer. "Look, Lex. I can see that he hurt you–"

"He did," I cut him off with fire flashing in my eyes.

"And I will make him pay for it, but don't leave. Give me a few more days for me to find out what the hell is going on with him. He loves you."

The features in my face lower, and for a split second, it feels like I've been slapped in the face. Reign is giving me the words that Killian refuses to let fall from his tongue and though it's not the man I need to hear them from, a spark of hope ignites in the empty shell that was once my heart.

"He doesn't love me," I reply with a croaking voice.

"He does. He's just scared to tell you." The comfort his eyes are giving me makes me want to believe him, as I wonder if there could be any truth in his words.

"Why?"

He throws his arms in the air, shaking his head. "I don't know. But I will find out."

I want to be strong and tell him to fuck off. That I'm done waiting for his brother, but my heart keeps protesting, dying to know if what he's saying is true. If there is one person who can get the truth out of Killian, it's Reign.

"Three days," I concede with a scowl. "After that, I'm on a Greyhound with an unknown destination."

41

It's a little before ten when my brothers and I walk into the restaurant as a unit. The few heads still enjoying their late dinner turn to watch us, their eyes widening when we stroll to the back, followed by half a dozen of our men.

Connor snaps his fingers in the air, his malicious gaze pointed at the few occupied tables one by one. "Everyone, *out.*"

We move through the curtain that hides the hallway to the back office from the restaurant as two men stay behind to guard it. Franklin leads the way, strutting into the office with an authority no one can replicate.

"Franklin Wolfe," I hear Shaun Murphy say in greeting.

When we walk through the door, his brown gaze flies up with a glint of worry noticeable in the blink of an eye. Usually this is the part I enjoy the most, when they are squirming in their seats, their simple minds trying to think of a way to survive what's coming. It never bores me, witnessing when arrogant tools realize they can't outsmart us.

But today, I just want to get back to my couch with a bottle in my hand.

"And brothers." He swallows with a tight jaw before he plasters a smile on his puffy face and the three other men in the room instantly seem on edge. "To what do I owe this pleasure?"

"A full pack, we must be in trouble." His skinny right-hand, Manuel, crosses his arms in front of his chest, his cheeks lifting in a mocking grin, reminding me of a weasel. He has annoyed me since the first time I laid eyes on his man bun and every time I come to collect, I ignore him like he's not even there, simply because he's a fucking nobody.

"Shut up, and get back to your corner, Manbun Manny," I bark, and it's followed by a chortle from Connor behind me, then I take a seat in front of Shaun's desk while Franklin takes the chair beside me.

"Isn't it payday?" Franklin loosens his peacoat, a question in his gaze.

"Yeah, but normally you just send one of your guys." Shaun locks eyes with me. "Or your brother."

"I thought I'd share in the fun today." I throw him a fabricated smile, and he eyes me in suspicion. Slowly, I see the worry creeping back into his eyes as he holds my gaze.

"How is business, Shaun?" Franklin asks.

"Good. I'm sure you've seen the big bags coming your way."

"I have. Definitely pleased with that. I'm just a little less pleased about the birdies chirping in my ear."

"What do you mean?" I can see a vein pulsing in his neck, and I roll my eyes at his lack of acting skills. These men should know by now that when we come with a full pack, you're not just in trouble. You're getting a permanent stay in Hell. For once I wish there was one of them who had enough balls to just say, *"You got me. It was worth a try."*

Reign lets out a snort, resting his shoulder against the side wall. "The birdies. Like Twitter. Jabbing shit. Some of it true, some of it just tacky gossip."

"Okay," Shaun replies carefully.

Manbun Manny clears his throat, flaring my aggravation to a new level when *he* has the balls to actually speak.

"A lot of people want to mix into things that aren't their business," he clarifies. "Get in good graces with the Wolfes."

"Didn't I tell you to shut up?" I snarl, pointing my gun at his face with crazed eyes and a cocked head. I hear Connor chuckle behind me, but keep pinning the asshole down as all the muscles in my back tense. In my head, I'm debating if I should shoot him, but when Franklin rests his palm on my shoulder, I listen to his silent plea and lower my gun.

"Luckily, I'm a star at finding the right bird with the right information," Reign adds, chipper as always.

"Can we stop dragging this out and just kill the motherfucker?" I grunt, pushing the air out of my lungs as I run a hand through my messy hair.

Panic settles in Shaun's expression. "What? No!"

"Reign found a birdie that told him you've been skimming off the top," Connor explains.

"Whoever it is, he's lying."

Reign shakes his head, a little skeptical. "I don't know, Shaun. He stuck with his story all the way through Connor's torture session."

I snap my head over my shoulder, giving Connor a glare.

"You went to torture someone without me?" Franklin and Reign hardly participate in the hard conversations, not really enjoying the mess. But Connor and I, we live for the mess. It's what keeps us sane during daily life, knowing that at some point we get to live out our urges on those who deserve it because they double-crossed us or think they can beat us.

"You were busy drowning yourself in Royal Blue." Connor shrugs his shoulders, and I flip him off, then snap my head back in front of me.

"You've been skimming off the top, Shaun," Franklin states.

Frantically, Shaun's head shakes, with terror etched in his eyes. "No, Franklin. I swear!"

"Do you have proof?" Manbun Manny questions with a slight scowl.

Without a second thought, I raise my gun, pulling the trigger. His head jerks, followed by blood spatter splashing over the white wall behind him before he falls to the floor with a loud thump. For a brief moment, you can hear a pin drop until Connor's laughter breaks the silence.

"What the fuck?" Shaun huffs with his eyebrows up to his hairline.

"No-suh," Reign chimes in.

"What?" My eyebrows knit together, swinging my head to Reign. "He was boring the hell out of me."

"We came to shoot *him*." Reign points at Shaun, indignant. "Not his little sidekick."

"Fine." *Bang*. Shaun's head falls forward, knocking against the desk. "There. He's dead."

"Killian!" Reign glances at the ceiling while I hear Franklin groan beside me. Connor's hysterical laughter now booms throughout the small room, and I turn around to give him a questioning brow raise. His face has a slight pink shade, barely able to catch his breath, and I twist my attention to Franklin.

He gives me a dull look, then pinches the bridge of his nose. "Fucking hell, Kill."

Rolling my eyes, I shake my head, completely done with this night. I glance around the room, finding the man who stood closest to Manbun Manny.

"You. What's your name?"

"Cian," he replies reluctantly, eyeing a wheezing Connor who seems to be having a hard time breathing as he almost chokes in his own guffaw.

"Nice to meet you. You're in charge now." I get to my feet. "Don't try to cheat us, or you'll end up like those two tools. Clean this up. We'll be back next week." I give my brothers another glare, then stalk out of there to call it a night.

"Connor," I hear Franklin call out as I walk past him.

"He's lost his mind," Connor shrieks, hysterically amused.

"Instruct them," Franklin says before their voices drown out and I make my way out of the restaurant. The cold air hits me in the face and I suck in a deep breath as I start walking down the pavement to get home. I barely make it two yards when the sound of someone following me outside makes my jaw clench.

"What is wrong with you?" Reign's voice sounds from behind me, the judgment clear as day.

I spin on my heels with a glare. “Can you stop with the dramatics?”

“Stop with the—you think *I’m* dramatic? There are two dead bodies inside.” His finger points at the building.

“It’s only one more than planned. No big deal.”

“You just shot an innocent person,” he deadpans, coming closer.

“He’s hardly innocent, Reign.” His sleazy grin told me he was in on it the minute we walked through the door. Reign might need proof for every kill he makes, but I can just read them and know right away if they’re innocent or guilty. The look on Manbun Manny’s face told me he was only an inch away from being caught red-handed.

“Who died and made you Connor?”

“That makes no sense.”

Reign grunts, balling his hands into fists. “You’re Killian Wolfe,” he hisses. “You are the strategic one. You can’t go on a rampage shooting whoever the fuck you want. People will want to retaliate.”

“I’m also the one they call ruthless!” I shout back, getting into his face. “*Cunning*. Don’t pretend I’m some prince like *you*.”

His expression softens. “You’re right. But up until now, you were never stupid either. “

“Shut the fuck up.”

“You could just go and see her, you know.” I want to punch him for bringing her up, but I should’ve expected a blow like that. Reign never knows when to stop talking.

“And do what? Fuck her into oblivion? Make love to her until dawn? I’m not you, Reign!”

“I know, I’m not half the asshole you are.” He shoots me a taunting smirk.

"Whatever." I twist, stomping away from him, because the other option is to give him a shiner that Sienna will hate me for. It's the only two options I have to keep some semblance of control over the sharp edge that fuels the pounding in my head.

"Where are you going?" Reign bellows as I keep walking.

"Home!"

"She sold the house." His words make me still, a tight knot settling in my stomach.

"What do you mean?" I swing my gaze back to my brother, who's giving me an expression filled with pity.

"She's leaving Boston."

42

Lexie

With a deep sigh, I glance one final time into the hallway of my home, then close the front door behind me. My weekender is feeling heavy in my grip as I close off this chapter in my life. I've been crying in the middle of the parlor for an hour, cross-legged, soaking up all the memories that were created between these four walls, until finally, my tears dried up. Feeling empty, I'm ready for the next step in my life, wherever that may lead me.

I turn around to descend down the small steps onto the street, but a pair of green eyes freeze me to the spot. Pebbles shower my skin, caused by a shiver running along my spine.

"Killian." He's leaning against his car, wearing his leather jacket and a penetrating glare. His brown hair sits messily on his head, like he just rolled out of bed, but it's his eyes that make my heart fall to the ground. They are bloodshot, tired, but mostly filled with a rage that tells me he's not here to tell me to stay.

"What the fuck are you doing?" he growls, his voice loud and clear, almost making me wince. But it quickly reminds me I'm not one of his men and I raise my chin with defiance as I let my feet take the remaining steps until they meet the cobblestone street.

"Leaving." I quickly turn left to continue my way, but he grabs my elbow, halting me in front of him.

"Why?" he barks. "I gave you your house. You can stay."

"For what?" I shout back, watching how his jaw clenches in frustration. "I got nothing left!"

"That's bullshit!" He lets go of me, walking a few steps away as he spins on his heels, a hand rubbing the back of his neck.

"It's not, Killian. What do I have left here? My family is all gone. My life is over."

"So build a new one!" He snaps his head back to me.

"I want to! Just not here. Not in Boston."

"You grew up here! You belong here."

"I'm all alone in a city I don't recognize as my own. I might have belonged here once upon a time, but not anymore."

"This is so fucked up." He looks up at the sky and for the first time, I can see the pain I've been feeling since we broke up reflected back at me. He feels the same way, slowly dying a little every day when we're not together. "I gave you your house!"

"It means nothing when you have no one to share it with." The tone in my voice is calmer this time, my anger slowly being replaced by the pain he represents.

"Fucking hell."

I keep my focus trained on him, watching him drip with frustration in the middle of the street. He looks like he's squirming in his own skin, dying to break free, but he can't push through the surface. It hurts to see him like this.

"Give me something to stay for," I offer, shrugging, that silly little girl inside of me rearing her head and feeling hopeful.

He stills with a straight face, the only emotion shown in his forest green gaze. As if he just saw a ghost, he never deviates his line of sight from mine, his chest slowly moving up and down. For a hot minute, we just stand there, the world around us blurring, the sounds of daily life getting drowned out. He looks lost. Confused. It feels like looking into a mirror with one big difference–I might be lost, but I'm going to fight to find my way back. I want to do it with him, because seeing him standing in front of me after all this time apart makes it undeniable that I love this man more than anything. But his lack of words tells me he either doesn't feel the same or he doesn't want to voice it. It doesn't matter. I can't put my life on hold any longer.

With pressed lips, and the corners of my eyes pooling, I lift my cheeks in a genuine smile at the same time tears fall over the edge.

"Goodbye, Killian," I tell him before I turn around and walk away. My heart is dying for him to call my name. To run after me, telling me to stay. When he doesn't, though, that's the waterworks truly start flowing, and my heart feels like it breaks again. But I continue walking with big and firm strides, knowing there is no other option than to keep going until I reach my new life.

43

The front door flies open and out of reflex I grab my gun, pointing it at the man stepping over the threshold.

"Honey, I'm home," Reign sings, not even giving the gun a second glance. He scrunches his nose, glancing around the parlor. "This is disgusting, Kill. Did you fire your cleaning lady?"

"What do you want?" Reign's weight moves the cushions next to me as he sits down.

"What I want is to slap your goddamn face, but I promised Sienna I wouldn't hit you. She didn't want you to start crying. Not any more than you have been doing for the last couple of weeks anyway."

"Don't you have somewhere to be?" I glare, then twist my head back to the TV.

"Yeah, but I'm kinda over this"—he moves his hand over my body with disdain—"look you're going for. I'm here to tell you to grow a pair of balls and either get the fuck over her or bring her back."

"Not gonna happen."

"Why not, Kill?"

"Because she wants something I can't give her."

I can almost hear his eyes rolling without looking at him.

"Fine, indulge me. What's that?"

"A happily ever after."

"Why can't you be her happily ever after?"

"Are you fucking serious right now?" I shoot him an incredulous look. "I'm a Wolfe. Her family got murdered because of us and our connection to a corrupt cop. She would never be safe with me. Besides, she wants a white picket fence and a bunch of babies. You don't do that with the villain. You do that with someone like you. Prince Charming."

"Whoa." Reign's mouth forms an 'O' in fake shock before he slaps the back of my head.

"Ouch, what the fuck did you do that for?" I bellow, balling my hand into a fist, ready to connect it with his eye.

"Do it!" he challenges. "Hit me. I know you want to."

We hold a stare-off, both with grinding teeth and our green eyes flaring with the same rage. I want to hit him so bad, finding someone to indulge my anger on. Instead, I shove him forward, not willing to play into his hands.

"She just wants you. You are all she wants. What if you are enough for her and you just *think* she wants everything else?" he continues. "Just because you are the villain in someone's story doesn't mean you're the villain in everyone's."

"Doesn't it?" I shout, the frustration that has been building in every fiber of my being getting the best of me. "Because it wasn't enough for Emma!"

I jump to my feet, swatting the bottle of whiskey from the coffee table. The glass shatters onto the floor and I start pacing the room.

"This is about Emma?" Reign frowns.

"No, it's not about Emma! It's about me not being willing to fucking give my life to someone who can decide it's not enough at any given time."

I can sense Reign's gaze never dropping, and I grind my teeth as I avoid eye contact. For the last few weeks, I've felt the pain slowly get the best of me and even though I don't want to fucking admit it, I'm not sure how to keep breathing.

I thought her leaving would give me the time and space to pick up where I left off, but every day the walls seem to close in a little more on me while the air becomes thick as syrup.

My mind keeps worrying where she is and my heart keeps telling me to go find her and I don't know how to handle it anymore, but I also don't know how to fix it.

"Is that what you think?" Reign's voice snaps me out of my mind-fuck. "That you weren't enough for Emma? That she didn't love you?"

"She fucking killed herself, Reign! Clearly, she didn't!" I yell.

I told her I loved her a month before she died. I didn't mean to, but it blurted out and when it did, it felt liberating. A feeling that only got magnified when a smile took over her expression that was vibrant as hell. I can still see it when I close my eyes. She said it back, and in my head, I made a silent plea that I would always protect her. A plea that I'd put into words when I found her a week later, staring into the sky with a vacant look. She didn't want to talk about it. She never wanted to talk about it. But there was a change in her eyes that scared me. She saw it too.

"Don't worry, baby. I won't leave you," she said.

"Promise?"

"I promise. It's hard. I have bad moments and I have good moments. The good moments are with you. They will make me better."

"Are they enough?"

She smiled, then pressed a bruising kiss to my lips. "You *are enough."*

But she fucking lied. The rope around her neck proved as much a month later.

Reign just shakes his head, pulling out his phone with a glare.

"What are you doing?"

He ignores me, the dial tone of his phone going to the speaker as he pushes the button.

"Hey, how is it going?" Sienna's voice is hesitant, as if she's bracing herself for bad news.

"Like shit. You wanna know why he's all fucked up?" I grind my teeth at the way he talks about me to Sienna, making it clear I've been the subject of their conversations more than once.

"Yeah?"

"Because of Emma," Reign says, locking his gaze with mine.

"Emma?" Sienna sounds surprised. "Why Emma? She loved him."

Reign's eyebrows lift in a smug expression, shooting me a look that says *told ya*.

"He thinks he wasn't enough for her." There is a sadness in his voice, and I just stand there, completely frozen.

"Ah, fuck," Sienna huffs. "Can he hear me? Kill, are you there?"

I purse my lips, wanting to kill my brother, but I concede with a growl.

"A green emerald."

Confused, I exchange a look with Reign, who then shrugs his shoulders.

"What?"

"A green emerald," she repeats, her voice echoing through the parlor. "It's what she wanted as an engagement ring if you ever asked her. It had to be a green one, because it reminded her of your eyes."

I try to process Sienna's words.

"She loved you more than anything, Killian. She was sick. Her lows were really low, and she felt really, really bad. But her highs were so high, no one could knock her off her cloud nine. They were always triggered by *you*. You two were only teenagers, but she wanted it all with you. She was planning your future together every chance she got." She pauses, a sigh coming through the line. "She didn't kill herself because she didn't love you. She killed herself because she couldn't handle the lows anymore. They sucked her in too deep, and she didn't know how to get back to the surface. It had nothing to do with you. You were part of her happy moments."

My eyes shut, and I roll my lips, putting my hands on the back of my neck, my chin facing the ceiling. I don't know what hits me first, the realization of my stupid decisions or the understanding of my relationship with Emma. My thoughts are jumbling through my mind and my skin burns up, making it impossible for me to breathe. I squat down, letting it all settle, with my chin to my chest, my elbows resting on my knees as I balance on my toes.

When Emma died, I felt betrayed. Lied to. *Rejected.*

Not once had I considered that her depression ran deeper than the love we shared. I'd let my feeling of inadequacy tear me up inside, thinking I wasn't enough for her to stay.

"It wasn't about me." Floored, I lift my head to Reign before Sienna's voice comes through the line once more.

"Of course it wasn't, Kill! She loved you! She loved all of us. We couldn't save her. We all tried, but no one could." Her voice breaks with every syllable and I can only blink at my brother. "She wouldn't want you to give up on the girl you love because of her."

The girl you love.

The girl I love.

A grin splits Reign's face when he sees the cogs turning in my head, followed by a grin of victory.

"I fucked up," I huff with wide eyes, rubbing my palms over my face. "Really, really bad."

"You did," Reign pitches in.

"You gonna let her walk away?" Sienna questions.

Not a goddamn chance in hell.

44

Lexie

"I'm going home, Lexie. Do you mind closing up?" Laura gives me a friendly smile, her bag draped over her shoulder as she stands in the doorway of the dance studio.

"Sure. I'll see you tomorrow."

"See you tomorrow." She closes the door behind her, and I smile with contentment, my favorite part of the day being the moment I have this place to myself.

I've been working at Laura's dance studio in Baltimore for three weeks now and every day I feel a little bit better. When I got on that bus, I had no clue where I was going, but when I woke up in Baltimore, it reminded me of Boston, so I got off to roam around the city. The peace that settled within me as I strolled down the street made me wonder if this was the city to stay in and when my eyes caught the sign of Laura's Dance Studio & Gym, something pulled me in. Without any plan, I asked her for a job and she gave me one without even a second thought. Turns out her receptionist was off on maternity leave and she hadn't found a replacement yet.

"You came at the perfect time," she told me, and I couldn't agree more.

Every day I start at eight, working the desk until five before I go up to the studio to dance. I've been dancing for three weeks straight and though it can't completely fix my damaged heart, it feels like slowly it's thawing just a little.

I turn the music on, pulling up my leggings as the first chords of Swan Lake reverberate through the room. Closing my eyes, I get into first position, sucking in a deep breath before I let the music take me away. My mind settles, enjoying every pull of my muscles as I start to dance. The rate of my heart speeds up, but the pounding of my heartbeat in my ears works to soothe. I used to live for ballet, feeling my most confident and clear-headed when I was dancing my sorrows away. Whatever worries I had, I'd lose them the moment my feet had me floating through the room. It gave me strength just as much as the act demanded from me and it gave me a sense of calm no other thing could ever provide.

Since I ended up in Baltimore, I'm slowly starting to get that back. Getting a little bit of myself back every time I get lost in the music.

I do a double pirouette facing the left wall, smiling with a lightheartedness I'm proud of, but as soon as I swing my arms up to initiate the next move, they fall to my sides in shock.

My heart literally stops beating, my smile falling, my eyes wide. I try to swallow the lump away before my lips part as I wonder if I'm hallucinating.

He looks more handsome than ever, and definitely more rested than the last time I saw him. His leather jacket hugs his broad shoulders, his hair sitting in a controlled mess on his head, with a few strands falling on his forehead. His back rests against the closed door, his hands tucked into his jeans.

My heart starts to race after the first moment of bewilderment while my mouth turns dry as I do my best to control my breath with every inhale and exhale. His green eyes peer at me intimidatingly, but I can see the smile haunting his face. It's tiny, and if you didn't know him, you wouldn't even see it, but I do.

"What are you doing here?"

"I could ask you the same." His cheeks lift into a full grin, as he pushes off the door to close the distance between us with determined steps.

Automatically, I counter each of them backwards, causing a flash of annoyance to run through his gaze. "You can't run away from me, baby."

I blink up at him, and when his hands fall to my waist, I bump against the wall as he crowds my space. His fresh scent attacks my nose, and I make my best effort to resist the need to wrap my arms around him to breathe him in.

God, I fucking missed him.

"What are you doing, *Killian*?" I repeat, grinding my teeth.

His tongue darts out, and my eyes lower to his lips as he does the same to mine.

"Taking you somewhere." Before I can reply, he squats down, pressing his shoulder into my stomach as he hauls me over his shoulder.

"What the fuck!" I shriek as he carries me out of the studio. Connecting my fists with his back, I try to squirm out of his grip, but he just slaps my ass.

"Stop fighting it, baby."

"Put me down, you asshole!'

"Not a chance, little Lexie."

He carries me down the stairs, not even skipping a beat.

"Where are we going?!" I cry as I keep my head up to see he's continuing out the door.

"Home."

"Home?" I screech. "Killian, I can't! I need to close up! Stop!"

Relentless, he strolls outside like he doesn't have a care in the world, then rounds his black car before he opens the passenger door and literally throws me in.

"What the hell, asshole! I can't leave, Killian. Laura is expecting me to lock up!" I hold on to the dash with one hand to push myself back on my feet, but his palm lands on my chest doing the complete opposite.

"Stay!" He scowls, then lifts my legs to place them inside the car with a grunt. His hands reach up to my chin, locking it in a firm grip as he crashes his mouth against mine. I tense at the sudden and unexpected movement, but it's only brief, because before I know it, I relax against his lips. My toes curl at the shot of endorphins that enters my body for the first time in weeks, and I can't hold back the moan that vibrates from my throat. Sooner that I want him to, he pulls his head back, his eyes pinning me down.

"Stay."

A little stunned, my lips part as he slams the door shut and I wince in the seat. Baring my teeth, I reach for the handle to open the door and tell the motherfucker that he can't command me like I'm some doormat. But the clicking of the doors and the smug grin on his face as he holds up the key fob have me roaring in frustration.

"Killian! Open the door!" I yell as I watch him step back toward the entrance. He ignores me something fierce, pretending I'm not even here.

"Asshole," I mutter.

I cross my arms in front of my chest, a big scowl taking permanent residence for the foreseeable future as I wait for him to get back.

45

Two minutes later, I close the door of the studio behind me, looking for the keys in her bag. I hear them clinking at the bottom and I pull them out, then turn around.

"Which one is it?" I shout at the car.

She replies by flipping me off with a sexy scowl on her freckled cheeks that only turns me on. Chuckling, I put my focus to the keys, trying them one by one before I find the right one and lock up.

The drive over here had me on edge, anxious to see her after too long apart, but when I found her, completely lost in her own world as she moved her feet along the wooden floor, I felt truly settled. She looked gorgeous, carrying herself with the grace of a queen. If I wasn't already convinced, it would've been that moment when I knew I wanted her to be mine.

Add in her black skin-tight leggings, and crop top that gave me enough skin to have my cock twitching, and I saw no other option than to toss her over my shoulder, ready to take her back home.

I get in the car, a scowl aimed my way, and I see the little jerk of her hand, quick enough for me to push the button to lock the doors before she tries to escape from me.

"Nice try, baby." I start the car. "Buckle up."

"No! What the fuck is wrong with you?"

I hold her angry gaze with a dull look. Her blue eyes are shooting daggers at me, but all I can think of is how much I missed them. How I missed them when they were staring up at me through her thick lashes. How they would glare at me every time I pissed her off.

"You're so sexy," I huff, cupping her cheek.

Rapidly, she slaps my hand away, flexing her palms in frustration.

"What are you doing here, Killian?" She sounds annoyed, but she can't hide the excitement in her navy-blue irises, and that alone has my lips curling.

"I'm taking you home."

"This is my home!"

I keep a straight expression, not even going to retort to that stupid reply. She might have been pretending this was her home for the last few weeks, and I had a huge part in that, but I'm not going to sit here pretending this will ever be her home.

"Let me out," she orders, folding her arms in front of her chest again with a clear defiance.

"No."

"You're kidnapping me," she states, as if that's about to shock me.

"I'm aware."

"You can't do this."

A grin cuts my face in half. "I can and I will."

"You're a fucking caveman." I can still hear her irritation, but her gaze softens a little, building a sense of victory inside of me.

"Look," I start, deciding I need to get this out before I piss her off even more—as fun as it may be. "I don't know how to do this shit."

"Well, you can start with *I'm sorry*," she interrupts like a little brat.

"Shut up, Lexie. I was talking." I ignore the rolling of her eyes as I continue. "I'm sorry. I'm sorry I treated you like shit and hurt you. I wanted to protect you."

"From what?" She blinks, her brow lifting.

Our gazes stay linked as I think about her question. The truth is, I don't even know. I wanna say *from me*, but this girl has shown me more than once that she doesn't need protection from anyone. She's fully capable of taking care of herself, but in the end, that probably was the reason I shut her out. Not to protect her from me. But to protect me from her, because I don't think I can cope with losing her.

"I'm not sure," I confess.

Her mouth is pinched, her glare still in place as she slowly shakes her head.

"You do not get to show up here, kidnap me, like I'm your fucking property and tell me we're going home!" Her voice raises with every word that follows, amusement creeping into my body. "You didn't want me! You made it perfectly clear!"

"I love you," I blurt out, my heart thumping as I wait for what her response might be. But she continues on her rampage, my admission not sinking in. My shoulders go rigid, containing the urge to just let her know how I feel by crashing my mouth against hers. But I know that won't cut it this time. She needs the words, and frankly, after my dick-ish behavior, she deserves it.

"You basically kicked me to the curb, telling me to go and live my life and find a new—wait... you love me?" Her perfect pink lips part, her lashes fluttering with her rapid blinking as she finally looks at me again.

"I love you," I repeat, a small smile hidden on my straight face.

"You love me." It's a mix between a question and a statement, and I take a mental picture of the shocked flush that colors her skin. She swallows hard, and I catch how her chest moves up and down with deep breaths.

"I'm sorry, *Alexandra*. You scare the living shit out of me." Her forehead creases with an incredulous frown, making her look cute as fuck. "Yeah, baby. You *scare* me. The way I feel around you, scare me. But I love you. It took me way too long to realize, but I do. I love you."

"You love me," she parrots.

"Yeah, but make no mistake. Not sure how long you're going to be pissed at me, and I can't blame you if it's going to be a wicked long time, but you're coming home with me. I don't care what kind of moral bullshit you throw at me, because we both know I don't have any. You. Are. Coming. Home. *Tonight.*" I finish, wanting to make it perfectly clear that she's got no choice in the matter. I'll woo her in the morning. Hell, I'll even grovel for as long as she wants me to, but there is not a chance in Hell she'll be living in a different city, let alone a different state.

"You don't do happily ever afters," she counters with a small voice.

I grab the back of her neck, pulling her lips close to mine. Her breath feels soft on my skin and my tongue darts out when her eyes lower to my mouth.

"If you're talking about pretty dresses and perfect lives, then no," I whisper, brushing my lips over hers, keeping our eyes locked. "But we can create our own. It will be unconventional as fuck, but I'll make it worth your while. I can be the anti-hero."

"I don't care if you're the villain, the monster, or the anti-hero. As long as it's you," she says, right before her lips crash against mine.

46

I'm lying on the couch, my face pointed at the door, when the front door opens. My heart jumps for joy and I pull my lip between my teeth when I glance at Killian entering with a seductive grin.

"Hey, baby."

"Hey," I reply as butterflies fly through my stomach. Before I came back to Boston, or should I say, before Killian dragged me back, I knew how I felt about him, but I never gave the tingling feelings inside of me free rein to do whatever they wanted. Now, they give me shivers every time he's near me. They give me a relentless flutter that keeps a permanent smile on my face, while also making me squirm.

It's awful.

It's amazing.

I can't live another day without it.

"What are you doing?" He sits down beside my feet, then gently pulls them around his waist as he crawls on top of me with a devilish glint in his beautiful green eyes.

"Looking for a dance studio." Our lips connect, and I take his face in my hands.

"Why? I don't mind you dancing around here. Especially if you're wearing those tight leggings while you do it."

"I'm serious." I try to glare but a smile creeps through.

"You want to dance at a studio?"

"I do."

He rubs his groin against my center, turning me on in the blink of an eye.

"I can buy you a studio?"

"Why would you do that?" I muse against his lips. His touch is both delicate and rough at the same time, the strokes of his palms snaking underneath my shirt, both firm and scorching.

"Because you like to dance. Because you wanted to become a professional dancer. Because I can." I smile at his words, loving the fact that he seems to know me better than I realize. I did want to become a professional dancer at some point in my life, but now I just want to dance as an outlet. Something to clear my mind.

His tongue licks the seam of my mouth, making it that much harder to think.

"I don't want my own studio. I just want a place to dance. I do want something else, though."

"Yeah, what's that? My cock between your legs? Or do you want my tongue?" He swirls his demanding tongue around mine, tilting my chin a little so he can deepen the kiss. A grunt rumbles against the back of my throat, and I can't hold back the giggle as I try to break loose.

"How about both?" I tell him with hooded eyes.

"Even better." He eagerly leans in, but I place my hand in front of his lips.

"Wait. You're distracting me."

He hums against my palm in agreement, nodding.

"I want to work for you."

His brows arch, and I lower my hand.

"What do you mean, *little Lexie*?"

"I want to work for you and your brothers. For the Wolfes."

"The Wolfes? You're part of us, baby."

That reply expands my heart, giving me the confidence to explain what I mean.

"Do you mean that?"

"Of course I mean that. You're mine. I know I said I don't do happy endings, but that doesn't mean you're not mine until the end. You are. And that means you're family. You're a Wolfe now. Besides, Franklin and Connor already asked me if you wanted to work for us."

"They did?" My heart swells at this piece of information. I didn't know his brothers trusted me enough to let me work for them, and I expected to have to convince them. It warms my heart that they accepted me before I even realized.

Killian nods before he gives me a tentative look. "And I'm not going to lie to you, you'll never get a big fairy tale wedding, but if you wanna wear a white dress when I drag you to city hall to change your last name, I'm not going to stop you."

"Wait, what?" I titter, not expecting him to move in that direction.

"Though, I prefer you in your black jeans and a hoodie."

"Why?" I laugh, unable to erase the beaming expression after everything he's disclosing.

"Because I like you like that. My little badass."

The hairs on my arms prick up as goosebumps shower my skin.

"So you do want to get married?"

He sighs, though I can still see the amusement in his eyes. They are staring at me with a kindness he doesn't show anyone but me, and it makes me swoon every single time. It makes me feel special, remembering that what we have is real. That he feels just as much for me as I do for him.

"I'm not going to lie, baby. I couldn't care less about getting married. You're my girl and no piece of paper is going to change that. But I do want you to become a Wolfe in front of the rest of the city. To make sure they know exactly who you are and to remind them not to mess with you."

"I'm a *badass*. No one dares to mess with me," I huff, jokingly.

"I know that." He chuckles. "But I need everyone to know that."

I rub the stubble on his jaw, gently brushing my thumb through it.

"I'd like that. I'd like to be part of your family now that I don't have one of my own."

The lightness in his gaze changes as his face falls a little.

"What?" My brows knit together, creasing the wrinkles on my forehead.

"You're a Wolfe now. Even if we haven't changed your last name yet. But you still have family, baby." I keep my mouth shut, waiting in anticipation. "You still have family on your mother's side."

"What do you mean?"

He clears his throat, then moves back to sit on the couch while taking me with him. Pulling me into his lap, he places my legs beside him so I'm straddling him, and I dip my chin to lock my eyes with his as I rest my hands on his neck.

"Your mother had a brother." He holds on to my hips.

"I know. He got murdered."

"Yeah. But he had a daughter. Your cousin."

I cock my head at this new piece of information. "I have a cousin? Why didn't you tell me?"

"I don't know," he replies with a guilty look. "Because I'm an asshole and I just got you back? I wanted you for myself for a few days."

My eyes narrow into a glare, but he gives me his seductive smirk I can't resist. It melts my resolve every fucking time I want to be pissed at him.

"I'm sorry," he offers, pulling my lips to his in a crushing kiss. "I'm not good at sharing."

"You don't have to share. I'm yours."

"Good." He tugs me closer against his chest, pressing his forehead against mine.

"Do you know her?"

"I do, actually. She's an old friend of Reign's. A little badass like you."

Excitement sparks in my eyes. "Can I meet her?"

"Sure, I'll have Reign give her a call."

"What's her name?"

"Callie Carrillo."

47

EPILOGUE

Killian

Our glasses lift in unison, a smirk on all our faces.

"Bottoms up, assholes." Connor brings the glass to his lips, pouring the contents down his throat without waiting for us.

"What are you doing, tool?" I scold. "You're supposed to wait for all of us."

"You guys take too long."

"It's a bachelor party! He hasn't even given a speech yet!" Reign screeches, indignant, as we still hold our shots in the air.

"I'm not going to make a fucking speech." Franklin gives him a look that says go fuck yourself and I snort, causing him to twist his attention to me.

"Yeah, you are," I disagree.

"Yeah, you definitely are," Reign chimes in, then nudges his chin to Connor. "Pour yourself a new one, asshole."

Connor does as he's instructed, though with a glare, while Franklin stares at us with a stoic gaze.

"I really don't want to be here," he tells us for the fiftieth time tonight. "Why do you two insist on making life hard for me?"

"Wait, that wasn't our sole purpose in this world?" Reign grabs his chest, faking his shock, and I chuckle, then finish my shot glass in one big gulp. The spirit burns through my chest, but I hide my discomfort.

"What the?" Reign looks like he's about to jump out of his skin, and I offer him a big smirk.

"Connor was right. We're taking too long."

"Oh, for fuck's sake." Giving up, Reign lifts his gaze to the ceiling, replicating my action by drinking the shot at once, then snatches the bottle of tequila out of his hand. "Give me that."

He takes big gulps, flipping all of us off as he holds our gazes. When he's finished about a quarter of the bottle, he lowers it. "Okay, I had my fill of shots for the night."

"That's not how it works," I say.

"I know. But you two assholes have less patience than Colin does, and he's a toddler." He points his finger at Connor and me while Franklin motions for the bartender.

"A bottle of whiskey, please. And four glasses. No ice."

"Speaking of Colin. I got news." Connor glances around at the three of us, beaming. "He's going to be a big brother. Lily is pregnant again."

The clear joy in his expression hits me like a ray of sunshine, the feeling leaving me a bit flustered.

"No-suh!" Reign's eyes pop out of his head before he wraps his arms around Connor. "Congratulations! Another Wolfe added to the pack!" he yells before Franklin and I follow behind him.

"I'm guessing this one wasn't a surprise?" I joke, slamming Connor's shoulder with a grin.

"No, she actually told me about this one," he jeers, and that has us all laughing.

"It's weird, isn't it?" I start as Franklin offers us all a glass of whiskey. I take the glass, slowly bringing it to my lips. "Connor never wanted to have kids, and now he's going to have two." I tear my attention to Franklin. "I remember a time when you didn't want to have kids."

"I didn't," Franklin concedes, "but then Kenny changed that."

"How?"

He shrugs. "I don't know, to be honest. I just know that she wrapped me around her finger and now I want it all. I want everything she wants. I want my name on her passport, my ring on her finger, and to grow our family. I'm even excited about the damn wedding."

"It just happens when you love someone. It changes your perspective on things," Reign adds.

"Do you want kids, Reign?" For the first time in like forever, there is no sarcasm on Connor's face.

"Ya-huh. Two or three. At least one girl." Reign's gaze grows vacant with a dreamy smile. "One that is a little copy and paste of Sienna. She'll probably give me a heart attack at sixteen, but I'm sure it'll be worth it."

"Really?" I huff, a little confused as to the feelings that are swirling around in my stomach as the conversation continues. “Even after all you’ve been through in Providence?”

“I learned from that,” he counters with a shrug, his glass hanging in front of his chest. “It was fucked up, but they showed me exactly what *not* to do. Same with Dad. I’ll be better than them.” He says it with so much ease that it has me glancing up at him in awe.

I never really thought about having kids. When I was still with Emma, I was only nineteen, and after Emma, I avoided any form of relationship that wasn’t family-based like the plague.

But today... things are different.

“Oh, look at that,” Connor titters, locking his gaze with mine as I swing it up. “Do you see that? He’s got baby fever.”

“What? Fuck no,” I lie.

“Yeah, you kinda do,” Reign nods.

“I don’t have fucking baby fever,” I growl, looking at Franklin for help.

A ghost of a smile haunts his face, and I roll my lips with a shake of my head.

“Really, Franklin?”

“You love Lexie. It makes sense. Would it be so bad?”

I don’t know. Would it?

“I guess not.”

“See! Baby fever!” Connor bellows, cheering.

“Shut the fuck up, you tool!”

Reign’s palms connect with my back in a forceful slap. “It’s okay, brother. We’ve all been there. You’re just a little late to the party.”

“Look, I don’t know, okay? I’m just not ruling it out anymore either.” In fact, a Colin-sized human with Lexie’s pretty face on it seems to melt my heart at a pretty quick rate right now.

"She's gonna be pregnant next year," Reign taunts to Connor.

"She's fucking nineteen. Even if we have kids one day, the mother of my child is not going to be a fucking teenager when we do."

"Aah, the mother of his child," Connor coos.

I rub my face, blowing out a breath. "Assholes."

"Do you want to buy a lap dance?" A skimpy dressed girl with black hair moves to stand beside me, glancing around my brothers and me with a seductive look shining from underneath her fake lashes. Last year, I would've eagerly thrown money at her, loving the type of girl that didn't come with any expectations other than what she could earn from me. But now I don't even know what we're doing here. I want to celebrate my brother's upcoming wedding, but spending it in a strip club doesn't sound appealing when it's not my girl who will be stripping for me.

We all eye the girl from bottom to top for a little too long and she keeps fluttering our lashes. The air grows a little icy and when she tries to persuade us by biting her lip, I can't resist rolling my eyes.

"Let's just find a sports bar and watch a game or something," I suggest, ignoring the stripper beside me.

"Great idea," Franklin mutters, followed by conceding murmurs from my brothers before we all rapidly down our drinks, and head out of there as fast as we can.

"Sorry, sweetheart. Maybe next time." I chuckle as I follow my brothers' trail.

It's a little past two in the morning when I get home, tiptoeing my way to the bedroom.

My heart pounds in excitement when I see Lexie peacefully asleep in my bed. Her brown hair is draped over her pillow and when I get closer, the features on her face make her look like an angel as she's sound asleep. I strip down to my boxers, then slide in behind her. Her warmth welcomes me like a hot bath after a long day, and I bury my nose in her hair as I pull her from sleep with kisses peppering her neck. She's wearing nothing more than some panties and a crop top, giving me easy access to every inch of her frame. My hands stroke the silky skin on her stomach, and it doesn't take long before she stirs awake with pleasured moans.

"How was your night?" she whispers, enjoying my touch.

"Lonely without you."

She pushes out a breath, and I can almost hear the smile forming on her lips. "I'm sure you had a stripper or two who would have kept you company."

"We went to a sports bar and watched the game instead."

"Really?" With her navy-blue eyes still a little sleepy, she rears her gaze to mine, and I take the moment to press a kiss to her lips with an agreeing hum.

"How was your night with the girls?"

"Good, we had fun." She continues to rest her head on the pillow, pushing her ass a little more against my cock. "The stripper was *hawt*."

My light mood gets swept away and my hands still on her body.

"What stripper?" I growl.

"The one we hired for Kendall."

The air gets slammed out of my chest as I grind my teeth. My fingers dig into her skin with a firm grip that only makes a giggle sound through the room. "You better not tell me you had a naked man sitting in your lap, *little Lexie*."

"It was a woman."

"No-suh." My scowl vanishes like snow in front of the sun.

"Hmm," she muses with a smug tone. "We didn't want a man stripping for us unless it was a Wolfe. So we hired a girl. She actually taught us some moves."

My cock jerks to life at that piece of information, the image of Lexie hanging on a pole flashing in my mind.

"Did she?" I lock my lips with the sensitive area below her ear, and she concedes with a moan.

"I love you," I groan against her skin between kisses, never stopping.

"I love you."

"Lily is pregnant."

"I know."

"She told you?" I pull back, grabbing her chin so I can look into her gorgeous eyes. They sparkle in the rays of moonlight that shine through the little crack of the blinds, fascinating me just as much as any other time.

"Right before the first shot," she explains.

"I think I want that."

"What?"

"Babies." My brothers were right. Connor's announcement made me realize I want that one day. I want to create life with her, feeling like it would be the perfect cherry on top of the already perfect cake. "With you. *Eventually*."

She spins in my arms, holding my face so she can examine every feature of my expression. "Who are you, and what did you do to my husband?"

A grin slides into place and I take her lip between my teeth, slowly pulling it before it's followed by a kiss. "I like it when you call me husband. But I'm serious."

"A few months ago, you didn't even want a relationship. Now, we're married and you're telling me you want to have kids?"

"*Eventually*," I clarify. I'm not ready for it now. I like having her for myself, knowing I can do whatever I want with her when I come home. I want to enjoy what we have a little while longer before we add anything else to the mix, but my stroll home showed me that I do want it someday. I want her belly to grow big with our child, to know that we're connected forever by the life we created.

"What changed?" The tone in her voice is curious and surprised, but to my relief, there is no rejection.

"You did. I never considered it, but here you are and now I realize I want it all. I want a little girl with your pretty face. A little warrior princess, strong like her mother. I want something that's ours. *Eventually.*"

"Eventually. I can do *eventually*." She smiles before a scowling. "But not before I'm legal to drink, okay? I don't want four-day benders, but I at least want to have been legally drunk once in my life before you and I start planning a bunch of babies."

"I said one," I deadpan. "Not a bunch."

"Let's start with one." Her lips fall against mine. "Eventually."

ACKNOWLEDGMENTS

The first and biggest thank you goes to you. Whether you are here from the beginning of the series or you just picked this one up (good choice!), it's the end for my Wolfe boys and boy, it was one hell of a ride. These four brothers creeped up on me long before I started writing for a living, and even though it's been hard, it's also been a blast. Thank you for loving these Boston boys as much as I do.

Thank you to my loving husband. The last year has been insane, but luckily we both know it was worth it. Thank you for supporting me in any way, rooting for me and sharing the joy it brings me. You truly are the best there is and know I'll never let you go. You can run, but you can't hide. You're mine. Tot het einde en terug.

Katie, superstar, you knew this was going to be the best when Killian said nothing more than two words and now, a year later, I couldn't agree more. He's my favorite of all, and you helped me see that until the very end was there. There is nothing more fun than throwing my plot ideas at your face and making them even better while we keep throwing it back and forth like mud. Thank you for being you. Thank you for everything.

Els, Eleanor, Ellie Kent, I think at this point I'm allowed to call you whatever I want, LOL. You crashed into my life last year without warning, and I'm so glad you did. You are such a blessing on this journey and I can't wait for your own to start. Though, I've been already pushing you over the start, because let's be honest? There is no time like today. Thank you for always being eager to binge my books, no matter what trope or plot. I feel like I could write you a political thriller and you'd still be showering me with voice notes, and they are always a blessing to receive! But most of all, thank you for being my friend.

Sheryn, your spirit always lifts me up, no matter what is going on. I love talking to you and how we continue to learn from each other. You always make time for my books and I appreciate every minute you spend on them and me. Thank you for being a great friend in this sometimes drama filled industry. P.S I just wish you lived closer.

Boston Lauren, one day, I'll wrap my arms around you and squeeze you as hard as I can. You've been such a good help with these books and you gave me the confidence I could do this. I couldn't have done it without you and I'm really grateful for the time you spend on my books. Or screaming about me on your social media. You are so much more than a super reader and I truly hope one day you'll be giving me a tour through your hometown.

Brianna, you never say no to my books even though I know sometimes you should. I like how you're not afraid to tell me what needs to change and for that you're one of the most valued beta's I have. Thank you, your effort, dedication and time means the world!

Thank you to my editor, MacKenzie. You truly are so easy to work with and everytime I get my manuscript back from you, I send it back with a content feeling. You made my life so much easier.

ABOUT THE AUTHOR

Billie Lustig is a dutch girl who has always had a thing with words: either she couldn't shut up or she was writing an adventure stuck in her head. She's pretty straight forward, can be a pain in the ass & is allergic to bullshit, but most of all, she's a sucker for love.

She is happily married to her own alpha male that taught her the truest thing about love:

when it's real, you can't walk away.

Check out www.billielustig.com for more info & sign up to my newsletter to be kept up to date or follow me on: Facebook, Instagram, Goodreads, Bookbub, Amazon and/or TikTok.

ALSO BY BILLIE LUSTIG

The Fire Series
Callous
Combust
Tormented
Torched

The Boston Wolfes
Franklin
Connor
Reign
Killian

The Sisters of Sin
Lush Rebel
Lush Angel
Lush Devil

Also By B. Lustig

I created B. Lustig to publish books that give you a heavy dose of angst, big-mouthed, heroes and women that like to challenge them. These are the stories without the guns, criminals, and dark worlds they come from. However, they bring you the same amount of sass and spice as any other Billie book.

Numbers:

8

9

5

7

Made in the USA
Columbia, SC
27 July 2023

20962304R00250